To

John Granville Mott

from his aunt

Ann J Stephens

Mary Winterbotham Mott

To her esteemed friend

Julia Morris with her Love

Auburn Aug 16 1882

FASHION AND FAMINE.

BY

MRS. ANN S. STEPHENS.

There is no sorrow for the earnest soul
That looketh up to God in perfect faith.

FORTIETH THOUSAND.

New York:
BUNCE & BROTHER, PUBLISHERS,
134 NASSAU STREET.

MDCCCLIV.

Republished in London by Richard Bentley, through special arrangement with the Author

W. H. TINSON,
STEREOTYPER,
24 Beekman Street.

Taws, Russell & Co., Printers,
26 Beekman and 18 Spruce St., N. Y.

To

MRS. LYDIA H. SIGOURNEY,

OF HARTFORD, CONN.,

THE MOST VALUED FRIEND THAT I HAVE,

AND ONE OF THE BEST WOMEN I EVER KNEW, THIS BOOK

Is Most Respectfully Dedicated.

ANN S. STEPHENS

Preface.

WHAT shall I say in this Preface to my book? Shall I make the usual half-sincere, half-affected apology of haste and inexperience, with hints of improvement in future efforts? Indeed I cannot. for though this volume really is the first novel ever printed in book form under my name. its imperfections, whatever they are, arise from no inexperience or undue haste, but from absolute lack of power to accomplish that which I have undertaken. Nor is it probable that the points in which I have failed here, would be very greatly improved were the same book to be written again.

I have endeavored to make this book a good one. If I have failed it is because the power has not been granted to me by the Source of all power, and for deficiency like this, the only admissible apology would be for having written at all. But excuses are out of place here. The book, with all its faults, is frankly surrendered to the public judgment, asking neither favoritism or forbearance, save that favoritism which deals gently with unintentional error, and that forbearance which no American ever withholds from a woman. Shall I say that this volume is launched on the world with fear and trembling? That would express an ungrateful want of faith in a class of readers who have generously sustained me through years of literary toil, and have nobly supported not only Peterson's Ladies' National Magazine now under my charge, but every periodical with which I have been connected. It would be ungrateful to the press that, without a single respectable exception, has always dealt generously by me, and would betray a weakness of character which I am not willing to acknowledge, for I have lived long enough to tremble at nothing which results from an honest intention, and to fear nothing but deserved disgrace—the death of beloved objects—or change in those affections that no literary fame or misfortune can ever reach.

But it is not without emotions that I present this book to the public, grateful and sweet emotions that liberal minds must respect more than a thousand insincere apologies. The thoughts of an author are the perfume of her own soul going forth on the winds of heaven to awaken other souls and renew itself in their kindred sympathies. I am more anxious for the effect which these thoughts, so long a portion of my own being, will have upon others, than for the return they may bring to myself. The American people are, in the mass, just and intelligent judges; always generous and perhaps over-indulgent to their authors. In writing this book I have endeavored to deserve their approbation and to cast no discredit upon a profession that I honor more than any other upon the broad earth. If I have succeeded, no human being can be more grateful than I shall be for the public opinion that assures me of it; but, to satisfy even my humble ambition, it must be an opinion honestly earned and frankly given. Popularity won without merit, and lost without blame, would be valueless to me, even while it lasted.

Contents.

CHAPTER		PAGE
I.	The Strawberry Girl and Market Woman	9
II.	The Old Couple in the Back Basement	26
III.	The Lone Mansion and its Mistress	43
IV.	The Astor House—the Ride—the Attic Room	54
V.	Mistress and Servant in Consultation	72
VI.	The Tempter and the Tempted—the young heart yields	81
VII.	The Old Homestead and Home Memories	89
VIII.	The City Cottage and its Strange Inmate	110
IX.	Mrs. Gray's Thanksgiving Dinner—Julia and Robert	126
X.	The Brother's Return—Questions and Answers	141
XI.	The Mother's Letter and the Son's Commentary	158
XII.	Strife for an Earl—Mrs. Sykes and Mrs. Nash	163
XIII.	The Morning Lesson—Doubt—Sympathy—Misery	179
XIV.	A Wedding Foreshadowed—Sunshine of the Heart	187
XV.	The Mother's Appeal—the Son's Falsehood	194
XVI.	The Bridal Wreath—Roses and Cypress	211
XVII.	An Hour before the Ball—Strides of Destiny	222
XVIII.	The Forged Check—Uncle and Nephew	228
XIX.	Night and Morning—Wild Heart Strife	234
XX.	The Last Interview—Parting—Death	251
XXI.	The City Prison—Examination for Murder	266
XXII.	The Imprisoned Witness in the Female Ward	282
XXIII.	The Three Old Women in Fulton Market	299
XXIV.	The First Night in Prison—Prayers—Tears—Dreams	311

CHAPTER		PAGE
XXV.	Little Georgie—his Mother and Julia Warren	319
XXVI.	Mrs. Gray and the Prison Woman	330
XXVII.	Struggles and Revels—Unquenched Anguish	338
XXVIII.	Ada Leicester and Jacob Strong	344
XXIX.	Ada's Solitary Breakfast—Desolation of Heart	350
XXX.	The Prison Woman in Ada's Dressing-Room	354
XXXI.	The Tombs Lawyer and his Client Mrs. Gray	366
XXXII.	The Lawyer's Visit to his Client	372
XXXIII.	The Trial for Murder—Opening Scenes	380
XXXIV.	The Two Witnesses—Recognition too Late	388
XXXV.	The Verdict—Stillness—Death-Shadows	399
XXXVI.	The Parents, the Child and Grandchild	405
XXXVII.	The Dawning of Light—Angelic Missions	412
XXXVIII.	Gathering for the Execution	414
XXXIX.	Hearts and Consciences at Rest	422

FASHION AND FAMINE.

CHAPTER I.

THE STRAWBERRY GIRL.

Like wild flowers on the mountain side,
Goodness may be of any soil;
Yet intellect, in all its pride,
And energy, with pain and toil,
Hath never wrought a holier thing
Than Charity in humble birth.
God's brightest angel stoops his wing,
To meet so much of Heaven on earth.

THE morning had not fully dawned on New York, yet its approach was visible everywhere amid the fine scenery around the city. The dim shadows piled above Weehawken, were warming up with purple, streaked here and there with threads of rosy gold. The waters of the Hudson heaved and rippled to the glow of yellow and crimson light, that came and went in flashes on each idle curl of the waves. Long Island lay in the near distance like a thick, purplish cloud, through which the dim outline of house, tree, mast and spire loomed mistily, like half-formed objects on a camera obscura.

Silence—that strange, dead silence that broods over a scene crowded with slumbering life—lay upon the city, broken only by the rumble of vegetable carts and the jar of milk-cans, as they rolled up from the different ferries; or the half-smothered roar of some steamboat putting into its dock, freighted with sleeping passengers.

After a little, symptoms of aroused life became visible about the wharves. Grocers, carmen, and huckster-women began to swarm around the provision boats. The markets nearest the water were opened, and soon became theatres of active bustle.

The first market opened that day was in Fulton street. As the morning deepened, piles of vegetables, loads of beef, hampers of fruit, heaps of luscious butter, cages of poultry, canary birds swarming in their wiry prisons, forests of green-house plants, horse-radish grinders with their reeking machines, venders of hot coffee, root beer and dough nuts, all with men, women and children swarming in, over and among them, like so many ants, hard at work, filled the spacious arena, but late a range of silent, naked and gloomy looking stalls. Then carts, laden and groaning beneath a weight of food, came rolling up to this great mart, crowding each avenue with fresh supplies. All was life and eagerness. Stout men and bright-faced women moved through the verdant chaos, arranging, working, chatting, all full of life and enterprise, while the rattling of carts outside, and the gradual accumulation of sounds everywhere, bespoke a great city aroused, like a giant refreshed, from slumber.

Slowly there arose out of this cheerful confusion, forms of homely beauty, that an artist or a thinking man might have loved to look upon. The butchers' stalls, but late a desolate range of gloomy beams, were reddening with fresh joints, many of them festooned with fragrant branches and gorgeous garden flowers. The butchers standing, each by his stall, with snow-white apron, and an eager, joyous look of traffic on his face, formed a display of comfort and plenty, both picturesque and pleasant to contemplate.

The fruit and vegetable stands were now loaded with damp, green vegetables, each humble root having its own peculiar tint, often arranged with a singular taste for color, unconsciously possessed by the woman who exercised no little skill in setting off her stand to advantage.

There was one vegetable stand to which we would draw the reader's particular attention ; not exactly as a type of the others, for there was something so unlike all the rest, both in this stall and its occupant, that it would have drawn the attention of any person possessed of the slightest artistical taste. It was like the arrangement of a picture, that long table heaped with fruit, the freshest vegetables, and the brightest flowers, ready for the day's traffic. Rich scarlet radishes glowing up through their foliage of tender green, were contrasted with young onions swelling out from their long emerald stalks, snowy and transparent as so many great pearls. Turnips, scarcely larger than a hen's egg, and nearly as white, just taken fresh and fragrant from the soil, lay against heads of lettuce, tinged with crisp and greenish gold, piled against the deep blackish green of spinach and water-cresses, all moist with dew, or wet with bright water-drops that had supplied its place, and taking a deeper tint from the golden contrast. These with the red glow of strawberries in their luscious prime, piled together in masses, and shaded with fresh grape leaves ; bouquets of roses, hyacinths, violets, and other fragrant blossoms, lent their perfume and the glow of their rich colors to the coarser children of the soil, and would have been an object pleasant to look upon, independent of the fine old woman who sat complacently on her little stool, at one end of the table, in tranquil expectation of customers that were sure to drop in as the morning deepened.

And now the traffic of the day commenced in earnest. Servants, housekeepers and grocers swarmed into the market. The clink of money—the sound of sharp, eager banter—the dull noise of the butcher's cleaver, were heard on every hand. It was a pleasant scene, for every face looked smiling and happy. The soft morning air seemed to have brightened all things into cheerfulness.

With the earliest group that entered Fulton market that morning was a girl, perhaps thirteen or fourteen years old, but tiny in her form, and appearing far more juvenile than that. A pretty quilted hood, of rose-colored calico, was turned back from her face, which seemed naturally delicate and pale ; but the fresh air, and perhaps a shadowy reflection from her hood, gave the glow of a rose-bud to her cheeks. Still there was anxiety upon her young face. Her eyes of a dark violet blue, drooped heavily beneath their black and curling lashes, if any one from the numerous stalls addressed her ; for a small splint basket on her arm, new and perfectly empty, was a sure indication that the child had been sent to make purchase ; while her timid air—the blush that came and went on her face—bespoke as plainly that she was altogether unaccustomed to the scene, and had no regular place at which to make her humble bargains. The child seemed a waif cast upon the market ; and she was so beautiful, notwithstanding her humble dress of faded and darned calico, that at almost every stand she was challenged pleasantly to pause and fill her basket. But she only cast down her eyes and blushed more deeply, as with her little bare feet she hurried on through the labyrinth of stalls, toward that portion of the market occupied by the huckster-women. Here she began to slacken her pace, and to look about her with no inconsiderable anxiety.

"What do you want, little girl ; anything in my way ?" was repeated to her once or twice, as she moved forward. At each of these challenges she would pause, look earnestly into the face of the speaker, and then pass on with a faint wave of the head, that expressed something of sad and timid disappointment.

At length the child—for she seemed scarcely more than that —was growing pale, and her eyes turned with a sort of sharp anxiety from one face to another, when suddenly they fell upon the buxom old huckster-woman, whose stall we have described. There was something in the good dame's appearance that brought an eager and satisfied look to that pale face. She drew close to the stand, and stood for some seconds, gazing timidly on the old woman. It was a pleasant face, and a comfortable, portly form enough, that the timid girl gazed upon. Smooth and comely were the full and rounded cheeks, with their rich autumn color, dimpled like an over-ripe apple. Fat and good humored enough to defy wrinkles, the face looked far too rosy for the thick, gray hair that was shaded, not concealed, by a cap of clear white muslin, with a broad, deep border, and tabs that met like a snowy girth to support the firm, double chin. Never did your eyes dwell upon a chin so full of health and good humor as that. It sloped with a sleek, smiling grace down from the plump mouth, and rolled with a soft, white wave into the neck, scarcely leaving an outline, or the want of one, before it was lost in the white of that muslin kerchief, folded so neatly beneath the ample bosom of her gown. Then the broad linen apron of blue and white check, girding her waist, and flowing over the smooth rotundity of person, was a living proof of the ripeness and wholesome state of her merchandise.—I tell you, reader, that woman, take her for all in all, was one to draw the attention, aye, and the love of a child, who had come forth barefooted and alone in search of kindness.

At length the huckster-woman saw the child gazing upon her with a look so earnest, that she was quite startled by it. She also caught a glance at the empty basket, and her little brown eyes twinkled at the promise of a new customer.

"Well, my dear, what do you want this morning?" she said, smoothing her apron with a pair of plump, little hands, and casting a well satisfied look over her stall, and then at the girl, who grew pale at her notice, and began to tremble visibly—"all sorts of vegetables, you see—flowers—strawberries--radishes—what will you have, child?"

The little girl crept round to where the woman stood, and speaking in a low, frightened voice, said—

"Please, ma'm, I want you to trust me!"

"Trust you!" said the woman, with a soft laugh that shook her double chin, and dimpled her cheeks. "Why, I don't know you, little one—what on earth do you want trust for? Lost the market money, hey, and afraid of a scolding—is that it?"

"No, no, I haven't lost any money," said the child eagerly; "please ma'm, just stoop down one minute, while I tell you!"

The little girl in her earnestness took hold of the woman's apron, and she, kind soul, sunk back to her stool: it was the most comfortable way of listening.

"I—I live with grandfather and grandmother, ma'm; they are old and poor—you don't know how poor; for he, grandpa, has been sick, and—it seems strange—I eat as much as any of them. Well, ma'm, I tried to get something to do, but you see how little I am; nobody will think me strong enough, even to tend baby; so we have all been without anything to eat, since day before yesterday."

"Poor thing!" muttered the huckster-woman, "poor thing!"

"Well, ma'm, I must do something. I can bear anything better than seeing them hungry. I did not sleep a wink all last night, but kept thinking what I should do. I never begged in my life; *they* never did; and it made me feel sick to think of it; but I could have done it rather than see them sit and look at each other another day. Did you ever see an old man cry for hunger, ma'm?"

"No, no, God forbid!" answered the dame, brushing a plump hand across her eyes.

"I have," said the child, with a sob, "and it was this that made me think that begging, after all, was not so very, very mean. So, this morning, I asked them to let me go out; but grandpa said he might go himself, if he were strong enough; but I never should—never—never!"

"Nice old man—nice old man!" said the huckster-woman.

"I did not ask again," resumed the child, "for an idea had come into my head in the night. I have seen little girls, no older than I am, selling radishes and strawberries, and things."

"Yes—yes, I understand!" said the old woman, and her eyes began to twinkle the more brightly that they were wet before.

"But I had no strawberries to sell, nor a cent of money to buy them with!"

"Well! well!"

"Not even a basket!"

"Poor thing!"

"But I was determined to do something. So I went to a

grocery, where grandpa used to buy things when he had money, and they trusted me with this basket."

"That was very kind of them!"

"Wasn't it very kind?" said the child, her eyes brightening, "especially as I told them it was all myself—that grandpa knew nothing about it. See what a nice new basket it is—you can't think how much courage it gave me. When I came into the market it seemed as if I shouldn't be afraid to ask anybody about trusting me a little."

"And yet you came clear to this side without stopping to ask anybody?"

"I was looking into their faces to see if it would do," answered the child, with meek simplicity, "but there was something in every face that sent the words back into my throat again."

"So you stopped here because it was almost the last stand."

"No, no, I did not think of that," said the child eagerly. "I stopped because something seemed to tell me that this was the place. I thought if you would not trust me, you would, any way, be patient and listen."

The old huckster-woman laughed—a low, soft laugh—and the little girl began to smile through her tears. There was something mellow and comfortable in that chuckle, that warmed her to the heart.

"So you were sure that I would trust you—hey, quite sure?"

"I thought if you wouldn't, there was no chance for me anywhere else," replied the child, lifting her soft eyes to the face of the matron.

Again the old woman laughed.

"Well, well, let us see how many strawberries will set you up in business for the day. Six, ten—a dozen baskets—your little arms will break down with more than that. I will let you have them at cost, only be sure to come back at night with the money. I would not for fifty dollars have you fail."

"But I may not sell them all!" said the child, anxiously.

"I should not wonder, poor thing. That sweet voice of

yours will hardly make itself heard at first ; but never mind, run down into the areas and look through the windows—people can't help but look at your face, God bless it !"

As the good woman spoke, she was busy selecting the best and most tempting strawberries from the pile of little baskets that stood at her elbow. These she arranged in the orphan's basket, first sprinkling a layer of damp, fresh grass in the bottom, and interspersing the whole with young grape leaves, intended both as an embellishment, and to keep the fruit fresh and cool. When all was arranged to her satisfaction, she laid a bouquet of white and crimson moss rose-buds at each end of the basket, and interspersed little tufts of violets along the side, till the crimson berries were wreathed in with flowers.

"There," said the old woman, lifting up the basket with a sigh of satisfaction, "between the fruit and flowers you must make out. Sell the berries for sixpence a basket, and the roses for all you can get. People who love flowers well enough to buy them, never cavil about the price ; just let them pay what they like."

The little girl took the basket on her arm ; her pretty mouth grew tremulous and bright as the moss rose-bud that blushed against her hand ; her eyes filled with tears.

"Oh, ma'm, I want to thank you so much, only I don't know how," she said, in a voice that went to the good woman's heart.

"There, there !—never mind—be punctual, that's a good girl. Now, my dear, what is your name ?"

"Julia—Julia Warren, ma'm !"

"A pretty name—very well—stop a moment, I had forgotten."

The child sat her basket down upon the stool which the huckster-woman hastily vacated, and waited patiently while the good dame disappeared in some unknown region of the market, eager to accomplish an object that had just presented itself to her mind.

"Here," she said, coming back with her face all in a glow, a small tin pail in one hand, and her apron gathered up in the other. "Just leave the strawberries, and run home with these. It will be a long time for the old folks to wait, and you will go about the day's work with a lighter heart, when you know that they have had a breakfast, to say nothing of yourself, poor thing! There, run along, and be back in no time."

Julia took the little tin pail and the rolls that her kind friend hastily twisted up in a sheet of brown paper.

"Oh! they will be *so* glad," broke from her, and with a sob of joy she sprang away with her precious burden.

"Well now, Mrs. Gray, you are a strange creature, trusting people like that, and absolutely laying out money too; I only wonder how you ever got along at all!" said a little, shrewish woman from a neighboring stand, who had been watching this scene from behind a heap of vegetables.

"Poh! it's my way; and I can afford it," answered the huckster-woman, rubbing her plump palms together, and twinkling her eyelashes to disperse the moisture that had gathered under them. "I haven't sat in this market fourteen years for nothing. The child is a good child, I'll stake my life on it!"

"I hope you may never see the pail again, that's all," was the terse reply.

"Well, well, I may be wrong—maybe I am—we shall know soon. At any rate I can afford to lose half a dozen pails, that's one comfort."

"Always chuckling over the money she has saved up," muttered the little woman, with a sneer; "for my part I don't believe that she is half as well off as she pretends to be."

The conversation was here cut short by several customers, who crowded up to make their morning purchases. During the next half hour good Mrs. Gray was so fully occupied, that she had no opportunity for thought of her protégé; but just as she obtained a moment's breathing time, up came the little girl panting for breath; her cheeks glowing like June roses; and her eyes sparkling with delight.

"They have had their breakfast; I told them all about it!" she said, in a panting whisper, drawing close up to the huckster-woman, and handing back the empty pail. "I wish you could have seen grandpa when I took off the cover, and let the hot coffee steam into the room. I only wish you could have seen him !"

"And he liked it, did he ?"

"Liked it ! Oh ! if you had been there to see !"

The child's eyes were brimful of tears, and yet they sparkled like diamonds.

Mrs. Gray looked over her stall to see if there was anything else that could be added to the basket. That pretty, grateful look expanded her warm heart so pleasantly, that she felt quite like heaping everything at hand upon the little girl. But the basket was already quite heavy enough for that slender arm, and the addition of a single handful of fruit or tuft of flowers, would have destroyed the symmetry of its arrangement. So with a sigh, half of disappointment, half of that exquisite satisfaction that follows a kind act, she patted little Julia on the head, lifted the basket from the stool, and kindly bade her begone to her day's work.

The child departed with a light tread and a lighter heart, smiling upon every one she met, and looking back, as if she longed to point out her benefactress to the whole world.

Mrs. Gray followed her with moist and sunny eyes ; then shaking the empty pail at her cynical neighbor, in the good-humored triumph of her benevolence, she carried it back to the coffee-stand whence it had been borrowed.

"Strawberries !—strawberries !"

Julia Warren turned pale, and looked around like a frightened bird, when this sweet cry first broke from her lips in the open street. Nobody seemed to hear—that was one comfort ; so she hurried round a corner, and creeping into the shadow of a house, leaned, all in a tremor, against an iron railing, quite confident, for the moment, that she should never find courage to open her mouth again. But a little reflection gave her strength. Mrs. Gray had told her that the morning was her harvest hour. She could not stand there trembling beneath the weight of her basket. The fruity scent—the fragrant breath of the violets that floated up from it, seemed to reproach her.

"Strawberries!—strawberries!"

The sound rose from those red lips more cheerily now. There was ripeness in the very tones that put you in mind of the fruit itself. The cry was neither loud nor shrill, but somehow people were struck by it, and turned unconsciously to look upon the girl. This gave her fresh courage, for the glances were all kind, and as she became accustomed to her own voice, the novelty of her position began to lose its terror. A woman called to her from the area of a house, and purchased two baskets of the strawberries, without asking any reduction in the price. Poor child, how her heart leaped when the shilling was placed in her hand! How important the whole transaction seemed to her; yet with what indifference the woman paid for the strawberries, and turned to carry them into the basement.

Julia looked through the railings and thanked this important customer. She could not help it; her little heart was full. A muttered reply that she was "welcome," came back; that was all. Notwithstanding the gruff answer, Julia took up her basket with a radiant face.

"Strawberries!—strawberries!"

Now the words came forth from red and smiling lips—nay, once or twice the little girl broke into a laugh, as she went along, for the bright shilling lay in the bottom of her basket. She wandered on unacquainted with the streets, but quite content; for though she found herself down among warehouses only, and in narrow, crowded streets, the gentlemen who hurried by would now and then turn for a bunch of violets, and she kept on bewildered, but happy as a bird.

All at once the strawberry girl found herself among the shipping; and a little terrified at the coarse and barren appearance of the wharves, she paused close by the water, irresolute what direction to pursue. It was now somewhat deep in the morning, and everything was life and bustle in that commercial district, for the child was but a few streets above the Battery, and could detect the cool wave of its trees through a vista in the buildings. The harbor, glowing with sunshine and covered with every species of water craft, lay spread before her gaze. Brooklyn Heights, Jersey City, and the leafy shores of Hoboken, half veiled in the golden haze of a bright June morning, rose before her like soft glimpses of the fairy land she had loved to read about. Never in her life had she been in that portion of the city before ; and she forgot everything in the strange beauty of the scene, which few ever looked upon unmoved. The steamboats ploughing the silvery foam of the waters, curving around the Battery, darting in and out from every angle of the shore ; the fine national vessels sleeping upon the waters, with their masts pencilled against the sky, and their great, black hulls, so imposing in their motionless strength ; the ferry-boats, the pretty barges and smaller kind of water craft shooting with arrowy speed across the waves—all these things had a strange and absorbing effect on the girl.

As she stood gazing upon the scene, there came looming up in the distant horizon, an ocean steamer, riding majestically on the waters, that seemed to have suddenly heaved the monster up into the bright June atmosphere. At first, the vast proportions of this sea monarch were lost in the distance ; but it came up with the force and swiftness of some wild steed of the desert, and each moment its vast size became more visible. Up it came, black, swift, and full of majestic strength, ploughing the waters with a sort of haughty power, as if spurning the element which had become its slave. Its great pipes poured forth a whirlwind of black, fleecy smoke, now and then flaked and lurid with fire, that whirled and whirled in the curling vapor, till all its glow went out, rendering the thick volumes of smoke that streamed over the water still more dense and murky.

At first the child gazed upon this imposing object with a sensation of affright. Her large eyes dilated ; her cheek grew pale with excitement ; she felt a disposition to snatch up her basket, and flee from the water's edge. But curiosity, and something akin to superstitious dread kept her motionless. She had heard of these great steamships, and knew that this must be one ; yet it seemed to her like some dangerous monster tortured with black, fiery venom. She turned to an old sailor that stood near, his countenance glowing with enthusiasm, and muttering eagerly to himself—

"Oh ! sir, it is only a ship—you are sure of that !" she said, for her childish dread of strangers was lost in wonder at a sight so new and majestic.

The man turned and gave one glance at the mild, blue eyes and earnest face of the child.

"Why, bless your heart, what else should it be ? A ship, to be sure it is—or at any rate, a sort of one, going by wind and fire both together ; but arter all, a clean rigged taut merchantman for me—that's the sort of craft for an old salt that's been brought up to study wind and water, not fire and smoke ! But take care of your traps, little one, she'll be up to her berth in no time."

The child snatched up her basket and gave a hurried glance around, seeking for some means of egress from the wharf ; but while she was occupied by the steamer, a crowd had gathered down to the water's edge, and she shrunk from attempting a passage through the mass of carts, carriages and people that blocked up her way to the city.

"Poh ! there's nothing to be afeared of !" said the good-natured tar, observing her terrified look ; "only take care of your traps, and it's worth while waiting."

By this time the steamer was opposite Governor's Island. She made a bold curve around the Battery, and came up to her berth with a slow and measured beat of the engine, blowing off steam at intervals, like a racer drawing breath after sweeping his course.

The deck of the steamer was alive with passengers, an eager crowd full of cheerfulness and expectation. Most of them were evidently from the higher classes of society ; for their rich attire and a certain air of refined indifference was manifest, even in the excitement of an arrival.

Among the rest, Julia saw two persons that fascinated her attention in a most singular degree, drawing it from the whole scene, till she heeded nothing else.

One of these was a woman somewhat above the common size, and of superb proportions, who leaned against the railing of the steamer with a heavy, drooping bend, as if occupied with some deep and painful feeling. One glove was off, and her eager grasp upon the black wood-work seemed to start the blue veins up to the snowy surface of a hand, whose symmetry was visible, even from the shore. Julia could not remove her eyes from the strange and beautiful face of this woman. Deep, but subdued agony was at work in every lineament. There was wildness in her very motion, as she lifted her superb form from the railing, and drew the folds of a cashmere shawl over her bosom, pressing her hand hard upon the rich fabric, as if to relieve some painful feeling that it covered.

The steamer now lay close in her berth. A sort of movable staircase was flung from the side of the wharf, and down this staircase came the passengers, eager to touch the firm earth once more. Among the foremost was the woman who had so riveted the attention of Julia Warren; and, behind her, bearing a silver dressing-case and a small embroidered satchel, came a tall and singular looking man. Though his form was upright enough in itself, he bent forward in his walk; and his arms, long and awkward, seemed like the members of some other body, that had, by mistake, been given up to his ungainly use. His dress was fine in material, but carelessly put on, ill-fitting and badly arranged in all its tints. A hat of fine beaver and foreign make, seemed flung on the back of his head, and settled tightly there by a blow on the crown; his great hands were gloveless; and his boots appeared at least a size too large for the feet they encased.

This man would now and then cast a glance from his small, gray eyes on the superb woman who preceded him; and it was easy to see by his countenance, that he observed, and after his fashion shared the anguish visible in her features. His own face deepened in its expression of awkward sadness with every glance; and he hugged the dressing case to his side with unconscious violence, which threatened to crush the delicate frost-work that enriched it.

With a wild and dry brightness in her large, blue eyes, the lady descended to the wharf, a few paces from the spot occupied by the strawberry girl. As her foot touched the earth, Julia saw that the white hand dropped from its hold on the shawl, and the costly garment half fell from her shoulders, trailing the dirty wharf with its embroidery. In the whole crowd there was no object but this woman to the girl. With a pale cheek and suspended breath she watched every look and motion. There was something almost supernatural in the concentration of her whole being on this one person. An intense desire to address the stranger—to meet the glance of her eyes—to hear her voice, seized upon the child. She sprang forward, obeying this strange impulse, and lifting the soiled drapery of the shawl, held it up grasped in her trembling hands.

"Lady, your shawl!"

The child could utter no more. Those large, blue eyes were bent upon her face. Her own seemed fascinated by the gaze Slowly, sadly they filled with tears, drop by drop, and the eyes of that strange, beautiful woman filled also. Still she gazed upon the child—her clean, poverty-stricken dress—her meek face, and the basket of fruit and flowers upon her arm; and as she gazed, a faint smile crept around her mouth.

"This sweet voice—the flowers—is it not a beautiful welcome?" she said, glancing through her tears upon the man who stood close by her side; but the uncouth friend, or servant, whatever he might be, did not answer. His eyes were riveted on the child, and some strange feeling seemed to possess him.

"Give me," said the lady, passing her hand over Julia's head with a caressing motion—"give me some of these roses; it is a long time since I have touched a flower grown in home soil!"

Julia selected her freshest bouquet and held it up. The

lady's hand trembled as she drew forth her purse, and dropping a bright coin into the basket, received the flowers.

"Take a few of the strawberries, lady, they are so ripe and cool!" said the little girl, lifting one of the baskets from its leafy nest.

Again the lady smiled through her tears, and taking the little basket, poured a few of the strawberries into her ungloved hand.

"Would not he like some?" questioned the child, offering the basket with its scarcely diminished contents to the man, who still kept his eyes fixed on her face.

"No, not them—but give me a bunch of the blue flowers—they grew around the rock-spring at the old homestead, thousands and thousands on 'em!" cried the man, with a strong Down East pronunciation, and securing a tuft of the violets he turned aside, as if ashamed of the emotion he had betrayed.

The lady turned away. Something in his words seemed to have disturbed her greatly. She gathered the shawl about her, and moved towards a carriage that had drawn close up to the wharf.

Julia's heart beat quick; she could not bear to see that strange, beautiful woman depart without speaking to her again.

"Lady, will you take this one little bunch?—some people love violets better than anything!"

"No, no, I cannot—I——" The lady paused, tears seemed choking her. She drew down the folds of a rich blonde veil over her face, and moved on.

Julia laid the violets back into her basket with a sigh. Feelings of vague disappointment were saddening her heart. When she looked up again, the lady had taken her seat in the carriage, and leaning out was beckoning to her.

"I will take the violets!" she said, reaching forth her hand, that trembled as the simple blossoms were placed in it.—"Heaven forbid that I should cast the sweet omen from me. Thank you child—thank you."

The lady drew back into the carriage. Her face was clouded

by the veil, but tears trembled in her voice, and that voice lingered upon Julia Warren's ear many a long month afterward. It had unlocked the deepest well-spring of her life.

The strawberry girl stood upon the wharf motionless and lost in thought minutes after the carriage drove away. She had forgotten the basket on her arm, everything in the strange regret that lay upon her young heart. Never, never would she meet that beautiful woman again. The thought filled her soul with unutterable loneliness. She was unconscious that another carriage had driven up, and that a Southern vessel, arrived that morning, was pouring forth luggage and passengers on the opposite side of the pier. She took no heed of anything that was passing around her, till a sweet, low voice close by, exclaimed—

"Oh! see those flowers—those beautiful, beautiful moss rose-buds!"

Julia looked up. A young girl with soft, dark eyes, and lips dewy and red as the buds she coveted, stood a few paces off, with her hand grasped by a tall and stately looking man, approaching middle age, if not a year or two on the other side, who seemed anxious to hurry his companion into the carriage.

"Step in, Florence, the girl can come to us!" said the man, restraining the eager girl, who had withdrawn her foot from the carriage steps. "Come, come, lady-bird, this is no place for us: see, half the crowd are looking this way."

The young lady blushed and entered the carriage, followed by her impatient companion, who beckoned Julia towards him.

"Here," he said, tossing a silver coin into her basket, "give me those buds, quick, and then get out of the way, or you will be trampled down."

Julia held up her basket, half terrified by the impatience that broke from the dark eyes bent upon her.

"There, sweet one, these might have ripened on your own smile: kiss them for my sake!" said the man, gently bending with his fragrant gift toward his lovely companion.

His voice, soft, sweet and harmonious, fell upon the child's heart also ; and while the tones melted into her memory, she shuddered as the flower may be supposed to shrink when a serpent creeps by.

CHAPTER II.

THE OLD COUPLE.

There is no spot so dark on earth,
But love can shed bright glimmers there,
Nor anguish known, of human birth,
That yieldeth not to faith and prayer.

In the basement of a rear building in one of those cross streets that grow more and more squalid as they stretch down to the water's edge, sat an aged couple, at nightfall, on the day when our humble heroine was presented to the reader. The room was damp, low and dark ; a couple of rude chairs, a deal table, and a long wooden chest were all the furniture it contained. A rough shelf ran over the mantel-piece, on which were arranged a half dozen unmatched cups and saucers, and a broken plate or two, and a teapot, minus half its spout, all scrupulously washed, and piled together with some appearance of ostentation.

A brown platter, which stood on the table, contained the only approach to food that the humble dwelling afforded. A bone of bacon thrice picked, and preserved probably from a wretched desire to possess something in the shape of food, though that something was but a mockery, this and a fragment of bread lay upon the platter, covered with a neat crash towel.

A straw bed made up on one corner of the floor partook of the general neatness everywhere visible in the wretched dwelling; the sheets were of homespun linen, such as our Down East house-wives loved to manufacture years ago, and the covering a patch-work quilt, formed of rich, old-fashioned chintz, was neatly turned under the edges. One might have known how more than precious was that fine old quilt, by the great care taken to preserve it. The whole apartment bespoke extreme poverty in its most respectable form. Perfect destitution and scrupulous neatness were so blended, that it made the heart ache with compassion.

The old couple drew their seats closer together on the hearth-stone, and looked wistfully in each other's faces as the darkness of coming night gathered around them. The bright morning had been succeeded by a chill, uncomfortable rain, and this increased tenfold the gloomy and dark atmosphere of the basement. Thus they sat gazing at each other, and listening moodily to the rain as it beat heavier and heavier upon the sidewalks.

"Come, come!" said the old woman, with a smile that she intended to be cheerful, but which was only a wan reflection of what she wished. "This is all very wrong; once to-day the Lord has sent us food, and here we are desponding again. Julia will be cold and wet, poor thing; don't let her find us looking so hungry when she comes in."

"I was thinking of her," muttered the old man, in a sad voice. "Yes, the poor thing will be cold and wet and wretched enough, but that is nothing to the disappointment; she had built up such hopes this morning."

"Well, who knows after all; something may have happened!" said the old woman, with an effort at hopefulness.

"No, no," replied the man, in a voice of touching despondency, "if she had done anything, the child would have been home long ago. She has no heart to come back."

The old man passed his hand over his eyes, and then flung a handful of chips and shavings on the fire from a scant pile that lay in a corner. The blaze flamed up, revealing the desolate room for a moment, and then died away, flashing over the pale and haggard faces that bent over it, with a wan brilliancy that made them look absolutely corpse-like.

Those two wrinkled faces were meagre and wrinkled from

lack of sustenance; still, in the faded lineaments there was nothing to revolt the heart. Patience, sweet and troubled affection, were blended with every grief-written line. But the wants of the body had stamped themselves sharply there. The thin lips were pale and fixed in an expression of habitual endurance. Their eyes were sharp and eager, dark arches lay around them, and these were broken by wrinkles that were not all of age.

As the flame blazed up, the old man turned and looked earnestly on his wife, a look of keen want, of newly whetted hunger broke from her eyes, naturally so meek and tranquil, and the poor old man turned his glance another way with a faint groan. It was a picture of terrible famine. Yet patience and affection flung a thrilling beauty over it.

One more furtive glance that old man cast on his wife, as the flame went down, and then he clasped his withered fingers, wringing them together.

"You are starving—you are more hungry than ever," he said, "and I have nothing to give you."

The poor woman lifted up her head and tried to smile, but the effort was heart-rending.

"It is strange," she said, "but the food we had this morning only seems to make me more hungry. Is it so with you, Benjamin? I keep thinking of it all the time. The rain as it plashes on the pavement seems like that warm coffee boiling over on the hearth; those shavings as they lie in the corner are constantly shifting before my eyes, and seem like rolls and twists of bread, which I have only to stoop forward and take."

The old man smiled wanly, and a tear started to his eyes, gliding down his cheek in the dim light.

"Let us try the bone once more," he said, after a brief silence, "there may be a morsel left yet."

"Yes, the bone! there may be something on the bone yet! In our good fortune this morning we must have forgotten to scrape it quite clean!" cried the old woman, starting up with eager haste, and bringing the platter from the table.

The husband took it from her hands, and setting it down before the fire, knelt on one knee, and began to scrape the bone eagerly with a knife. "See, see !" he said, with a painful effort at cheerfulness, as some strips and fragments fell on the platter, leaving the bone white and glistening like ivory. "This is better than I expected ? With a crust and a cup of clear cold water, it will go a good way."

"No, no," said the woman, turning her eyes resolutely away, "we had forgotten Julia. She scarcely ate a mouthful this morning !"

"I know," said the old man, dropping his knife with a sigh.

"Put it aside, and let us try and look as if we had been eating all day. She would not touch it if—if——" Here the good old woman's eyes fell upon the little heap of food—those precious fragments which her husband had scraped together with his knife. The animal grew strong within her at the sight ; she drew a long breath, and reaching forth her bony hand, clutched them like a bird of prey ; her thin lips quivered and worked with a sort of ferocious joy, as she devoured the little morsel, then, as if ashamed of her voracity, she lifted her glowing eyes to her husband, and cast the fragment of food still between her fingers back upon the platter.

"I could not help it ! Oh, Benjamin, I could *not* help it !" Big tears started in her eyes, and rolled penitently down her cheek. "Take it away ! take it away !" she said, covering her face with both hands. "You see how ravenous the taste of food makes me !"

"Take it !" said the old man, thrusting the platter into her lap.

"No ! no ! You haven't had a taste; you—you—I am better now, much better !"

For one instant the old man's fingers quivered over the morsel still left upon the platter, for he was famished and craving more food, even as his wife had been; but his better nature prevailed, and dashing his hand away, he thrust the plate more decidedly into her lap.

"Eat!" he said. "Eat! I can wait, and God will take care of the child!"

But the poor woman waved the food away, still keeping one hand resolutely over her eyes. "No—no!" she said faintly, "no—no!"

Her husband lifted the plate softly from her lap: she started, looked eagerly around, and sunk back in her chair with a hysterical laugh.

"The strawberries! the strawberries, Benjamin! Only think, if Julia could not sell the strawberries she will eat them, you know, all—all. Only think what a feast the child will have when she has all those strawberries! Bring back the meat; what will she care for that?"

The old man brought back the plate, but with a sorrowful look. He remembered that the strawberries entrusted to his grandchild were the property of another; but he could not find the heart to suggest this to the poor famished creature before him, and he rejoiced at the brief delusion that would induce her to eat the little that was left. With martyr-like stoicism he stifled his own craving hunger, and sat by while his wife devoured the remainder of the precious store.

"And you have had none," she said, with a piteous look of self-reproach, when her own sharp want was somewhat appeased.

"Oh, I can wait for Julia and the strawberries."

"And if that should fail," answered the poor wife, filled with remorse at her selfishness, or what she began to condemn as such, "if anything should have happened, you may pawn or sell the quilt to-morrow—I will say nothing against it—not a word. It was used for the first time when—when *she* was a baby, and—"

"And we have starved and suffered rather than part with it!" cried the old man, moving gloomily up and down the room, "while she—"

"Is dead and buried, I am afraid," said the woman, interrupting him.

"No," answered the old man, solemnly, "or we should not have been left behind. It is not for nothing, wife, that you and I, and her child too, have starved and pined, and prayed in this cellar. God has an end to accomplish, and we are His instruments; how, I cannot tell. It is dark, as yet; but all in His good time, His work will be done. Let us be patient."

"Patient!" said the old woman, dolefully; "I haven't strength to be anything but patient."

"She will yet return to us—our beautiful prodigal—our lost child," continued the old man, lifting his meek eyes heavenward "We have waited long; but the time will come."

"If I could only think so," said the woman, shaking her head drearily—"If I could but think so!"

"I know it," said the old man, lifting his clasped hands upward, while his face glowed with the holy faith that was in him; "God has filled my soul with this belief. It has given me life when food was wanting. It grows stronger with each breath that I draw. The time will come when I shall be called to redeem our child, even to the laying down of life, it may be. I sometimes had a thought, wife, that her regeneration will be thus accomplished."

"How? What do you mean to say, husband?"

"How, I cannot tell that; but the God of heaven will, in His own good time. Let us wait and watch."

"Oh! if she comes at last, I could be so patient! But think of the years that are gone, and no news, not a word. While we have suffered so much, every month, more and more—ah, husband, how can I be patient?"

"Wait," said the old man, solemnly; "keep still while God does his work. We know that our child has committed a great sin; but she was good once, and—"

"Oh, how kind, how good she was! I think she was more like an angel than any thing on earth, till *he* came."

"Hush! When he is mentioned, bitter wrath rises in my bosom; I cannot crush it out—I cannot pray it out. God help me! Oh, my God, help me to hear this one name with charity."

"Benjamin—my husband!" cried the old woman, regarding the strong anguish in his face with affright, as his uplifted hands shook in their tight grip on each other, and his whole frame began to tremble.

He did not heed her pathetic cry, but sat down again by the hearth, and with a thin hand pressed hard upon each knee, bent forward, gazing into the smouldering fire, gloomy and silent. The old woman stole one hand over his and pressed it gently. It returned no answering token of her sympathy, but still rigidly held its grasp on his knee.

Again she touched his hand, and the loved name, that had been so sweet to her in youth, filled his ear with pathetic tenderness.

"Benjamin!"

He lifted his head, looked earnestly in her face, and then sunk slowly to his knees. With his locked hands pressed down upon the hearth, and his head bent low like one preparing to cast off a heavy weight, he broke forth in a prayer of such stern, passionate entreaty, that the very storm seemed to pause and listen to the outbreak of a soul more impetuous than itself. Never in God's holiest temple has the altar been sanctified by a prayer, more full of majestic eloquence, than that which rose from the hearth of the miserable cellar that night. The old man truly wrestled with the angels, and called for help against his own rebellious nature, till his forehead was beaded with drops of anguish, and every word seemed to burn and quiver like fire upon his meagre lips.

She, in her weaker and more timid nature, fell down by his side, pouring faint ejaculations and low moans into the current of his eloquence. But while he prayed for strength to endure, for divine light by which he could tread on beneath the burden of life, she now and then broke forth into a moaning cry, which was,

"Bread! bread! oh God, give us this day our daily bread!"

All at once, in the midst of his pleading, the old man's voice broke; a glorious smile spread over his features, and dropping his forehead between both hands, he murmured in the fulness of a heart suddenly deluged with love,

"Oh, my God, I thank thee, thou hast indeed rendered me worthy to redeem our child!"

Then he arose feebly from his knees, and sat down with her withered hand in his, and gazed tranquilly on the sparks of fire that shot, at intervals, through the black shaving ashes.

"Wife," he said, and his voice was so changed from its sharp accents, that she lifted her eyes to his in wonder; "wife, you may speak of him now, God has given me strength; I can hear it without a vengeful wish."

"But I don't want to mention his name, I didn't mean to do it, then," answered the wife with a shudder.

"You see," rejoined Father Warren, with a grave, sweet smile, "You see, wife, how long the Lord has been chastening us before he would drive the fiend from my heart. How could I expect God to make me the instrument to save our child while this hate of her husband lay coiled up like a viper in my bosom?"

"And did you hate him so terribly?" she asked, not able to comprehend the strength of a nature like his.

"Hate!" exclaimed the old man, "did you not see how I toiled and wrestled to cast that hate out from my soul?"

"Yes, I saw," answered the wife, timidly, and they sunk into silence. Thus minutes stole on; the rain came down more furiously; the winds shook the loose window panes, and the fire grew fainter and fainter, only shedding a smoky gloom over those two pale faces.

All at once there came a faint noise in the area—the moist plash of a footstep mingled with the sound of falling rain. Then the outer door opened, admitting a gush of damp wind into the hall that forced back the door of the basement, and there stood little Julia Warren, panting for breath, but full of wild and beautiful animation. The rain was dripping from her hood, and down the heavy braids of her hair, and her little feet left a wet print on the floor at every step.

The old man started up, and flung some fresh fuel on the fire,

2*

which instantly filled the basement with a brilliant but transitory light. There she stood, that brave little girl, dripping with wet, and deluged with sudden light. Her cheeks were all in a glow, warm and wet, like roses in a storm. Her eyes were absolutely star-like in their brilliancy, and her voice broke through the room in a joyful gush that made everything cheerful again.

"Did you think I was lost, grandpa, or drowned in the rain—don't it pour, though? Here, grandma, come help me with the basket. Stop, till I light a candle, though."

The child knelt down in her dripping garments to ignite the candle, which she had taken somewhere from the depths of her basket. But her little hands shook, and the flame seemed to dance before her; she really could not hold the candle still enough for her purpose, that little form thrilled and shook so with her innocent joy.

"Here, grandpa, you try," she said, surrendering the candle, while her laugh filled the room like the carol of birds, when all the trees are in blossom, "I never shall make it out; but don't think, now, that I am shivering with the wet, or tired out—don't think anything till I have told you all about it. There, now, we have a light; come, come!"

The little girl dragged her basket to the hearth, and no fairy, telling down gold and rubies to a favorite, ever looked more lovely. Down by the basket the old grandparents fell upon their knees—one holding the light—the other crying like a child.

"See, grandpa, see; a beef-steak—a great, thick beef-steak, and pickles, and bread, and—and—do look, grandmother, this paper—what do you think is in it? oh! ha! I thought you would brighten up! tea, green tea, and sugar, and—why grandfather, is that you crying so? Dear, dear, how can you? Don't you see how happy I am? Why, as true as I live, if I ain't crying myself all the time! Now, ain't it strange; every one of us crying, and all for what? I—I believe I shall die, I'm so happy!"

The excited little creature dropped the paper of tea from her hands, as she uttered these broken words, and flinging herself on the old woman's bosom, clung to her, bathed in tears, and shaking like an aspen leaf, literally strengthless with the joy that her coming had brought to that desolate place.

While her arms were around the poor woman's neck, the grandmother kept her eyes fixed upon the basket, and she contrived to break a fragment from one of the loaves it contained, and greedily devour it amid those warm caresses.

Joy is often more restless than grief; Julia was soon on her feet again.

"There, there, grandmother! just let the bread alone, what is that to the supper we will have by-and-bye. I'll get three cents' worth of charcoal, and borrow a gridiron, and—and—now don't eat any more till I come back, because of the supper!"

The little girl darted out of the room as she uttered this last injunction, and her step was heard like the leap of a fawn, as she bounded through the passage. When she returned, the larger portion of a loaf had disappeared, and the old couple were in each other's arms, while fragments of prayer and thanksgiving fell from their lips. It was a beautiful picture of the human heart, when its holiest and deepest feelings are aroused. Gratitude to God and to his creatures shed a touching loveliness over it all.

Julia, with her bright eyes and eager little hands, bustled about, quite too happy for a thought of the fatigue she had endured all the day. She drew forth the little table. She furbished and brightened up the cups and saucers, and gave an extra rub to the iron candlestick, which was, for the first time in many a day, warmed up by a tall and snowy candle. The scent of the beef-steak as it felt the heat, the warm hiss of the tea-kettle, the crackling of the fire, made a cheerful accompaniment to her quick and joyous movements. The cold rain pattering without—the light gusts of wind that shook the windows, only served to render the comfort within more delightful.

"There now," said Julia, wiping the bottom of her broken-spouted tea-pot, and placing it upon the table, "there now, all is ready !. I'm to pour out the tea, grandpa must cut the steak, and you, grandma—oh, you are company to-night. Come, every thing is warm and nice."

The old people drew up to the humble board. A moment their gray heads were bent, while the girl bowed her forehead gently downward, and veiled her eyes with their silken lashes, as if the joy sparkling there were suddenly clouded by a thought of her own forgetfulness in taking a seat before the half-breathed blessing was asked.

But her heart was only subdued for a moment. Directly her hands began to flutter about the tea-pot, like a pair of humming birds, busy with some great, uncouth flower. She poured the rich amber stream forth with a dash, and as each lump of sugar fell into the cups, her mouth dimpled into fresh smiles. It was quite like a fairy feast to her. Too happy for thoughts of her own hunger, she was constantly dropping her knife and fork to push the bread to her grandfather, or heap the old grandma's plate afresh, and it seemed as if the broken tea-pot was perfectly inexhaustible, so constantly did she keep it circulating around the table.

"Isn't it nice, grandma, green tea, and such sugar. What, grandpa ! you haven't got through yet ?" she was constantly saying, if either of the old people paused in the enjoyment of their meal, for it seemed to her as if such unusual happiness ought to last a long, long time.

"Yes," said the old man at length, pushing back his plate with a pleasant sigh, and more pleasant smile ; "yes, Julia; now let us see you eat something, then tell us how all these things came about. You must have been very lucky to have earned a meal like this with one day's work."

"A meal !" cried the child ; "oh, the supper. You relished the supper, grandpa ?"

"Yes ; you couldn't have guessed how hungry we were, or how keenly we should have relished anything."

"But—but, you are wondering where the next will come from. You think me like a child in having spent so much in this one famous supper."

"Yes, like a child, a good, warm-hearted child—who could blame you?"

"Blame!" cried the grandmother, with tears in her eyes;—"blame! God bless her!"

"But then," said the child, shaking her head and forcing back a tear that broke through the sunshine in her eyes, "one should not spend everything at once; grandpa means that, I suppose?"

"No, no!" answered the old woman, eagerly, "he does not mean to find the least fault. How should he?"

"It would have been childish, though; but perhaps I should have done it, who knows?—one don't stop to think with a bright half dollar in one's hand, and a poor old grandfather and grandmother, hungry at home. But then look here!"

The child drew a coin from her bosom, and held it up in the candle-light.

"Gold!" cried the astonished grandfather, absolutely turning pale with surprise.

"A half eagle, a genuine half eagle, as I am alive!" exclaimed the old woman, taking the coin between her fingers and examining it eagerly.

"Yes, gold—a half eagle," said the exulting child, clasping her small hands on the table, "worth five dollars—the old woman in the market told me so!—five dollars! only think of that!"

"But you did not earn it," said the old man, gravely.

"Earn it—oh, no," answered the little girl with a joyous laugh, "who ever thought of a little girl like me earning five dollars in a day? Still I don't know. That good woman at the market told me to let every one give what he liked for the flowers, and so I did. The most beautiful lady you ever set eyes on, took a bunch of rose-buds from my basket, and flung that money in its place."

"But who was this lady? There may be some mistake.

She might not have known that it was gold !" said the old man, reaching over, and taking the half eagle from his wife.

"I think she knew; indeed I am quite sure she did," answered the child, "for she looked at the piece as she took it from her purse. She knew what it was worth, but I didn't."

"Well, that we may know what to think, tell us more about this wonderful day," said the old man, still examining the gold with an anxious expression of countenance. "Your grandmother has finished her tea, and will listen now."

Julia was somewhat subdued by her grandfather's grave air; but spite of this, tears and smiles struggled in her eyes, and her mouth, now tremulous, now dimpling, could hardly be trained into anything like serious narrative.

"Well," she said, shaking back the braids of her hair, and resolutely folding both hands in her lap. "Very well; please don't ask any questions till I have got through, and I'll do my best to tell everything just as it happened. You know how I went out this morning, about the basket that I got trusted for at the grocery, and all that. Well, I went off with the new basket on my arm, making believe to myself as bold as a lion. Still I couldn't but just keep from crying—everything felt so strange, and I was frightened too—you don't know how frightened !

"Grandma, I think the babes in the woods must have felt as I did, only I had no brother with me, and it is a great deal more lonesome to wander through lots of cold looking men and women that you never saw before, than to be lost among the green woods, where flowers lie everywhere in the moss, and the trees are all sorts of colors, with birds hopping and singing about—dear little birds, such as covered the poor babes with leaves, and—and—finally grandmother, as I was saying, I felt more lonesome and down-hearted than these children could have done, for they had plenty of blackberries, you know, but I was dreadful hungry—I was indeed, though I would not own it to you; and then all the windows were full of nice tarts and candies, just as if the people had put them there to see how bad they could make me feel. Well, I have told you about going into the market, and how my heart seemed to get colder and colder, till I saw that good woman—that dear, blessed woman——"

"God bless her, for that one kind act!" exclaimed the old man, fervently.

"He *will* bless her; be sure of that," chimed in the good grandame.

"I wish you could have seen her—I only wish you could!" cried the child, in her sweet, eager gratitude, "perhaps you will some day, who knows?"

And in the same sweet, disjointed language, the child went on relating her adventures along the streets, and on the wharf, where for the first time she had seen an ocean steamer.

When she spoke of the lady and her strange attendant, the old people seemed to listen with more absorbing interest. They were keenly excited by the ardent admiration expressed by the child, yet to themselves even this feeling was altogether unaccountable. When the little girl spoke of the strange man whom she had met on the wharf also, her voice become subdued, and there was a half terrified look in her eyes. The singular impression which that man had left upon her young spirit seemed to haunt it like a fear; she spoke almost in whispers, and looked furtively toward the door, as if afraid of being overheard; but the moment she related how he drove away with his beautiful companion, her courage seemed to return, she glanced brightly around, and went on with her narrative with renewed spirit.

"He had just gone," she said, "and I was beginning to look around for some way to leave the wharf, when I saw a handkerchief lying at my feet. The carriage wheel had run over it, and it was crushed down in the mud. I picked it up, and run after the carriage, for the handkerchief was fine as a cobweb, and worth ever so much, I dare say. In and out, through the carts, and trunks, and people, I ran with my basket on my arm, and the muddy handkerchief in one hand. Twice I saw the carriage, but it was too far ahead, and at last I turned a corner—I lost it there, and stood thinking what I should do, when the very carriage which I had seen go off with the lady in it, passed by; the lady had stopped for something, I suppose, and that kept her back. She was looking from the window that minute. I thought perhaps the handkerchief was hers, after all; so I ran off the sidewalk and shook it, that she might take notice. The carriage stopped; down came the driver and opened the door, and then the lady leaned out, and smiling with a sort of mournful smile, said—

"'Well, my girl, what do you want now?'"

"I held up the handkerchief, but was quite out of breath, and could only say, 'this—this—is it yours, ma'am?'

"She took the handkerchief, and turned to a corner where a name was marked. Then her cheek turned pale as death, and her mouth, so full, so red, grew white. I should have thought that she was dying, she fixed her eyes on me so wildly.

"'Come in, come in, this instant,' she said, and before I could speak, she caught hold of my arm, and drew me—basket and all—into the carriage. The door was shut, and in my fright I heard her tell the man to drive fast. I did not speak; it seemed like dreaming. There sat the lady, so pale, so altered, with the handkerchief, all muddy as it was, crushed hard in her white hand—sometimes looking with a sort of wild look at me, sometimes seeming to think of nothing on earth. The carriage went faster and faster; I was frightened and began to cry. She looked at me very kindly then, and said—

"'Hush, child, hush! no one will harm you.' Still I could not keep from sobbing, for it all seemed very wild and strange.

"Then the carriage stopped before a great stone house, with so many long windows, and iron-work fence all before it. A good many trees stood around it, and a row of stone steps went up half way from the gate to the front door. The windows of the house were painted all sorts of colors, and at one corner was a kind of steeple, square at the top and full of narrow windows, and half covered with a green vine that crept close to the stone-work almost to the top.

"No one came to the door. The strange man who rode with the driver let us in with a key that he had, and everything was as still as a meeting-house. When we got inside, the lady took my hand and led me into a great square entry-way, with a marble floor checked black and white; then she led me up a great high stair-case, covered from top to bottom with a carpet that seemed made of roses and wood-moss. Everything was still and half dark, for all the windows were covered deep with silk curtains, and it had begun to cloud up out of doors.

"The lady opened a door, and led me into a room more beautiful that anything I ever set my eyes on. But this was dark and dim like the rest. My feet sunk into the carpet, and everything I touched seemed made of flowers, the seats were so silken and downy.

"The lady flung off her shawl, and sat down upon a little sofa covered with blue silk. She drew me close to her, and tried to smile.

"'Now,' she said, 'you must tell me, little girl, exactly where you got the handkerchief!'

"'I found it—indeed I found it on the wharf,' I said, as well as I could, for crying. 'At first I thought it must belong to the tall gentleman, but he drove away so fast; then I saw your carriage, and thought——'

"She stopped me before I could say the rest—her eyes were as bright as diamonds, and her cheeks grew red again.

"'The tall gentleman! What tall gentleman?' she said.

"I told her about the man with the beautiful lady. Before I had done, she let go of my hand and fell back on the sofa; her eyes were shut, but down through the black lashes the great tears kept rolling till the silk cushion under her head was wet with them. I felt sorry to see her so troubled, and took the handkerchief from the floor—for it fell from her hand as she sunk down. With one corner that the wheel had not touched, I tried to wipe away the tears from her face, but she started up, all in a tremble, and pushed me away ; but not as if she were angry with me ; only as if she hated the handkerchief to touch her face.

"She walked about the room a few times, and then seemed to get quite natural again. By-and-bye the queer looking man came up with a satchel and a silver box, under his arm ; and she talked with him in a low voice. He seemed not to like what she said ; but she grew positive, and he went out. Then she lay down on the sofa again, as if I had not been by ; her two hands were clasped under her head ; she breathed very hard, and the tears now and then came in drops down her cheeks.

"It was getting dark, and I could hear the rain pattering outside. I spoke softly, and said that I must go ; she did not seem to hear ; so I waited and spoke again. Still she took no notice. Then I took up my basket and went out. Nobody saw me. The great house seemed empty—everything was grand, but so still that it made me afraid. Nothing but the rain dripping from the trees made the least noise. All around was a garden, and the house stood mostly alone, among the trees on the top of a hill and lifted up from the street. I had no idea where I was, for it seemed almost like the country, trees all around, and green grass and rose bushes growing all about the house !

"A long wide street stretched down the hill toward the city. I noticed the street lamp posts standing in a line each side, and just followed them till I got into the thick of the houses once more. After this I went up one street and down another, inquiring the way, till after a long, long walk, I got back to the market, quite tired out and anxious.

"The good market woman was *so* pleased to see me again. I gave her all my money, and she counted it, and took out pay for the flowers and strawberries. There was enough without the gold piece ; she would not let me change that, but filled the basket with nice things, just to encourage me to work hard next week. There, now, grandfather, I have told you all about this wonderful day. Isn't it quite like a fairy tale?"

The old man sat gazing on the sweet and animated face of his grandchild; his hands were clasped upon the table, and his aged face grew luminous with Christian gratitude. Slowly his forehead bent downward, and he answered her in the solemn and beautiful words of Scripture, "I have been young, and now I am old; yet I have never seen the righteous forsaken, or his seed begging bread." There was pathos and fervency in the old man's voice, solemn even as the words it syllabled. The little strawberry girl bowed her head with gentle feeling, and the grandmother whispered a meek "Amen."

CHAPTER III.

THE LONE MANSION.

There are some feelings all too deep,
  For grief to shake, or torture numb,
Sorrows that strengthen as they sleep,
  And struggle though the heart is dumb.

Little Julia Warren had given a very correct description of the house to which she had been so strangely conveyed. Grand, imposing, and unsurpassed for magnificence by anything known in our city, it was nevertheless filled with a sort of gorgeous gloom that fell like a weight upon the beholder. Most of the shutters were closed, and where the glass was not painted, rich draperies muffled and tinted the light wherever it penetrated a crevice, or struggled through the reversed fold of a blind.

As you passed through those sumptuous rooms, so vast, so still, it seemed like traversing a flower-garden by the faintest starlight; you knew that beautiful objects lay around you on every side, without the power of distinguishing them, save in shadowy masses. All this indistinctness took a strong hold on the imagination, rendered more powerful, perhaps, by the profound stillness that reigned in the dwelling.

Since the great front door had fallen softly to its latch after the little girl left the building, no sound had broken the intense hush that surrounded it. Still the lady, who had so marvelously impressed herself upon the heart of that child, lay prone upon the couch in her boudoir in the second story. She was the only living being in that whole dwelling, and but for the quick breath that now and then disturbed her bosom, she appeared lifeless as the marble Flora that seemed scattering lilies over the cushion where she rested.

After a time the stillness seemed to startle her. She lifted her head and looked around the room.

"Gone!" she said, in a tone of disappointment, which had something of impatience in it—"gone!"

The lady started up, pale and with an imperious motion, as one whose faintest wish had seldom been opposed. She approached a window, and flinging back the curtains of azure damask, cast another searching look over the room. But the pale, sweet features of the Flora smiling down upon her lilies, was the only semblance to a human being that met her eye. She dropped the curtain impatiently. The statue seemed mocking her with its cold, classic smile. It suited her better when the wind came with a sweep, dashing the rain-drops fiercely against the window.

The irritation which this sound produced on her nerves seemed to animate her with a keen wish to find the child who had disappeared so noiselessly. She went to the door, traversed the hall and the great stair-case ; and her look grew almost wild when she found no signs of the little girl ! Two or three times she parted her lips, as if to call out ; but the name that she would have uttered clung to her heart, and the parted lips gave forth no sound.

It was strange that a name, buried in her bosom for years, unuttered, hidden as the miser hides his gold, at once the joy, and agony of his life, should have sprung to her memory there and then ; but so it was, and the very attempt to syllable that name seemed to freeze up the animation in her face. She grew much paler after that, and her white fingers clung to the silver knob like ice as she opened the great hall-door and looked into the street.

The entrance to the mansion was sheltered, and though the rain was falling, it had not yet penetrated to the threshold. Up and down the broad street no object resembling the strawberry girl could be seen ; and with an air of disappointment, the lady was about to close the door, when she saw upon the threshold a broken rose-bud, which had evidently fallen from the child's basket, and beside it the prints of a little, naked foot left in damp tracery on the granite. These foot-prints descended the steps, and with a sigh the lady drew back, closing the door after her gently as she had opened it.

She stood awhile musing in the vestibule, then slowly mounting the stairs, entered the boudoir again. She sat down, but it was only for a minute ; the solitude of the great house might have shaken the nerves of a less delicate woman, now that the rain was beating against the windows, and the gloom thickening around her, but she seemed quite unconscious of this. Some new idea had taken possession of her mind, and it had power to arouse her whole being. She paced the room, at first gently, then with rapid footsteps, becoming more and more excited each moment ; though this was only manifested by the brilliancy of her eyes, and the breathless eagerness with which she listened from time to time. No sound came to her ears, however—nothing but the rain beating, beating, beating against the plate-glass.

The lady took out her watch, and a faint, mocking smile stole over her lips. It seemed as if she had been expecting the return of her servant for hours ; and lo ! only half an hour had passed since he went forth.

" And this," she said, with a gesture and look of self-reproach —" this is the patience—this the stoicism which I have attained —Heaven help me !" She walked slower then, and at length sunk upon the couch with her eyes closed resolutely, as one who forced herself to wait and be still. Thus she remained, perhaps fifteen minutes, and the marble statue smiled upon her through its chill, white flowers.

She had wrestled with herself and conquered. So much time! Only fifteen minutes, but it seemed an hour. She opened her eyes, and there was that smiling face of marble peering down into hers; it seemed as if something human were scanning her heart. The fancy troubled her, and she began to walk about again.

As the lady was pacing to and fro in her boudoir, her foot became entangled in the handkerchief which she had so passionately wrested from the strawberry-girl, when in her gentle sympathy the child would have wiped the tears from her eyes. She took the cambric in her hand, not without a shudder; it might be of pain; it might be that some hidden joy blended itself with the emotion; but with an effort at self-control she turned to a corner of the handkerchief, and examined a name written there with attention.

Again some powerful change of feeling seemed to sweep over her; she folded the handkerchief with care, and went out of the room, still grasping it in her hand. Slowly, and as if impelled against her wishes, this singular woman mounted a flight of serpentine stairs, which wound up the tower that Julia had described as a steeple, and entered a remote room of the dwelling. Even here the same silent splendor, the same magnificent gloom that pervaded the whole dwelling, was darkly visible. Though perfectly alone, carpets thick as forest moss muffled her foot-steps, till they gave forth no echo to betray her presence. Like a spirit she glided on, and but for her breathing she might have been taken for something truly supernatural, so singular was her pale beauty, so strangely motionless were her eyes.

For a moment the lady paused, as if calling up the locality of some object in her mind, then she opened the door of a small room and entered.

A wonderful contrast did that little chamber present to the splendor through which she had just passed. No half twilight reigned there ; no gleams of rich coloring awoke the imagination ; everything was chaste and almost severe in its simplicity. Half a shutter had been left open, and thus a cold light was admitted to the chamber, revealing every object with chilling distinctness :—the white walls ; the faded carpet on the floor ; and the bed piled high with feathers, and covered with a patchwork quilt pieced from many gorgeously colored prints, now somewhat faded and mellowed by age. Half a dozen stiff maple chairs stood in the room. In one corner was a round mahogany stand, polished with age, and between the windows hung a looking-glass framed in curled maple. No one of these articles bore the slightest appearance of recent use, and common-place as they would have seemed in another dwelling, in that house they looked mysteriously out of keeping.

The lady looked around as she entered the room, and her face expressed some new and strong emotion ; but she had evidently schooled her feelings, and a strong will was there to second every mental effort. After one quick survey her eyes fell upon the carpet. It was an humble fabric, such as the New England housewives manufacture with their own looms and spinning wheels ; stripes of hard, positive colors contrasted harshly together, and even time had failed to mellow them into harmony ; though faded and dim, they still spread away from the feet harsh and disagreeable. No indifferent person would have looked upon that cheerless object twice ; but it seemed to fascinate the gaze of the singular woman, as no artistic combination of colors could have done. Her eyes grew dim as she gazed ; her step faltered as she moved across the faded stripes; and reaching a chair near the bed, she sunk upon it pale and trembling. The tremor went off after a few minutes, but her face retained its painful whiteness, and she fell into thought so deep that her attitude took the repose of a statue.

Thus an hour went by. The storm had increased, and through the window which opened upon a garden, might be seen the dark sway of branches tossed by the roaring wind, and blackened with the gathering night. The rain poured down in sheets, and beat upon the spacious roof like the rattle of artillery. Gloom and commotion reigned around. The very elements seemed vexed with new troubles as that beautiful woman entered the room whose humble simplicity seemed so unsuited to her.

Ada saw nothing of the storm, or if she did, the wildness and gloom seemed but a portion of the tumult in her own heart. Yet how still and calm she was—that strange being! At length the chain of iron thought seemed broken; she turned toward the bed, laid her hand gently down upon the quilt, and gazed at the faded colors till some string in her proud heart gave way, and sinking down with her face buried in the scant pillows, she wept like a child. Every limb in her body began to tremble. The bed shook under her, and notwithstanding the stormy elements, the noise of her bitter sobs filled the room. The voice of her grief was soon broken by another sound—the sound of passionate kisses lavished upon the pillows, the quilt, and the homespun linen upon the bed. She looked at them through her tears; she smoothed them out with her trembling hands; she laid her cheek against them lovingly, as a punished child will sometimes caress the very garments of a mother whose forgiveness it craves; yet in all this you saw that this strange, almost insane excitement was not usual to the woman—that she was not one to yield her strength to a light passion; and this made her grief the more touching. You felt that if such storms often swept across her track of life, she did not bow herself to them without a fierce struggle.

She lay upon the bed weeping and faint with exhausted emotion, when the sound of a closing door rang through the building. This was followed by stumbling footsteps so heavy that even the turf-like carpets could not muffle them. The lady started up, listened an instant, and then hurried from the room, closing the door carefully after her. It was now almost dark, and but for the angular figure and ungainly attitude of the person she found in her boudoir, she might not have recognized her own servant, who stood waiting her approach.

"Jacob, you have come—well!" said the lady in a low voice.

"Yes, and a pretty time I have had of it," said the man, drawing back from the hand which she had almost placed upon his arm, and shaking himself with much of the surliness, and all the indifference of a mastiff, till the rain fell in showers from his coat. "I am soaking wet, ma'm, and dangerous to come near—it might give you a cold."

"It is raining then?" said the lady, subduing her impatience.

"Raining! I should think it was, and blowing too. Why, don't you hear the wind yelling and tusseling with the trees back of the house?"

"I have not noticed," answered the lady, mournfully; "I was thinking of other things."

"Of *him*, I suppose!" There was something husky in the man's voice as he spoke, the more remarkable that his strong Down East pronunciation was usually prompt, and clear from any signs of feeling.

"Yes, of him and of them! Jacob, this has been a terrible day to me."

"And to me, gracious knows!" muttered the man, giving his coat another rough shake.

"Yes, you have been upon your feet all day—you are wet through, my kind friend, and all to serve me—I know that it is hard!"

"Nothing of the sort!—nothing of the sort! Who on earth complained, I should like to know? A little rain, poh!" exclaimed the man, evidently annoyed that his vexation, uttered in an under tone, should have reached the lady's ear.

"No, you never do complain, Jacob; and yet you have often found me an exacting mistress—or friend, I should rather say—for it is long since I have considered you as anything else. I have often taxed your strength and patience too far!"

"There it is again!" answered the man, with a sort of rough impatience, which, however, had nothing unkind or disrespectful in it—"jist as if I was complaining or discontented—jist as if I wasn't your hired man—no, servant, that is the word—*to* serve, wait, tend on you; and hadn't been ever since the day—but no matter about that—jist now I've been down town as you ordered."

"Well!"

Oh! how much of exquisite self-control was betrayed by the low, steady tone in which that little word was uttered.

"Of course," said the man, "I could do nothing without help. The little girl's story was enough to prove that—that he was in town, but it only went so far. She neither knew which way he drove, or how the coach was numbered; so it seemed very much like searching for a needle in a hay-mow. But you wanted to know where he was, and I determined to find out. Wal, this morning, as we left the steamer, I saw a man in the crowd with a great, gilt star on his breast, and as the thing looked rather odd for a republican, I asked what it meant. It was a policeman; they have got up a new system here in the city, it seems, and from what was said on the wharf, I thought it no bad idea to get some of these men to help me to search for Mr. Leicester."

"Hush, hush; don't speak so loud," said the lady, starting as a name her lips had not uttered for years was thus suddenly pronounced.

"I inquired the way, and went to the police office at once: it is in the Park, ma'm, under the City Hall. Wal, there I found the chief, a smart, active fellow as I ever set eyes on; I told him what brought me there, and who I wanted to find. He called a young man from the out room; wrote on a slip of paper; gave it to the man, and asked me to sit down. Wal, I sat down, and we began to talk about my travels, and things in gineral, like old acquaintances, till by-and-bye in came the very policeman that I had seen on the wharf.

"'Mr. Johnson,' says the chief, 'a Southern vessel arrived to-day at the same wharf where the steamer lies. Did you observe a tall gentlemen with a young lady on his arm, leave that vessel?'

"'Dark hair; large eyes; a black coat?' says the man, looking at me.

"'Exactly,' says I.

"'The lady beautiful; eyes you could hardly tell the color of; lashes always down; black silk dress; cashmere scarf; cottage-bonnet!' says he, again.

"'Jist so!' says I.

"'Yes,' says he to the chief, 'I saw them.'

"'Where did they go?' questions the chief.

"'Hack No. 117 took three fares from the vessel and steamer, one to the City Hall, one to the New York, one to the Astor. This was the second, he went to the Astor.'"

"And the young girl—did she go with him?" cried the lady, striving in vain to conceal the keen interest which prompted the question.

"That was just what the chief asked," was the reply.

"And the answer—was she with him?"

"Wal, the chief put that question, only a little steadier; and the man answered that the young lady——"

"Well."

"That the coachman first took the young lady to a house in —I believe it was Ninth street, or Tenth, or——"

"No matter, so she was not with him," answered the lady, drawing a deep breath, while an expression of exquisite relief came to her features; "and he is there alone at the Astor House. And I in the same city! Does nothing tell him?—has his heart no voice that clamors as mine does? The Astor House! Jacob, how far is the Astor House from this?"

"More than a mile—two miles. I don't exactly know how far it is."

"A mile, perhaps two, and that is all that divides us. Oh! God, would that it were all!" she cried, suddenly clasping her hands with a burst of wild agony.

The servant man recoiled as he witnessed this burst of passion, wherefore it were difficult to say; for he remained silent, and the twilight had gathered fast and deep in the room. For several minutes no word was spoken between the two persons so unlike in looks, in mind, in station, and yet linked together by a bond of sympathy strong enough to sweep off these inequalities into the dust. At length the lady lifted her head, and looked at the man almost beseechingly through the twilight.

The storm was still fierce. The wind shook and tore through the foliage of the trees; and the rain swept by in sheets, now and then torn with lightning, and shaken with loud bursts of thunder.

"The weather is terrible!" said the lady, with a sad, winning smile, and with her beautiful eyes bent upon the man.

He thought that she was terrified by the lightning, and this brought his kind nature back again.

"This—oh! this is nothing, madam. Think of the storms we used to have in the Alps, and at sea."

A beautiful brilliancy came into the lady's eyes.

"True, this is nothing compared to them: and the evening, it is not yet entirely dark!"

"The storm makes it dark—that is all. It isn't far off from sun-down by the time!" answered Jacob, taking out an old silver watch, and examining it by the window.

"Jacob, are you very tired?"

"Tired, ma'm! What on earth should make me tired? One would think I had been hoeing all day, to hear such questions!"

The lady hesitated. She seemed ashamed to speak again, and her voice faltered as she at length forced herself to say—

"Then, Jacob, as you are not quite worn out—perhaps you will get me a carriage—there must be stables in the neighborhood."

"A carriage!" answered the man, evidently overwhelmed with surprise: "a carriage, madam, to-night, in all this rain!"

"Jacob—Jacob, I must see him—I must see him now, to-night—this hour! The thought of delay suffocates me—I am not myself—do you not see it? All power over myself is gone. Jacob, I must see him now, or die!"

"But the storm, madam," urged poor Jacob, from some cause almost as pale as his mistress.

"The better—all the better. It gives me courage. How can we two meet, save in storm and strife? I tell you the tempest will give me strength."

"I beg of you, I—I——"

"Jacob, be kind—get me the carriage!" pleaded the lady, gently interrupting him: "urge nothing more, I entreat you; but instead of opposing, help me. Heaven knows, but for you I am helpless enough!"

There was no resisting that voice, the pleading eloquence of those eyes. A deep sigh was smothered in that faithful breast, and then he went forth perfectly heedless of the rain; which, to do him justice, had never been considered in connection with his own personal comfort.

He returned after a brief absence; and a dark object before the iron gate, over which the rain was dripping in streams, bespoke the success of his errand. The lady had meantime changed her dress to one of black silk, perfectly plain, and giving no evidence of position, by which a stranger might judge to what class of society she belonged; a neat straw bonnet and a shawl completed her modest costume.

"I am ready, waiting!" she cried, as Jacob presented himself at the door, and drawing down her veil that he might not see all that was written in her face, she passed him and went forth.

But Jacob caught one glance of that countenance with all its eloquent feeling, for a small lamp had been lighted in the boudoir during his absence; and that look was enough. He followed her in silence.

CHAPTER IV.

THE ASTOR HOUSE AND THE ATTIC ROOM.

When woman sinneth with her heart,
Some trace of heaven still lingers there;
The angels may not all depart
And yield her up to dark despair.

But man—alas, when thought and brain
Can sin, and leave the soul at ease:
Can sneer at truth and scoff at pain!—
God's angels shrink from sins like these!

Alone in one of the most sumptuous chambers of the Astor House, sat the man who had made an impression so powerful upon little Julia Warren that morning. Though the chill of that stormy night penetrated even the massive walls of the hotel, it had no power to throw a shadow upon the comforts with which this man had found means to surround himself. A fire blazed in the grate, shedding a glow upon the rug where his feet were planted, till the embroidered slippers that encased them seemed buried in a bed of forest moss.

The curtains were drawn close, and the whole room had an air of snugness and seclusion seldom found at a hotel. Here stood an open dressing-case of ebony, with its gold mounted and glittering equipments exposed; there was a travelling desk of ebony, inlaid with mother-of-pearl, opal-tinted and glittering like gems in the uncertain light. Upon the mantel-piece stood a small picture-frame, carved to a perfect net-work, and apparently of pure gold, circling the miniature of a female, so exquisitely painted, so beautiful in itself, that the heart warmed to a glow while gazing upon it. It was a portrait of the very girl whom Julia had seen supported by that man's arm in the morning—new and fresh was every tint upon the ivory. Alas! no female face ever had time to grow shadowy and mellow in that little frame; with almost every change of the moon some new head was circled by the glittering net-work—and this spoke eloquently of one dark trait in the character of the man.

He sat before the fire, leaning back in his cushioned easy-chair, now glancing with an indolent smile at the picture—now leaning toward a small table at his elbow, and helping himself to the fragments of some tiny game-birds from a plate where several were lying, all somewhat mutilated, as if he had tried each without perfectly satisfying his fastidious appetite. Various foreign condiments, and several flasks of wine stood on the table, with rich china and glasses of unequal shape and variously tinted. For at the hotel this man was known to be as fastidious in his taste as in his appetite ; with him the appointments of a meal were equally important with the viands.

No lights were in the room, save two wax tapers in small candle-sticks of frosted silver, which, with various articles of plate upon the table, composed a portion of his travelling luxuries. If we have dwelt long upon these small objects, it is be cause they bespoke the character of the man better than any philosophical analysis of which we are capable, and from a feeling of reluctance to come in contact with the hard and selfish, even in imagination.

Oh ! if the pen were only called upon to describe the pure and the good, what a pleasant task might be this of authorship; but while human life is made up of the evil and the good, in order to be true, there must be many dark shadows in every picture of life as it exists now, and has existed from the beginning of the world. In humanity, as in nature herself, there is midnight darkness contrasting with the bright and pure sunshine.

There was nothing about the person of Leicester that should make the task of describing him an unpleasant one. He had reached the middle age, at least was fast approaching it : and on a close scrutiny, his features gave indication of more advanced years than the truth would justify ; for his life had been one that seldom leaves the brow smooth, or the mouth perfectly flexible. Still to a casual observer, Leicester was a noble-looking and elegant man. The dark gloss and luxuriance of his hair was in nothing impaired by the few threads of silver that begun to make themselves visible ; his forehead was high, broad and white ; his teeth perfect, and though the lips were somewhat heavy, the smile that at rare intervals stole over them was full of wily fascination, wicked, but indescribably alluring. That smile had won many a new face to the little frame from which poor Florence Craft seemed to gaze upon him with mournful tenderness.

As he looked upward it deepened, spread and quivered about his mouth, that subtle and infatuating smile. There was something of tenderness, something of indolent scorn blended with it then, for his eyes were lifted to that beautiful face gazing upon him so immovably from the ivory. He caught the mournful expression, cast, perhaps, by the position of the candles, and it was this that gave a new character to his smile. He stretched himself languidly back in his chair, clasped both hands behind his head, and still gazed upward with half closed eyes.

This change of position loosened the heavy cord of silk with which a dressing-gown, lined with crimson velvet, and of a rich cashmere pattern, had been girded to his waist, thus exposing the majestic proportions of a person strong, sinewy and full of flexible vigor. His vest was off, and the play of his heart might have been counted through the fine and plaited linen that covered his bosom. Something more than the rise and fall of a base heart, had that loosened cord exposed. Protruding from an inner pocket of his dressing-gown the inlaid butt of a revolver was just visible.

Thus surrounded by luxuries, with a weapon of death close to his heart, William Leicester sat gazing with half-shut eyes upon the mute shadow that returned his look with such mournful intensity. At length the smile upon his lip gave place to words full of meaning, treacherous and more carelessly cruel than the smile had foreshadowed.

"Oh! Flor, Flor," he said, "your time will soon come. This

excessive devotion—this wild love—it tires one, child—you are unskilful, Flor—a little spice of the evil-one—a storm of anger—now a dash of indifference—anything but this eternal tenderness. It gets to be a bore at last, Flor, indeed it does."

And Leicester waved his head at the picture, smiling gently all the time. Then he unsealed one of the wine-flasks, filled a glass and lifted it to his mouth. After tasting the wine with a soft, oily smack of the lips, and allowing a few drops to flow down his throat, he put aside the glass with a look of disgust, and leaning forward, rang the bell.

Before his hand left the bell-tassel, a servant was at the door, not in answer to his summons, but with information that a carriage had stopped at the private entrance, and that some one within wished to speak with him.

Leicester seemed annoyed. He drew the cords of his dressing-gown, and stood up.

"Who is in the carriage? What does he seem like, John?"

The mulatto smiled till his teeth glistened in the candle-light.

"Why don't you speak, fellow?"

The waiter cast a shy glance toward the picture on the mantel-piece, and his teeth shone again.

"The night is dark as pitch, sir; I couldn't see a yard from the door; but I heard a voice. It wasn't a man's voice."

"A woman!—in all this storm too. Surely *she* cannot have been so wild," cried Leicester, casting aside his dressing-gown, and hurriedly replacing it with garments more befitting the night, "Go, John, and say that I will be down presently, and listen as you give the message; try and get a glimpse of the lady."

John disappeared, and threaded his way to the entrance with wonderful alacrity. A man stood upon the steps, apparently indifferent to the rain that beat in his face. By changing his position he might have avoided half the violence of each new gust, but he seemed to feel a sort of pleasure in braving it, for a stern pallor lay upon the face thus steadily turned to the storm.

This was the man who had first spoken to the servant, but instead of addressing him, John was passing to the carriage, intent on learning something of its inmate. But as he went down the steps a strong grasp was fixed on his arm, and he found himself suddenly wheeled, face to face, with the powerful man upon the upper flag.

"Where are you going?"

There was something in the man's voice that made the mulatto shake.

"I was going to the carriage, sir, with Mr. Leicester's message to the—the——" Here John began to stammer, for he felt the grasp upon his arm tighten like a vice.

"I sent for Mr. Leicester to come down; give *me* his answer!"

"Yes—yes, sir, certainly. Mr. Leicester will be down in a minute," stammered John, shaking the rain from his garments, and drawing back to the doorway the moment he was released, but casting a furtive glance into the darkness, anxious, if possible, to learn something of the person in the carriage.

That moment, as if to reward his vigilance, the carriage window was let down, and by the faint light that struggled from the lanterns, the mulatto saw a white hand thrust forth; and a face of which he could distinguish nothing, save that it was very pale, and lighted by a pair of large eyes fearfully brilliant, gleamed on him through the illuminated mist.

"What is it? Will he not come? Open the door—open the door," cried a voice that rang even through his inert heart.

It was a female's voice, full and clear, but evidently excited to an unnatural tone by some powerful feeling.

Again the mulatto attempted to reach the carriage.

"Madam—Mr. Leicester will——"

Before the sentence was half uttered, the mulatto found him self reeling back against the door, and the man who hurled him there, darted down the steps.

"Shut the window—sit further back, for gracious' sake."

"Is he coming? Is he here?" was the wild rejoinder.

"He *is* coming; but do be more patient."

"I will—I will!" cried the lady, and without another word she drew back into the darkness.

Meanwhile the mulatto found his way back to the chamber, where Mr. Leicester was waiting with no little impatience. The very imperfect report which he was enabled to give, relieved Leicester from his first apprehension, and excited a wild spirit of adventure in its place.

"Who in the name of Heaven can it be?" broke from him as he was looking for his hat. "The face, John, you saw the face, ha!"

"Only something white, sir; and the eyes—such eyes, large and shining—a great deal brighter than the lamp, that was half put out by the rain!"

"It cannot be Florence, that is certain," muttered Leicester, as he took up his dressing-gown from the floor and transferred the revolver to an inner pocket of his coat—"some old torment, perhaps, or a new one. Well, I'm ready."

Leicester found the carriage at the entrance, its outlines only defined in the surrounding darkness by the pale glimmer of a lamp, whose companion had been extinguished by the rain. Upon the steps, but lower down, and close by the carriage, stood the immovable figure of that self constituted sentinel. As Leicester presented himself, on the steps above, this man threw open the carriage door, but kept his face turned away, even from the half dying lamp-light.

Leicester saw that he was expected to enter; but though bold, he was a cautious man, and for a moment held back with a hand upon his revolver.

"Step in—step in, sir," said the man, who still held the door; "the rain will wet you to the skin."

"Who wishes to see me?—what do you desire?" said Leicester, with one foot on the steps. "I was informed that a lady waited. Is she within the carriage?"

A faint exclamation broke from the carriage, as the sound of his voice penetrated there.

"Step in, sir, at once, if you would be safe!" was the stern answer.

"I am always safe," was the haughty reply, and Leicester touched his side pocket significantly.

"You are safe here. Indeed, indeed you are!" cried a sweet and tremulous voice from the carriage. "In Heaven's name, step in, it is but a woman."

He was ashamed of the hesitation that might have been misunderstood for cowardice, and sprang into the vehicle. The door was instantly closed; another form sprang up through the darkness and placed itself by the driver. The carriage dashed off at a rapid pace, for, drenched in that pitiless rain, both horses and driver were impatient to be housed for the night.

Within the carriage all was profound darkness. Leicester had placed himself in a corner of the back seat. He felt that some one was by his side shrinking back as if in terror or greatly agitated. It was a female, he knew by the rustling of a silk dress—by the quick respiration—by the sort of thrill that seemed to agitate the being so mysteriously brought in contact with him. His own sensations were strange and inexplicable; accustomed to adventure, and living in intrigue of one kind or another continually, he entered into this strange scene with absolute trepidation. The voice that had invited him into the carriage was so clear, so thrillingly plaintive, that it had stirred the very core of his heart like an old memory of youth, planted when that heart had not lost all feeling.

He rode on then in silence, disturbed as he had not been for many a day, and full of confused thought. His hearing seemed unusually acute. Notwithstanding the rain that beat noisily on the roof, the grinding wheels, and loud, splashing tread of the horses, he could hear the unequal breath of his companion with startling distinctness. Nay, it seemed to him as if the very beating of a heart all in tumult reached his ear also : but it was not so. That which he fancied to be the voice of another soul, was a powerful intuition knocking at his own heart.

Leicester had not attempted to speak; his usual cool self-posses sion was lost. His audacious spirit seemed shamed down in that unknown presence. But this was not a state of things that could exist long with a man so bold and so unprincipled. After the carriage had dashed on, perhaps ten minutes, he thought how singular this silence must appear, and became ashamed of it. Even in the darkness he smiled in self derision ; a lady had called at his hotel—had taken him almost per force into her carriage—was he to sit there like a great school-boy, without one gallant word, or one effort to obtain a glimpse at the face of his captor ? He almost laughed as this thought of his late awkward confusion presented itself. All his audacity returned, and with a tone of half jeering gallantry he drew closer to the lady.

"Sweet stranger," he said, "this seems a cold reception for your captive. If one consents to be taken prisoner on a stormy night like this, surely he may expect at least a civil word."

He had drawn close to the lady, her hand lay in his cold as ice. Her breath floated over his cheek—that, too, seemed chilly, but familiar as the scent of a flower beloved in childhood. There was something in the breath that brought that strange sensation to his heart again. He was silent—the gallant words seemed freezing in his throat. The hand clasped in his grew warmer, and began to tremble like a half frozen bird taking life from the humane bosom that has given it shelter. Again he spoke, but the jeering tone had left his voice. He felt to his innermost soul that this was no common adventure, that the woman by his side had some deeper motive than idle romance or ephemeral passion for what she was doing.

"Lady," he said, in a tone harmonious with gentle respect, "at least tell me why I am thus summoned forth. Let me hear that voice again, though in this darkness to see your face is impossible. It seemed to me that your voice was familiar. Is it so ? Have we ever met before ?"

The lady turned her head, and it seemed that she made an effort to speak ; but a low murmur only met his ear, followed by a sob, as if she was gasping for words.

With the insidious tenderness which made this man so dangerous, he threw his arm gently around the strangely agitated woman, not in a way to arouse her apprehensions had she been the most fastidious being on earth, but respectfully, as if he felt that she required support. She was trembling from head to foot. He uttered a few soothing words, and bending down, kissed her forehead. Then her head fell upon his shoulder, and she burst into a passion of tears. Her being seemed shaken to its very centre ; she murmured amid her tears soft words too low for him to hear. Her hand wove itself around his tighter and more passionately ; she clung to him like a deserted child restored to its mother's bosom.

Libertine as he was, Leicester could not misunderstand the agitation that overwhelmed the stranger. It aroused all the sleeping romance—all the vivid imagination of his nature ; unprincipled he certainly was, but not altogether without feeling. Surprise, gratified vanity, nay, some mysterious influence of which he was unaware, held the deep evil of his nature in abeyance. Strange as this woman's conduct had been, wild, incomprehensible as it certainly was, he could not think entirely ill of her. He would have laughed at another man in his place, had he entertained a doubt of her utter worthlessness ; but there she lay against his heart, and spite of that, spite of a nature always ready to see the dark side of humanity, he could not force himself to treat her with disrespect. After all, there must have been some few sparks of goodness in that man's heart, or he could not so well have comprehended the better feelings of another.

She lay thus weeping and passive, circled by his arm ; her tears seemed very sweet and blissful. Now and then she drew a deep, tremulous sigh, but no words were uttered. At length he broke the spell that controlled her with a question.

"Will you not tell me now, why you came for me, and your name ? If not that, say where we have ever met before ?"

She released herself gently from his arm at these words, and drew back to a corner of the seat. He had aroused her from the sweetest bliss ever known to a human heart. This one mo ment of delusion was followed by a memory of who she was, and why she sought him, so bitter and sharp that it chilled her through and through. There was no danger that he could recognize her voice then, even if he had known it before. Nothing could be more faint and changed than the tone in which she answered—

"In a little time you shall know all."

He would have drawn her toward him again, but she resisted the effort with gentle decision; and, completely lost in wonder, he waited the course this strange adventure might take.

The horses stopped before some large building, but even the outline was lost in that inky darkness; something more gloomy and palpable than the air loomed before them, and that was all Leicester could distinguish. He sat still and waited.

The carriage door was opened on the side where the female sat, and some words passed between her and a person outside, but she leaned forward, and had her tones been louder, they would have been drowned by the rain dashing over the carriage. The man to whom she had spoken closed the door and seemed to mount a flight of steps. Then followed the sound of an opening door, and after that a gleam of light now and then broke through a chink in that black mass, up and up, till far over head it gleamed through the blinds of a window, revealing the casement and nothing more.

Again the carriage door was opened. The lady arose and was lifted out. Leicester followed, and without a word they both went through an iron gate and mounted the granite steps of a dwelling. The outer door stood open, and, taking his hand, she led him through the profound darkness of what appeared to be a spacious vestibule. Then they ascended a flight of stairs winding up and up, as if confined within a tower; a door was opened, and Leicester found himself in a small chamber, furnished after a fashion common to country villages in New England, but so unusual in a large city that it made him start.

We need not describe this chamber, for it is one with which the reader is already acquainted. The woman who now stood upon the faded carpet, over which the rain dripped from her cloak, had visited it before that day.

One thing seemed strange and out of keeping. A small lamp that stood upon the bureau was of silver, graceful in form, and ornamented with a wreath of flowers chased in frosted silver, and raised from the surface after a fashion peculiar to the best artists of Europe. Leicester was a connoisseur in things of this kind, and his keen eye instantly detected the incongruity between this expensive article and the cheap adornments of the room.

"Some waiting maid or governess," he thought, with a sensation of angry scorn, for Leicester was fastidious even in his vices. "Some waiting-maid or governess who has borrowed the lamp from her mistress' drawing-table ; faith ! the affair is getting ridiculous !"

When Leicester turned to look upon his companion, all the arrogant contempt which this thought had given to his face still remained there. But the lady could not have seen it distinctly; she had thrown off her cloak, and stood with her veil of black lace, so heavily embroidered that no feature could be recognized through it, grasped in her hand, as if reluctant to fling it aside. She evidently trembled from head to foot : and even through the heavy folds of her veil, he felt the thrilling intensity of the gaze she fixed upon him.

The look of scornful disappointment left his face ; there was something imposing in the presence of this strange being that crushed his suspicions and his sneers at once. Enough of personal beauty was revealed in the superb proportions of her form to make him more anxious for a view of her face. He advanced toward her eagerly, but still throwing an expression of tender respect into his look and manner. They stood face to face—she lifted her veil.

He started, and a look of bewilderment came upon his face. Those features were familiar, so familiar that every nerve in his strong frame seemed to quiver under the partial recognition. She saw that he did not fully recognize her, and flinging away both shawl and bonnet, stood before him.

He knew her then! You could see it in the look of keen surprise—in the color as it crept from his lips—in the ashy pallor of his cheek. It was not often that this strong man was taken by surprise. His self-possession was marvellous at all times; but now, even the lady herself did not seem more profoundly agitated. She was the first to speak. Her voice was clear and full of sweetness.

"You know me, William?"

"Yes!" he said, after a brief struggle, and drawing a deep breath—"yes."

She looked at him: her large eyes grew misty with tenderness, and yet there was a proud reserve about her as if she waited for him to say more. She was keenly hurt that he answered her only with that brief "yes."

"It is many years since we met," she said at length, and in a low voice.

"Yes, many years," was his cold reply; "I thought you dead."

"And mourned for me! Oh! Leicester, for the love of Heaven, say that I was mourned when you thought me dead!"

Leicester smiled—oh, that cruel smile! It pierced that proud woman's heart like the sting of a venomous insect, she seemed withered by its influence. He was gratified, gratified that his smile could still make that haughty being cower and tremble. He was rapidly gaining command over himself. Quick in association of ideas, even while he was smiling he had began to calculate. Selfish, haughty, cruel, with a heart fearful in the might of its passion, yet seldom gaining mastery over nerves that seemed spun from steel, even at this trying moment he could reason and plan. That power seldom left him. With all his evil might, he was cautious. Now he resolved to learn more, and deal warily as he learned.

"And if I did mourn, of what avail was it, Ada?" He uttered the name on purpose, knowing that, unless she were marvellously changed, it would stir her heart to yield more certain signs of his power. He was not mistaken. She moved a step toward him as he uttered the name in the sweet, olden tone that slept ever in her heart. The tears swelled to her eyes—she half extended her arms.

Again he was pleased. The chain of his power had not been severed. Years might have rusted but not broken it—thus he calculated, for he could reason now before that beautiful, passionate being, coldly as a mathematician in his closet. The dismay of her first presence disappeared with the moment.

"Oh! had I but known it! Had I but dreamed that you cared for me in the least!" cried the poor lady, falling into one of the hard chairs, and pressing a hand to her forehead.

"What then, Ada—what then?"

He took her hand in his: she lifted her eyes—a flood of mournful tenderness clouded them.

"What then, William?"

"Yes, what then? How would any knowledge of my feelings have affected your destiny?"

"How? Did I not love—worship—idolize? Oh! Heavens, how I did love you, William!"

Her hands were clasped passionately: a glorious light broke through the mist of her unshed tears.

"But you abandoned me!"

"Abandoned *you*—oh, William!"

"Well, we will not recriminate—let us leave the past for a moment. It has not been so pleasant that we should wish to dwell upon it."

"Pleasant! oh! what a bitter, bitter past it has been to me!"

"But the present. If you and I can talk of anything, it must be that. Where have you been so many years?"

"You know—you know—why ask the cruel question?" she answered.

"True, we were not to speak of the past."

"And yet it must be before we part," she said, gently, "else, how can we understand the present?"

"True enough; perhaps it is as well to swallow the dose at once, as we shall probably never meet again."

She cast upon him a wild upbraiding look. The speech was intended to wound her, and it did—that man was not content with making victims, he loved to tease and torture them. He sat down in one of the maple chairs, and drew it nearer to her.

"Now," he said, "tell me all your history since we parted—your motive for coming here."

She lifted her eyes to his, and smiled with mournful bitterness; the task that she had imposed upon herself was a terrible one. She had resolved to open her heart, to tell the whole harrowing, mournful truth, but her courage died in his presence. She could not force her lips to speak all.

He smiled; the torture that she was suffering pleased him—for, as I have said, he loved to play with his victims, and the anguish of shame which she endured had something novel and exciting in it. For some time he would not aid her, even by a question, but he really wished to learn a portion of her history, for during the last three years he had lost all trace of her, and there might be something in the events of those three years to affect his interest. It was his policy, however, to appear ignorant of *all* that had transpired.

But she was silent; her ideas seemed paralyzed. How many times she had fancied this meeting—with what eloquence she had pleaded to him—how plausible were the excuses that arose in her mind—and now where had they fled? The very power of speech seemed abandoning her. She almost longed for some taunting word, another cold sneer—at least they would have stung her into eloquence—but that dull, quiet silence chained up her faculties. She sat gazing on the floor, mute and pale; and he remained in his seat coldly regarding her.

At length the stillnes grew irksome to him.

"I am waiting patiently, Ada; waiting to hear why you abandoned your husband!"

She started: her eye kindled, and the fiery blood flashed into her cheek.

"I did *not* abandon my husband. He left me."

"For a journey, but for a journey !" was the calm reply.

"Yes, such journeys as you had taken before, and with a like motive, leaving me young, penniless, beset with temptation, tortured with jealousy. On that very journey you had a companion."

She looked at him as if eager even then, against her own positive knowledge, to hear a denial of her accusations ; but he only smiled, and murmured softly—

"Yes, yes, I remember. It was a pleasant journey."

"It drove me wild—I was not myself—suspicions, such suspicions haunted me. I thought—I believed, nay, believe now that you wished me to go—that you longed to get rid of me—nay, that you encouraged—I cannot frame words for the thought even now. He had lent you money, large sums—William, William, in the name of Heaven, tell me that it was not for this I was left alone in debt and helpless. Say that you did not yourself thrust me into that terrible temptation !"

She laid her hand upon his arm and grasped it hard ; her eyes searched his to the soul. He smiled—her hand dropped—her countenance fell—and oh ! such bitter disappointment broke through her voice.

"It has been the vulture preying on my heart ever since. A word would have torn it away, but you will not take the trouble even to deceive me. You smile, only smile !"

"I only smile at the absurdity of your suspicion."

She looked up eagerly, but with doubt in her face. She panted to believe him, but lacked the necessary faith.

"I asked *him* to deny this on his death-bed, and he could not !"

"Then he *is* dead," was the quick rejoinder. "He *is* dead !"

"Yes, he is dead," she answered in a low voice.

"And the daughter, his heiress ?"

"She too is dead !"

He longed to ask another question. His eyes absolutely gleamed with eagerness, but his self-control was wonderful. A direct question might expose the unutterable meanness of his hope. He must obtain what he panted to know by circuitous means.

"And you staid by him to the last?"

She turned upon him a sharp and penetrating look. He felt the whole force of her glance, and assumed an expression well calculated to deceive a much less excitable observer.

"I thought," he said, "that you had been living in retirement. That you left the noble villain without public disgrace. It was a great satisfaction for me to know this."

"I did leave him. I did live in retirement, toiled for my own bread; by wrestling with poverty I strove to win back some portion of content."

"Yet you were with him when he died!"

"It was a mournful death-bed—he sent for me, and I went. Oh! it was a mournful death-bed!"

Tears rolled down her cheeks; she covered her face with both hands.

"I had been the governess of his daughter—her nurse in the last sickness."

"And you lived apart, alone—you and this daughter."

"She died in Florence. We were alone. She was sent home for burial."

"And to be a governess to this young lady you abandoned your own child—*only* to be governess. Can you say to me, Ada, that it was only to be a governess to this young lady?"

There was feeling in his voice, something of stern dignity—perhaps at the moment he did feel—she thought so, and it gave her hope.

She had not removed her hands; they still covered her face, and a faint murmur only broke through the fingers—oh! what cowards sin makes of us! That poor woman dared not tell the truth—she shrunk from uttering a positive falsehood, hence the humiliating murmur that stole from her pallid lips—the sickening shudder that ran through her frame.

"You do not answer," said the husband, for Leicester *was* her husband—"you do not answer."

She had gathered courage enough to utter the falsehood, and dropping her hands, replied in a firm voice, disagreeably firm, for the lie cost her proud spirit a terrible effort, and she could not utter it naturally as he would have done.

"Yes, I can answer. It was to be the young lady's governess that I went—only to be her governess!—penniless, abandoned, what else could I do?"

He did not believe her. In his soul he knew that she was not speaking the truth; but there was something yet to learn, and in the end it might be policy to feign a belief which he could not feel.

"So after wasting youth and talent on his daughter—paling your beauty over her death-bed and his—this pitiful man could leave you to poverty and toil. Did he expect that I would receive you again after that suspicious desertion?"

"No, no. The wild thought was mine—you once loved me, William!"

The tears were swelling in her eyes again; few men could have resisted the look of those eyes, the sweet pleading of her voice—for the contrast with her usual imperious pride had something very touching in it.

"You were very beautiful then," he said—"very beautiful."

"And am I so much changed?" she answered, with a smile of gentle sweetness.

In his secret heart he thought the splendid creature handsomer than ever. If the freshness of youth was gone, there was grace, maturity, intellect, everything requisite to the perfection of womanhood, in exchange for the one lost attraction.

It was a part of Leicester's policy to please her until he had mastered all the facts of her position; so he spoke for once sincerely, and in the rich tones that he knew so well how to modulate, he told how superbly her beauty had ripened with time. She blushed like a girl. He could feel even that her hand was glowing with the exquisite pleasure given by his praise. But he had a point to gain—all her loveliness was nothing to him, unless it could be made subservient to his interest. What was her present condition?—had she obtained wealth abroad?—or could she insanely fancy that he would receive her penniless? This was the point that he wished to arrive at, but so far she had evaded it as if unconsciously.

He looked around the room, hoping to draw some conclusion by the objects it contained. The scrutiny was followed by a faint start of surprise; the hard carpet, the bureau, the bed all were familiar. They had been the little "setting out" that his wife had received from her parents in New England. How came they there, so well kept, so neatly arranged in that high chamber! Was she a governess in some wealthy household, furnishing her own room with the humble articles that had once been their own household goods? He glanced at her dress. It was simple and entirely without ornament; this only strengthened the conclusion to which he was fast arriving. He remembered the marble vestibule through which they had reached the staircase, the caution used in admitting him to the house. The hackney-coach, everything gave proof that she would be an incumbrance to him. She saw that he was regarding the patchwork quilt that covered the bed; the tears began to fall from her eyes.

"Do you remember, William, we used it first when our darling was a baby? Have you ever seen her since—since?"

He dropped her hand and stood up. His whole manner changed.

"Do not mention her, wretched, unnatural mother—is she not impoverished, abandoned? Can you make atonement for this?"

"No, no, I never hoped it—I feel keenly as you can how impossible it is. Oh, that I had the power!"

These words were enough; he had arrived at the certainty that she was penniless.

"Now let this scene have an end. It can do no good for us to meet again, or to dwell upon things that are unchangeable. You have sought this interview, and it is over. It must never be repeated."

She started up and gazed at him in wild surprise.

"You do not mean it," she faltered, making an effort to smile away her terror—"your looks but a moment since—your words. You have not so trifled with me, William!"

He was gone—she followed him to the door—her voice died away—she staggered back with a faint wail, and fell senseless across the bed.

CHAPTER V.

MISTRESS AND SERVANT.

With hate in every burning thought,
There, shrouded in the midnight gloom,
While every pulse its anguish brought,
He guarded still that attic room.

Jacob stood upon the steps of that tall mansion, till his mistress disappeared in the darkness that filled it. His eyes followed her with an intense gaze, as if the fire smouldering at his heart could empower his vision to penetrate the black night that seemed to engulf her, together with the man to whose hand she was clinging. The rain was pouring around him. The winds sweeping through the drops, lulled a little, but were still violent. He stood motionless in the midst, allowing both rain and wind to beat against him without a thought. He was list ening for another sound of their footsteps, from the marble floor, and seemed paralyzed upon the great stone flags, over which the water was dripping.

The carriage wheels grinding upon the pavement, as the coach man attempted to turn his vehicle, aroused Jacob from his abstraction. He turned, and running down the steps, caught one of the horses by the bit.

"Not yet—you will be wanted again!" he shouted.

"Wanted or not, I am going home," answered the driver.

gruffly ; "as for sitting before any lady's door on a night like this, nobody knows how long—I won't, and wouldn't for twice the money you'll pay me."

Jacob backed the horses, till one of the carriage wheels struck the curbstone.

"There," he said resolutely, "get inside if you are afraid of the rain ; but as for driving away, that's out of the question !"

"We'll see, that's all," shouted the driver, giving his dripping reins a shake.

"Stop," said Jacob, springing up on one of the fore-wheels, and thrusting a silver dollar into the man's hand. "This is for yourself beside the regular pay ! Will that satisfy you for now waiting ?"

"I shouldn't wonder," answered the man, with a broad grin, thrusting the coin into the depths of a pocket that seemed unfathomable, "that's an argument to reconcile one to cold water : because, do you mind, there's a prospect of something stronger after it. Hallo, what are you about there ?"

"Only looking to the lamp," answered Jacob, holding the little glass door open as he spoke.

"But it's out !"

"So it is !" answered Jacob, dismounting from the wheel.

"And what's worse, there isn't a lamp left burning in the neighborhood to light up by !" muttered the driver, peering discontentedly into the darkness.

"Exactly !" was the terse rejoinder.

"I shall break my neck, and smash the carriage."

"Keep cool—keep cool," said Jacob, "and when we get safely back to the Astor, there'll be another dollar to pay for the mending—do you hear ?"

"Of course I do !" answered the man, with a chuckle, and gathering himself up in his overcoat like a turtle in its shell, he cowered down in his seat quite contented to be drenched at that price to any possible extent.

Relieved from all anxiety regarding the carriage, Jacob fell back into the state from which this little contention had, for the moment, diverted him. He looked upward—far, in a gable overhead a single beam of light quivered and broke amid the rain-drops—it entered his heart like a poignard.

What was he saying to her?—was he harsh?—or worse, oh, a thousand times worse, could that light be gleaming upon their reconciliation? Jacob writhed with the thought; he tried to be calm; to quench the fire that broke up from the depths of his heart. His nature strong, and but slowly excited, grew ungovernable when fully aroused. Never till that hour had his imagination been so glowing, so terribly awake. A thousand fears flashed athwart his usually cool brain. Alone, in that great, silent house, with a man like Leicester, was she safe?—his mistress—was she? This thought—the latest and least selfish—goaded him to action.

He strode hurriedly up the steps, crossed the vestibule and groped his way up through the darkness till he reached the attic. A single ray of light penetrating a key-hole, guided him to the door of that singular chamber. He drew close and listened, unconscious of the act, for his anxiety had become intense, and Jacob thought of no forms then.

The rain beating upon the roof overpowered all other sounds; but now and then a murmur reached his ear, broken, but familiar as the pulses of his own heart. This was followed by tones that brought his teeth sharply together. They might be mellowed by distance, but to him they seemed soft and persuasive to a degree of fascination. He could not endure them; they glided through his heart like serpents distilling poison from every coil. He laid his hand upon the latch, hesitated, and turning away, crept through the darkness, ashamed of what he had done. He an eaves-dropper, and with her, his mistress! He paused on the top of the winding staircase beyond ear-shot, but with his eyes fixed upon that ray of light, humbled and crushed in spirit, for he had awoke as from a dream, and found himself listening. There the poor man sat down pale and faint with self-reproach.

Poor Jacob; his punishment was terrible! Minute after minute crept by, and each second seemed an hour. Sometimes he sat with both hands clasped over his face, and both knees pressed hard by his elbows. Then he would stand up in the darkness quiet as a statue ; not a murmur could possibly reach his ear from the room. Still he held his breath, and bent forward like one listening. Cruel anxiety forced the position upon him, but it could not impel him one step nearer the door.

He was standing thus, bending forward with his eyes, as it were, devouring the little gleam of light that fell so tranquilly through the key-hole, when the door was suddenly opened and Leicester came out. With the abrupt burst of light rushed a cry, wild and quivering with anguish. Jacob sprang forward, seized Leicester by the arm, and after one or two fruitless efforts—for every word choked him as it rose—he said—

" Have you killed her? Is it murder ?"

" A fit of hysterics, friend, nothing more !" was the cool reply.

Jacob strode into the chamber. His mistress lay prone upon the bed, her face pale as death, and a faint convulsion stirring her limbs.

He bent over her, and gently put the hair back from her temples with his great, awkward hand.

" She is not dead, nor hurt !" he murmured, and though his face expressed profound compassion, a gleam of wild joy broke through it all. " His scorn has wounded her, not his hand."

Still the poor lady remained insensible. There was a faint quivering of the eyelids, but no other appearance of life. Jacob looked around for some means of restoration, but none were there. He flung up the window, and dashing open a shutter, held out his palm. It was soon full of water-drops, and with these he bathed her forehead and her pale mouth, while a gust of rain swept through the open sash. This aroused her ; a shudder crept through her limbs, and her eyes opened. Jacob was bending over her tenderly, as a mother watches her child.

She saw who it was, and rising feebly to her elbow, put him

back with one hand, while her eyes wandered eagerly around the room.

"Where—where is he?" she questioned; "oh, Jacob, call him back."

"No!" answered the servant, firmly, notwithstanding that his voice shook—"no, I will not call him back! To-morrow you would not thank me for doing it!"

She turned her head upon the pillow, and closing her eyes, murmured—

"Leave me then—leave me!"

Jacob closed the window, and folding the quilt softly over her, went out. He had half descended the coil of steps, when a voice from below arrested his attention.

"Here yet!" he muttered, springing down into the darkness, and like a wild beast guided by the instinct of his passion, he seized Leicester by the arm.

"Softly, softly, friend," exclaimed that gentleman, with a low calm intonation, though one hand was upon his revolver all the time. "Oblige me by relaxing your hand just the least in the world; my arm is tender as a lady's, and your fingers seem made of iron."

"We grasp rattlesnakes hard when we do touch them,' muttered Jacob, fiercely, "and close to the throat, it strangles back the poison."

"Never touch a rattlesnake at all, friend, it is a desperate business, I assure you; they are beautiful reptiles, but rather dangerous to play with. Oh, I am glad that your fingers relax, it would have been unpleasant to shoot a fellow creature here in the dark, and with a gentle lady close by."

"Would it?" muttered Jacob, between his teeth.

The answer was a light laugh, that sounded strangely in that silent dwelling.

"Your hand once more, friend; after all, this darkness makes me quite dependent on your guidance," said the voice again.

There was a fierce struggle in Jacob's bosom; but at last his hand was stretched forth and clasped with the soft, white fingers whose bare touch filled his soul with loathing.

"This way—I will lead you safely !"

"Why, how you tremble, friend—not with fear, I hope."

"No, with hate !" were the words that sprang to the honest lips of Jacob Strong ; but he conquered the impulse to utter them, and only answered—"I'm not afraid !"

"Faith, but it requires courage to grope one's way through all this darkness—every step puts our necks in danger."

Jacob made no observation ; he had reached the lower hall, and moved rapidly across the tessellated floor toward the front entrance. The moment they gained the open air, Jacob wrenched his hand from the other's grasp, and hurrying down the steps, opened the carriage door. The rain prevented any further questioning on the part of Leicester, and he took his seat in silence.

Jacob climbed up to the driver's seat, and took possession of the reins. The man submitted quietly, glad to gather himself closer in his overcoat. A single crack of the whip, and off went the dripping horses, plunging furiously onward through the darkness, winding round whole blocks of buildings, doubling corners, and crossing one street half a dozen times, till it would have puzzled a man in broad daylight to guess where he was going, or whence he came. At length the carriage dashed into Broadway, and downward to the Astor House.

The coachman kept his seat, and Jacob once more let down the carriage steps. The drive had given him time for deliberation. He was no longer a slave to the rage that an hour before seemed to overpower his strength—rage that had changed his voice, and even his usual habits of language.

"Come in—come in !" said Leicester, as he ran up the steps "I wish to ask a question or two."

Jacob made no answer, but followed in a heavy indifferent manner. All his faculties were now under control, and he was prepared to act any part that might present itself.

Leicester paused in the lobby, and turning round, cast a

glance over Jacob's person. It was the first time he had obtained a full view of those harsh features. Leicester was perplexed. Was this the man who had guided him through the dark passages of the mansion-house, or was it only the coachman? The profound darkness had prevented him seeing that another person occupied the driver's seat when he left the carriage; and Jacob's air was so like a brother of the whip, that it puzzled even his acute penetration. The voice—Leicester had a faultless ear, and was certain that in the speech he should detect the man. He spoke, therefore, in a quiet, common way, and took out his purse.

"How much am I to pay you, my fine fellow?"

"What you please. The lady paid, but then it's a wet night, and——"

"Yes, yes, will that do?" cried Leicester, drawing forth a piece of silver. The voice satisfied him that it was the coachman only. The former tone had been quick, peremptory, and inspired with passion; now it was calm, drawling, and marked with something of a Down-East twang. Nothing could have been more unlike than that voice then, and an hour before.

Jacob took the money, and moving toward the light, examined it closely.

"Thank you, sir; I suppose it's a genuine half dollar," he said, turning away with the business-like air he had so well assumed.

Leicester laughed—"Of course it is—but stop a moment, and tell me—if it is within the limits of your geographical knowledge—where I have been travelling to night?"

"Sir!" answered Jacob, turning back with a perplexed look.

"Where have I been? What number and street was it to which you drove me?"

"The street. Wal, I reckon it was nigh upon Twenty Eighth street, sir."

"And the number?"

"It isn't numbered just there, sir, I believe."

"But you know the house?"

"Yes, sir, that is, I suppose I know it. The man told me when to stop, so I didn't look particularly myself."

"The man, what was he, a servant or a gentleman?"

"Now raly, sir, in a country where all are free and equal, it is dreadful difficult to tell which is which sometimes. He acted like a hired man to the lady, and like a gentleman to me, that is in the way of renunciation!"

"Renunciation—remuneration, you mean!"

"Wal, yes, maby I do!" answered Jacob, shaking the rain from his hat, "one word is jest as good as t'other, I calculate, so long as both on 'em are about the same length."

"So you could find the house again?" persisted Leicester, intent upon gaining some information regarding his late adventure.

"Wal, I guess so."

"Very well—come here to-morrow, and I will employ you again."

"Thank you, sir!"

"Stop a moment, leave me your card—the number of your hack, and——"

A look of profound horror came over Jacob's face. "Cards, sir, I never touched the things in my hull life."

Leicester laughed.

"I mean the tickets you give to travellers, that they may know where to get a carriage."

Jacob began to search his pockets with great fervor, but in vain, as the reader may well suppose.

"Wal, now, did you ever—I hain't got the least sign of one about me."

"No matter, tell me your number, that will do!"

The first combination of figures that entered Jacob's head, was given with a quiet simplicity that left no suspicion of their truthfulness.

"Very well—come to-morrow, say at two o'clock."

Jacob made an awkward bow. In truth, with his loose

joints and ungainly figure, this was never a very difficult exploit.

"A minute more. Should you know that lady again?"

"Should I know her!" almost broke from Jacob's lips; but he forced back the exclamation, and though his frame trembled at the mention of his mistress, he answered naturally as before.

"Wal, it was dark, but I guess that face ain't one to forget easy."

"You may be sent for again, perhaps, by the same person."

"Jest as likely as not!"

"You seem a shrewd, sensible fellow, friend!"

"Wal, yes, our folks used to say I was a cute chap."

"And pick up a little information about almost everybody, I dare say!"

"Sartainly, I am generally considered purty wide awake!"

"Very well, just keep an eye on this lady—make a little inquiry in the shops and groceries about the neighborhood—I should like to learn more about her. You understand!"

Jacob nodded his head.

"You shall be well paid for the trouble—remember that!"

"Jest so!" was the composed answer.

"Very well, call to-morrow—the man will bring you to my rooms," said Leicester, turning away.

"I will," muttered Jacob, in a voice so changed, that Leicester's suspicions must have returned, had it reached his ear.

The next moment the fictitious driver came rushing down the Astor House steps. He dashed the silver impetuously upon the pavement, and plunged into the carriage.

"Drive up the Fifth avenue, till I tell you to stop and let me out," he shouted to the coachman; then sinking back in the seat and knitting his great hands hard together, he muttered through his teeth—"the villain!—oh the villain, how cool, how etarnally cool he was!"

CHAPTER VI.

THE TEMPTER AND THE TEMPTED.

The serpent, coiled within the grass,
With open jaw and eager eyes,
Watches the careless wild bird pass,
And lures him from his native skies.

Leicester went to his room humming a tune as he moved along the passages. Soft and low the murmurs fell from his lips, like the suppressed cooing of a bird. Now and then he paused to brush the moisture from his coat. Once he fell into thought, and stood for more than a minute with his eyes bent upon the floor. One of those lone wanderers in hotels, that sit up to help off early travellers, happened to pass just then, and interrupted his reverie.

"Oh, is it you Jim," said Leicester, starting, "I hope there is a fire still in my room."

"Yes, sir, I just looked in to see if the young gentleman was comfortable," answered the man.

"What young gentleman, Jim?"

"Why, one that called just after you went out, sir. I told him you left no word, and might be in any minute, so he has been waiting ever since."

This information seemed to disturb Leicester, but he checked a visible impulse to speak again, and moved on.

Leicester found in his chamber a young man, or rather lad, for the intruder did not seem to be more than nineteen. His complexion was fair as an infant's, and silky as an infant's were the masses of chestnut curls, rich with a tinge of gold, that lay upon his white forehead. The boy was sound asleep in the large, easy chair. One cheek lay against the crimson dressing-gown, which Leicester had flung across the back of this chair on going out. The other was warmed to a rich rose tint by the heat. His lips, red and lustrous as over-ripe cherries, were just parted, till the faintest gleam of his teeth became visible. The lad was tall for his age, and every limb was rounded almost to a tone of feminine symmetry. His hands, snowy, somewhat large, and dimpled at the joints, lay on his chest indolently, as if they had been clasped and were falling apart in his slumber, while each elbow fell against, rather than rested upon the arms of his seat.

An air of voluptuous quiet hung about the boy. Wine gleamed redly in the half filled glasses, fragments of Leicester's supper were scattered about, and all the rich tints that filled the room floated around him, like the atmosphere in a warmly toned picture. Leicester observed this, as he entered the room, and, with the feelings of an artist, changed one of the candles, that its beams might fall more directly on the boy's face, and fling a deeper shadow in the background.

The deep, sweet slumber of youth possessed the boy, and even the increased light did not arouse him ; he only stretched himself more indolently, and, while one of his hands fell down, began to breathe deep and freely again. The motion loosened several folds of the dressing-gown, adding a more picturesque effect to the position.

Leicester smiled, and leaning against the mantel-piece, began to study the effect quietly ; for he was one of those men whose refinement in selfishness, forbade the abridgment of a pleasurable sensation, however ill-timed it might be. The boy smiled in his sleep. He was evidently dreaming, and the glow that spread over his cheek grew richer, as if the slumbering thought was a joyous one.

Leicester's brow darkened. There was something in that soft sleep, in the warm smile, that seemed to awake memories of his own youth. He gazed on, but his eye grew vicious in its ex pression, as if he were beginning to loathe the youth for the innocence of his look. Again the boy moved and muttered in his sleep—something about a picture; Leicester heard it, and laughed softly.

At another time, Leicester would not have hesitated to arouse the youth, for it was deep in the night, and he was not one to break his own rest for the convenience of another ; but he had been greatly excited, notwithstanding that cool exterior. Old memories were stirred up in his heart—pure as some memories of youth ever must be, even though breaking through a nature vile as his—like water-lilies dragged up from the depths of a dark pool. Those memories disturbed the very dregs of his heart, and when thus disturbed, some pure waters gushed up, mingled with much that was black and bitter. He had no inclination for sleep, none for solitude, and with his whole being thus aroused, anything which promised to occupy thought, without touching upon feeling, was a relief.

It would not do. The exquisite taste, the intense love of artistical effect that brightened his nature, could not long rob his spirit of those thoughts that found in everything a stimulus In vain he strove to confine himself to simple admiration, as he gazed upon each new posture assumed by the sleeping boy. His own youth rose before him in the presence of youth asleep. He made a powerful effort at self-control. He said to his thought, so far shalt thou go and no farther. But the light which gleamed across the throat of that sleeping boy, exposed by the low collar and simple black ribbon, was something far more intense than the beams of a waxen candle. Spite of himself, it illuminated the many dark places in his own soul, and forced him to see that which existed there.

Thus he fell into a reverie, dark and sombre, from which he awoke at length with a profound sigh. The boy still smiled in his sleep. Leicester could no longer endure this blooming human life, so close to him, and yet so unconscious. He laid his hand on the youth's shoulder and aroused him.

"Robert !"

"Ha ! Mr. Leicester—is it you?" cried the boy starting up and opening a pair of large gray eyes to their fullest extent.—"Really, I must have been asleep in your chair, and dreaming too. It was not the wine, upon my honor. I only drank half a glass."

"And so you were dreaming?" said Leicester, with a sort of chilly sadness. "The vision seemed a very pleasant one!"

The lad glanced at the miniature on the mantel-piece, and his eyes flashed under their long lashes.

"The last object I saw was that," he said. "It haunted me, I suppose."

"You think it pretty, then?" was the quiet rejoinder.

"Pretty! beautiful! I dreamed she was with me in one of those far off isles of the ocean, which Tom Moore talks about. Such fruit, ripe, luscious, and bursting with fragrance—flowers moist with dew, and fairly dripping with sunshine—grass upon the banks softer than moss, and greener than emerald—water so pure, leaping——"

"It was a pleasant dream, no doubt," said Leicester, quietly interrupting the lad.

"Pleasant—it was Heavenly. That lovely creature, so bright, so——"

"Do you know how late it is?" said Leicester, seating himself in the easy chair, and bringing the boy down from his fancies with the most ruthless coldness.

"No, really. I had been waiting some time, that is certain. Then the dream—but one never guesses at the length of time when——"

"It is near one o'clock!"

"And you are sleepy—wish me away—well, good bye then!"

"No; but I wish to talk of something beside childish visions!"

"Childish!" The boy's cheek reddened.

"Well, youthful, then; that is the term, I believe. Now tell me what you have been doing. How do you like the counting-house?"

"Oh, very well. I'm sure it seems impossible to thank you enough for getting me in."

"Has the firm raised your salary yet?"

"No—I have not ventured to mention it."

"You have won confidence, I trust."

"I have tried my best to deserve it," answered the boy modestly.

Leicester frowned. The frank honesty of this speech seemed to displease him.

"They are beginning to trust you in things of importance—with the bank business, perhaps?"

"Yes, sometimes!"

"That looks very well, and your writing—I hope you have attended to the lessons I gave you. Without faultless penmanship, a clerk is always at disadvantage."

"I think you will not be displeased with my progress, sir."

"I am glad of it. It would grieve me, Robert, should you fall short in anything, after the recommendation I procured for your employers."

"I never will, sir, depend upon it—I never will if study and hard work will sustain me," answered the youth, earnestly.

"I do not doubt it. Now tell me about your companions, your amusements."

"Amusements, sir, how can I afford them?"

"Certainly the salary is too small!"

"I did not complain. In fact, I suppose it is large enough for the services!"

"Still you work all the time?"

"Of course I do!"

"And those who receive twice—nay, three times your salary do no more."

"That is true," answered the boy, thoughtfully, "but then I am so young!"

"But you have more abilities than many of those above you who are far better paid."

"Do you think so—really think so, Mr. Leicester?" said the youth, blushing with honest pleasure.

"I never say what I do not think!" answered the crafty man with quiet dignity, and keeping his eyes fixed upon the boy, for he was reading every impulse of that warm young heart. "You have abilities of a high order, industry, talent, everything requisite for success—but remember, Robert, the reward for those qualities comes slowly as society is regulated, and sometimes never comes at all. The rich blockhead often runs far in advance of the poor genius."

The youth looked grave. A spirit of discontent was creeping into his heart. "I thought that with integrity and close application, I should be sure to succeed like others," he said, "but I suppose poverty will stand in the way. Strange that I did not see that before."

"See what, Robert?"

"Why, that starting poor I am only the more likely to be kept in poverty. I remember now one of our clerks, no older than I am, was promoted only last week. His father was a rich man, and it was whispered that he would sometime be a junior partner in the concern."

"You see, then, what money can do."

"Well, after all, my good old aunt has money, more than people imagine, I dare say!" cried the boy, brightening up.

"What, the old lady in the market? Take my advice, Robert, and never mention her."

"And why not?" questioned the boy

"Because selling turnips and cabbage sprouts might not be considered the most aristocratic way of making money among your fellow clerks."

The boy changed countenance; his eye kindled and his lip began to curve.

"I shall never be ashamed of my aunt, sir. She is a good, generous woman——"

"No doubt, no doubt. Go and proclaim her good qualities among your companions, and see the result. For my part, I think the state of society which makes any honest occupation a cause of reproach, is to be condemned by all honorable men. But you and I, Robert, cannot hope to change the present order of things, and without the power to remedy we have only to submit. So take my advice and never talk of that fine old huckster-woman among your fellow clerks."

Robert was silent. He stood gazing upon the floor, his cheeks hot with wounded feeling, and his eyes half full of tears. When he spoke again there was trouble in his voice.

"Thank you for the advice, Mr. Leicester, though I must say it seems rather cold-hearted. I will go now; excuse me for keeping you up so late."

"You need not go on that account," said Leicester, "I am not certain of going to sleep at all before morning!"

"And I," said Robert, with a faint smile, "somehow this conversation makes me restless. That sweet dream from which you aroused me, will not be likely to come back again to-night!"

Robert glanced at the miniature as he spoke, and a glow of admiration kindled the mist still hanging about his eyes.

"Perhaps," said Leicester, quietly, and with his keen glance fixed upon the boy, "perhaps I may introduce you to her some day."

"To her," cried the youth. "Alive! is there any being like that alive?"

His face was in a glow, and a bright smile flashed over it. Nothing could have been more beautiful than the boy that moment.

Leicester regarded him with a faint smile. Like a chemist, he was experimenting upon the beautiful nature before him, and like a chemist he watched the slow, subtle poison that he had administered.

"Alive and breathing, Robert; the picture does not quite equal her in some things. It is a little too sad. The quick sparkle of her more joyous look no artist can embody. But you shall see her."

"I shall see her," muttered Robert, turning his eyes from the miniature. "What if my dream were to prove correct?"

"What—the lone island, the flowers, the magical fruit!" said Leicester with a soft laugh that had a mocking tone in it.

"That was not all my dream. It seemed to me that she

was in trouble, and in all her beauty and her grief, became my guardian angel."

"You could not select anything more lovely for the office, I assure you," answered Leicester.

"She must be good as she is beautiful," answered the boy, turning an earnest glance on his companion; for without knowing it, his sensitive nature had been stung by the sarcasm lurking beneath the soft tones in which Leicester had spoken.

"At your age, all women are angels," was the rejoinder.

"And at yours, what are they then?" questioned the lad.

"Women!" answered Leicester with a scornful curve of the lip, and a depth of sarcasm in his voice, that made the youth shrink.

The arch hypocrite saw the impression his unguarded bitterness had made, and added, "but this one really is an angel. I may not admire her as much as you would, Robert, but she is an exquisite creature, timid as a young fawn, delicate as a flower!"

"I was sure of it!" exclaimed Robert with enthusiasm, for this frank praise had obliterated all impression made by the sarcasm in Leicester's voice.

"And now," said Leicester taking his hat from the table, "as you seem quite awake, and as I positively cannot sleep, what if we take a stroll?"

"Where could we go at this time of night?" said Robert, surprised by the proposition.

"I have a great fancy to let you see the inside of a gambling house for once," was the quiet reply.

"A gambling house? Oh, Mr. Leicester!"

"I have often thought," said Leicester, as if speaking to himself, "that the best way of curing that ardent curiosity with which youth always regards the unseen, is to expose evil at once, in all its glare and iniquity. The gambling house is sometimes a fine moral school. Robert, have you never heard grave men assert as much?"

Robert did not answer, but a cloud settled on his white forehead, and taking his cap from Leicester, who held it toward him, he began to crush it nervously with his hand.

"The storm is over, I believe," observed Leicester, without seeming to observe his agitation. "Come, we shall be in time for the excitement when it is most revolting."

Robert grew pale and shrunk back.

"Not with me?" cried Leicester, turning his eyes full upon the boy with a look of overwhelming reproach, "are you afraid to go with *me*, Robert?"

"No. I will go anywhere with you?" answered the youth, almost with a sob, for that look of reproach from his benefactor wounded him to the heart. "I will go anywhere with you!"

And he went.

CHAPTER VII.

THE OLD HOMESTEAD.

There was not about her birth-place,
  A thicket, or a flower,
But childish game, or friendly face,
  Had given it a power
To haunt her in her after life,
  And be to her again,
A sweet and bitter memory
  Of mingled joy and pain.

It was a wild and lovely spot in the heart of Maine, a state where the rural and the picturesque are more beautifully blended than can be found elsewhere upon the face of the earth. The portion we speak of is broken, and torn up, as it were, by undulating ridges of the White Mountains, that seem to cast their huge shadows half over the state. The valleys are bright with a wealth of foliage, which, in the brief summer time, is of a deeper and richer green than ever was found elsewhere on this side the Atlantic. Hills, some of them bold and black with naked rocks, others clothed down the side with soft waving ridges of cultivation, loomed over fields of Indian corn, with buckwheat, all in a sea of snowy blossoms. Patches of earth newly ploughed for the next year's crop, blended their brown tints with mountain slopes, rich with rye and oats. Wild, deep lakes, sleeping in their green basins among the hills ; mountain streams plunging downward, and threading the dark rocks together as with a thousand diamond chains closely entangled and struggling to get free, shed brightness and music among these hills ; and the Androscoggin, gliding calmly on, winding through the hills, and rolling softly beneath the willows that here and there give its banks a park-like beauty, and a thousand broken hollows —sheltered and secluded nooks of cultivated ground, sometimes containing a single farm, sometimes a small village ; such is the country, and such are the scenes to which our story tends.

In one spot the mountainous banks loomed close and dark over the river ; but there was a considerable depth of rich soil among the rocks, and thrifty trees crowded the poverty-stricken yellow pine up to the very summit of each beautiful acclivity ; for half a mile the shadows of this rough bank fell nearly across the river, but all at once it parted as if some earthquake had torn it, centuries before; and there lay a little valley opening upon the stream, walled on one hand by an abrupt precipice, and on the other by a steep and broken hill, its crevices choked up by wild grape-vines, mosses, and every species of forest tree that can be found among the high grounds of Maine. This little valley was perhaps half a mile in width, and cut back into the mountains twice that distance. From thence the highway wound up the broken bank, and was lost sight of among the pine trees bristling along the horizon.

The river was broad at this point, as a rich flat of groves and meadow land lay on the opposite side. This was threaded by a turnpike, connected with the road we have mentioned by a ferry-boat, or rather ancient scow, in which two old men of the neighborhood picked up a tolerable subsistence.

A few weeks after the events already related in the course

of our story, a plain, one-horse chaise came slowly along the highway, and bent its course toward the ferry. The scow had been hauled up beneath a clump of willows, and two old men sat in the shade, waiting for customers. They saw the chaise, and instantly sprang to work, pushing the scow out into the stream, and bringing it up with a clumsy sweep against the carriage track.

The chaise contained two persons ; one was a female, in a neat, unostentatious travelling dress, and with her face partially concealed by a green veil. The old men had never travelled far beyond the river which afforded them support, but there was something in the air and general appearance of the lady, which aroused them to an unusual degree of curiosity.

The man, too—there was much in his air and dress to attract observation ; a degree of rustic awkwardness, mingled with self-confidence and a sort of rude strength, that struck the old men as unnatural and foreign. The chaise was soon recognized as belonging to the landlord in a neighboring village ; but the two persons who rode in it puzzled them exceedingly. The man in the chaise drove at once into the scow, and, stepping out, he took his horse by the bit.

"Now move on!" he said, addressing the old men with the air of one who understood the place and its customs. "If the horse stands steady, I will lend a hand directly."

"Oh, he's steady enough ; we've rowed the critter across here more than once ; he ain't shiey, that horse ain't," answered one of the men, ready to open a conversation on any subject.

"That may be, but I'll hold him just now and see how he stands the water."

There was nothing in this to open a fresh vein of conversation ; so, taking up their poles, the two old men pushed their lumbering craft into the river, casting now and then a furtive glance at the lady, who had drawn her veil aside, and sat with her eyes fixed on the opposite shore, apparently unmindful of their scrutiny.

"Purty, ain't she ?" whispered one of the men.

The other nodded his head.

"A sort of nat'ral look about her," continued the man, drawing back, as if to give a fresh plunge with his pole.

"Just so," was the rejoinder.

The lady, who had, up to this time, kept her eyes eagerly bent on the little village to which they seemed creeping over the water, suddenly addressed them—

"There are three houses in the valley now—that nearest the water, to whom does it belong?"

"That, ma'am! oh, that's the new tavern; the sign isn't so well seen when the leaves are out, yet if you look close, it's swinging to that ar willow agin the house

The lady cast a glance toward the willow, then her eyes seemed to pierce into the depths of the valley. Beyond the tavern lay an apple orchard, and back of that rose the roof of an old gray house. The ridge and heavy stone chimney alone were visible; but the old building seemed to fascinate her gaze—she bent forward, her hands were clasped, her features grew visibly pale. She cast an earnest look at the old man, and attempted to speak; but the effort only made her parted lips turn a shade whiter. She uttered no sound.

"You needn't be afraid, ma'am, there's no arthly danger here!" said one of the men, mistaking the source of her emotion. "I've been on this ferry sixteen years, and no accident has ever happened in my time. You couldn't drown here if you was to try."

The lady looked at him with a faint quivering smile, that died gently away as her gaze became more earnest. She dwelt upon his withered old face, as if trying to study out some familiar feature in its hard lines.

"Sixteen years!" she said, and the smile returned, but with an additional tinge of sadness, "sixteen years!"

"It seems a long time to you, like enough; but wait till you get old as I am, and see how short it is."

The lady did not reply; but sinking back into her seat, drew the veil over her face.

All this time, the traveller, who still held the horse by the bit, had been regarding the lady with no ordinary appearance of anxiety. He overheard the whispers passing between the ferrymen, and seemed annoyed by their import. He was evidently ill at ease. When the scow ran with a grating noise upon the shore, he gave the usual fare in silence, and entering the chaise with a swinging leap, drove toward the tavern.

The landlord, who had just arisen from an early supper, washed down by a cup of hard cider, came indolently from the front stoop and held the horse while the travellers dismounted.

"Want to bait the horse?" he inquired, pointing toward a wooden trough built against the huge trunk of the willow.

"Put him up—we shall stay all night, replied the guest."

The landlord's face expanded ; it was not often that his house was honored by travellers of a higher grade than the teamsters, who brought private fare for man and horse with them ; the same bag usually containing oats or corn in one end, and a box of baked beans, a loaf of bread, and a wedge of dried beef in the other—man and beast dividing accommodations equally on the journey.

"Oats or grass?" cried the good man, excited by the rich prospects before him.

"Both, with two rooms—supper for the lady in her own chamber—for me, anywhere."

"Supper!" cried the landlord, with a crest-fallen look, "supper! We haven't a morsel of fresh meat, nor a chicken on the place."

"But there is trout in the brook, I suppose," answered the traveller.

"Wal, how did you know that? Been in these parts afore mebby."

"These hills are full of trout streams, everybody knows that, who ever heard of the state," was the courteous reply. "If you have a pole and line handy perhaps I can help you."

"There is one in the porch—I'll just turn out the horse, and show you the way."

The traveller seemed glad to be relieved from observation. He turned hurriedly away, and taking a rude fishing-rod from the porch went round the house, and crossing a meadow behind it, came out upon the banks of a mountain stream, that marked the precipitous boundaries of the valley. A wild, sparkling brook it was—broken up by rocks sinking into deep, placid pools, and leaping away through the witch-hazels and brake leaves that overhung it with a soft, gushing murmur so sweet and cheerful, that it seemed like the sunshine laughing, as it was drawn away to the hill shadows.

Jacob Strong looked up and down the stream with a sad countenance. "How natural everything seems," he muttered. "She used to sit here on this very stone, with her little fish-pole, and send me off yonder after box-wood blossoms and wild honey-suckles, while she dipped her feet in and out of the water, just to hurry me back again. Those white little feet—how I did love to see her go barefooted! By and by, as she grew older, how she would laugh at my awkward way of baiting her hook—she didn't know what made my hand tremble—no, nor never will!"

Jacob sat down upon the stone on which his eyes had been riveted. With his face resting between his hands, an elbow supported by each knee, and his feet buried in a hollow choked up with wood moss, he fell into one of those profound reveries, that twine every fibre of the heart around the past. The fishing rod lay at his feet, unheeded. Just beneath his eye, was a deep pool, translucent as liquid diamond, and sleeping at the bottom, were three or four fine trout, floating upon their fins, with their mottled sides now and then sending a soft rainbow gleam through the water.

At another time, Jacob, who had been a famous angler in his day, would have been excited by this fine prospect of sport; but now those delicate creatures, balancing themselves in the waves, scarcely won a passing notice. They only served to remind him more vividly of the long ago.

He was aroused by the landlord, who came up the stream, pole in hand, baiting his hook as he walked along. He cast two fine trout, strung upon a forked hazel twig, on the moss at Jacob's feet, and dropped his hook into the pool.

Jacob watched him with singular interest. His eyes gleamed as he saw the man pull his fly with a calm, steady hand over the surface of the water, now dropping it softly down, now aiding it to float lazily on the surface, then allowing it to sink insidiously before the graceful creatures, that it had as yet failed to excite.

All at once, a noble trout, that had been sleeping beneath a tuft of grass over which the water flowed, darted into the pool with a swiftness that left a ripple behind him, and leaped to the fly. Jacob almost uttered a groan, as he saw the beautiful creature lifted from the wave, his fins quivering, his jewelled sides glistening with water drops, and every wild evolution full of graceful agony. He was drawing a parallel between the tortured trout and a human being, whose history filled his heart. This it was that wrung the groan from his heart.

"This will do!" said the landlord, gently patting the damp sides of his prize, and thrusting the hazel twig under his gills. "You're sartin of a supper, sir, and a good one too—they'll be hissing on the gridiron long before you get to the house, I reckon, without you make up your mind to go along with me."

"Not yet; I will try my luck further up the stream," answered Jacob, and snatching up the rod, he plunged through a clump of elders, and disappeared on the opposite bank. But the man was scarcely out of sight, when he returned again and resumed his old position.

Again he fell into thought—deep and painful thought. You could see it in the quiver of his rude features, in the mistiness that gathered over his eyes.

The afternoon shadows were beginning to lengthen across the valley, but they only served to plunge poor Jacob into memories still more bitter and profound. Everything within sight seemed clamoring to him of the past. Near by was a clover-field ruddy with blossoms, and broken with clumps and ridges of golden butter-cups and swamp lilies. Again the little girl stood before him—a fair, sweet child, with chestnut curls and large earnest eyes, who had waited in a corner of the fence, while he gathered armsful of these field-blossoms, for her to toss about in the sunshine. On the other hand lay an apple orchard, with half a dozen tall pear trees, ranging along the fence. He remembered climbing those trees a hundred times up to the very top, where the pears were most golden and ripe. He could almost hear the rich fruit as it went tumbling and rustling through the leaves, down to the snow-white apron held up to receive it. That ringing shout of laughter, as the apron gave way beneath its luscious burden—it rang through his heart again, and made a child of him.

The shadows grew deeper upon the valley, dew began to fall, and every gush of air that swept over the fields, became more and more fragrant. Still Jacob dwelt with the past. The lady at the inn was forgotten. He was roaming amid those sweet scenes with that wild, mischievous, beautiful girl, when a hand fell upon his shoulder.

He started up and began to tremble as if caught in some deep offence.

"Madam—oh, madam! what brought you here?"

"I could not stay in that new house, Jacob. It was so close I could not breathe. The air of this valley penetrates my very heart—but I cannot shed a tear. Is it so with you, Jacob Strong?"

Jacob turned his head away; he could not all at once arouse himself from the deep delirium of his memories; his strong brain ached with the sudden transition her presence had forced upon it. Ada looked searchingly up the valley, and made a step forward.

"Where are you going, madam, not up yonder—not to the old house?"

"I must go, Jacob—this suspense is choking me—I could not live another hour without learning something of them."

"No, not yet, I beg of you, do not go yet."

Ada Leicester turned abruptly toward her humble friend; her lips grew very pale.

"Why, why? have you inquired? have you heard anything?"

"No, I did not like to ask questions at first."

"Then you know absolutely nothing?"

"Nothing yet!"

"But you have seen the old house. It should be visible from this hollow!"

"Not now, madam. The orchard has grown round since—since——"

"Have the saplings grown into trees since then, Jacob? Indeed it seems but like yesterday to me," said the lady, with a sad wave of the hand. "I thought to get a view of the house from this spot, just as one ponders over the seal of a letter, afraid to read the news within. Let me sit down, I feel tired and faint."

Jacob moved back from the stone, and tears absolutely came into his eyes as she sat down.

"How strangely familiar everything is," said the lady, looking around, "this tuft of white flowers close by the stone—it scarcely seems to have been out of blossom since I was here last, I remember. But why have you crushed them with your feet, Jacob?"

"Because *I* remember!" answered the man, removing his heavy foot from the bruised flowers, and regarding them with a stern curve of the lip, which on his irregular mouth was strangely impressive. The lady raised her eyes, filled with vague wonder, to his features. Jacob was troubled by that questioning glance.

"I never loved flowers," he faltered.

"You never loved flowers! Oh, Jacob, how can you say so?"

"Not that kind, at any rate, ma'am," answered Jacob, almost vehemently, pointing down with his finger. "The last time I came this way, a snake was creeping round among those very flowers. That snake left poison on everything it touched, at least in this valley."

The lady gazed on his excited face a moment very earnestly. Then the broad, white lids drooped over her eyes, and she only answered with a profound sigh.

The look of humble repentance that fell upon Jacob's face was painful to behold. He stood uneasily upon his feet, gazing down upon the tuft of flowers his passion had trampled to the earth. His large hands, with their loosely knit joints, became nervously restless, and he cast furtive glances at the face and downcast features of the lady. He could not speak, but waited for her to address him again, in his heart of hearts sorry for the painful thoughts his words had aroused. At length he ventured to speak, and the humble, deprecating tones of his voice were almost painful to hear.

"The dews are falling, ma'am, and you are not used to sitting in the damp."

"There was a time," said the lady, "when a little night dew would not drive me in doors."

"But now you are tired and hungry."

"No, Jacob, I can neither taste food nor take rest till we have been yonder—perhaps not then, for Heaven only knows what tidings may reach us. Go in and get some supper for yourself, my good friend."

Jacob shook his head.

"I *am* wrong," persisted the lady; "let me sit here till the dusk comes on; then I will find my way to the house—perhaps I may sleep there to-night, Jacob, who knows?" She paused a moment, and added, "If they are alive, but surely I need not say if. They must be alive."

"I hope so," answered Jacob, pitying the wistful look with which the poor lady searched his features, hoping to gather confidence from their expression.

"And yet my heart is so heavy, so full of this terrible pain, Jacob. Leave me now; if any thing can make me cry, it will be sitting here alone."

Jacob turned away, without a word of remonstrance. His own rude, honest heart was full, and the sickening anxiety manifest in every tone and look of his mistress was fast undermining his own manhood. He did not return to the tavern, however, but clambering over a fence, leaped into the clover field, and wading, knee-deep, through the fragrant blossoms, made his way toward the old farm-house, whose chimney and low, sloping roof became more and more visible with each step.

On he went, with huge, rapid strides, resolute to carry back some tidings to the unhappy woman he had just left. "I will see them first," he muttered; "they might not know her, or may have heard. It ain't likely, though—who could bring such news into these parts? Anyhow, I will see that nothing is done to hurt her feelings."

Full of these thoughts, Jacob drew nearer and nearer to the old house. He crossed the clover lot, and a fine meadow, whose thick, waving grass was still too green for the scythe, lay before him, bathed in the last rays of a midsummer sunset. Beyond this meadow rose the farm-house, silent and picturesque in the waning day, with gleams of golden light here and there breaking over the mossed old roof. Jacob paused, with his hand upon an upper rail of the fence. His heart misgave him. Every object was so painfully familiar, that he shrunk from approaching nearer. There was the garden sloping away from the old dwelling, with a line of cherry trees running along the fence, and shading triple rows of currant and gooseberry bushes, now bent to the ground with a load of crimson and purple fruit. There was the well sweep, with its long, round bucket swinging to the breeze, and the pear tree standing by, like an ancient sentinel staunch at his post, and verdant in its thrifty old age. A stone or two had fallen from the rough chimney, and on the sloping roof lay a greenish tinge, betraying the velvety growth of moss with which time had dotted the decayed shingles, while clumps of house-leeks clustered here and there in masses from under their warped edges.

Silent and solemnly quiet stood that old dwelling amid the dying light which filled the valley. A few jetty birds were fluttering in and out of a martin-box at one end, and that was all the sign of life that appeared to the strained eyes of Jacob Strong. He stood, minute after minute, waiting for a sight of some other living object—a horse grazing at the back door—a human being approaching the well, anything alive would have given relief to his full heart.

He could contain himself no longer: a desperate wish to learn at once all that could give joy or pain to his mistress possessed him. He sprang into the meadow, found a path trodden through the grass, and sweeping the tall, golden lilies aside, where they fell over the narrow way, he strode eagerly forward, and soon found himself in a garden. It was full of coarse vegetables, and gay with sun-flowers; tufts of "love-lies-bleeding" drooped around the gate, and flowering beans, tangled with morning-glories, half clothed the worm-eaten fence.

Coarse and despised as some of these flowers are, how eloquently they spoke to the heart of Jacob Strong! The very sun-flowers, as they turned their great dials to the West, seemed to him redolent and golden with the light of other days. They filled his heart with new hope; since the earliest hour of his remembrance, those massive blossoms had never been wanting at the old homestead.

Again the objects became more and more familiar. The plantain leaves about the well seemed to have kept their greenness for years. The grindstone, with a trough half full of water, stood in its old place by the back porch. Surely, while such things remained, the human beings that had lived and breathed in that lone dwelling, could not be entirely swept away!

Jacob Strong entered the porch and knocked gently at the door. A voice from within bade him enter, and, lifting the latch, he stood in a long, low kitchen, where two men, a woman, and a chubby little girl, sat at supper. One of the men, a stout, sun-burned fellow, arose, and placing a splint-bottomed chair for his guest, quietly resumed his place at the table, while the child sat with a spoon half way to its mouth, gazing with eyes full of wonder at the strange man.

Jacob stood awkwardly surveying the group. A chill of keen

disappointment fell upon him. Of the four persons seated around that table, not one face was familiar. He sat down and looked ruefully around. A single tallow candle standing on the table shed its faint light through the room, but failed to reveal the troubled look that fell upon the visitor. The silence that he maintained seemed to astonish the family. The farmer turned in his chair, and at last opened a discourse after his own hospitable fashion.

"Sit by and take a bite of supper," he said, while his wife arose and went to a corner cupboard.

"No, I thank you," answered Jacob, with an effort; for the words seemed blocking up his throat.

"You had better sit by," observed the wife, modestly, coming from the cupboard with a plate and knife in her hands. "There's nothing very inviting, but you'll be welcome."

"Thank you," said Jacob, rising, "I'm not hungry; but if you've got a cup handy, I will get a drink at the well."

The farmer took a white earthen bowl from the table, and, reaching forward, handed it to his guest.

"And welcome! but you'll find the well-pole rather hard to pull, I calculate."

Jacob took the bowl and went out. It seemed to him that a draught from that moss-covered bucket would drive away the chill that had fallen on his heart at the sight of those strange faces.

He sat the bowl down among the plantain leaves, and seizing the pole, plunged the old bucket deep into the well. When it came up again, full and dripping, he balanced it on the curb and drank. After this, he lingered a brief time by the well, filled with disappointment, and striving to compose his thoughts. At length he entered the house again with more calm and fixed resolution.

"This seems to be a fine place of yours," he said, taking the chair once more offered to his acceptance, and addressing the farmer. "That was as pretty a meadow I just crossed as one might wish to see!"

"Yes, there is some good land between this and the brook," answered the man, pleased with these commendations of his property.

"You keep it in good order, too; such timothy I have not seen these five years."

"Wal, true enough, one may call that grass a little mite superior to the common run, I do think!" answered the farmer, taking his chubby little daughter on one knee, and smoothing her thick hair with both his hard palms. "Considering how the old place was run down when we took it, we haven't got much to be ashamed of, anyhow."

"You have not always owned the farm?" Jacob's voice shook as he asked the question, but the farmer was busy caressing his child, and only observed the import of his words, not the tone in which they were uttered.

"I rayther think you must be a stranger in these parts, for everybody knows how long I've been upon the place; nigh upon ten years, isn't it, Mabel?"

"Ten years last spring," replied the woman, in a pleasant, low tone; "jist three years before Lucy was born."

"That's it! she's as good as an almanac at dates; could beat a hull class of us boys at cyphering when we went to school together, couldn't you, Mabel?"

The wife answered with a blush, and a good-humored smile divided cordially between her husband and Jacob.

"You must not think us over-shiftless," she said, "for living in the old house so long; we've talked of building every year, but somehow the right time hasn't come yet; besides, my old man don't exactly like to tear the old house down."

"Tear it down!" cried Jacob, with a degree of feeling that surprised the worthy couple—"tear the old homestead down! don't do it—don't do it, friend. There are people in the world who would give a piece of gold for every shingle on the roof rather than see a beam loosened."

"I guess you must have been in this neighborhood afore this," said the farmer, looking at his wife with shrewd surprise;

"know something about the old homestead, I shouldn't wonder!"

"Yes, I passed through here many years ago; a man at that time, older than you are now, lived on the place; his name was —let me think——"

"Wilcox—was that the name?"

"Yes, that was it—a tall man, with dark eyes."

"That's the man, poor old fellow; why we bought the farm of him."

"I wonder he ever brought himself to part with it! His wife seemed so fond of the place, and—and his daughter: he had a daughter, if I recollect right?"

"Yes, we heard so; I never saw her; but the folks around here talk about her wild, bright ways, and her good looks, to this day; a harnsome, smart gal she was if what they say can be relied on."

"But what became of her? Did she settle anywhere in these parts?"

"Wal, no, I reckon not. A young fellow from somewhere about Boston or York, come up the river one summer to hunt and fish in the hills, he married the gal, and carried her off to the city."

"And did she never come back?"

"No; but a year or two after, the young man come and brought a little girl with him, the purtyest creature you ever sat eyes on. Hard words passed between him and the old man, for Wilcox wouldn't let any human being breathe a whisper agin his daughter. Nobody ever knew exactly what happened, but the young man went away and left his child with the old people. It wasn't long after this before the old man kinder seemed to give up, he and his wife too, just as if that bright little grandchild had brought a canker into the house.

"After that things went wrong, nothing on earth could make the old people neighborly; they gin up going to meeting, and sat all Sunday long on the hearth, there, looking into the fire. Wal, you know the best of us will talk when anything happens that is not quite understood. Some said one thing, and some another, and Wilcox, arter a while, got so shy of his neighbors that they took a sort of distaste to him."

"Did the old people live alone after their daughter went away?" asked Jacob, in a husky voice. "There was a young man or boy in the family when I knew anything about it."

"Oh, yes, I jist remember, there was a young chap that Mr. Wilcox brought up—a clever critter as ever lived. He went away just arter the gal was married, and nobody ever knew what became of him. People thought the old man pined about that too: at any rate, one thing and another broke him down, and his wife with him."

"You do not mean to say that Mr. Wilcox and his wife are dead?"

The farmer turned his eyes suddenly on the form of Jacob Strong, as these words were uttered, for there was something in the tone that took his honest heart by surprise. Jacob sat before him like a criminal, pale, and shrinking in his chair.

"No, I did not mean to say that they died, but when a tough, cheerful man, like Wilcox, gives up, it is worse than death."

"What happened then—where did he go? is the child living?" almost shouted Jacob Strong, unable to control the agony of his impatience a moment longer; but the astonished look of his auditors checked the burst of impetuous feeling, and he continued more quietly—

"I took an interest in this family long ago, and stopped in the valley over night, on purpose to visit the old gentleman. I had no idea he would ever leave the farm, and was surprised to find strangers here, more so than you could have been at seeing me. Tell me now where the Wilcox family can be found?"

"That is more, by half, than I know myself," answered the farmer. "I bought the farm, paid cash down for everything, land, stock, furniture, and all."

"But where did they go?" cried Jacob, breathless with suspense.

"To Portland; they took one wagon load of things, and

when the teamster came back, he said they were left in the hold of a schooner lying at the wharf."

"But where was she bound?—what was her name?"

"That was exactly what we asked the teamster, but he could tell nothing about it; and from that day to this, no person in these parts has ever heard a word about them!"

Jacob arose and supported himself by his chair.

"And is this all? Gone, no one knows where? Is this all?"

"All that I or any one else can tell you," answered the kind-hearted farmer.

"But the teamster, where is he?"

"Dead!"

Jacob left the house without another word. He knew that these tidings would be more terrible to another than they had been to him, and yet that seemed scarcely possible, for all the rude strength of his nature was prostrated by the news that he heard.

The twilight had given place to a full moon, and all the valley lay flooded in a sea of silver. The meadows were full of fire-flies, and a whip-poor-will on the mountain-side poured his mournful cry upon the air. Jacob could not endure the thought of meeting his friend and mistress, with tidings that he knew would rend her heart. He left the homestead, tortured by all that he had heard, and plunged into a hollow which opened to the trout stream. In this hollow stood a tall elm tree, with great, sweeping branches, that drooped almost to the ground. A spring of never-failing water gushed out from a rocky bank, which it shaded, and the sweet gurgle of its progress as it flowed away through the cowslips and blue flag that choked up the outlet to the mountain streams, fell like the memory of an old love upon his senses.

He drew near the tree, and there, sitting upon the fragment of rock, with her head resting against the rugged trunk of the elm, sat Ada Leicester. Her face shone white in the moon-beams, and Jacob could hear her sobs long before she was con scious of his presence.

She heard his approach, and starting to her feet, came out into the full light. The hand with which she wildly seized his was damp and cold, and he could see that heavy tear-drops were trembling on her cheek.

"You—you have seen them—are they alive? I saw you go in, and have been waiting all this time. Tell me, Jacob, will they let me sleep in the old house to-night?"

"They are all gone; no one of the whole family are there!" answered Jacob Strong, too much excited for ordinary prudence.

A wild cry, scarcely louder than the scream of a bird, but oh, how full of agony! rang down the valley, and terror-stricken at what he had done, Jacob saw his mistress lying at his feet, her deathly face, her lifeless hands, and the white shawl which she had flung about her, huddled together in the pale moonlight.

The strong man lost all self-control. He looked fiercely around, as if some one might attempt to stop him; then gathered Ada Leicester up in his huge arms, and folded her close to his bosom. It was not a light burden to carry; but he neither wavered nor paused, but strode down the hollow, folding her tighter and tighter against his heart; and a joy broke over his features, as the moonlight fell upon them, that seemed scarcely human.

"Ada Wilcox—little Ada—I have carried you so a thousand times. Then, Ada, you would lift up your little arms, and fold them over my neck, and lay your cheek against mine, as it is now, Ada."

His face sunk slowly toward hers. He gave a sudden start.

"God forgive me! oh, Ada, forgive me!" broke from him, as he looked down upon the pale forehead which his lips had almost pressed.

He stood still, holding his breath, trembling in all his limbs, and beginning to move to and fro, as he perceived that her pale eyelids began to quiver in the moonlight.

It was a delusion; the fainting fit had been too sudden; the exhaustion complete. She lay in his arms like one from whom life had just departed—her pale limbs relaxed—her eyelids closed. He stood thus awhile, and then she began to move in his arms.

"Do not move, Ada—Ada Wilcox; it is Jacob, your father's bound boy. We are all alone, in the home meadow. He has carried you down to the brook a thousand times, when you knew all about it and laughed and—and——; not yet—not yet," he said passionately; "you are not strong enough to stand alone."

Still she struggled, for in his excitement he girded her form with those strong arms, till the pain restored her to consciousness.

"Not yet—oh, not yet," he pleaded, feeling the strong heart within him sink with each faint struggle that she made; "you cannot stand—the grass is deep and damp—be still—I am strong as an ox, Ada—I can carry you."

"Is it you, Jacob Strong?" she said, but half conscious.

"Yes," said Jacob in a choked voice, "it's me, your father's bound boy; we are in the old home lot again. I—I—it is a long time since I have carried you in my arms, Ada Wilcox."

"Ada Wilcox!" said the woman, with a start; "let me down, Jacob Strong; my name is not Ada Wilcox; all that bore that name are gone; the homestead is full of strangers; Wilcox is a dead name; that of Leicester has crept over it like night-shade over a grave."

Jacob Strong unfolded his arms so abruptly, that Ada almost fell to the earth.

"I had forgotten that name," he said with mournful sternness.

The poor woman attempted to stand up, but she wavered, and her pale face was lifted with piteous helplessness toward him.

"No, Jacob, I tremble—this blow has taken all my life. Help me to stand up, that I may look on the old homestead once more. How often have we looked upon it from this spot!"

"I remember," answered Jacob, "the moonlight lies upon the roof as it did that night; the old pear tree had stretched its shadow just to the garden fence."

Jacob Strong grew pale in the moonlight. Ada felt his arm shake beneath the grasp of her hand.

"You shiver with the cold," she said.

"It is cold, madam; the dew is heavy; I will go forward and break a path through the grass. It will not be the first time."

Jacob moved on, tramping down the grass, and casting his long, uncouth shadow before her, in the moonlight. She followed him in silence, casting back mournful glances at the old homestead.

Jacob paused to let down a heavy set of bars that divided the meadow from the trout stream. He jerked them fiercely from their sockets in the tall chestnut posts, dropping them down on each other with a noise that rang strangely through the stillness. Ada Leicester passed through the opening, and moved slowly toward the tavern. She reached the door, but turned again to her attendant.

"Jacob," she said, very sorrowfully, "I am all alone now, in the wide world; you will not leave me?"

"Ada Wilcox, I have not deserved that question," said Jacob, pushing open the door.

She shrunk through timidly, perhaps expecting her servant to follow; but he closed the door and rushed away, leaping the pile of bars with a bound, and plunging back into the meadow.

"Leave her!" he said, dashing the tall herds-grass aside with his hand; "Leave her, as if I warn't her slave—her dog—her jackall, and had been ever since I was a shaver, so small that this very grass would have closed over my head; and yet she don't know why—thinks it's the wages, may be. It never enters her head that I've got a soul to love and hate with. What did I follow her and that man to foreign parts for, but to stand ready when her time of trouble came? What did I give up my free-born American birthright for, and put that gold lace, and darn'd etarnal cockade over my hat, like an English white nigger, only because I couldn't stand by her in any other way? What is it that makes me humble as a rabbit, sometimes, and then, again, snarling around like a dog? She don't see it; she believes me when I tell her that it was a hankering to see foreign parts, that sent me over sea; and that I, a freeborn American citizen, have a nat'ral fancy to gold bands and cockades, as if the thing wasn't jist impossible! True enough, she don't want me to wear them now; but if she did, it's my solemn belief that I should do it, jist here, in sight of the old homestead.

"The old homestead," he continued, standing still in the grass, and looking toward the old home, till the bitter mood passed from his heart, and his eyes filled with tears. "Oh, if I was only his bound boy again, and she a little girl, and the old folks up yonder. I would be a nigger—a hound—anything, if she could only stand here, as she did then—as innocent and sweet a critter as ever drew breath. But he did it—that villain! Oh, if he could be extarminated from the face of the earth! It wan't her fault—I defy the face of man to say that. It was the original sin in her own heart."

Poor Jacob! All his massive strength was exhausted now. He even ceased to mutter over the sad, sad memories that crowded on him. But all that night he wandered about the old homestead—now lost beneath its pear trees—now casting his uncouth shadow across the barn-yard, where half a dozen slumbering cows lifted their heads and gazed earnestly after him, as if waiting for the intruder to be gone. There was not a nook or corner of the old place that he did not visit that night, and the morning found him cold, sad and pale, waiting for his mistress at the tavern door.

Just after daylight, the one-horse chaise crossed the ferry again. The old boatmen would gladly have conversed a little with its inmates, but Jacob only answered them in monosyllables, and they could not see the lady's face, so closely was it shrouded with the folds of her travelling veil.

CHAPTER VIII.

THE CITY COTTAGE.

Alas, that woman's love should cling
  To hearts that never feel its worth,
As prairie roses creep and fling
  Their richest bloom upon the earth.

OVERLOOKING one of those small parks or squares that lie in the heart of our city like tufts of wild flowers in a desert, stands one of those miniature palaces, too small for the very wealthy, and too beautiful in its appointments for any idea but that of perfect taste, which wealth does not always give. A cottage house it was, or rather an exquisite mockery of what one sees named as cottages in the country. The front, of a pale stone color, was so ornamented and netted over with the lace-work of iron balconies and window-gratings, that it had all the elegance of a city mansion, with much of the rustic beauty one sees in a rural dwelling.

A little court, full of flowers, lay in front, with a miniature fountain throwing up a slender column of water from the centre of a tiny grass-plat, that, in the pure dampness always raining over it, lay like a mass of crushed emeralds hidden among the flowers. The netted iron-work that hung around the doors, the windows, and fringed the eaves, as it were, with a valance of massive lace, was luxuriously interwoven with creeping plants. Prairie roses, crimson and white, clung around the lower balconies. Ipomas wove a profusion of their great purple and rosy bells around the upper windows; cypress vines, with their small crimson bells; petunias of every tint; rich passion flowers, and verbenas with their leaves hidden in the light balconies, wove and twined themselves with the coarser vines, blossoming each in its turn, and filling the leaves with their gorgeous tints. Crimson and fragrant honeysuckles twined in massive wreaths up to the very roof, where they grew and blossomed in the lattice-work, now in masses, now spreading out like an embroidery, and everywhere loading the atmosphere with fragrance.

The cool, bell-like dropping of the fountain, that always kept the flowers fresh ; the fragrance of half a dozen orange trees, snowy with blossoms and golden with heavy fruit ; the gleam of white lilies ; the glow of roses, and the graceful sway of a slender labarnum tree, all crowded into one little nook scarcely large enough for the pleasure-grounds of a fairy, were enough to draw general attention to the house, though another and still more beautiful object had never presented itself at the window.

On a moonlight evening, especially when a sort of pearly veil fell upon the little flower nook, an air of quiet beauty impossible to describe, rested around this dwelling—beauty not the less striking that it was so still, so lost in profound repose, that the house might have been deemed uninhabited but for the gleam of light that occasionally broke through the vines about one or another of the windows. Sometimes it might be seen struggling through the roses around the lower balcony, but far oftener it came in faint gleams from a window in the upper story, and at such times the shadow of a person stooping over a book, or lost in deep thought, might be seen through the muslin curtains.

No sashes, flung open in the carelessness of domestic enjoyment, were ever seen in the dwelling ; no voices of happy childhood were ever heard to ring through those clustering vines. Sometimes a young female would steal timidly out upon the balconies, and return again, like a bird afraid to be detected beyond the door of its cage. Sometimes an old lady in mourning might be seen passing in and out, as if occupied with some slight household responsibility. This was all the neighborhood ever knew of the cottage or its inmates. The face of the younger female, though always beautiful, was not always the same, but no person knew when one disappeared and another took her place.

The cottage had been built by a private gentleman, and its first occupant was the old lady. She might have been his mother, his tenant, or his housekeeper, no one could decide her exact position. He seldom visited the house. Sometimes during months together he never crossed the threshold. But the old lady was always there, scarcely ever without a young and lovely companion; and, what seemed most singular, year after year passed and her mourning garments were never changed.

Servants, the universal channel through which domestic gossip circulates in the basement strata of social life, were never seen in the cottage. An old colored woman came two or three times a week and performed certain household duties; but she spoke only in a foreign language, and probably had been selected for that very reason. Thus all the usual avenues of intelligence were closed around the cottage. True, a colored man came occasionally to prune and trim the little flower nook, but he was never seen to enter the house, and appeared to be profoundly ignorant of its history and its inmates. Some of the most curious had ventured far enough into the fairy garden to read the name on a silver plate within the latticed entrance. It was a single name, and seemed to be foreign; at any rate, it had no familiar sound to those who read it, and whether it belonged to the owner of the cottage or the old lady, still continued a mystery.

Thus the cottage remained a tiny palace, more isolated amid the surrounding dwellings than it could have been if buried in the green depths of the country. But at the season when our story commences, the profound quietude of the place was broken by the appearance of a new inmate. A fair young girl about this time was often noticed early in the morning, and sometimes after dusk hovering about the little fountain, as if enticed there by the scent of the orange trees; still, though her white garments were often seen fluttering amid the shrubbery, which she seemed to haunt with the shy timidity of a wild bird, few persons ever obtained a distinct view of her features.

On the night, and at the very hour when Ada Leicester and Jacob Strong met beneath the old elm tree in sight of the farm-house which had once sheltered them, two men gently approached this cottage and paused before the gate. This was nothing singular, for it was no unusual thing, when that lovely fountain was tossing its cool shower of water-drops into the air, and the flowers were bathed in the moonlight, for persons to pause in their evening walk and wonder at the gem-like beauty of the place. But these two persons seemed about to enter the little gate. One held the latch in his hand, and appeared to hesitate only while he examined the windows of the dwelling. The other younger by far and more enthusiastic, grasped the iron railing with one hand, while he leaned over and inhaled the rich fragrance of the flower garden with intense gratification.

"Come," said Leicester, gently opening the gate, "I see a light in the lower rooms—let us go in!"

"What, here? Is it here you are taking me?" cried the youth, in accents of joyful surprise—"how beautiful—how very, very beautiful. It must be some queen of the fairies you are leading me to!"

"You like the house then?" said Leicester, in his usual calm voice, gently advancing along the walk. "It does look well just now, with the moonlight falling through the leaves, but these things become tiresome after a while!"

"Tiresome!" exclaimed the youth, casting his glance around. "Tiresome!"

"I much doubt," added Leicester, turning as he spoke, and gliding, as if unconsciously, along the white gravel walk that curved around the fountain—"I much doubt if any thing continues to give entire satisfaction, even the efforts of our own mind, or the work of our own hands, after it is once completed. It is the progress, the love of change, the curiosity to see how this touch will affect the whole, that gives zest to enjoyment in such things. I can fancy the owner of this faultless little place now becoming weary of its prettiness."

"Weary of a place like this—why the angels might think themselves at home in it!"

"They would find out their mistake, I fancy!"

As Leicester uttered these words the moonlight fell full upon his face, and the worm-like curl of his lip which the light revealed, had something unpleasant in it. The youth happened to look up at the moment, and a sharp revulsion came over his feelings. For the moment he fell into thought, and when he spoke, the change in his spirit was very evident.

"I can imagine nothing that is not pure and good, almost as the angels themselves, living here!" he said, half timidly, as if he feared the scoff that might follow his words.

"We shall see," answered Leicester, breaking a cluster of orange flowers from one of the plants. He was about to fasten the fragrant sprig in his button-hole, but some after-thought came over him, such as often regulated his most trivial actions, and he gave the branch to his companion.

"Put it in your bosom," he said, with a sort of jeering good humor, as one trifles with a child: "who knows but it may win your first conquest?"

The youth took the blossoms, but held them carelessly in his hand. There was something in Leicester's tone that wounded his self-love; and without reply he moved from the fountain. They ascended to the richly latticed entrance, and Leicester touched the bell knob.

The door was opened by a quiet, pale old lady, who gravely bent her head as she recognised Leicester. After one glance of surprise at his young companion, which certainly had no pleasure blended with it, she led the way into a small parlor.

Nothing could be more exquisitely chaste than that little room. The ceilings and the enamelled walls were spotless as crusted snow, and like snow was the light cornice of grape leaves and fruit, that scarcely seemed to touch the ceiling around which they were entwined. No glittering chandelier, no gilded cornices or gorgeous carpets disturbed the pure harmony of this little room; delicate India matting covered the floor; the chairs, divans and couches were of pure white enamel. Curtains of soft, delicate lace, embroidered, as it were, with snow-flakes, draped the sashes. Those at the bay window, which opened on the flower-garden, were held apart by two small statues of Parian marble that stood guarding the tiny alcove, half veiled in clouds of transparent lace.

Upon a massive table of pure alabaster, inlaid with softly clouded agate, stood a Grecian vase, in which a lamp was burning, and through its sculpture poured a subdued light that seemed but a more lustrous kindling of the moonbeams that lay around the dwelling.

The youth had not expressed himself amiss. It did seem as if an angel might have mistaken this dwelling, so chaste, so tranquilly cool, for his permanent home. The clouds of Heaven did not seem more free from earthly taint than everything within it. Robert paused at the threshold; a vague feeling of self-distrust came over him. It seemed as if his presence would soil the mysterious purity of the room. The old lady, with her grave face and black garments, was so at variance with the dwelling, that the very sight of her moving so noiselessly across the room chilled him to the heart.

Leicester sat down on a divan near the window.

"Tell Florence I am here!" he said, addressing the old lady.

For a moment the lady hesitated; then, without having spoken a word, she went out. Directly there was a faint rustling sound on the stairs, a quick, light footstep near the door, and with every appearance of eager haste a young girl entered the room. A morning dress of white muslin, edged with a profusion of delicate lace, clad her slender form from head to foot; a tiny cameo of blood-red coral fastened the robe at her throat, and this was all the ornament visible upon her person.

She entered the room in breathless haste, her dark eyes sparkling, her cheeks warm with a rich crimson, and with both hands extended, approached Leicester. Before she reached the divan the consciousness that a stranger was present fell upon her. She paused, her hands fell, and all the beautiful gladness faded from her countenance.

"A young friend of mine," said Leicester, with an indolent wave of the hand toward Robert. "The evening was so fine, we have been rambling in the park, and being near, dropped in to rest awhile."

The young lady turned with a very slight inclination, and Robert saw the face he had so admired in Leicester's chamber, the beautiful, living original of a picture still engraven on his heart. The surprise was overpowering. He could not speak; and Leicester, who loved to study the human heart in its tumults, smiled softly as he marked the change upon his features.

As if overcome by the presence of a stranger, the young lady sat down near the divan which Leicester occupied. The color had left her cheek; and Robert, who was gazing earnestly upon her, thought that he could see tears gathering in her eyes.

"It is a long time since you have been here," she said, in a low voice, bending with a timid air toward Leicester. "I—I—that is, we had begun to think you had forgotten us."

"No, I have been very busy, that is all!" answered Leicester, carelessly. "I sent once or twice some books and things—did you get them?"

"Yes; thank you very much—but for them I should have been more sad than, than—"

She checked herself, in obedience to the quick glance that he cast upon her; but, spite of the effort, a sound of rising tears was in her voice; the poor girl seemed completely unnerved with some sudden disappointment.

"And your lessons, Florence, how do you get along with them?"

"I cannot study," answered the girl, shaking her head mournfully. "Indeed I cannot, I am so, so——"

"Homesick!" said Leicester, quietly interrupting her. "Is that it?"

"Homesick!" repeated the girl, with a faint shudder. "No, I shall never be that!"

"Well—well, you must learn to apply yourself," rejoined Leicester, with an affectation of paternal interest; "we must have a good report of your progress to transmit when your father writes."

Florence turned very white, and, hastily rising, lifted the lace drapery, and concealing herself in the recess behind, seemed to be gazing out upon the flower-garden. A faint sound now and then broke from the recess; and Robert, who keenly watched every movement, fancied that she must be weeping.

Leicester arose, and sauntering to the window, glided behind the lace. A few smothered words were uttered in what Robert thought to be a tone of suppressed reproof, then he came into the room again, making some careless observation about the beauty of the night. Florence followed directly, and took her old seat with a drooping and downcast air, that filled the youth with vague compassion.

"Now that we are upon this subject," said Leicester, quietly resuming the conversation, "you should, above all things, attend to your drawing, my dear young lady. I know it is difficult to obtain really competent masters; but here is my young friend, who has practised much, and has decided genius in the arts; he will be delighted to give you a lesson now and then."

Florence lifted her eyes suddenly to the face of the youth. She saw him start and change countenance, as if from some vivid emotion. A faint glow tinged her own cheek, and, as it were, obeying the glance of Leicester's eye, which she felt without seeing, she murmured some gentle words of acknowledgment.

"I shall be most happy," said the poor youth, blushing, and all in a glow of joyous embarrassment—"that is, if I thought—if I dreamed that my imperfect knowledge—that—that any little talent of mine could be of service."

"Of course it will!" said Leicester, quietly interrupting him; "do you not see that Miss Craft is delighted with the arrangement? I was sure that it would give her pleasure!"

Florence turned her dark eyes on the speaker with a look of gratitude that might have warmed a heart of marble.

"Ah, how kind you are to think of me thus!" she said, in a low tone, that, sweet as it was, sent a painful thrill through the listener. "I was afraid that you had forgotten those things that I desire most."

"It is always the way with very young ladies; they are sure to think a guardian too exacting or too negligent," said Leicester, with a smile.

Again Florence raised her eyes to his face, with a look of vague astonishment; she seemed utterly at a loss to comprehend him, and though a faint smile fluttered on her lip, she seemed ready to burst into tears.

You should have seen Leicester's face as he watched the mutations of that beautiful countenance. It was like that of an epicure who loves to shake his wine, and amuse himself with its rich sparkle, long after his appetite is satiated. It seemed as if he were striving to see how near he could drive that young creature to a passion of tears, and yet forbid them flowing.

"Now," he said, turning upon her one of his most brilliant smiles, "now let us have some music. You must not send us away without that, pretty lady; run and get your guitar."

"It is here," said Florence, starting up with a brightened look. "At least, I think so—was it not in this room I played for you last?"

"And have you not used the poor instrument since?" questioned Leicester, as she brought a richly inlaid guitar from the window recess.

"I had no spirits for music," she answered softly, as he bent over the ottoman on which she seated herself, and with an air of graceful gallantry, threw the broad ribbon over her neck.

"But you have the spirits now," he whispered.

A glance of sudden delight and a vivid blush was her only reply, unless the wild, sweet burst of music that rose from the strings of her guitar might be deemed such.

"What will you have?" she said, turning her radiant face

toward him, while her small hand glided over the strings after this brilliant prelude. "What shall it be?"

It was a fiendish pleasure, that of torturing a young heart so full of deep emotions; but the pleasures of that man were all fiendish; the cold refinement of his intellect made him cruel. With his mind he tortured the soul over which that mind had gained ascendancy. He named the song very gently which that poor young creature was to sing. It was her father's favorite air. The last time she had played it—oh! with what a pang she remembered that time. It sent the color from her lips. Her hand seemed turning to marble on the strings.

This was what Leicester expected. He loved to see the hot, passionate flashes of a heart all his own thus frozen by a word from his lip or a glance of his eye. A moment before she had been radiant with happiness—now she sat before him drooping and pale as a broken lily. That was enough. He would send the fire to her cheek again.

"No, let me think, there was a pretty little air you sometimes gave us on shipboard—do you remember I wrote some lines for it! Let me try and catch the air."

He began to hum over a note or two, as if trying to catch an almost forgotten air, regarding her all the while through his half-closed eyes. But even the mention of that song did not quite arouse her; it is easier to give pain than pleasure; easier to dash the cup of joy from a trembling hand than to fill it afterward. She sighed deeply, and sat with her eyes bent upon the floor. That bad man was half offended. He looked upon her continued depression as an evidence of his waning power, and was not content unless the heart-strings of his victim answered to every glowing or icy touch of his own evil spirit.

"Ah, you have forgotten the air—I expected it," he said, in a tone of thrilling reproach, but so subdued that it only reached the ear for which it was intended. He had stricken that young heart cruelly. Even this but partially aroused her. His vicious pride was pained. He leaned back on the divan, and the words of a song, sparkling, passionate and tender with love broke from his lips. His voice was superb ; his features lighted up ; his dark eyes flashed like diamonds beneath the half-closed lashes.

You should have seen Florence Leicester then. That voice flowed through her chilled heart like dew upon a perishing lily—like sunshine upon a rose that the storm has shaken ; her drooping form became more erect ; her hand began to tremble; her pale lips were softly parted, and grew red as if the warm breath, flashing through, kindled a richer glow with each short, eager gasp. Deeper and deeper those mellow notes penetrated her soul ; for the time, her very being was given up to the wild delusion that had perverted it.

All the time that his spirit seemed pouring forth its tender memories, he was watching the effect, coldy as the physician counts the pulse of his patient. She was very beautiful as the bloom came softly back to her cheek like a smile growing vivid there ; it was like watching a flower blossom, or the escape of sunbeams from underneath a summer cloud. He loved a study like this; it gratified his morbid taste; it gave him mental excitement, and yielded a keen relish to his inordinate vanity.

A doubt that his hitherto invincible powers of attraction might fall away with the approach of age, had began to haunt him about this time, and the thought stimulated his hungry self-love into more intense action. He was testing his own powers in the beautiful agitation of that young creature. The rich vibrations of his voice were still trembling upon the air, when the old lady returned to the room. Her manner was still quiet, but her large and very black eyes were brighter than they had been, and her tread, though still, was more firm as she crossed the room. She advanced directly toward Leicester, whose back was partly turned toward her, and touched his shoulder.

" William !"

Leicester started from his half reclining position and sat upright ; his song was hushed the instant that low, but ringing voice fell upon his ear, and, with some slight display of embarrassment, he looked in the old lady's face. Its profound gravity seemed to chill even his self-possession.

"Not here, William; you know I do not like music!" added the old lady, in her firm, gentle tones.

Florence leaned back in her seat and drew a deep breath. It seemed as if she had been disturbed in the sweet bewilderment of some dream; Robert was gazing fixedly upon her, wondering at all he saw. To him she appeared like the birds he had read of fluttering around the jaws of a serpent; spite of himself, this delusion would come upon him. Yet he had boundless faith in the honor and goodness of the man on whom her eyes were fixed, while she was a profound stranger.

"I did not know—indeed, madam, I thought you liked music!" said Florence, casting the ribbon from her neck, and addressing the old lady.

"Only when we are alone; then I love to hear you both sing and play, dear child; but William—Mr. Leicester's voice; it is that I do not like."

"Not like *his* voice?" exclaimed Florence, turning her eyes upon him with a look that made Robert press his lips hard together—"not like that—oh, madam?"

"Well—well, madam, you shall not be annoyed by it again," said Leicester, with a slight shrug of their shoulders, "I forgot myself, that is all!"

The old lady bent her head and sat down, but her coming cast a restraint upon the little group, and though she attempted to open a conversation with Robert, he was too much pre-occupied for anything more than a few vague replies that were sadly out of place.

From the moment of the old lady's entrance, Leicester changed his whole demeanor. He joined in the efforts she was making to draw the youth out, and that with a degree of quiet gravity that seemed by its respect to win upon her favor. He took no further notice of Florence, and seemed unconscious that she was sitting near watching this change with anxious eyes and drooping spirits.

" I have," said Leicester, after a few common-place remarks, 'I have just been proposing that the young gentleman should give our pretty guest here some drawing lessons during the season, always under your sanction, madam, of course."

The old lady cast a more searching glance at the youth than she had hitherto bestowed on him, then bending her eyes upon the floor, she seemed to ponder over the proposal that had been made. After this her keen glance was directed to Leicester; then she seemed once more lost in thought.

" Yes," she said, at length, looking full and hard at Leicester, "it will occupy her—it will be a benefit, perhaps to them both."

Leicester simply bent his head. He conquered even the expression of his face, that the keen eyes bent upon him might not detect the hidden reason which urged this proposal. That some motive of self interest was there, the old lady well knew, but she resolved to watch closer. His projects were not to be fathomed in a moment. She did not leave the room again, and her presence threw a constraint upon the group, which prompted the visitors to depart.

Florence rose as they prepared to go out. Her dark eyes were beseechingly turned upon Leicester. With a mute glance she sought to keep him a few minutes longer, though she had no courage to utter the wish. He took her soft, little hand gently in his, held it a moment, and went away, followed by Robert and the old lady, who accompanied her guests to the door.

Florence had crept into the window recess, and while her panting breath clouded the glass, gazed wistfully at these two dark shadows as they glided through the flower-garden. She was keenly disappointed ; his visit, the one great joy for which she had so waited and watched, was over ; and how had it passed ? With the keen, cold eyes of that old lady upon them—beneath the curious scrutiny of a stranger. Tears of vexation gathered in her eyes ; she heard the old lady return, and tried to crush them back with a pressure of the silken lashes, shrink ing still behind the cloud of lace that her discomposure might not be observed.

The old lady entered the room, and, believing it empty, sat down in a large easy-chair. She sighed profoundly, shading her face with one of the thin delicate hands, that still bore an impress of great beauty. Her eyes were thus shrouded, and, though she did not appear to be weeping, one deep sigh after another heaved the black neckerchief folded over her bosom. As these sighs abated, Florence saw that the old lady was sinking into a reverie so deep, that she fancied it possible to steal away, unnoticed, to her room. So, timidly creeping out from the drapery, that in its cloud-like softness fell back without a rustle, she moved toward the door. The old lady looked suddenly up, and the startled girl could see that the usual serious composure of her countenance was greatly disturbed.

"Is it you, my dear?" she said, in her usual kindly tones, "I thought you had gone up stairs."

Florence was startled by the suddenness of this address, and turned back, for there was something in the old lady's look that seemed to desire her stay.

"No," she said, "I was looking out upon—upon the night. It is very lovely!"

"Paradise was more lovely, and yet serpents crept among the flowers, even there!" said the old lady, thoughtfully.

A vivid blush came into Florence's pale cheek.

"I—I do not understand you," she said, in a faltering voice.

"No, I think not—I hope not," answered the lady, bending her eyes compassionately on the young girl, "come here, and sit by me."

Florence sat down upon the light ottoman which the old lady drew near her chair. The blushes, a moment before warm upon her cheeks, had burned themselves out. She felt herself growing calm and sad under the influence of those serious, but kind eyes.

"You love Mr. Leicester!" This was uttered quietly, and rather as an assertion, than from any desire for a reply. As she spoke, the old lady pressed her hand upon the coil of raven hair that bound that graceful head; the motion was almost a caress, and it went to the young creature's heart. "Has he ever said that he loved you?"

"Loved me, oh yes! a thousand times," cried the young creature, her eyes and her cheek kindling again, "else how could you know—how could any one guess how very, very much I think of him?"

"And how do you expect this to end?" questioned the old lady, while a deeper shade settled on her pale brow.

"End?" repeated Florence, and her face was bathed with blushes to the very temples; "I have never really thought of that—he loves me!"

"Have you never doubted that?" questioned the old lady, with a faint wave of the head.

"What, his love? I—I—how could any one possibly doubt?"

"And yet to-night—this very evening?"

"No—no, it was only disappointment—regret, the—the flurry of his sudden visit—not doubt—oh, not doubt of his love!"

"Has this man—has Leicester ever spoken to you of marriage? Have his professions of love ever taken this form?" persisted the old lady, becoming more and more earnest.

"Of marriage? yes—no—not in words."

"Not in words then?"

"No, I never thought of that before—but what then?"

"Then," said the old lady, impressively—"then he is one shade less a villain than I had feared!"

"Madam!" exclaimed the young girl, all pallid and gasping with anger and affright.

"My child," said the old lady, taking both those small, trembling hands in hers, "William Leicester will never marry you, nor any one."

"How do you know, madam? how can you know? Who are you that tells me this with so much authority?"

"I am his mother, poor child. God help me, I am his mother!"

The young girl sat gazing up into that aged face, so pale, so still, that her very quietude was more painful than a burst of passion could have been.

"His mother!" broke from her parted lips. "It is his mother who calls him a villain!"

"Even so," said the old lady, with mournful intensity. "Look up, girl, and see what it costs a mother to say these things of an only son!"

Florence did look up, and when she saw the anguish upon that face usually so calm, her heart filled with tender pity, notwithstanding the tumult already there, and taking the old lady's hands in hers, she bent down and kissed them.

"If you are indeed his mother," she said, with a sort of fond anguish, "to-morrow you will unsay these bitter words—you are only angry with him now—something has gone wrong. You will not repeat such things of him to-morrow—for oh, they have made me wretched."

"I am cruel only that I may be kind!" said the old lady with mournful earnestness. "And now, dear child, let us talk no more, you are grieved, and I suffer more than you think."

With these words, the old lady arose and led her guest from the room.

CHAPTER IX.

MRS. GRAY'S THANKSGIVING DINNER.

Oh, I love an old-fashioned thanksgiving,
  When the crops are all safe in the barn;
When the chickens are plump with good living,
  And the wool is all spun into yarn.

It is pleasant to draw round the table,
  When uncles and cousins are there,
And grandpa, who scarcely is able,
  Sits down in his old oaken chair!

It is pleasant to wait for the blessing,
  With a heart free from malice and strife,
While a turkey, that's portly with dressing,
  Lies, meekly awaiting the knife.

AMID all the varieties of architecture—Grecian, Gothic, Swiss, Chinese, and even Egyptian, to be met with on Long Island, there yet may be found some genuine old farms, with barns instead of carriage-houses, and cow sheds in the place of pony stables. To these old houses are still attached generous gardens, hedged in with picket fences, and teeming with vegetables, and front yards full of old-fashioned shrubbery, with thick grass half a century old mossing them over. These things, primitive, and full of the olden times, are not yet crowded out of sight by sloping lawns, gravel walks, and newly acclimated flowers; and if they do not so vividly appeal to the taste, those, who have hearts, sometimes find them softened by these relicts of the past, to warmer and sweeter feelings than mere fancy ever aroused.

One of these old houses, a low roofed, unpretending dwelling, exhibiting unmistakable evidence of what had once been white paint on the edges of its clap-boards, and crowned by a huge stone chimney, whose generous throat seemed half choked up with swallows' nests, belonged to a character in our story which the reader cannot have forgotten without breaking the author's heart.

It was autumn—but a generous, balmy autumn, that seemed to cajole and flatter the summer into keeping it company close up to Christmas. True, the gorgeous tints of a late Indian summer lay richly among the trees, but some patches of bright green were still left, defying the season, and putting aside, from day to day, the red and golden veil which the frost was constantly endeavoring to cast over them.

In front of the old house stood two maples—noble trees, such as have had no time to root themselves around your modern cottages. These maples, symmetrical as a pair of huge pine cones, rose against the house a perfect cloud of gorgeous foliage. One was red as blood, and with a dash of the most vivid green still keeping its hold down the centre of each leaf—the other golden all over, as if its roots were nourished in the metallic soil of California, and its leaves dusted by the winds that drift up gold in the valley of Sacramento. These superb trees blended and wove their ripe leaves together, now throwing out a wave of red, now a mass of gold, and here a tinge of green in splendid confusion.

All around, under these maples, the grass was littered with a fantastic carpet of leaves, showered down from their branches. They hung around the huge old lilac bushes. They fluttered down to the rose thickets, and lay in patches of torn crimson and crumpled gold among the house-leeks and mosses on the roof.

In and out, through this shower of ripe leaves, fluttered the swallows. In and out along the heavy branches, darted a pair of red squirrels, who owned a nest in one of the oldest and most stately trees. In and out, through the long, low kitchen, the parlor, the pantries, and the milk-room, went and came our old friend, Mrs. Gray, the comely huckster-woman of Fulton market. That house was hers. That great square garden at the back door was hers. How comfortable and harvest-like it lay, sloping down toward the south, divided into sections, crowded with parsnips, beets, onions, potatoes, raspberry thickets, and strawberry patches; in short, running over with a stock in trade that had furnished her market stall during the year.

The season was late. The frost had been there nipping, biting and pinching up the noble growth of vegetables that was to supply Mrs. Gray's stall in the winter months. Half the great white onions lay above ground, with their silvery coats exposed. The beet beds were of a deep blackish crimson; and the cucumber vines had yielded up their last delicate gherkins. All her neighbors had gathered in their crops days ago, but the good old lady only laughed and chuckled over the example thus offered for her imitation. New England born and accustomed to the sharp east winds of Maine, she cared nothing for the petty frosts that only made the leaves of her beet and parsnip beds gorgeous, while their precious bulbs lay safely bedded in the soil. No matter what others did, she never gathered her garden crop till Thanksgiving. That was her harvest time, her great yearly jubilee—the season when her accounts were reckoned up—when her barns and cellars were running over with the wealth of her little farm.

Christmas, New Year, the Fourth of July, in short, all the holidays of the year were crowded into one with Mrs. Gray. During the whole twelve months, she commemorated Thanksgiving only. The reader must not, for a moment, suppose that the Thanksgiving Mrs. Gray loved to honor, was the miserable counterfeit of a holiday proclaimed by the governor of New York. No! Mrs. Gray scorned this poor attempt at imitation. It made her double chin quiver only to think of it. If ever a look of contempt crept into those benevolent eyes, it was when people would try to convince her that any governor out of New England, could enter into the spirit of a regular Down East Thanksgiving; or, that any woman, south of old Connecticut, could be educated into the culinary mysteries of a mince pie. Her faith was boundless, her benevolence great, but in these things Mrs. Gray could not force herself to believe.

You should have seen the old lady as Thanksgiving week

drew near—not the New York one, but that solemnly proclaimed by the governor of Maine. Mrs. Gray heeded no other. That week the woman of a neighboring stall took charge of Mrs. Gray's business. The customers were served by a strange hand; the brightness of her comely face was confined to her own roof tree. She gave thanks to God for the bounties of the earth, heartily, earnestly; but it was her pleasure to render these thanks after the fashion of her ancestors.

You should have seen her then, surrounded by raisins, black currants, pumpkin sauce, peeled apples, sugar boxes, and plates of golden butter, her plump hand pearly with flour dust, the whole kitchen redolent with ginger, allspice, and cloves! You should have seen her grating orange peel and nutmegs, the border of her snow-white cap rising and falling to the motion of her hands, and the soft gray hair underneath, tucked hurriedly back of the ear on one side, where it had threatened to be in the way.

You should have seen her in that large, splint-bottomed rocking-chair, with a wooden bowl in her capacious lap, and a sharp chopping-knife in her right hand; with what a soft, easy motion the chopping-knife fell! with what a quiet and smiling air the dear old lady would take up a quantity of the powdered beef on the flat of her knife, and observe, as it showered softly down to the tray again, that "meat chopped too fine for mince pies was sure poison." Then the laugh—the quiet, mellow chuckle with which she regarded the astonished look of the Irish girl, who could not understand the mystery of this ancient saying.

Yes, you should have seen Mrs. Gray at this very time, in order to appreciate fully the perfections of an old-fashioned New England housewife. They are departing from the land. Railroads and steamboats are sweeping them away. In a little time, providing our humble tale is not first sent to oblivion, this very description will have the dignity of an antique subject. Women who cook their own dinners and take care of the work hands are getting to be legendary even now.

6*

The day came at last, bland as the smile of a warm heart, a breath of summer seemed whispering with the over-ripe leaves. The sunshine was of that warm, golden yellow which belongs to the autumn. A few hardy flowers glowed in the front yard, richly tinted dahlias, marigolds, chrysanthemums, and China-asters, with the most velvety amaranths, still kept their bloom, for those huge old maples sheltered them like a tent, and flowers always blossomed later in that house than elsewhere. No wonder! Inside and out, all was pleasant and genial. The fall flowers seemed to thrive upon Mrs. Gray's smiles. Her rosy countenance, as she overlooked them, seemed to warm up their leaves like a sunbeam. Everything grew and brightened about her. Everything combined to make this particular Thanksgiving one to be remembered.

Now, all was in fine progress, nothing had gone wrong, not even the awkward Irish girl, for she had only to see that the potatoes were in readiness, and for that department she was qualified by birth.

Mrs. Gray had done wonders that morning. The dinner was in a most hopeful state of preparation. The great red crested, imperious looking turkey, that had strutted away his brief life in the barn-yard, was now snugly bestowed in the oven—Mrs. Gray had not yet degenerated down to a cooking-stove—his heavy coat of feathers was scattered to the wind. His head, that arrogant, crimson head, that had so often awed the whole poultry yard, lay all unheeded in the dust, close by the horse-block. There he sat, the poor denuded monarch—turned up in a dripping pan, simmering himself brown in the kitchen oven Never, in all his pomp, had that bosom been so warmed and distended—yet the huge turkey had been a sad gourmand in his time. A rich thymy odor broke through every pore of his body ; drops of lucious gravy dripped down his sides, filling the oven with an unctuous stream that penetrated a crevice in the door, and made the poor Irish girl cross herself devoutly. She felt her spirit so yearning after the good things of earth, and never having seen Thanksgiving set down in the calendar, was shy of surrendering her heart to a holiday that had no saint to patronize it.

No wonder! the odor that stole so insidiously to her nostrils was appetising, for the turkey had plenty of companionship in the oven. A noble chicken-pie flanked his dripping pan on the right; a delicate sucking pig was drawn up to the left wing; in the rear towered a mountain of roast beef, while the mouth of the oven was choked up with a generous Indian pudding. It was an ovenful worthy of New England, worthy of the day.

The hours came creeping on when guests might be expected. Mrs. Gray, who had been invisible a short time after filling the oven, appeared in the little parlor perfectly redolent with good humor, and a fresh toilet. A cap of the most delicate material, trimmed with satin ribbons, cast a transparent brightness over her bland and pleasant features. A dress of black silk, heavy and ample in the skirt, rustled round her portly figure as she walked. Folds of the finest muslin lay upon her bosom, in chaste contrast with the black dress, and just revealing a string of gold beads which had reposed for years beneath the caressing protection of her double chin.

Mrs. Gray, was ready for company, and tried her best to remain with proper dignity in the great rocking chair, that she had drawn to a window commanding a long stretch of the road; but every few moments she would start up, bustle across the room, and charge Kitty, the Irish girl, to be careful and watch the oven, to keep a sharp eye on the sauce-pans in the fire-place, and, above all, to have the mince pies within range of the fire, that they might receive a gradual and gentle warmth by the time they were wanted. Then she would return to the room, arrange the branches of asparagus that hung laden with red berries over the looking glass, or dust the spotless table with her handkerchief, just to keep herself busy, as she said.

At last she heard the distant sound of a wagon, turning down the cross road toward the house. She knew the tramp of her own market horse even at that distance, and seated herself by the window ready to receive her expected guests with becoming dignity.

The little one-horse wagon came down the road with a sort of dash quite honorable to the occasion. Mrs. Gray's hired man was beginning to enter into the spirit of a holiday; and the old horse himself made every thing rattle again, he was so eager to reach home, the moment it hove in sight.

The wagon drew up by the door yard gate with a flourish worthy of the Third avenue. The hired man sprang out, and with some show of awkward gallantry, lifted a young girl in a pretty pink calico and a cottage bonnet, down from the front seat. Mrs. Gray could maintain her position no longer; for the young girl glanced that way with a look so eloquent, a smile so bright, that it warmed the dear old lady's heart like a flash of fire in the winter time. She started up, hastily shook loose the folds of her dress, and went out, rustling all the way like a tree in autumn.

"You are welcome, dear, welcome as green peas in June, or radishes in March," she cried, seizing the little hand held toward her, and kissing the heavenly young face.

The girl turned with a bright look, and making a graceful little wave of the hand toward an aged man who was tenderly helping a female from the wagon, seemed about to speak.

"I understand, dear, I know all about it! the good old people—grandpa and grandma, of course. How could I help knowing them?" Mrs. Gray went up to the old people as she spoke, with a bland welcome in every feature of her face.

"Know them, of course I do!" she said, enfolding the old gentleman's hand with her plump fingers. "I—I—gracious goodness, now, it really does seem as if I had seen that face somewhere!" she added, hesitating, and with her eyes fixed doubtingly on the stranger, as if she were calling up some vague remembrance, "strange, now isn't it? but he looks natural as life."

The old man turned a warming glance toward his wife, and then answered, with a grave smile, "that, at any rate, Mrs. Gray could never be a stranger to them, she who had done so much——"

She interrupted him with one of her mellow laughs. Thanks for a kind act always made the good woman feel awkward, and she blushed like a girl. "No, no; but somehow I can't give it up; this isn't the first time we have seen each other!"

"I hope that it will not be the last!" said old Mrs. Warren, coming gently forward to her husband's assistance. "Julia has seen you so often, and talked of you so much—no wonder we seem like old acquaintances. I always thought Julia looked very much like her grandfather!"

"Yes, I reckon it must be that," answered Mrs. Gray, evidently but half giving up her prepossession. "Her face isn't one to leave the mind: I dreamed about it the first night after she came into the market, poor thing—poor thing!"

Mrs. Gray repeated the last words with great tenderness, for Julia Warren had crept close to her, and taking one of her hands, softly lifted it to her lips.

"Come, come, let us go in," cried the good woman, gently withdrawing her hand, with which she patted Julia on the shoulder. "There, there, pick your grandmother a handful of China-asters. I believe the frost left them just for you."

Julia was about to obey the welcome command, but her glance happened to fall on the face of her grandfather, and she hesitated. There was something troubled in his look, an expression of anxiety that struck her as remarkable.

"Grandpa, what is the matter?—you look pale!" she said, in a low voice, for, with delicate tact, she saw he wished to escape observation.

"Nothing, child, nothing," he answered hurriedly, but with kindness. "Do not mind me."

Julia cast one more anxious look into his face, and then stooped to the flowers. The old gentleman followed Mrs. Gray and his wife into the house.

"A sweet, pretty creature, isn't she?" said Mrs. Gray, watching Julia from the parlor window, after she had put aside Mrs. Warren's things; "and handsome as a picture! Just watch her now as she turns her face this way."

"You are kind to praise her," said Mrs. Warren, with a gentle smile; "you know how much it pleases us."

Mrs. Gray laughed and shook her head. "I know how much it pleases me, and that's all I think about it," she answered; and the two warm-hearted women stood together watching Julia as she gathered and arranged her humble bouquet.

The child did indeed look very lovely in her pink dress—only a shilling calico, but fresh and becoming for all that. You never saw a more interesting picture in your life. The long ringlets of her hair swept from underneath her bonnet, while its delicate rose-colored tinge and the ride had given her cheek a bloom fresh as an almond flower when it first opens. Still she was a slender, fragile little creature, and you saw that the rude winds of life had swept too early over her. Feeling and intellect had prematurely developed themselves in her nature. In her face—in her smile—in her eyes, with their beautiful curling lashes, there was something painfully spiritual. Within the last few months this expression had grown upon her wonderfully. Her loveliness was of a kind to make you thoughtful, sometimes even sad. Mrs. Gray felt all this without understanding it, and her heart yearned strangely toward the child.

"It's a truth," she said, addressing the grandmother. "I feel almost as if she were my own daughter, and yet I never had a child, and didn't use to care for other people's children much. I really believe that some day I shall up and give her these. It's come into my mind more than once, I can tell you, and yet they were my mother's, and her mother's before that." Here Mrs. Gray ran her fingers along the gold beads on her neck. "It's strange, but I always want to be giving her something."

"You *are* always giving her something," said Mrs. Warren, gratefully.

"No, no, nothing to speak of."

"That pretty dress and the bonnet—are they nothing?"

"And who told you that?—who told you they came from me?"

"We have not so many friends that there could be much doubt," answered Mrs. Warren, with a sigh. "Julia was sure of it from the first; and the other things!" continued the old lady, in a low voice, glancing at her own neat dress, "who else would have thought of them?"

All truly benevolent persons shrink from spoken thanks. The gratitude expressed by looks and actions may give pleasure, but there is something too material in words—they destroy all the refinement of a generous action. Good Mrs. Gray felt this the more sensitively, because her own words had seemed to challenge the thanks of her guest. The color came into her smooth cheek, and she began to arrange the folds of her dress with both hands, exhibiting a degree of awkwardness quite unusual to her. When she lifted her eyes again, they fell upon a young man coming down the cross road on foot, with an eager and buoyant step.

"There he comes, I thought he would not be long on the way," she cried, while a flash of gladness radiated her face. "It's my nephew; you see him there, Mrs. Warren—no, the maple branch is in the way! Here he is again—now look! a noble fellow, isn't he?"

Mrs. Warren looked, and was indeed struck by the free air and superior appearance of the youth. He had evidently walked some distance, for a light over-sacque hung across his arm, and his face was flushed with exercise. Seeing his aunt, the boy waved his hand; his lips parted in a joyous smile, and he hastened his pace almost to a run.

Mrs. Gray's little brown eyes glistened; she could not turn them from the youth, even while addressing her guest.

"Isn't he handsome?—not like your girl, but handsome for a boy," she exclaimed with fond enthusiam, "and good—you have no idea, ma'am, *how* good he is. There, that is just like him, the wild creature!" she continued, as the youth laid one hand upon the door yard fence, and vaulted over, "right into my flower-beds, trampling over the grass there—did you ever?"

"Couldn't help it, Aunt Sarah," shouted the youth, with a careless laugh, "I'm in a hurry to get home, and the gate is too far off. Three kisses for every flower I tramp down—will that do? Ha, what little lady is this?"

The last exclamation was drawn forth by Julia Warren, who had seated herself at the root of the largest maple, and with her lap full of flowers, was arranging them into bouquets. On hearing Robert's voice she looked up with a glance of pleasant surprise, and a smile broke over her lips. There was something so rosy and joyous in his face, and in the tones of his voice, that it rippled through her heart as if a bird overhead had just broken into song. The youth looked upon her for a moment with his bright, gleeful eyes, then, throwing off his hat and sweeping back the damp chestnut curls from his forehead, he sat down by her side, and cast a glance of laughing defiance at his relative.

"Come out here and get the kisses, Aunt Sarah, I have made up my mind to stay among the flowers!"

Mrs. Gray laughed at the young rogue's impudence, as she called it, and came out to meet him.

"Now this is too bad," exclaimed the youth, starting up: "don't box my ears, aunt, and besides paying the kisses, I will embrace you dutifully—upon my life I will—that is if my arms are long enough," and with every appearance of honest affection, the youth cast one arm around the portly person of his aunt, and pressed a warm kiss on her cheek.

"You are welcome home, Robert, always welcome; and I wish you a happy Thanksgiving with my whole heart. Julia dear, this is my nephew, Mr. Robert Otis. His mother and I were sisters—only sisters; there were three of us in all, two daughters and a son. He is the only child among us, that is the reason I spoil him so."

Julia, who had just recovered from the blush that crimsoned her cheek at his first approach, came forward and extended her hand to the youth with a timid and gentle grace, that seemed too composed for her years.

"And Miss Julia Warren, who is she, dear aunt?" questioned the youth, in a half whisper, as the girl moved toward the house, holding the loose flowers to her bosom with one hand.

"The dearest and best little girl that ever lived, Robert; that is all I know about her!" was the earnest reply.

"And enough, who wants to know any more about any one," returned the youth; "and yet Mr. Leicester would say that something else is wanting before we invite strangers to eat Thanksgiving dinners with us. *He* would say that all this is imprudent."

"Mr. Leicester is very wise, I dare say, and I am but a simple old woman, Robert; but somehow that which seems right for me to do always turns out for the best."

"Because what seems right to the good always *is* best, my darling old aunt. I only wanted to prove how prudent and wise a city life has made me."

"Prudent and wise—don't set up for that character, Bob. These things never did run in our family, and never will. Just content yourself with being good and happy as you can!"

All at once Robert became grave. Some serious thought seemed pressing upon his mind.

"I always was happy when you were my only adviser," he said, looking in her face with a thoughtful sort of gloom.

"Now don't, Robert, don't joke with your old aunt. One would think by your looks that there was something in it. I'm sure it would break my heart to think you unhappy in earnest!"

"I know it would!" answered the affectionate youth, casting aside his momentary depression. "Just box my ears for teasing you, and let us go in—I must help the little girl tie up her flowers."

Mrs. Gray seemed about to press the conversation a little more earnestly; but that moment the Irish girl came through the front door with an expression of solemn import in her face.

She whipered in a flustered manner to her mistress, and the words "spoilt entirely," reached Robert's ear.

Away went the aunt all in a state of excitement to the kitchen. The nephew watched her depart, and then turning thoughtfully back, begun to pace up and down the footpath leading from the front door to the gate. The first wild flash of spirits consequent on a return home had left him, and from that time the joyousness of his look grew dim. He was gay only by starts, and at times fell into thought that seemed unnatural to his youth, and his usual merry spirit.

Whatever mischief had happened in the kitchen, the dinner turned out magnificently. The turkey came upon the table a perfect miracle of cookery. The pig absolutely looked more beautiful than life, crouching in his bed of parsely, with his head up, and holding a lemon daintily between his jaws. The chicken-pie, pinched around the edge into a perfect embroidery by the two plump thumbs of Mrs. Gray, and then finished off by an elaborate border done in key work, would have charmed the most fastidious artist.

You have no idea, reader mine, how beautiful colors may be blended on a dinner-table, unless you have seen just the kind of feast to which Mrs. Gray invited her guests. The rich brown of the meats ; the snow white bread; the fresh, golden butter; the cranberry sauce, with its bright, ruby tinge, were daintily mingled with plates of pies, arranged after a most tempting fashion. Golden custard; the deep red tart; the brown mince and tawny orange color of the pumpkin, were placed in alternate wedges, and radiating from the centre of each plate like a star, stood at equal distances round the table. Water sparkling from the well; currant wine brilliantly red—contrasted with the sheeted snow of the table-cloth; and the gleam of crystal; then that old arm-chair at the head of the table, with its soft crimson cushions. I tell you again, reader, it was a Thanksgiving dinner worthy to be remembered. That poor family from the miserable basement in New York, did remember it for many a weary day after. Mrs. Gray remembered it, for she had given delicious pleasure to those old people. She had, for that one day at least, lifted them from their toil and depression. Besides, the good woman had other cause to remember the day, and that before she closed her eyes in sleep.

Robert too. In his heart there lingered a remembrance of this dinner long after such things are usually forgotten. And Julia! even with her it was an epoch, a mile-stone in the path of her life—a mile-stone wreathed with blossoms, to which in after days she loved to wander back in her imagination, as pilgrims journey to visit a shrine.

When old Mr. Warren took the great crimson easy-chair at the head of the table, and folding his hands earnestly and solemnly, asked a blessing on the food, Mrs. Gray could not forbear stealing another, and more searching glance at his face. She could not be mistaken, somewhere those features had met her eye before; it might be years ago, she could not fix the time or place, but she had seen that forehead and heard the voice—of that she became certain.

I will not dwell upon that dinner—the warm, almost too warm hospitality! No wine was wanted to keep up the general cheerfulness; the sparkle of champagne; the dash of crystals; the gush of song were all unnecessary there.

Everything was fresh, earnest, and full of pure enjoyment; even old Mr. Warren smiled happily more than once; and as for Robert, he was perfectly brilliant during the whole meal, saying the drollest things to his aunt, and making Julia laugh every other minute with his sparkling nonsense.

There was one thing that, for a moment, cast a shadow upon the general hilarity. By the great easy-chair occupied by Mr. Warren, stood an empty seat; a plate, knife, and glass was before it; but when Mr. Warren asked if any other guest was expected, a profound sigh arose from the recesses of Mrs. Gray's bosom, and she answered sadly that one guest was always expected on Thanksgiving day, but he never came. All the company saw that this was a painful subject, and no more questions were asked; but after dinner, when Robert and Julia were under the old maples, he told her in a low voice that this seat was always kept standing for an uncle of his—Mrs. Gray's only brother—who left home when a youth, and had been a wanderer ever since. For him this empty seat was ever in readiness.

Mrs. Gray, with all her good common sense, had a dash of romance buried deep somewhere in her capacious bosom. It was an old-fashioned, hearty sort of romance, giving depth and vigor to her affections ; people might smile at it, but what then ? It beautified, and gave wholesome refinement to a character which required something of this kind to tone down its energies, and soften even its best impulses.

Thanksgiving, in New England, is a holiday of the hearth-stone, a yearly Sabbath, where friends that are scattered meet with a punctuality that seems almost religious. It is a season of little, pleasant surprises; unexpected friends often drop in to partake of the festival. It was not very singular, considering all these things, that good Mrs. Gray should have cherished a fancy, as each of these festive holidays came round, that her long absent brother might return to claim his seat at her table. They were orphans—and her home was all that he could claim in his native land. She did hope—and there was something almost of religious faith in the idea—that some day her only brother would surprise them with his presence.

And now the day was over, the landmark of another year was planted, her guests had departed, and Mrs. Gray sat down in her little parlor alone. There was something melancholy in the solitude to which she was left. Every footfall of the old market horse as he bore away those whom she had made so happy, seemed to trample out a sweet hope from her heart. There stood the chair—empty, empty, empty—her brother, her only brother, would he never come again? As these thoughts stole through her mind, Mrs Gray folded her arms, and, leaning back in the old arm-chair that had been her father's, wept, but so gently that one sitting by her would hardly have been aware of it.

CHAPTER X.

THE BROTHER'S RETURN.

My soul is faint beneath its unshed tears;
The earth seems desolate amid its flowers;
Oh, better far wild hope and racking fears,
Than all this leaden weight of weary hours.

Miss Landon says, in one of her exquisite novels, that the history of a book—the feelings, sufferings, and experience of its author—would, if truly revealed, be often more touching, more romantic, and full of interest, than the book itself. Alas, alas, how true this is with me! How mournful would be the history of these pages, could I write of that solemn under-current of grief that has swept through my heart, while each word has fallen, as it were, mechanically from my pen. I have written in a dream; my mind has been at work while my soul dwelt wholly with another. Between every sentence fear, and grief, and keen anxiety have broken up, known only to myself, and leaving no imprint on the page which my hand was tracing. My brother, my noble young brother, so good, so strong, once so full of hopeful life! How many times have I said to my heart, as each chapter was commenced, Will he live to see the end? By his bedside I have written—with every sentence I have turned to see if he slept, or was in pain. We had began to count his life by months then, and as each period of mental toil came round, the wing of approaching death fell more darkly over my page and over my heart. Reader, do you know how we may live and suffer while the business of life goes regularly on, giving no token of the tears that are silently shed?

Here, here! between this chapter and the last he died. The flowers we laid upon his coffin are scarcely withered; the vibrations of the passing bell have but just swept through the beautiful valley where we laid him down to sleep. While I am yet standing bewildered and grief-striken in "the valley and shadow of death,"—for we followed that loved one even to the brink of eternity, rendering him up to God when we might go no further,—even there comes this cry from the outer world, "Write—write!"

And I must write—my work, like his young life, must not be broken off in the middle. Here, in the desolate room, where he was an object of so much care, I must gather up the tangled thread of my story. There is nothing to interrupt me now—no faint moan, no gentle and patient call for water or for fruit. The couch is empty—the room silent; nothing is here to interrupt thought save the swell of my own heart—the flow of my own tears.

And she sat waiting for *her* brother, that kind-hearted old huckster-woman, waiting for him on that Thanksgiving night, with the beautiful faith which will not yield up hope even when everything that can reasonably inspire it has passed away.

The hired man had escorted the Irish girl on a visit to some "cousin from her own country," and Robert was acting as charioteer to the Warren family. Thus it happened that Mrs. Gray was left entirely alone in the old farm-house.

The twilight deepened, but the good woman, lost in profound memories, sat gazing in the fire, unconscious of the gathering darkness; even her housewife thrift was forgotten, and she sat quiet and unconscious for the time as it passed. There stood the table, still loaded with the Thanksgiving supper—nothing had been removed—for Mrs. Gray had no idea of more than one grand course at her festive board. Pies, puddings, beef, fowl, everything came on at once, a perfect deluge of hospitality, and thus everything remained. It was a feast in ruins. When her guests went away, the good lady, partly from fatigue, partly from the rush of thick-coming memories, forgot that the table was to be cleared. The lonesome stillness suited her frame of mind, and thus she sat, motionless and sorrowful, brooding amid the vestiges of her Thanksgiving supper.

She was aroused from this unusual state of abstraction by a

slight noise among the dishes, and supposing that the sleek old house cat had broken bounds for once, she stamped her foot upon the hearth too gently for much effect, and brushing the tears from her eyes, uttered a faint "get out," as if that hospitable heart smote her for attempting to deprive the cat of a reasonable share in the feast.

Still the noise continued, and added to it was the faint creaking of a chair. She looked around, eagerly arose from her seat, and stood up motionless, with her eyes bent on the table. A man sat in the vacant chair—not the hired man—for his life he dared not have touched that seat. The apartment was full of shadows, but through them all Mrs. Gray could detect something in the outline of that tall figure that made her heart beat fast. The face turned toward her was somewhat pale, and even through the gloom she felt the flash of two dark eyes riveted upon her.

Mrs. Gray had no thought of robbers—what highwayman could be fancied bold enough to seat himself in that chair? She had no fear of any kind, still her stout limbs began to shake, and when she moved toward the table it was with a wavering step. As she came opposite her brother's chair the intruder leaned forward, threw his arms half across the table, and bent his face toward her. That moment the hickory fire flashed up; she rushed close to the table, seized both the large hands stretched toward her, and cried out, "Jacob, brother Jacob—is that you?"

"Well, Sarah, I reckon it isn't anybody else!" said Jacob Strong, holding his sister's hand with a firm grip, though she was trying to shake his over the table with all her might. "You didn't expect me, I suppose?"

It would not do; with all his eccentricity, the warm, rude love in Jacob Strong's heart would force its way out. His voice broke; he suddenly planted his elbows on the table, and covering his face with both hands, sobbed aloud.

"Jacob, brother Jacob, now don't!" cried Mrs. Gray, coming round the table, her buxom face glistening with tears. "I'm sure it seems as if I should never feel like crying again. Why, Jacob, *is* it you? I can't seem to have a realizing sense of it yet."

Jacob arose, opened his large arms, and gathered the stout form of Mrs. Gray to his bosom, as if she had been a child.

"Sarah, it is the same heart, with a great deal of love in it yet. Does not that seem real?"

"Yes," said Mrs. Gray, in a soft, deep whisper, "yes, Jacob, that is nat'ral, but I want to cry more than ever. It seems as if I couldn't stop! I always kind of expected it, but now that you are here, it seems as if I had got you right back from heaven."

Jacob Strong held his sister still closer to his bosom, and putting up his hand, he attempted to smooth her hair with a sort of awkward caress, probably an old habit of his boyhood, but his hand fell upon the muslin and ribbons of her cap, and the touch smote him like a reproach. "Oh, Sarah," he said, in a broken voice, "you have grown old. *Have* I been away so many years?"

"Never mind that now," answered Mrs. Gray, whose kindly heart was moved by the sigh that seemed lifting her from the bosom of her brother. "I have had trouble, and, sure enough, I have grown old, but it seems to me as if I was never so happy as I am now."

Jacob tightened his embrace a moment, and then released his sister.

"Get a light, Sarah, let us look at each other."

Mrs. Gray took a brass candlestick from the mantel-piece and kindled a light. Her face was paler than usual, and bathed with tears as she turned it toward Jacob. For a time the two gazed on each other with a look of intense interest; an expression of regretful sadness settled on their features, and, without a word, Mrs. Gray sat down the light.

"Is it age, Sarah, or trouble, that has turned your hair so grey?" said Jacob, a moment after, when both were seated at the hearth. He paused, a choking sensation came in his throat, and he added with an effort, "have I helped to do it? was it mourning because I went off and never wrote?"

"No, no, do not think that," was the kind reply, "I always knew that there must be some good reason for it; I always expected that you would come back, and that we should grow old together."

"Then it was not trouble about me?"

"Nothing of the kind; I knew that you would never do anything really wrong; something in my heart always told me that you were alive and about some good work, what, I could not tell; but though I longed to see you, and wondered often where you were, I was just as sure that all would end right, and that you would come back safe, as if an angel from heaven had told me so!"

"Yet I was doing wrong all the time, Sarah," answered Jacob, smitten to the heart by the honest sisterly faith betrayed in Mrs. Gray's speech. "It was cruel to leave you—cruel not to write. But it appeared to me as if I had some excuse. You were settled in life—and so much older. It did not seem as if you could care so much for me with a husband to think of. I was a boy, you know, and could not realize that two full grown married women really could care much about me."

"You knew when poor Eunice died?" answered Mrs. Gray. "You heard, I suppose, that she was buried by her husband not three months after the fever took him off; and about the baby?"

"No, no, I never heard of it, I was too full of other things. I did not even know that your husband was gone, till a man up yonder called you the Widow Gray, when I inquired if you lived here. The last news I heard was years ago, when your husband left home and settled here on the Island."

"He died that very year," answered Mrs. Gray, with a gentle fall of her voice; "I have been alone ever since—all but little Robert."

"Little Robert—have you a child, then, Sarah? I did not know that!"

"No, it wasn't my child, poor Eunice left a boy behind her, the dearest, little fellow. I wish you could have seen him when he first came here, a nussing baby, not three months old, so feeble and helpless. In his mother's sickness he hadn't been tended as children ought to be; and he was the palest thinnest little creature. I wasn't much used to babies, but somehow God teaches us a way when we have the will—and no creature ever prayed for knowledge as I did. Sometimes when the little thing fell to sleep, moaning in my arms, it sounded as if it must wake up with its mother in heaven; but good nussing and new milk, warm from the cow, soon brought out its roses and dimples. He grew, I never did see a child grow like him, when he once took a start—and so good-natured too!"

"But now—where is the boy now?" questioned Jacob.

"He was here this forenoon, almost a man grown. You have been away *so* long, Jacob. He was here and ate his Thanks giving dinner. A perfect gentleman, too; I declare, I was almost ashamed to kiss him, he's grown so."

"Then you have brought him up on the place?"

"No, Jacob, we never had a gentleman in our family that I ever heard on, so I determined to make one of Robert."

"And how did you go to work?" questioned Jacob, with a grim smile, "I've tried it myself; but we're a tough family to mould over; I never could do more than make a tolerably honest man out of my share of the old stock."

"Oh, Robert was naturally gifted," answered Mrs. Gray, with great complacency.

"He did not get it from our side of the house, that's certain," muttered Jacob; "the very gates on the old farm always swung awkwardly."

"But his father—he was an 'Otis,' you know—Robert looks a good deal like his father, and took to his learning just as naturally as he did to the new milk. He was born a gentleman. I remember Mr. Leicester said these very words the first time he came here."

Jacob gave a start, and clenching his hand, said, only half letting out his breath—"Who, who ?"

"Mr. Leicester, the best friend Robert ever had. He used to come over to the Island to board sometimes for weeks together, for there was deer in the woods then, and fish in the ponds, enough to keep a sportsman busy at least four months in the year. He took a great notion to Robert from the first, and taught him almost everything—no school could have made Robert what he is."

"And this man has had the teaching of my sister's child!" muttered Jacob, shading his face with one hand. "Everywhere —everywhere, he trails himself in my path."

Mrs. Gray looked at her brother very earnestly. "You are tired," she said.

"No, I was listening. So this man, this Mr. Leicester— you like him then ? he has been good to you ?"

Mrs. Gray hesitated, and bent her eyes upon the fire. "Good —yes he has been good to us ; as for liking him I ought to. I know how ungrateful it is, but somehow, Jacob, I'll own it to you, I never did like Mr. Leicester with my whole heart, I'm ashamed to look you in the face and say this, but it's the living truth : perhaps it was his education, or something."

"No, Sarah, it was your heart, your own upright heart, that stirred within you. I have felt it a thousand times, struggled against it, been ashamed of it, but an honest heart is always right. When it shrinks and grows cold at the approach of a stranger, depend on it, that stranger has some thing wrong about him. Never grieve or blush for this heart warning. It is only the honest who feel it. Vile things do not tremble as they touch each other."

"Why, Jacob, Jacob, you do not mean to say that it was right for me to dislike Mr. Leicester—to dread his coming—to feel sometimes as if I wanted to snatch Robert from his side and run off with him! I'm sure it has been a great trouble to me, and I've prayed and prayed not to be so ungrateful. Now you speak as if it was right all the time ; but you don't know all ; you will blame me as I blame myself after I tell you it was through Mr. Leicester that Robert got his situation with one of the richest and greatest merchants in New York, and that he was paid a salary from the first, though hundreds and hundreds of rich men's sons would have jumped at the place without pay ; now, Jacob, I'm sure you'll think me an ungrateful creature."

"Ungrateful !" repeated Jacob with emphasis, "but no matter now ; the time has gone by when it would do good to talk all this over. But tell me, Sarah, what studies did he seem most earnest that Robert should understand ? What books did they read together ? What was the general discourse ?"

"I'm sure it's impossible for me to tell ; they read all sorts of books, some of 'em are on the swing shelf—you can look at 'em for yourself."

Jacob arose, and taking up a light, examined the books pointed out to him, while his sister stood by, gazing alternately upon his face and the volumes, as if some new and vague fear had all at once possessed her.

There was nothing in the volumes which Jacob beheld to excite apprehension, even in the most rigid moralist. Some of the books were elementary; the rest purely classical; a few were in French, but they bore no taint of the loose morals or vicious philosophy which has rendered the modern literature of France the shame of genius.

Jacob drew a deep breath, and replacing the light on the mantel-piece, sat down. His feelings and suspicions were not in the least changed, but the inspection of those books had baffled him. Mrs. Gray sat watching him with great anxiety.

"There is nothing wrong in the books, is there ?" she said, at length.

"No !" was the absent reply,

"You could tell, I suppose, for it seemed as if you were reading. It is foreign language, isn't it ?"

"Yes."

"And you can read it ?"

"Yes !"

"But how—where did you get so much learning?"

Jacob did not hear her. He was lost in profound thought, striving to search out some clue which would reveal the motives of that evil man for the interest he had taken in Robert Otis.

"And these were all my nephew studied?" he said, at length, still pondering upon what had been told him.

"No, not all. Those were the books; but then Mr. Leicester thought a good deal of music and drawing, but most of all, writing. Hours and hours he would spend over that. Every kind of writing, not coarse hand and fine hand as you and I learned to write—but everything was given him to copy. Old letters, names. I remember he practised one whole month writing over different names from a great pile of letters that Mr. Leicester brought for copies."

"Ha!" ejaculated Jacob Strong, now keenly interested, "so he was taught to copy these names?"

"Yes, and he did it so beautifully, sometimes, you could not have known one from the other. The more exactly alike he made them, the more Mr. Leicester was pleased. I used to tell Robert to beat the copy if he could, and some of the names were crabbed enough, but Mr. Leicester said that wasn't the object."

"No, it wasn't the object," muttered Jacob, and now his eyes flashed, for he had obtained the clue.

"One week, I remember," persisted Mrs. Gray, "he wrote and wrote, and all the time on one name. I fairly got tired of the sight of it, and Robert too; but Mr. Leicester said that he would never be a clerk without perfect penmanship."

"And this one name, what was it?" inquired Jacob, with keen interest.

Mrs. Gray opened a stand drawer, and took out a copy-book filled with loose scraps of paper.

Jacob examined the book and the scraps of paper separately and together. Mrs. Gray was wrong when she said it was a single name only. In the book, and on loose fragments were notes of hand, evidently imitated from some genuine original, with checks on various city banks, apparently drawn at random, and merely as a practice in penmanship; but one bank was more frequently mentioned than the others, and this fact Jacob treasured in his mind.

"This name," he said, touching a signature to one of these papers—"whose is it?"

"Why it is the merchant that Robert is with," answered Mrs. Gray. "That is the one he wrote over so often!"

"I thought so," said Jacob, dryly; and laying the copy-book down, he seemed to cast it from his mind.

Mrs. Gray had become unfamiliar with the features of her relative, or she would have seen that deep and stern feelings were busy within him; but now she only thought him anxious and tired out with the excitement of returning home after so many years of absence.

They sat together on the hearth, more silent than seemed natural to persons thus united, when a footstep upon the crisp leaves brought a smile to Mrs. Gray's face.

"I thought there was a sound of wheels," she said, eagerly. "It is Robert come back from the ferry—how he will be surprised!"

"Not now!" said Jacob Strong. "I would rather not see him to-night—do not tell him that I am here!"

"But he will stay all night!" pleaded Mrs. Gray, whose kind heart was overflowing with the hope of presenting the youth to his uncle without delay.

"So much the better; I can see something of him without being known. Where does that door lead?"

"To a spare bed-room!"

"His bed-room?"

"No. Robert will sleep up stairs in his own chamber—he always does."

"Very well, I will take that room; say nothing of my return. When he is in bed I will come out again."

"Dear me, how strange all this is—how can I keep still?—

how can I help telling him?" murmured the good woman, half following Jacob into the dark bedroom; "I never kept a secret in my life. He will certainly find me out."

"Hush!" said Jacob in an emphatic whisper, from the bedroom; "I will lay down upon the bed—leave the door partly open—now take your seat again where the light will fall on you both. Go—go?"

Mrs. Gray took her seat again, looking very awkward and conscience-stricken. Robert came in flushed with his ride. It was a sharp autumnal evening, and his drive home had been rapid; a brilliant color lay in his cheeks, and the rich hair was blown about his forehead. He flung off his sacque, and cast it down with the heavy whip he carried in one hand.

"Well, aunt, I am back again—that old horse, like wine I have tasted, grows stronger and brighter as he gets old."

"But where is he? the hired-man went away at dark," said Mrs. Gray, anxious for the comfort of her horse.

"Never mind him. I put the blessed pony up myself. You should have heard the old fellow whinney as I gave out his oats. He knew me again."

"Of course he did. I should like to see anything on the place forget you, Robert; it wouldn't stay here long, I give my word for it."

"Oh, aunt, I would not have even a horse or dog sent from the old place for a much greater sin—I know what it is!"

"But you never were sent off, Robert."

"No, aunt, but I went. Instead of superintending the place, and taking the labor from your shoulders, who have no one else to depend on—I must set up for a gentleman—see city life, aunt. I wish from the bottom of my heart that I had never left you!"

"Why, Robert—what makes you wish this? or if you really are homesick, why not come back again?"

"Come back again, aunt!" said the youth, with sudden and bitter earnestness. "Is there any coming back in this life? When we are changed, and places are changed—always ourselves most—how can a return to one spot be called coming back?"

"But I am not changed—the place is just as it was," pleaded the kind aunt.

"But I am changed, aunt—I can throw myself by your side, and lay my head upon your lap as if I were a petted child still, but it would not be natural—we could not force ourselves into believing it natural."

"How strangely you talk, Robert; to me you are a child yet."

"But to myself I am *not* a child, I have thought, felt—yes, I have suffered only as men think, feel and suffer. Oh, aunt, if I had never lived with any one but you, how much better it would have been!"

The youth had cast himself on the hearth by his aunt, and rested his beautiful head upon her knee. Tears—those warm bright tears that youth alone can shed—filled his eyes without impairing their brightness.

The old lady pressed her hand upon his hair, and looked lovingly into those brimming eyes. "And this comes of being a gentleman!" she whispered, shaking her head with a gentle motion.

The youth gave a faint shudder, and turning his head so that his eyes were buried in the folds of her dress, sobbed aloud.

"Why, Robert, Robert, what is this?—what trouble is upon you?"

"None, aunt—nothing. I am only in a fit of the blues just now. It makes me home-sick to see you all alone here, that is all!" answered the youth, lifting his face, and shaking back the curls from his forehead, while he attempted one of his old careless smiles, but vainly enough.

The old lady was distressed. "Is it money, Robert?—have you been extravagant? The salary is a very nice one; but if you want more clothes, or anything, I wouldn't mind giving you twenty or thirty dollars. There, now, will that do?"

Blessed old woman, she did not understand the half sad, half comic smile that curled those young lips, and thinking, in her innocence, that she had dived to the heart of his mystery, her own face beamed with satisfaction.

"That is it; I see through it all now; come, how much shall it be—twenty, thirty, forty? It's extravagant, I know, but this day, of all others, I feel as if it would do me good to give somebody everything I've got in the world; there, nephew, there—two tens—three fives—a three, and, and—yes, I have it—here is a two. Now brighten up, and next time don't be afraid to come and tell me; only, Robert, remember the fate of the prodigal son—the husks, the tears—not that I wouldn't kill the fatted calf—not that I wouldn't forgive you, Bob—I couldn't help it; but it would break my heart. If I was to be called on for the sacrifice, I couldn't eat a morsel of the animal, I'm sure. So you won't be extravagant and spend the hard earnings of your old aunt, at any rate, till after she's dead and gone."

The good woman had worked herself up to a state of almost ludicrous sorrow with the future her fancy was coloring. Her hands shook as she drew an old black pocket-book from some mysterious place in the folds of her dress, and counting out the bank-notes as they were enumerated, crowded them into Robert's hand.

The youth had altered very strangely while she was speaking. His face was pale and red in alternate flashes; his lips quivered, and with a convulsive movement he pressed his eyelids down, thus crushing back the tears that swelled against them. Mrs. Gray attempted to press the bank-notes upon him, but his hand was cold, and his fingers refused to clasp the money. Drawing back with a faint struggle, he said, "No, no, aunt, I do not want it! Indeed it would do me no good!"

"Do you no good! What! is it not money that you want?" cried the kind woman. "Nonsense, nonsense, Robert; here, take it—take it. I wouldn't mind ten dollars more—it does seem as if I was crazy, but then really I would not mind it scarcely at all."

Robert was more composed now. The hot flushes had

left his face very pale, and with a look of firm resolve upon it.

"No, aunt, he said," gently putting back the money, "I will not take it. The salary I receive ought to be enough for my support, and it shall; besides, I tell you but the simple truth, that money would do me no good whatever."

The old lady took up the crushed notes, smoothed them across her knee with both hands, over and over, in a puzzled and dissatisfied way.

"What is it that you are worried about, if money will not answer?" she said, at length.

"Nothing, aunt—why should you think it?" He spoke slowly and in a wavering voice at first, then with a sort of reckless impetuosity he broke into a laugh. It was not his old gleeful laugh, and Mrs. Gray only looked startled by it.

"There, now, put up the old pocket-book, and give me a hearty good-night kiss," he said hurriedly, "I shall be off in the morning before you are up."

"Good night, Robert," said Mrs. Gray, with a meek and disappointed air. "That kiss is the first one that ever fell heavily on your old aunt's heart. You are keeping something back from me."

"No, aunt, no!" The words were uttered faintly, and Mrs. Gray felt that the ardor of truth was not there. For a moment both were silent; Robert had lighted a candle, and stood on the hearth looking hard into the blaze; he turned his eyes slowly upon his aunt. She sat with one hand upon the pocket-book, gazing into the fire. There was anxiety and doubt in her features. Robert sighed heavily.

"Good night, aunt."

"Good night."

She listened to each slow footstep, as her nephew went up stairs. When his chamber door closed, she buckled the strap around her pocket-book, and dropped it with a deep sigh into its repository among her voluminous skirts.

"I can't understand it," she murmured—"I can't make out what ails him!"

All at once she remembered the presence of her brother, and her face brightened up. "Jacob will know what it means. Jacob, Jacob!"

Mrs. Gray uttered the name of her brother in a whisper, but it brought him forth at once.

"Well Jacob, you have seen him—you have heard him talk. Isn't he something worth loving?"

"He is worth loving and worth saving too," answered Jacob. "Sarah, I do not think anything on earth could make my heart beat as the sight of that boy did."

"He is in trouble, you see that, Jacob, and would not take money! What can it mean?"

"I saw all—heard all. His nature is noble—his will strong—have no fear. He needs a firmer hand than yours, Sarah; I will take care of him."

"I did not give a hint about you."

"That was right. It is best that he shouldn't know about me, at any rate, jest now."

"But I should so like to tell him!" said Mrs. Gray.

"And you shall in time, but not yet. I must know more and see more first."

"Well, you ought to know best," answered the sister, in a tone of gentle submission. "I'm sure he puzzles me!"

"Now," said Jacob, seating himself, "let us leave the boy to his rest. I wish to talk with you about old times—about the people Down East."

"It is a good while since I was in Maine, Jacob; I've almost forgotten all about the folks."

"But there was one family that you will remember. Old Mr. Wilcox's, I want to hear about him."

There was something constrained and unnatural in Jacob's manner; he had evidently forced himself to appear calm when every word was sharpened with anxiety.

Mrs. Gray shook her head; Jacob's heart fell as he saw the

motion. "Nothing—can you tell me nothing?" he said, with an expression of deep anguish. "Oh, Sarah, try, try! you do not know how much happiness a word from you would bring!"

"If I could but speak it," said Mrs. Gray, "how glad I should be. Mr. Wilcox sold out and left Maine about the time we moved on to the Island; where he went, no one ever heard. It was a very strange thing, everybody thought so at the time; but that story about his daughter set people a-talking, and I suppose he couldn't bear it."

Jacob uttered a faint groan—her words had taken the last hope from his heart. "And this is all you know, Sarah?"

"It is all anybody knows of old Mr. Wilcox or his family. As for his daughter.—let me think, that was just before you left the old gentleman; nobody ever heard of her either. What is the matter are you going away, Jacob?"

"Yes, I will talk over these things another time. Good night, Sarah. I will just throw myself on the bed till day-break."

"But you are not going away to live?"

"Yes; but you will see me every now and then; I shall stay near you—in the city, may be."

"Why not here? I have enough for us both, and we two are all that is left, almost. It seems kind of hard for you to leave me so soon."

"Not now, Sarah, by and by we will settle down and grow old together; but the time has not come yet."

"I forgot to ask, are you married, Jacob?"

"Married!" answered Jacob Strong, and a grim, hard smile crept over his lips. "No, I was never married. Good night, Sarah."

"There, now, I suppose I've been inquisitive, and worried him," thought Mrs. Gray, as the bed-room door closed upon her brother. "What a Thanksgiving it has been? Who would have thought this morning that *he* would sleep under my roof to-night and Robert close by, without knowing a word of it?

Well, faith is a beautiful thing after all—I was certain that he would come back alive, and sure enough he has!"

Thus Mrs. Gray ruminated, unconscious of the lapse of time, till a sense of fatigue crept over her. Still she was keenly wakeful, for, unused to excitement of any kind, the agitation that crowded upon her that day forbade all inclination to sleep. There was a large moreen couch in the room, and as the night wore on she lay down upon it, still thoughtful and oppressed with the weight of her over-wrought feelings. Thus she lay till the candle burned out, and there was no light in the room save that which came from a bed of embers and the rays of a waning moon, half exhausted in the maple boughs.

A sleepy sensation was at length conquering the excitement that had kept her so long watchful, when she was aroused by the soft tread of a foot upon the stairs. Quietly, and with frequent pauses, it came downward; the door opened, and Mrs. Gray saw her nephew, in his night clothes, and barefooted, glide across the room. He went directly to an old-fashioned work-stand near the bed-room door, and opened one of the drawers. Then followed a faint rustle of papers, and he stole back again softly, and with something in his hand.

It was strange that Mrs. Gray did not speak, but some unaccountable feeling kept her silent, and after she heard him cautiously enter his room again, the reflection that there was nothing but his own little property in the stand, tranquilized her. "He wanted something from the drawer, and so came down softly, that I might not be disturbed," she thought.

Thus the kind lady reassured herself, and with these gentle thoughts in her mind she fell asleep.

Mrs. Gray awoke early in the morning, and softly entered the spare bed-room. It was empty. No vestige of her brother's visit remained. Like a ghost he came, like a ghost he had departed. She went up stairs—the nephew was gone. Some time during that day she happened to think of his visit to the work-stand. It was only the old copy book that he had taken.

CHAPTER XI.

THE MOTHER'S LETTER.

What though her gentle heart is breaking!
  What though her form grows pale and thin!
His iron heart knows no awaking,
  Nor tears nor anguish moveth him.

It was two nights after Thanksgiving. Leicester had thrown himself upon a couch in his chamber. A little sofa-table was by his elbow, and upon it a small and richly chased salver, overflowing with notes and letters. Most of them were unopened, for he had been absent several days, and it often happened that when he once knew a handwriting, and did not fancy the correspondence, letters remained for weeks unread, on that little table, even when he was at home.

But this morning Leicester seemed to have nerved himself to read everything that came to hand. Bills, letters heavy with red wax from the counting-room, and even dirty, square-shaped missives, stamped with keys or thimbles, passed successively through his hands. These coarse letters he took up first, sorting them out with his white fingers from the rose-tinted and azure notes, glittering with gold and fancy seals, with which they were interspersed. These notes, breathing a voluptuous odor, eloquent of that sentimental foppery from which deep, pure feeling recoils, Leicester flung aside in disgust.

When all the business letters were read, he selected from this perfumed mass three little snow-white notes, traced in delicate characters, that seemed yet unsteady with the trembling hand that had written them. A single drop of pale green wax, stamped with a gem, held the envelopes, and in all things these notes were singularly chaste, and unlike those he had left so contemptuously unread. He broke the seals coldly, and perused each note according to its date. The contents must have been full of eloquence, wild and passionate; for they brought the color even to his hardened cheek, and toward the last he became somewhat excited.

"By Jove, it is a pity these could not be published. How the creature writes—a perfect nightingale pouring forth her heart in tears. After all, it is amusing to see downright, earnest love like this. One—two—three—I wonder if there are no more!"

He began tossing over the notes again. "Yes, yes, here is another, like a snow-drop in a cloud of buttercups. How is this?—the seal black, the handwriting delicately rigid—that of my lady mother."

He spoke a little anxiously, and, unfolding the note, read the few lines it contained with a darkened brow.

"Ill—is she, poor girl?—ill, and delirious at times—unfortunate that—physicians must be called, nurses—all a torment and a plague. My friend Robert has been of little use here, after all; I did think his handsome face might have helped me safely out of the whole business. Now, here is the question—shall I go up—re-assure her—take her away from the old lady—brave her friends? No, it is not worth while; a bullet through the brain must be unpleasant, especially to a reflecting mind; and these haughty southerners make short settlements. Besides, I hate scenes. But then the girl is ill, has fretted herself to the brink of the grave. These are the very words—I wonder my stately mamma ever brought herself to utter anything so pathetic. Well, she *has* suffered—the worst is over. When all hope is extinguished she will find consolation, or die. Die—that would end all; but then death is so gloomy, and she does write exquisite letters."

His lips ceased to utter these cold thoughts, and falling back on his couch he closed his eyes, still holding the open note in one hand. It was terrible to see how calm and passionless his features remained while he settled in his mind the destiny of one who had loved him so much. After some ten minutes, he opened his eyes, turned softly on the couch, and laid down his mother's letter.

"No, I will not go near her," he said, "and yet this is another heart that I am casting away—another that has loved me. How soon—how soon shall I have need of affection? A whole life—conquest upon conquest, and yet never truly loved save by these two women—the first and the last. It is strange but this moment my heart softens toward them both. What, a tear in Leicester's eye!" and with a look of thrilling self-contempt the bad man started up, scoffing at the only pure feeling that had swelled his bosom for months.

A waiter stood in the door. "Sir, there is a man below, who says you told him to call."

"What does he seem like?"

"A hack-driver. He says you employed him one rainy night, a long time ago, and ordered him to come again when he had news to bring?"

"What, a tall, awkward fellow, with a stoop in the shoulders—tremendous feet and hands?"

"That's the man, sir."

"Send him up, I did tell him to call."

A few minutes, and Jacob Strong stood in Leicester's chamber, self-possessed even in his exaggerated awkwardness, and with a look of shrewd intelligence which recommended itself to Leicester at once. In their previous acquaintance, the man of the world had seen this applied solely to self-interest in the supposed hackman, and he hoped to make this rude, sharp intellect useful to himself.

It would have been a strange contrast to one acquainted with them both—the deep, wily, elegant man of the world—the honest, firm, shrewd man of the people. These two were pitted together in the game of life; and though one was unconscious, looking upon his antagonist as an instrument—nothing more—and though the other was often compelled to grapple hard with his passions, that they might lead him to no false move—the game was a trial of skill worth studying.

"You told me to find out who the lady was, and where she lived, sir. It took time, for these great people are always moving about, but I have done it."

"I was sure that you were to be depended on, my good fellow; there is your money. Now tell me all about her. Who is she? Where does she live, and when have you seen her?"

Jacob took the offered piece of gold, turned it over in his palm, as if estimating its value, and then laid it on the table, before Leicester

"I don't jest like to give up the money," he said—eyeing the gold with well-acted greed; "but perhaps you will help me in a way I like better."

"How!—what can be better than money?" questioned Leicester. "I thought you Yankees considered the almighty dollar above all things."

"Once in a while there may be things that we like better than that, though we do love to plant the root of evil whenever we can get seed, jest as I want to plant that are gold eagle where it will bring a crop of the same sort."

"Oh, that is it!" said Leicester, laughing, "I thought there must be something to come. But do you remember the old proverb about a 'bird in the hand?'"

"Wal, yes. It seems to me as if I did remember something about it," answered Jacob, putting his huge hand to his forehead; "'a bird in the hand is worth two in the bush,' isn't that the poetry you mean?"

"Yes, that is quite near enough. Now tell me about this lady, and we will talk of the reward after. You found the number of the house?"

"No. It wasn't numbered; but that made no difference, she didn't live there; only staid there one night. Besides, she wasn't a lady, only a kind of help, you know!"

"A governess or waiting-maid—I thought so," exclaimed Leicester. "Very well, where is she now?"

"She went away with the folks that she had been living with, up to Saratoga, and about; then she came back, and they all went off together across the water, to where she came from."

"What, to Europe? Then that is the last of her! Very well, my good fellow, you have earned the money."

Jacob looked keenly at the gold, but did not take it.

"Maybe," said he, shifting his weight from one foot to the other—"maybe you can tell me of some one that wants a hired-man, to drive carriage, or do almost any kind of chores. I'm out of work jest now, and it costs all creation to live here in New York."

Leicester was interested. His personal habits rendered an attendant necessary, and yet he had of late been unable to supply himself with one that could at the same time be useful and discreet. Here was a person, evidently new to the world, honest and with a degree of shrewdness that might be invaluable, ready to accept any situation that might offer. Could he but attach this man to his person, interest his affections, what more useful agent, or more serviceable dependent could be found? Still there was risk in it. Leicester with his lightning habit of thought revolved the idea in his mind, while Jacob stood looking upon the floor, inly a-fire with intense excitement, but to all outward appearance calm.

"You don't know of any one then?" he said, at last, with assumed indifference. "Wal, I don't see how on arth I shall get along."

Leicester looked at him searchingly. Jacob felt the glance, and met it with a calm, dull expression of the eye, that completely deceived the man who was trying with such art to read him to the soul.

"What if I were to engage you myself?"

"Wal, now, I should be awful glad!"

"Do you read? Of course! what Down Easter does not? But are you fond of reading?—in the habit of picking up books and papers?"

Jacob saw the drift of this question at once.

"Wal, yes. I can read a chapter in the Bible, or a piece in

the English reader, I suppose, as well as most folks, though I haven't tried much of late years. But then, if you want a feller to read books for you, why I don't think we should agree I was set agin them at school, and haven't got over it yet."

"You know how to write, of course?"

He made one of his shuffling bows, and began to brush his hat with the sleeve of his coat

"You need not wait; we will talk about the wages to-morrow," said Leicester. "Meantime if you can gather any more information about—about the lady, you know it would be a praiseworthy introduction to your new duties."

Jacob bowed again and edged himself toward the door. "I will do my best, you may be sartain. What time o' day shall I come to-morrow?"

"At ten or two, it does not signify. If I am not in, wait!"

"I will!" muttered Jacob, when he found himself alone. "It is something to have learned how to wait, as you shall find, my new master—*master*!" and Jacob laughed.

CHAPTER XII.

STRIFE FOR AN EARL.

Thistledown—Thistledown!—join the pursuit;
  While fashion flies onward, let wisdom be mute.
All pleasure is fleeting, and life's but a span,
  Come gather up, Thistledown, souls, while you can!

It had been a brilliant season in the fashionable world that year. Saratoga and Newport were perfect hot-beds of gaiety, splendor and trivial ambition. A thorough bred nobleman or two from England—a German countess—the greatest and most popular statesmen of our own land, had flung a dazzling splendor over these places. But even amid all this false life and *éclat* there was one person whose dress, wit and beauty became the theme of general comment. She had taken rooms at Saratoga late in the season. Accommodations for half a dozen servants—stabling for almost as many horses, all was in preparation long before the lady herself appeared.

There was something about this to puzzle and bewilder the most thorough-bred gossip of a watering-place. The servants were foreign, and thoroughly educated to their vocation. When questioned regarding their mistress, they spoke of her without apparent restraint, and always as my lady. But there was no title attached to the name under which the superb suite of apartments had been engaged. Mrs. Gordon! Nothing could be more simple and unpretending. If there was a title behind it, as the indiscretion of the servants seemed to intimate, she was only the more interesting.

Mrs. Gordon's servants had lounged about the United States a whole fortnight; her horses had been exercised by the grooms often enough to attract attention to their superb beauty, and to keep the spirit of gossip and curiosity alive. A lady's maid had for days been making a sensation at the servant's table by her broken English and Parisian finery. Yet no one had obtained a sight of the lady. At last she appeared in the drawing-room, very simply dressed, quiet and self-reliant, neither courting attention nor seeming in the least desirous of avoiding it. She presented no letters, sought no introductions. The various fashionable cliques, with their reigning queens, seemed scarcely to attract the notice of this singular woman, though a mischievous smile would sometimes dawn upon her beautiful mouth, as some petty manœuvering for superiority passed before her.

A creature so calm, so tranquil, so quietly regardless of contending cliques and fashionable factions, was certain to become an object of peculiar attention, even though rare personal beauty, and all the appliances of great wealth had been wanting. The reputation of a title, the graceful repose of manners just enough tinged with foreign grace to be piquant, and, above all, the novelty of a face and position singularly unlike anything known at the Springs that season, could not fail to excite a sensation.

If the lady had designed to secure for herself with one graceful fling a place among the *élite* of American fashion, she could not have managed more adroitly. But even the design was doubtful; she scarcely seemed conscious of the position after it had been awarded to her, and accepted it with a sort of graceful scorn at last, as if yielding herself to the caprice of others, not to her own wishes.

In less than three weeks after her domestication at the Springs, this stranger, announced without introduction, and with no seeming effort, became the reigning belle and toast of the higher circles. Her dress was copied—her wit quoted—her manners became a model to aspiring young ladies, and, with all her power, she was the most popular creature in the world, for she was affable to all, and peculiarly gentle and unassuming to those whom other fashionable leaders were ready to crush with a look and wither by a frown. Sometimes a dash of haughty contempt was visible in her manner, but this was only when thrown in contact with assumption and innate coarseness, which soon shrunk from her keen wit and smiling sarcasms. She was feared by the few, but loved, nay, almost worshipped, by the many.

When the season broke up and the waves of high life ebbed back to the cities, this woman had attained a firm social position, unassailable even by the most envious and the most daring. Still she was as completely unknown as on the first day of her appearance. Of herself she never spoke, and from the strange serving-man, who, maintaining the most profound respect, always hovered about her, nothing but vague hints could be obtained. These hints, apparently won from a simple and hesitating nature, always served to inflame rather than satisfy curiosity. One thing was certain. The lady had seen much of foreign life—had travelled in every penetrable country, and her wealth seemed as great as her beauty. More than this no one knew; and this very ignorance, strange as it may seem, added strength to her position.

The way in which Mrs. Gordon shrouded herself had its own fascination. True, it might conceal low birth, even shame, but it had pleased the fashionable world to bury a high European title under all this mystery, and this belief the lady neither aided nor contradicted, for she seemed profoundly unconscious of its existence. With no human being had she become so intimate that a question on the subject might be directly hazarded. With all her graceful kindliness, there was some thing about her that forbade intrusion or scrutiny. She came to Saratoga beautiful, wealthy, unknown. She left it a brilliant enigma, only the more brilliant that she continued to be mysterious, though a title still loomed mistily in the public mind.

This mysteriousness was rather increased in its effect, and her position wholly established at the annual fancy ball given the last week of her stay at the springs.

During the whole of that season the United States Hotel had been kept in a state of delightful commotion by the rivalry of two leaders in the fashionable world, who had taken up their head-quarters in that noble establishment.

Never was a warfare carried on with such amiable bitterness, such caressing home-thrusts. Everything was done regally, and with that sublime politeness which duellists practice when most determined to exterminate each other. Of course, each lady had her position and her followers, and no military chieftains ever managed their respective forces more adroitly.

Mrs. Nash was certainly the oldest incumbent, and had a sort of preëmption right as a fashionable leader. She had won her place exactly as her husband had obtained his wealth, first plodding his way from the work-shop to the counting-room, thence into the stock market, where, by two or three dashing speculations worthy of the gambling-table, and entered upon in the same spirit, he became a millionaire.

Exactly by the same method Mrs. Nash worked her way upward as a leader of ton. Originally uneducated and assuming,

She had exercised unbounded sway over her husband's work-people, patronizing their wives, and practising diligently the airs that were to be transferred with her husband's advancement into higher circles.

Through the rapid gradations of her husband's fortune, she held her own in the race, and grew important, dressy, and presuming, but not a whit better informed or more refined. When her husband became a millionaire, she made one audacious leap into the midst of the upper ten thousand, hustled her way upward, and facing suddenly about, proclaimed herself a leader in the fashionable world.

People looked on complacently. Some smiled in derision; some sneered with scorn; others, too indolent or gentle for dispute, quietly admitted her charms; while to that portion of society worth knowing, she retained her original character—that of a vulgar, fussy, ignorant woman, from whom persons of refinement shrunk instinctively. Thus, through the forbearance of some, the sneers of others, and the carelessness of all, she fought her way to a position which soon became legitimate and acknowledged.

But this year Mrs. Nash met with a very formidable rival, who disputed the ground she had usurped inch by inch. If Mrs. Nash was insolent, Mrs. Sykes was sly and fascinating. With tact that was more than a match for any amount of arrogant presumption, and education which gave keenness to art, founded upon the same hard purpose and coarse-grained character that distinguished Mrs. Nash, she was well calculated to make a contest for fashionable superiority, exciting and piquant.

Women of true refinement never enter into these miserable rivalries for notoriety, but they sometimes look on amused. In this case the ladies were beautifully matched. The audacity of one was met with the artful sweetness of the other. If Mrs. Nash had power and the prestige of established authority, Mrs. Sykes opposed novelty, unmatched art, and a species of serpent-like fascination difficult to cope with; and much to her astonishment, the former lady found her laurels dropping away leaf by leaf before she began to feel them wither.

Always on the alert for partisans, both these ladies had looked upon Mrs. Gordon with calculating eyes. Beautiful, undoubtedly wealthy, and with that slight foreign air—above all, with a title dropping now and then unconsciously from the lips of her servants—she promised to be an auxiliary of immense value to either faction.

For a week or two they hovered about her, much as two cautious trouts might coquette with a fly on the surface of a mountain pool. Both were afraid to dart at the fly, and yet each was vigilant to keep the other from securing the precious morsel.

Thus, while they were manœuvering around her, drawing public attention that way, Mrs. Gordon became an object of very general admiration, and bade fair, without an effort, and wholly against her will, to rival both the combatants, and like the dancing horse of a Russian chariot, to carry away all the admiration, while the other two bore the toil and burden of the road.

But a few days before the fancy ball, a new fly was cast into the fashionable current, that quite eclipsed anything that had appeared before. An English earl, fresh from the continent, came up to Saratoga, one day, in a train from New York, and would be present at the fancy ball.

Here was new cause for strife between the Nashes and the Sykeses. Which of these ladies should secure the nobleman for the fancy ball? True, the earl was very young, awkward as the school-boy he was, and really looked more like a juvenile horse-jockey than a civilized gentleman. But he was an *earl;* would assuredly have a seat in the House of Lords, if ever he became old enough; besides, he had already lost thirty thousand dollars at the gaming-table, and bore it like a prince.

Here was an object worth contending for. What American lady would be immortalized by leaning upon the arm of an earl as she entered the assembly room? No minor claims could be put in here. The earl undoubtedly belonged to Mrs. Nash or Mrs. Sykes—which should it be? This was the question that agitated all fashionable life at the Springs to its centre. Partisans were brought into active operation. Private ambassadors went and came from the gambling saloons to the drawing-rooms, looking more portentous than any messenger ever sent from the allied powers to the Czar.

The innocent young lord, who had escaped from his tutor for a lark at the Springs, was terribly embarrassed by so many attentions. Too young for any knowledge of society in his own land, he made desperate efforts to appear a man of the world, and feel himself at home in a country where men are set aside, while society is converted into a paradise for boys. It is rumored that some professional gentlemen took advantage of this confusion in the young lordling's ideas, and his losses at the gambling-table grew more and more princely.

But the important night arrived. The mysterious operations of many a private dressing-room became visible. A hundred bright and fantastic forms trod their way to music along the open colonnade of the hotel toward the assembly-room. The brilliant procession entered the folding-doors, and swept down the room two rivers of human life, flowing on, whirling and retiring, beneath a shower of radiance cast from the wall, and the chandeliers that seemed literally raining light. In her toilet, the American lady is not a shade behind our neighbors of Paris; and no saloon in the world ever surpassed this in picturesque effect and richness of costume. Diamonds were plentiful as dew-drops on a rose thicket. Pearls embedded in lace that Queen Elizabeth would have monopolised for her own toilet, gleamed and fluttered around those republican fairies, a decided contrast to the checked handerchief that Ben. Franklin used at the European court, or the bare feet with which our revolutionary fathers trod the way to our freedom through the winter snows. After the gay crowd had circulated around the room awhile, there was a pause in the music, a breaking up of

8

the characters into groups ; then glances were cast toward the door, and murmurs ran from lip to lip. Neither Mrs. Nash or her rival had yet appeared ; as usual their entrance was arranged to make a sensation. How Dodsworth's leader knew the exact time of this fashionable's advent, I do not pretend to say. Certain it is, just as the band struck up an exhilarating march, Mrs. Z. Nash entered the room with erect front and pompous triumph, holding the English earl resolutely by the arm. Mrs. Theodore Sykes came in a good deal subdued and crestfallen, after the dancing commenced. She was escorted by one of the most illustrious of our American statesmen, which somewhat diminished the bitterness of her defeat. Her fancy dress was one blaze of diamonds, and when Mrs. Nash sailed by, holding the young earl triumphantly by the arm, she seemed oblivious of the noble presence, but was smiling up into the eyes of her august companion, as if an American statesman really were some small consolation for the loss of a schoolboy nobleman, who looked as if he would give his right arm, which however, belonged to Mrs. Nash just then, to be safe at home, even with his tutor. When Mrs. Gordon entered the room, no one could have told. When first observed, she was sitting at an open window which looked into the public grounds. The light was striking aslant the white folds of a brocaded silk, and on the delicate marabout feathers in her hair, with the brilliancy of sunshine, playing upon wreaths of newly fallen snow. She evidently had no desire to enter into the spirited competition going on between the rival factions. When a crowd of admirers gathered around the window, she received them quietly, but without empressment. At length, as if weary with talking, she took the first arm offered, and sauntered into the crowd, searching it with her eyes, as if she feared or expected some one. The first dance had broken up ; all was gay confusion, when unwittingly she came face to face with Mrs. Nash, who was sailing down the room with her captive. The young earl, who had remained awkwardly shy since his entrance, gave a start of recognition, his sullen features lighted up, and freeing his arm from the grasp of Mrs. Nash, with an unceremonious "Excuse me, Madam!" he advanced with both hands extended.

"My dear, dear lady, I am so glad to see you!"

The lady reached out her hand, smiling and cordial. "You, here?" she answered, shaking her head, "and alone, ah truant!"

"It wasn't my fault; I was deluded off—kidnapped—but by the best fellow in the world; I will tell you all about it." With a hurried bow to the party he was about to leave. The youth placed himself in a position to converse with Mrs. Gordon, as she passed with her previous escort, quite unconscious of her triumph, or of the rage it had occasioned. The lady bent her head with matronly grace, and resumed her walk. "And so you have run away from the good tutor?" she said.

"Run away? oh, nothing of the sort; he consented to let me come. Leicester can do anything with him. A deuced clever fellow, that Leicester; you know him of course! Everybody knows Leicester, I believe. Ha, what is the matter? Did I tread on your dress?"

"No no! you were saying something of—"

"Yes, yes, of Leicester—a wonderful fellow—we have only known him a week or two, and he can do anything with my tutor—got me off up here like magic!"

"And do you like him?"

"Well, now, you'll confess it's rather hard to like a man who has won ten thousand dollars from you, in one night; but I do rather fancy him, in spite of it."

"Has he won this money from you?" inquired the lady, in a low voice—"you, a minor!"

"*Entre nous*, yes; but it was all above-board, and in the most gentlemanly manner."

"Is Mr. Leicester at the hotel? Has he ever presented himself in the drawing-room?"

"No; he thinks the ladies a bore. I thought so myself, ten minutes ago; but now, with an old friend, it is different. The sight of you brought me back to Florence. You were kind to me there : I shall never, never forget the days and nights of that terrible fever ; but for you, I must have died."

"I was used to sickness, you know," answered the lady, in a faltering voice.

"I remember," answered the earl, "that lovely girl—your relative, I believe—did she recover in Florence ?"

"She died there," was the low reply.

"As I might have done, but for you," he answered, with feeling. "It was the first idea I ever had of a mother's kindness."

"And do you really feel this little service so much ?"

"I only wish it were in my power to prove how much !"

"You can, easily."

"How, lady ?"

"Return to your tutor in the morning—break off all acquaintance with this gentleman."

"What—Leicester ?"

"Yes, Leicester.'

"That is easy ; he left for New York this evening, and I go forward to Canada. Is there nothing more difficult by which I can prove my gratitude ?"

"Yes ; tell me all that has passed between you and this Mr. Leicester, but not here—let us walk down into the drawing-room."

A few moments after, Mrs. Sykes drew softly up to Mrs. Nash, with one of her sweetest smiles : "His lordship, after all, glides back to his own countrywomen ; we Americans stand no chance," she said.

Mrs. Nash bit her lip, and gave the folds of her gold-colored moire a backward sweep with her hand.

"I fancy the earl is not anxious to extend his attention beyond its present limit ; I always said she was worth knowing. Mrs. Gordon seems an old acquaintance. We may, perhaps, now find out who she really is ; I will ask him in the morning."

"Do !" cried half a dozen voices—"we always thought her somebody, but really, she quite patronises the earl himself : do ask all about her, when his lordship comes back."

It was a vain request—the young earl had left the ball-room for good; and long before the persons grouped around Mrs. Nash had left their beds in the morning, he was passing up Lake Champlain, sleepily regarding the scenery along its shore.

That same morning, Mrs. Gordon left Saratoga, so early that no one witnessed her departure. But two or three young men, who had finished up their fancy ball in the open air, reported that she was seen at daybreak, on the colonnade, talking very earnestly to her tall, awkward serving-man, for more than half an hour.

Mrs. Gordon—for thus the lady continued to be known—came to New York early in the autumn, and in the great emporium began a new phase of her erratic and brilliant life.

A mansion, in the upper part of the city; had been in the course of erection during the previous year. It was a castellated villa in the very suburbs, standing upon the gentle swell of a hill, and commanding a fine view both of the city, and the beautiful scenery that lies upon the North and East Rivers.

A few ancient trees, rooted when New York was almost a distant city, stood around this dwelling, sheltering with their old and leafy branches the glowing flowers and rare shrubbery with which grounds of considerable extent were crowded.

This dwelling, so graceful in its architecture, so fairy-like in its grounds, had risen as if by magic among those old trees. Lavish was the cost bestowed upon it; rich and faultless was the furniture that arrived from day to day after the masons and artists had completed their work. Statues of Parian marble, rich bronzes, antique carvings in wood, and the most sumptuous upholstery were arranged by the architect who had superintended the building, and who acted under directions from some person abroad.

When all was arranged, drawing-rooms, library, ladies' boudoir and sleeping chambers, that might have sheltered the repose of an Eastern princess, the house was closed. Those who passed it could now and then catch a glimpse of rich fresco paintings, upon the walls, through a half-fastened shutter; and through the hot-house windows might be seen a little world of exotic plants, dropping their rich blossoms to waste; while the walls beyond were laden with fruit ripening in the artificial atmosphere. Grapes and nectarines fell from bough and vine, untasted, or only to be gathered stealthily by the old man who had temporary charge of the grounds.

Thus everything remained close and silent, like some enchanted palace of fairy land, week after week, till the autumn came on. Since the architect left it, no person save the old gardener, had ever been observed to enter even the delicate iron railing that encompassed the grounds. True, the neighbors, to whom this dwelling had become an object of great interest, were heard to assert that at a time, early in the summer, lights had been observed one stormy night, in the second-story, and even high up in the principal tower. Some even persisted that before it was quite dark, a close carriage had been driven up to the door and away again, leaving two or three persons, who certainly entered the house. After that, carriage wheels had more than once been heard above the storm, rolling to and fro, as if people were coming and going all night.

The next morning, when all the neighborhood was alive with curiosity, this dwelling stood as before—stately and silent, amid the old forest trees. The shutters were closed; the gate locked. Not a trace could be found proving that any human being had entered the premises. So the whole story was generally set down as an Irish fiction, though the servant girl, who originated it, persisted stoutly that she had not only seen lights and heard the wheels, but had caught glimpses of a cashmere shawl within the door; and of a little barefooted girl, with a basket on her arm, coming out half an hour after, and alone. But there stood the closed and silent house—and there was the talkative old gardener in contradiction of this marvellous tale. Besides, carriages were always going up and down the avenue upon which the dwelling stood, and out of this the girl had probably found material for her fiction. Certain it was, that from this time till October no being was seen to enter the silent palace.

Then, in the first golden flush of autumn, the house was flung open. Carriages came to and fro almost every hour. Saddle-horses, light phætons, and an equipage yet more stately, drove in and out of the stables. The windows, with all their wealth of gorgeously tinted glass, were open to the hazy atmosphere; grooms hung around the stables; footmen glided over the tesselated marble of the entrance-hall.

Conspicuous among the rest, was one tall, awkwardly-shaped man, who came and went apparently at pleasure. His duties seemed difficult to define, even by the curious neighbors. Sometimes he drove the carriage, but never unless the lady of the mansion rode in it. Sometimes he opened the door. Again he might be seen in the conservatory, grouping flowers with the taste and delicacy of a professed artist; or in the hot-houses, gathering fruit and arranging it in rich masses for the table. It was marvellous to see the beautiful effect produced by those great, awkward hands. The very japonicas and red roses seemed to have become more glowing and delicate beneath his touch. But after the first week this man almost wholly disappeared from the dwelling. Sometimes he might be seen stealing gently in at nightfall, or very early in the morning; but his active superintendence was over; he seemed to be no longer an inmate, but one who came to the place occasionally to inquire after old friends.

But the mistress of all this splendor—the beautiful woman who sometimes came smilingly forth to enter her carriage, who sauntered now and then into the conservatory, blooming as the flowers that surrounded her, mature in her loveliness as the fruit that hung upon the walls bathed in the golden sunshine—who was this woman, with her unparalleled attractions, her almost fabulous wealth? The world asked this question without an answer, for the Mrs. Gordon of Saratoga, and the Ada Leicester of our story, satisfied no curiosity regarding her personal history. She visited no one who did not first seek her companionship, and thus deprived society of its right to question her.

We, who know this woman by her right name, and in her true character—that of a disappointed, erring, but still affectionate being—might wonder at her bloom, her smiling cheerfulness, her easy and gentle repose of look and manner; but human nature is full of such contradictions, teeming with serpents, absolutely hidden and bathed in the perfume of flowers.

If Ada Leicester smiled, she was not the less sad at heart. If her manners were easy and her voice sweet, it was habit—the necessity of pleasing others—that had rendered these things a second nature to her. With one great, and, we may add, almost holy object at heart, she pursued it earnestly, while all the routine of life went on as if she had no thought but for the world, and no pleasure or aim beyond the luxurious life which seemed to render her existence one continued gleam of Paradise.

Hitherto we have seen this woman in the agony of perverted love—perverted, though legal, for its object was vile; and worship of a base thing is hideous according to its power. We have seen her bowed down with grief, grovelling to the very soil of her native valley, in passionate agony. But these were phases in her life, and extremes of character which seldom appeared before the world.

It is a mistake when people fancy that any life can be made up of unmitigated sorrow. Even evil has its excitement and its gleams of wild pleasure, vivid and keen. The sting of conscience is sometimes forgotten; the viper, buried so deeply in flowers that his presence is scarcely felt, till, uncoiling with a fling, he dashes them all aside, withered by his hot breath and spotted with venom. This heart-shock, while it lasts, is terrible; but those who have no strength to cast forth the serpent bury him again in fresh flowers, and lull him to a poisonous sleep in some secret fold of the heart, till he grows restless and fierce once more.

With all her splendor, Ada Leicester was profoundly unhappy. The deep under-current of her heart always welled up bitter waters. Let the surface sparkle as it would, tears were constantly sleeping beneath. There is no agony like that of a heart naturally pure and noble, which circumstance, weakness, or temptation has warped from its integrity. To know yourself possessed of noble powers, to appreciate all the sublimity of goodness, and yet feel that you have undermined your own strength, and cast a veil over the beautiful through which you can never see clearly, this is deep sorrow—this is the darkness and punishment of sin. If we could but know how evil is punished in the heart of the evil-doer, charity would indeed cover a multitude of sins.

Ada Leicester was unhappy—so unhappy that the beggar at her gate might have pitied her. The pomp, the adulation which surrounded her, had become a habit; thus all the zest and novelty of first possession was gone, and these things became necessary, without gratifying the hungry cry of her soul.

At this period of her life she was utterly without objects of attachment; and what desolation is equal to this in a woman's heart? The thwarted affections and warm sympathies of her nature became clamorous for something to love. Her whole being yearned over the blighted affections of other days; maternal love grew strong within her. She absolutely panted to fold the child, abandoned in a delirium of passionate resentment, once more to her bosom. But that child could nowhere be found. Her parents, too—that noble, kind old man, who had loved her so—that meek and loving woman, her mother—had the earth opened and swallowed them up? was she never to see them more? —to what terrible destitution might her sin have driven them.

The time had been when this proud woman shrunk from meeting persons so deeply injured—but oh, how fervently loved! Now she absolutely panted to fling herself at their feet, and crave forgiveness for all the shame and anguish her madness had cast upon them. In all this her exertions had been cruelly thwarted; parents, child, everything that had loved her and suffered for her, seemed swept into oblivion. The past was but a painful remembrance, not a wreck of it remained save in her own mind.

Another feeling more powerful than filial or maternal love—more absorbing—more ruthlessly adhesive, was the love she could not conquer for the man who had been the first cause of all the misery and wrong against which she was struggling. It was the one passion of a life-time—the love of a warm, impulsive heart—of a vivid intellect, and, say what we will, this is a love that never changes—never dies. It may be perverted—it may be wrestled with and cast to the earth for a time; but such love once planted in a woman's bosom, burns there so long as a spark is left to feed its vitality; burns there, it may be, for ever and ever, a blessing or a curse.

To Ada Leicester it was a curse, for it outlived scorn. It crushed her self-respect—it fell like a mildew upon all the good resolutions that, about this time, began to spring up and brighten in her nature. You would not have supposed that proud, beautiful woman so humble in her love—her hopeless love—of a bad man, and that man the husband whom she had wronged! Yet so it was. Notwithstanding the past: notwithstanding all the perfidy and cruel scorn with which he had deliberately urged her on to ruin, she would have given up anything, everything for one expression of affection, such as had won the love of her young heart. But even here, where the accomplishment of her wish would surely have proved a punishment, her affections were flung rudely back.

And now, when all her efforts were in vain, when no one could be found to accept her penitence, or return some little portion of the yearning tenderness that filled her heart, she plunged recklessly into the world again. The arrow was in her side; but she folded her silken robes over it, and strove to feed her great want with the husks of fashionable life; alas, how vainly! To persons of her passionate nature, the very attempt thus to appease the soul's hunger is a mockery. Ada Leicester felt this, and at times she grew faint amid her empty splendor. She had met with none of the usual retributions which are the coarser and more common result of faults like hers. No disgrace clung to her name: she had wealth, beauty, position, homage.

But who shall say that the punishment of her sin was not great even then? for there is no pain to some hearts so great as a consciousness of undeserved homage. Still this was but the silver edging to the cloud that had begun to rise and darken over her life. Her own proud, warm heart was doomed to punish itself to the utmost.

CHAPTER XIII.

THE MORNING LESSON.

Like some poor cherub gone astray,
From out his native paradise,
Her gentle soul had lost its way,
And fed itself on tears and sighs.

Jacob Strong was alone in Mr. Leicester's chamber. His master had gone out hurriedly, and left the room in considerable disarray. Papers were scattered about loose upon the table. The small travelling desk, which usually stood upon it, was open, and on the purple lining lay an open letter, bearing a Southern post-mark, that had evidently arrived by the morning mail.

We do not pretend to justify our friend Jacob, though he is an especial favorite, in the course he pursued on that occasion. His reasons may possibly be deemed justifiable by the reader, but in our minds there still rests a doubt. Be this as it may, Jacob took up the open letter, and glanced hurriedly over its contents: then he read it more deliberately, while a new and singular expression stole over his features. This did not seem sufficient gratification of his curiosity, for he even opened a compartment of the desk, and pursued his research among notes, visiting cards, bills and business papers, for a good half hour, dotting down a hasty memorandum now and then, with a gold and amethyst pen, which he took from Leicester's inkstand. Then he read the open letter a third time, muttering over the words as if anxious to fix them on his mind by the additional aid of sound.

"That will do—that will clinch the matter; he will never let this escape!" he said, at last, replacing the letter. "Cautious, subtle as he is, this temptation will be too strong. Then, then——"

Jacob's eyes flashed; he pressed the knuckles of one large hand hard upon the desk, and firmly shut his teeth.

That moment a stealthy tread was heard near the door. Jacob instantly commenced making a terrible noise and confusion among the chairs, and while he was occupied in setting things right, after his awkward fashion, Leicester glided into the chamber. Remembering the letter, he had hurried back to secure it from the possible curiosity of his servant. But Jacob was busy with the furniture, muttering his discontent against the untidy chamber-maid, and seemed so completely occupied with an old silk handkerchief, which he was flourishing from one object to another, that all suspicion forsook Leicester. He quietly closed the desk, therefore, and placing the letter in his pocket, sunk into an easy chair, which Jacob had just left clouded in a dusky haze, while he commenced operations on a neighboring sofa.

Something more exciting than usual must have occupied Leicester's thoughts; or, with his fastidious habits, he would not for a moment have endured the perpetual clouds of dust that floated over his hair and clothes, whenever Jacob discovered a new object upon which to exercise his handkerchief. As it was, he sat lost in thought, apparently quite unconscious of the annoyance, or of the keen glances which the servant now and then cast upon him.

"It will do," thought Jacob, gathering the duster up in his hand, with an eager clutch; and while he seemed looking around for something to employ himself with, those keen grey eyes were bent upon Leicester's face. "I was sure of it; he has almost made up his mind. Let me hear the tone of his voice, and I shall know how."

Jacob had not long to wait. After a reverie that was disturbed by many an anxious thought, Leicester turned in his chair, opened the little travelling desk, and began to write, pausing now and then, as if the construction of his language was more than usually difficult. The note did not please him. He tore it in two, and casting the fragments upon the hearth-rug, selected another sheet from the perfumed paper that lay at his elbow. This time he was more successful. The note was carefully folded, secured with a little antique seal, and directed in a light and flowing hand. Leicester smiled as he wrote, and his face brightened as if he had flung off a load of annoying doubts. "Here," he said, holding the letter over his shoulder with a carelessness that was certainly more than half assumed, "take this note, and observe how it is received. You understand?"

Jacob took the snowy little billet, and bent over it wistfully, as if the direction could only be made out with great effort.

"Well!" said Leicester, turning sharply upon him, "what keeps you? Surely you understand enough to make out the address?"

"Well, yes!" answered Jacob, holding the note at arm's length, and eyeing it askance; "it's rather too fine, that are handwriting; but then I can manage to cipher it out if you give me time enough."

"Very well—you have had time enough. Go! and remember to observe all that passes when you deliver it."

Jacob took up his drab beaver, planted it firmly on the back of his head, and disappeared, holding the note between his thumb and finger.

While our friend Jacob is making his way up town, we will precede him, and enter the pretty cottage which, with its fairy garden, has before been an object of description.

In the parlor of this beautiful but monotonous dwelling sat Florence Craft. Cold as it was becoming, she still wore the pretty morning dress of fine India muslin, with its profusion of soft lace, but over it was a scarf of scarlet cashmere, that gave to her cheek its rosy shadow, as a crimson camilla sometimes casts a trace of its presence on the marble urn against which it falls. But for this warm shadow her face was coldly white, and even traced with mournful lines, as if she had been suffering from illness or some grief unnatural to her youth, and weighing sadly upon her gentle nature. Her soft brown eyes seemed misty and dulled by habitual tears, and the long curling lashes flung a deeper shadow on the cheek just beneath; for a faint circle, such as disease or grief often pencils, was becoming definitely marked around those sad and beautiful eyes. The imprint of many a heavy heart-ache might have been read in those shadowy circles, and the paler redness of a mouth that smiled still—but oh, how mournfully!

Florence sat by a sofa-table, one foot, too small now for the satin slipper that had so beautifully defined its proportions a little while before, rested upon the richly carved supporter. She had become painfully fragile, and the folds of her dress fell around her drooping form like a white cloud, so transparent that but for the red scarf, you might have defined the slender arms and marble neck underneath with startling distinctness. She was occupied with her drawing lesson, but even the pencil seemed too heavy for the slender and waxen fingers that guided it; and to one that undertsood the signification, there was something ominous in the bright, feverish tinge that spread over her palm, as if she had been crushing roses in that little hand, and might not hope to wash the stain away.

Robert Otis leaned over the unhappy girl. He too was changed, but not like her. The flesh had not wasted from his limbs; the fire of youth had not burned out prematurely in those bright eyes; but his look was unsettled, restless, nay, sometimes wild. His very smile was hurried and passed quickly away; all its soft, mellow warmth was gone. The change was different, but terribly perceptible both in the youth and the young girl.

It was no boyish passion which marked the features of that noble face as it bent lower and lower over the drooping girl. Tenderness, keen, deep sympathy was there, but none of the ardent feeling that had fired his whole being when only the semblance of that beautiful form first met his eye. If Robert Otis loved Florence Craft, it was with the tender earnestness of a brother, not with the fiery ardor natural to his age and temperament.

"You seem tired; how your hand trembles; rest awhile, Miss Craft. This stooping posture must be oppressive," said Robert, gently attempting to remove the pencil from the fair hand that could really guide it no longer.

"No, no," said Florence, raising her eyes with a sad smile, "you do not give lessons every day, now, and we must improve the time. When Mr. Leicester comes he should find me quite an artist, I must not disgrace you with my idleness. He would feel hurt if we did not meet his expectations. Don't you think so?"

"Perhaps, I cannot exactly tell. Mr. Leicester is so unlike other men, it is difficult to decide what his wishes really are," said Robert. "He certainly did take great interest in your progress at first!"

"And now that interest has ceased! Is that what you mean to say, Robert?" questioned the young girl, and even the scarlet reflection of her shawl failed to relieve the deadly paleness of her countenance.

"No, I did not say that!" answered Robert, gently, "he questions me of your progress often."

Florence drew a deep breath, and now there was something more than a scarlet reflection on her cheek.

"But then," continued Robert, "he contents himself with questions; he does not come to witness the progress you are making."

"You have noticed it, then?—you have thought it strange?" said Florence, while the red upon her cheek began to burn painfully, and tears rushed to her eyes. "Yet you do not know—you cannot even guess how hard this is to bear!"

"Perhaps I can guess," answered Robert, casting down his eyes and trembling visibly.

Florence started from her chair, and stood upright. In the violence of her agitation, she lost the languid, willowy stoop of frame that had become habitual. For a moment the full energies of her nature were lighted up, stung into sharp vitality by surprise and terror. But she did not speak, she only stood upright a single moment, and then sunk to the couch helplessly and sobbing like a child. Robert knelt by her greatly agitated, for he had anticipated no such violent effect from his words.

"Do not weep, Miss Craft, I did not intend to pain you thus. What have I said?—what have I done that it should bring so much grief?"

She looked at him earnestly, and whispered in a low voice, while the lashes fell over her eyes, sweeping the tears downward in fresh gushes. "What was it that you said? Something that you could guess, was not that it? Now tell me all you guess. What is it that you think?"

"Nothing that should overwhelm you in this manner," said Robert, struggling against the convictions her agitation was calculated to produce. "I thought—I have long thought—that you were greatly attached to Mr. Leicester, more than a ward usually is to her guardian."

"You are with him so much—surely you did not think that my love—for I do not deny it, Robert—was unwelcome or unsought?"

Robert hesitated; he could not find it in his heart to give utterance to his thoughts.

"No, I did not think that," he said; "but Mr. Leicester is a strange man, so much older than we are—so much wiser. I can fathom neither his motives nor his feelings."

"And I—I have felt this so often—that is, of late," said Florence, "at times I am almost afraid of him, and yet this very fear has its fascination."

"Yes," answered Robert, thoughtless of the meaning that might be given to his words, "the bird shivers with fear even as the serpent lures it, and in this lies some subtle mystery; for while the poor thing seems to know its danger, the knowledge yields it no power of resistance. Here lies the serpent with its eyes burning and its jaws apart, exposing all its venom ; but the spell works in spite of this."

"Hush ! hush !" said Florence, with a look of terror, "this is a cruel comparison. It makes me shudder !"

"I did not intend it as a comparison," answered Robert. "With you it can never be one, and with me such ideas would be very ungrateful, applied to my oldest friend. I wish to heaven, no thought against him would ever enter my head again."

"Conquer them—never breathe them even to yourself !" said Florence, with sudden impetuosity. "They have killed me—those weary, base suspicions—not mine ! not mine ! Oh, I am so thankful that they were not formed in my heart ?—they were whispered to me—forced on me. I would not believe them—but the evil thing is here. I have no strength to cast it out alone, and he never comes to help me."

"Perhaps he does not know how deeply you feel for him," said Robert, anxious to console her.

Florence shook her head, and leaning forward, shrouded her eyes with one hand. After a while, she turned her gaze upon Robert, and addressed him more quietly.

"You must not think ill of him," she said, with a dim smile. "See what suspicion and pining thoughts can do, when they have crept into the heart." The poor girl drew up the muslin sleeve from her arm, and Robert was startled to see how greatly the delicate limb was attenuated. Tears came into his eyes, and bending down he touched the snowy wrist with his lips. "I must tell him that you are ill—that you suffer—surely he cannot dream of this !"

"Not yet—we must not importune him ; besides, I am becoming used to this desolate feeling. You will come oftener now. It is something to know that he has been near you—touched your clothes—held your hand—the atmosphere of his presence hangs about your very garments, and does me good. This seems childish, does it not ? but it is true. Sometime, when you have given up your being to another, this will appear less strange. Oh, how I sometimes envy you!"

"I might have loved, young as you think me, even as you love this man," said Robert, annoyed, spite of his sympathy, by the words which she had unconsciously applied to his youth; "but that which has wounded you, saved me. You do not know, Miss Craft, all that I have felt since the evening when Mr. Leicester brought me here. What I saw that night awoke me from the first sweet dream of passion I ever knew. I could have loved you then, even as you loved Mr. Leicester."

"*Me!*" said Florence, and a momentary smile lighted her eyes—as if the very thought of his young love amused her, sad as she was; "how strange! to me you seemed so young and embarrassed—a mere boy—now——"

"Now I am changed, you would say—now I am a different person—older, firmer, more self-possessed; yet it is only a few months ago. I may seem older and less timid—for in this little time I have thought and suffered—but then, I was more worthy of your love, for I had not learned to distrust my oldest friend. Like you, I have struggled against suspicion—and like you, I have failed to cast it forth. It has withered your gentle nature —mine it has embittered."

"Ah! but you had not my temptation. It was not his own mother who poisoned your mind against him."

"His mother? I did not know that either of his parents were living."

"That quiet, cold lady; the woman whom you have seen here! Did he never tell you that she was his mother?"

"He never even hinted it!" said Robert, greatly surprised.

"She told me so with her own lips: she warned me against him—she, his mother."

"Indeed!" said Robert, thoughtfully. "Yet with what coldness she received him!"

"It is not her nature," answered Florence, and her eyes filled with grateful tears. "To me, her kindness has been unvaried; there is something almost holy in her calm, sweet affection : but for this I had not been so unhappy. Had I detected prejudice, temper, anything selfish mingled with her words, they would never have reached my heart; but now, I cannot turn from her. With all her stately coldness she had something of his power—I dare not doubt her. But I will not believe the warning she gave me."

Robert walked up and down the room. New and stern thoughts were making their way in his mind. Gratitude is a powerful feeling, but it possesses none of the infatuation and blindness which characterizes the grand passion. Suspicions that had haunted his conscience like crimes, were beginning to shape themselves into stubborn facts. Still he would not yield to them. Like the gentle girl, drooping before his eyes, he dared not believe anything against William Leicester. Humiliation, nay, almost ruin, lay in the thought

CHAPTER XIV.

A WEDDING FORESHADOWED.

When her heart was all dreary and burdened with fears,
Hope came like a seraph and touched it with light,
Like sunshine or rain-drops it kindled her tears
Till they trembled like stars 'mid her soul's quick delight.

Florence had taken up her pencil again, but still remained inactive, gazing wistfully through the lace curtains, at the little fountain flinging up a storm of spray amid flowers gorgeous with autumn tints and the crisp brown that had settled on the little grass-plat. Notwithstanding the dahlias were in a glow of rich tints, and the chrysanthemums sheeted with white, rosy, and golden blossoms, there was a tinge of decay upon the leaves, very beautiful, but always productive of mournful feelings Florence had felt this influence more than usual that morning, and now to her excited nerves there was something in the glow of those flowers, and the soft rush of water-drops, that made her heart sink.

If the autumn and summer had been so dreary, with all the warmth and brightness of sunshine and blossoms, what had the winter of promise to her ? Spite of herself she looked down to the thin, white hand that lay so listlessly on the paper, and gazed on it till tears swelled once more against those half-closed eye-lids. " How desolate to be buried in the winter, and away from all——" These were the thoughts that arose in that young heart. The objects that gave rise to them were flowers, autumn flowers, the richest and most beautiful things on earth. Thus it often happens in life, that lovely things awake our most painful and bitter feelings, either by a mocking contrast with the sorrow that is within us, or because they are associated with the memory of wasted happiness.

As Florence sat gazing upon the half veiled splendor of the garden flowers, she saw a man open the little gate, and move with a slow, heavy step toward the door. The face was unfamiliar, and the fact of any strange person seeking that dwelling was rare enough to excite some nervous trepidation in a young and fragile creature like Florence.

" There is some one coming," she said, addressing Robert, who was thoughtfully pacing the room, with a tone and look of alarm quite disproportioned to the occasion. " Will you go to the door, I believe every one is out except us ?"

Robert shook off the train of thought that had made him unconscious of the heavy footsteps now plainly heard in the veranda, and went to the door.

Jacob Strong did not seem in the least embarrassed, though nothing could be supposed further from his thoughts than an encounter with the young man in that place. Perhaps he lost something of the abruptness unconsciously maintained during his walk, for his mien instantly assumed a loose, almost slouching carelessness, such as had always characterized it in the presence of Leicester or his protégé.

"Well, how do you do, Mr. Otis? I didn't just expect to find you here! Hain't got much to do down at the store, I reckon?"

"Never mind that, Mr. Strong," answered the youth, good-humoredly, "but tell me what brought you here. Some message from Mr. Leicester, ha!"

"Well, now, you do beat all at guessing," answered Jacob, drawing forth the billet-doux with which he was charged. "Ain't there a young gal a-living here, Miss Flo—Florence Craft? If that ain't the name, I can't cipher it out any how!"

"Yes, that is the name—Miss Craft does live here," said Robert. "Let me have the note—I will deliver it."

"Not as you know on, Mr. Otis," replied Jacob, with a look of shrewd determination. "Mr. Leicester told me to give this ere little concern into the gal's own hand, and I always obey orders though I break owners. Jest be kind enough to show me where the young critter is, and I'll do my errand and back again in less than no time."

"Very well, come this way; Miss Craft will receive the note herself."

Florence was standing near the window, her bright, eager eyes were turned upon the door, she had overheard Leicester's name, and it thrilled through every nerve of her body.

Jacob entered with his usual heavy indifference. He looked a moment at the young girl, and then held out the note. Robert fancied that a shade of feeling swept over that usually composed face, but the lace curtains were waving softly to a current of air let in through the open doors, and it might be the transient shadows thus flung upon his face. Still there was something keen and intelligent in the glance with which Jacob regarded the young girl while she bent over the note.

Suddenly he bent those keen, grey eyes, now full of meaning, and almost stern in their searching power, upon the youth himself. Robert grew restless beneath that strict scrutiny, the color mounted to his forehead, and as a relief he turned toward Florence

She was busy reading the note, apparently unconscious of the person, but oh, how wildly beautiful her face had become! Her eyes absolutely sparkled through the drooping lashes; her small mouth was parted in a glowing smile—you could see the pearly edges of her teeth behind the bright red of lips that seemed just bathed in wine. She trembled from head to foot, not violently, but a blissful shiver, like that which stirs a leaf at noonday, in the calm summer time, wandered over her delicate frame. Twice—three times, she read the note, and then her soft eyes were uplifted and turned upon Robert, in all their glorious joy.

"See!" she said, and her voice was one burst of melody—"Oh, what ingrates we have been to doubt him!" In her bright triumph, she held forth the note, but as Robert advanced to receive it, she drew back. "I had forgotten," she said, "I alone was to know it; but you can guess—you can see how happy it has made me."

Robert Otis turned away, somewhat annoyed by this half confidence. Florence, without heeding this, sat down by the table, and, with the open note before her, prepared to answer it, but her excitement was too eager—her hand too unsteady. After several vain efforts, she took the note and ran up stairs.

Thus Jacob and Robert were left alone together. The youth, possessed by his own thoughts, seemed quite unconscious of the companionship forced upon him. He sat down on the couch which Florence had occupied, and, leaning upon the table, supported his forehead with one hand. Jacob stood in his old place, regarding the varied expressions that came and went on that young face. His own rude features were greatly disturbed, and at this moment bore a look that approached to anguish. Twice he moved, as if to approach Robert—and then fell back irresolute; but at last, he strode forward, and before the youth was aware of the movement, a hand lay heavily upon his shoulder.

"So you love her, my boy?"

Robert started. The drawling tone, the rude Down East enunciation was gone. The man who stood before him seemed to have changed his identity. Rude and uncouth he certainly was—but even in this, there was something imposing. Robert looked at him with parted lips and wondering eyes—there was something even of awe in his astonishment.

"Tell me, boy," continued Jacob, and his voice was full of tenderness—"tell me, is it love for this girl, that makes you thoughtful? Are you jealous of William Leicester?"

Robert lost all presence of mind—he did not answer—but sat motionless, with his eyes turned upon the changed face bending close to his.

"Will you not speak to me, Robert Otis? You may—you should, for I am an honest man."

"I believe you are!" said Robert, starting up and reaching forth his hand—"I know that you are, for my heart leaps toward you. What was the question? I will answer it now. Did you ask if I loved Florence Craft?"

"Yes, that was it—I would know; otherwise events may shape themselves unluckily. I trust, Robert, that in this you have escaped the snare."

"I do not understand you, but can answer your question a great deal better than I could have done three days ago. I do love Miss Craft as it has always seemed to me that I should love a sister, had one been made an orphan with me: I would do any thing for her, sacrifice anything for her. Once I thought this love, but now I know better. There was another question—am I jealous of William Leicester? I do not know; my heart sinks when I see them together—I cannot force myself to wish her his wife, and yet this repugnance is unaccountable to myself. He is my friend—she something even dearer than a sister; but my very soul revolts at the thought of their union. It was this that made me thoughtful: I do not love Florence in your meaning of the word; I am not jealous of Mr. Leicester; but God forgive me! there is something in my heart that rises up against him! There, sir, you have my answer. I may be imprudent—I may be wrong; but it cannot be helped now."

"You have been neither imprudent nor wrong," answered Jacob, laying his hand on the bent head of the youth. "I am a plain man, but you will find in me a safer counsellor than you imagine—a wiser one—though not more sincere—than your good aunt."

"Then you know my aunt?" cried Robert, profoundly astonished.

"It would have been well had you confided even in her, on Thanksgiving night, when you were so near confessing the difficulties that seem so terrible to you. A few words then, might have relieved all your troubles."

"Then Mr. Leicester has told—has betrayed me to—to his servant, I would not have believed it!" Robert grew pale as he spoke; there was shame and terror in his face; deep bitterness in his tone; he was suffering the keen pangs which a first proof of treachery brings to youth.

"No, you wrong Mr. Leicester there—he has not betrayed you, never will, probably, nor do I know the exact nature of your anxieties."

"But who are you then? An hour ago I could have answered this question, or thought so. Now, you bewilder me; I can scarcely recognize any look or tone about you—which is the artificial? which the real?"

"Both are real; I *was* what you have hitherto seen me, years ago. I *am* what you see now; but I can at will throw off the present and identify myself with the past. You see, Robert Otis, I give confidence when I ask it—a breath of what you have seen or heard to-day, repeated to Mr. Leicester, would send me from his service. But I do not fear to trust you!"

"There is no cause of fear—I never betrayed anything in my life—only convince me that you mean no evil to him."

"I only mean to prevent evil! and I will!"

"All this perplexes me," said Robert, raising one hand to his forehead—"I seem to have known you many years; my heart warms toward you as it never did to any one but my aunt."

"That is right; an honest heart seldom betrays itself. But

hush! the young lady is coming; God help her, *she* loves that man."

"It is worship—idolatry—not love; that seems but a feeble word; it gives one the heart-ache to witness its ravages on her sweet person."

"And does she feel so much?" said Jacob, with emotion.

Before Robert could answer, the light step of Florence was heard on the stairs; when she entered the room, Jacob stood near the window, holding his hat awkwardly between both hands, and with his eyes bent upon the floor.

"You will give this to Mr. Leicester," she said, still radiant and beautiful with happiness, placing a note in Jacob's hand—"here is something for yourself, I only wish it could make you as happy as—as—that it may be of use, I mean." Blushing and hesitating thus in her speech, she placed a small gold coin upon the note. Poor girl, it was a pocket-piece given by her father, but in her wild gratitude she would have cast thousands upon the man whose coming had brought so much happiness.

Jacob received the coin, looked at her earnestly for a moment, half extended his hand, and then thrust it into his pocket.

"Thank you, ma'am, a thousand times—I will do the errand right off!" and putting on his hat, Jacob strode from the house, muttering, as he cast a hurried glance around the little garden, "It seems like shooting a robin on her nest—I must think it all over again."

Robert would have followed Jacob Strong, for his mind was in tumult, and he panted for some more perfect elucidation of the mystery that surrounded this singular man. But Florence laid her hand gently on his arm, and drew him into the window recess: her face was bright with smiles and bathed in blushes. "You were ready to go without wishing me joy," she said; "and yet you must have guessed what was in that precious, precious note!"

Robert felt a strange thrill creep through his frame. He turned his eyes from the soft orbs looking into his, for their brilliancy pained him.

"No," he said, almost bitterly, "I cannot guess—perhaps I do not care to guess !"

"Oh, Robert ! you do not know what happiness is ; no human being ever was so happy before. How cold—how calm you are ! You could feel for me when I was miserable, but now—now it is wrong : he charged me to keep it secret, but my heart is so full, Robert ; stoop and let me whisper it—tell nobody, he would be very angry—but this week we are to be married !"

"Now," said Robert, drawing a deep breath, and speaking in a voice so calm that it seemed like prophecy—"now I feel for you more than ever."

The little, eager hand fell from his arm, and in a voice that thrilled with disappointment, Florence said,

"Then you will not wish me joy !"

Robert took her hand, grasped it a moment in his, and flinging aside the cloud of lace that had fallen over them, left the room. Florence followed him with her eyes, and while he was in sight a shade of sadness hung upon her sweet face—but her happiness was too perfect even for this little shadow to visit it more than a moment. She sunk upon an ottoman in the recess, and, with her eyes fixed upon the autumn flowers without, subsided into a reverie, the sweetest, the brightest that ever fell upon a youthful heart.

CHAPTER XV.

THE MOTHER'S APPEAL.

Wrong to one's self but wrongs the world;
God linketh soul so close to soul,
That germs of evil, once unfurled,
Spread through the life and mock control.

Pen, ink, and paper lay upon the table. The curtains were flung back, admitting the broad sunshine that revealed more clearly than the usual soft twilight with which Leicester was in the habit of enveloping himself, the lines which time and passion sometimes allowed to run wild, sometimes curbed with an iron will, had left on his handsome features. Papers were on the table, not letters, but scraps that bore a business aspect, some half printed, others without signature, but still in legal form, as notes of hand or checks are given.

Leicester took one of these checks—a printed blank—and gazed on it some moments with a fixed and thoughtful scrutiny He laid it gently down, took up a pen, and held the drop of ink on its point up to the light, as if even the color were an object of interest. He wrote a word or two, merely filling up the blank before him, but simple as the act seemed, that hand, usually firm as marble, quivered on the paper, imperceptibly, it is true, but enough to render the words unsteady. His face, too, was fiercely pale, if I may use the term, for there was something in the expression of those features that sent a sort of hard glow through their whiteness. It was the glow of a desperate will mastering fear.

With a quick and scornful quiver of the lip, he tore the half-filled check in twain, and cast the fragments into the fire. "Am I growing old?" he said aloud, "or is this pure cowardice? Fear!—what have I to fear?" he continued, hushing his voice. "It *cannot* be brought back to me. A chain that has grown, link by link, for years, will not break with any common wrench. Still, if it could be avoided, the boy loves me!—well, and have not others loved me? Of what use is affection, if it adds nothing to one's enjoyments? If the old planter had left my pretty Florence the property at once, why then—but till she is of age—that is almost two years—till she is of age we must live."

Half in thought, half in words, these ideas passed through the brain and upon the lip of William Leicester. When his mind was once made up to the performance of an act, it seldom paused even to excuse a sin to his own soul, but this was not exactly a question of right and wrong: that had been too often decided with his conscience to admit of the least hesitation. There was peril in the act he meditated—peril to himself—this made his brow pale and his hand unsteady. During a whole life of fraud and evil-doing, he had never once placed himself within the grasp of the law. His instruments, less guilty, and far less treacherous than himself, had often suffered for crimes that his keen intellect had suggested. For years he had luxuriated upon the fruit of iniquities prompted by himself, but with which his personal connection could never be proved. But for once his subtle forethought in selecting and training an agent who should bear the responsibility of crime while he reaped the benefit, had failed. The time had arrived when Robert Otis was, if ever, to become useful to his teacher. But evil fruit in that warm, generous nature had been slow in ripening. With all his subtle craft, Leicester dared not propose the fraud which was to supply him with means for two years' residence in Europe

There was something in the boy too clear-sighted and prompt even for his wily influence, and now, after years of training worthy of Lucifer himself, Leicester, for the first time, was afraid to trust his chosen instrument. Robert might be deluded into wrong—might innocently become his victim, but Leicester despaired of making him, with his bright intellect and honorable impulses, the principal or accomplice of an act such as he meditated.

A decanter of brandy stood upon the table—Leicester filled a goblet and half drained it. This in no way disturbed the pallor of his countenance, but his hand grew firm, and he filled up several of the printed checks with a rapidity that betrayed the misgivings that still beset him.

He examined the papers attentively after they were written, and, selecting one, laid it in an embroidered letter-case which he took from his bosom; the others he placed in an old copy-book that had been lying open before him all the time; it was the same book that Robert Otis had taken from his aunt's stand-drawer on Thanksgiving night.

When these arrangements were finished, Leicester drew out his watch, and seemed to be waiting for some one that he expected.

Again he opened the copy-book and compared the checks with other papers it contained. The scrutiny seemed to satisfy him, for a smile gleamed in his eyes as he closed the book.

Just then, Robert Otis came in. His step had become quiet, and the rosy buoyancy of look and manner that had been so interesting a few months before, was entirely gone. There was restraint—nay, something amounting almost to dislike in his air as he drew a seat to the table.

"You are looking pale, Robert; has anything gone amiss at the counting-house?" said Leicester, regarding his visitor with interest.

"Nothing!"

"Are you ill then?"

"No, I am well—quite well!"

"But something distresses you; those shadows under the eye, the rigid lines about the mouth—there is trouble beneath them. Tell me what it is—am I not your friend?"

Robert smiled a meaning, bitter smile, that seemed strangely unnatural on those fresh lips. Leicester read the meaning of that silent reproach, and it warned him to be careful.

"Surely," he said, "you have not been at F—— street, without your friend?—you have not indulged in high play, and no prudent person to guide you?"

"No!" said Robert, with bitter energy—"that night I did play—how, why, it is impossible for me to remember. Those few hours of wild sin were enough—they have stained my soul—they have plunged me into debt—they have made me ashamed to look a good man in the face."

"But I warned, I cautioned you!"

Robert did not answer, but by the gleam of his eyes and the quiver of his lips, you could see that words of fire were smothered in his heart.

"You would have plunged into the game deeper and deeper, but for me.

"Perhaps I should—it was a wild dream—I was mad—the very memory almost makes me insane. I, so young, so cherished, in debt—and how—to what amount?"

"Enough—I am afraid," said Leicester, gently—"enough to cover that pretty farm, and all the bank stock your nice old aunt has scraped together. But what of that?—she is in no way responsible, and gambling debts are only debts of honor—no law reaches them?"

"I will not make sin the shelter of meanness," answered the youth, with a wild flash of feeling; "these men may be villains, but they did not force themselves upon me. I sought them of my own free choice; no—I cannot say that either, for heaven knows I never wished to enter that den!"

"It was I that invited, nay, urged you!"

"Else I had never been there!"

"But I intended it as a warning—I cautioned you, pleaded with you."

"Yes, I remember—you said I was ignorant, awkward, a novice—Mr. Leicester; your advice was like a jeer—your caution a taunt; your words and manner were at variance; I played that night, but not of my own free will. I say to you, it was *not* of my free will!"

"Is it me, upon whom your words reflect?" said Leicester, with every appearance of wounded feeling.

Robert was silent.

"Do you know," continued Leicester, in that deep, musical tone, that was sure to make the heart thrill—"do you know, Robert Otis, why it is that you have not been openly exposed?—why this debt has not been demanded long ago?"

"Because the note which I gave is not yet due!"

"The note—a minor's note—what man in his senses would receive a thing so worthless? No, Robert—it was my endorsement that made the paper valuable. It is from me, your old friend, Robert, that the money must come to meet the paper at its maturity."

Tears gushed into the young man's eyes—he held out his hand

across the table—Leicester took the hand and pressed it very gently.

"You know," he said, "this note becomes due almost immediately."

"I know—I know. It seems to me that every day has left a mark on my heart; oh, Mr. Leicester, how I have suffered!"

"I will not say that suffering is the inevitable consequence of a wrong act, because that just now would be unkind," said Leicester, with a soft smile, "but hereafter you must try and remember that it is so."

Robert looked upon his friend; his large eyes dilated, and his lips began to tremble; you could see that his heart was smitten to the core. How he had wrought that man! Tears of generous compunction rushed to his eyes.

"It will be rather difficult, but I have kept this thing in my mind," said Leicester. "To-morrow I shall draw a large sum; a portion must redeem your debt, but on condition that you never play again!"

Robert shuddered. "Play again!" he said, and tears gushed through the fingers which he had pressed to his eyes. "Do you fear that a man who has been racked would of his own free will seek the wheel again? But how am I to repay you?"

"Confide in me; trust me. Robert, the suspicions that were in your heart but an hour since—they will return."

Robert shook his head, and swept the tears from his eyes.

"No, no! even then I hated myself for them: how good, how forgiving, how generous you are! I am young, strong, have energy. In time this shameful debt can be paid—but kindness like this—how can I ever return that?"

"Oh! opportunities for gratitude are never wanting: the bird we tend gives back music in return for care, yet what can be more feeble? Give me love, Robert, that is the music of a young heart—do not distrust me again!"

"I never will!"

Leicester wrung the youth's hand. They both arose.

"If you are going to the counting-room, I will accompany you," he said, "my business must be negotiated with your firm."

"I was first going to my room," said Robert.

"No matter, I will walk slowly—by the way, here is your old copy-book; I have just been examining it. Those were pleasant evenings, my boy, when I taught you how to use the pen."

"Yes," said Robert, receiving the book, "my dear aunt claims the old copies as a sort of heir-loom. I remembered your wish to see it, and so took it quietly away. I really think she would not have given it up, even to you."

"Then she did not know when you took it?"

"No, I had forgotten it, and so stole down in the night. She was sound asleep, and I came away very early in the morning."

"Dear old lady," said Leicester, smiling; "you must return her treasure before it is missed. Stay; fold your cloak over it. I shall see you again directly."

Leicester's bed-chamber communicated with another small room, which was used as a dressing-closet. From some caprice he had draped the entrance with silken curtains such as clouded the windows. Scarcely had he left the room when this drapery was flung aside, revealing the door which had evidently stood open during his interview with Robert Otis.

Jacob Strong closed the door very softly, but in evident haste; dropped the curtains over it, and taking a key from his pocket, let himself out of the bed-chamber. He overtook Robert Otis, a few paces from the hotel, and touched him upon the shoulder.

"Mr. Otis, that copy-book—my master wishes to see it again—will you send it back?"

"Certainly," answered Robert, producing the book. "But what on earth can he want it for?"

"Come back with me, and I will tell you!"

"I will," said Robert; "but remember, friend, no more hints against Mr. Leicester, I cannot listen to them."

"I don't intend to *hint* anything against him now!" said Jacob, dryly, and they entered the hotel together.

Jacob took the young man to his own little room, and the two were locked in together more than an hour. When the door opened, Jacob appeared composed and awkward as ever, but a powerful change had fallen upon the youth. His face was not only pale, but a look of wild horror disturbed his countenance.

"Yet I will not believe it," he said, "it is too fiendish. In what have I ever harmed him?"

"I do not ask you to *believe*, but to know. Keep out of the way a single week, it can do harm to no one."

"But in less than a week this miserable debt must be paid!"

"Then pay it!"

Robert smiled bitterly.

"How? by ruining my aunt? Shall I ask her to sell the old homestead?"

"She would do it—she would give up the last penny rather than see you disgraced, Robert Otis!"

"How can you know this?"

"I do know it, but this is not the question. Here is money to pay your debt, I have kept it in my pocket for weeks."

Robert did not reach forth his hand to receive the roll of bank-notes held toward him, for surprise held him motionless.

"Take the money, it is the exact sum," said Jacob, in a voice that carried authority with it. "I ask no promise that you never enter another gambling hall—you never will!"

"Never!" said Robert, receiving the money; "but how—why have you done this?"

"Ask me no questions now; by-and-bye you will know all about it; the money is mine. I have earned it honestly; as much more is all that I have in the world. No thanks! I never could bear them, besides it will be repaid in time!"

"If I live," said Robert, with tears in his eyes.

"This week, remember—this week you must be absent. A visit to the old homestead, anything that will take you out of town."

"I will go," said Robert, "it can certainly do no harm."

And they parted.

Ada Leicester fled from the keen disappointment which almost crushed her for a time, and sought to drown all thought in the whirl of fashionable life. Her reception evenings were splendid. Beauty, talent, wit, everything that could charm or dazzle gathered beneath her roof. She gave herself no time for grief. Occasionally a thought of her husband would sting her into fresh bursts of excitement—sometimes the memory of her parents and her child passed over her heart, leaving a swell behind like that which followed the angels when they went down to trouble the still waters. Her wit grew more sparkling, her graceful sarcasm keener than ever it had been. She was the rage that season, and exhausted her rich talent in efforts to win excitement. She did not hope for happiness from the homage and splendor that her beauty and wealth had secured; excitement was all she asked.

When all other devices for amusement failed to keep up the fever of her artificial life, she bethought her of a new project. Her talent, her wealth must achieve something more brilliant than had yet been dreamed of, she would give a fancy ball, something far more picturesque than had ever been known in Saratoga or Newport.

At first Ada thought of this ball only as a something that should pass like a rocket through the upper ten thousand; but as the project grew upon her, she resolved to make it an epoch in her own inner life. The man whom she had loved, the husband who had so coldly trampled her to the earth in her seeming poverty—he should witness this grand gala—he should see her in the full blaze of her splendid career. There was something of proud retaliation in this; she fancied that it was resentful hate that prompted this desire to see and triumph over the man who had scorned her. Alas! poor woman, was there no lurking hope ?—no feeling that she dared not call by its right name in all that wild excitement ?

She sent for Jacob, and besought him to devise some means by which Leicester should be won to attend the ball, without suspecting her identity.

Let it be superb—let it surpass everything hitherto known in elegance," she said—" he shall be here—he shall see the poor governess, the scorned wife in a new phase."

There was triumph in her eyes as she spoke.

" You love this man, even now, in spite of all that he has done ?" said Jacob Strong, who stood before her while she spoke.

" No," she answered—" no, I hate—oh ! how I do hate him !"

Jacob regarded her with a steady, fixed glance of the eye ; he was afraid to believe her. He would not have believed her but for the powerful wish that gave an unnatural impulse to his faith.

" He may be dazzled by all this splendor ; the knowledge of so much wealth will make him humble—he will be your slave again !"

Ada glanced around the sumptuous array of her boudoir. Her eyes sparkled ; her lip quivered with haughty triumph.

" And I would spurn him even as he spurned me in that humble room over-head—that room filled with its wealth of old memories."

Jacob turned away to hide the joy that burned in his eyes.

" Oh ! my mistress, say it again. In earnest truth, you hate this man; do not deceive yourself. Have you unwound the adder from your heart ? Did that night do its work ?"

Ada Leicester paused ; she was ashamed to own, even before that devoted servant, how closely the adder still folded himself in her bosom. She turned pale, but still answered with unfaltering voice, " Jacob, I hate him !"

" Not yet—not as you ought to hate him," answered Jacob, regarding her palid face so searchingly that his own cheek whitened, "but when you see him in all his villany, as I have seen him ; when you know all !"

"And do I not know all ? What is it you keep from me ? What is there to learn more vile—more terrible than the past ?"

"What if I tell you that within a month, William Leicester, your husband, will be married to another woman ?"

"Married ! married to another !—Leicester—my——" she broke off, for her white lips refused to utter another syllable. After a momentary struggle she started up—"does he think that I am dead ?—does he hope that night has killed me ?"

"He knows that you are living; but thinks you have returned to England."

"But this is crime—punishable crime."

"I know that it is."

A faint, incredulous smile stole over her lips, and she waved her hand. "He will not violate the law; never was a bad man more prudent."

"He will be married to-morrow night."

"And to that girl ? Does he love her so much ? Is her beauty so overpowering ? What has she to tempt Leicester into this crime ?"

"Her father is dead. By his will a large property falls to this poor girl. The letter came under cover to Leicester ; he opened it. After the marriage they will sail for the north of Europe—there the letter will follow them, telling the poor orphan of her father's death. How can she guess that her husband has seen it before !"

"But I—I am not dead !"

"You love him, he knows that better than you do. Death is no stronger safeguard than that knowledge. In your love or in your death he is equally safe."

"God help me ; but I will not be a slave to this abject love forever. If this last treachery be true, my soul will loathe him as he deserves."

"It is true."

"But my ball is to-morrow night. He accepted the invitation. You are certain that he will come?"

"He accepted the invitation eagerly enough," said Jacob, dryly; "but what then?"

"Why, to-morrow night—this cannot happen before to-morrow night—then I shall see him; after that—no, no, he dare not. You see, Jacob, it is in order to save him from deeper crime; we must not sit still and allow this poor girl to be sacrificed; that would be terrible. It must be prevented."

"Nothing easier. Let him know that the brilliant, the wealthy Mrs. Gordon, is his wife; say that she has millions at her disposal; this poor girl has only one or two hundred thousand, the choice would be soon made."

"Do you believe it? can you think it was belief in my poverty, and not—not a deeper feeling that made him so cruel that night? would he have accepted me for this wealth?"

A painful red hovered in Ada's cheek, as she asked this question; it was shaping a humiliating doubt into words. It was exposing the scorpion that stung most keenly at her heart.

Jacob drew closer to his mistress; he clasped her two hands between his, and his heavy frame bent over her, not awkwardly, for deep feeling is never awkward.

"Oh, my mistress, say to me that you will give up this man—utterly give him up; even now you cannot guess how wicked he is; do not, by your wealth, help him to make new victims; do not see him and thus give him a right over yourself and your property—a right he will not fail to use; give up this ball; leave the city—this is no way to find that poor old man, that child——"

"Jacob! Jacob!" almost shrieked the unhappy woman, "do you see how such words wound and rankle? I may be wild—the wish may be madness—but once more let me meet him face to face——"

Jacob dropped her hands; two great tears left his eyes, and rolled slowly down his cheeks.

"How she loves that man!" he said, in a tone of despondency.

"Remember, Jacob, it is to serve another. What if, thinking himself safe, he marries that poor girl?" said Ada, in an humble, deprecating tone.

"Madam," answered Jacob, "do you know that the law gives this man power over you—a husband's power—if he chooses to claim it?" Jacob broke off, and clenched his huge hand in an agony of impatience, for his words had only brought the bright blood into that eloquent face. Through those drooping lashes he saw the downcast eyes kindle.

"She hopes it! she hopes it!" he said, in the bitterness of his thought; "but I will save her—with God's help I will save them both!"

When Ada Leicester looked up to address her servant, he had left the room.

Among other things, Jacob had been commissioned to procure a quantity of hot-house flowers; for the conservatories at Mrs. Gordon's villa were to be turned into perfect bowers. Besides, Ada was prodigal of flowers in every room of her dwelling, even when no company was expected. In order to procure enough for this grand gala evening, Jacob had resource to Mrs. Gray, who trafficked at times in everything that has birth in the soil.

Mrs. Gray was delighted with this commission, for it promised a rich windfall to her pretty favorite, Julia Warren. So, after the market closed that day, she went up to Dunlap's, and bargained for all the exotics his spacious greenhouse could produce. She informed Julia of her good luck, and returned home with a warmth about the heart worth half a dozen Thanksgiving suppers, bountiful as hers always were.

The next day Julia was going up town, with a basket loaded with exotics on her arm. It was late in the afternoon, for the blossoms had been left on the stalk to the latest hour, that no sweet breath of their perfume should be wasted before they reached the boudoir they were intended to embellish.

It was a sweet task that Julia had undertaken. With her love of flowers, it was a delicious luxury to gaze down upon her dewy burden, as she walked along, surrounded by a cloud of fragrance invisible as it was intoxicating. A life of privation had rendered her delicate organization keenly susceptible of this delicate enjoyment. It gratified the hunger of sensations almost ethereal. She loitered on her way, she touched the flowers with her hands, that, like the blossoms, were soon bathed in odor. Rich masses of heliotrope, the snowy cape jessamine, clusters of starry daphne, crimson and white roses, with many other blossoms strange as they were sweet, made every breath she drew a delight. A glow of exquisite satisfaction spread over her face, her dreamy eyes were never lifted from the blossoms, except when a corner was to be turned or an obstacle avoided.

"Where are you going, girl? Are those flowers for sale?"

Julia started and looked up. She was just then before a cottage house, laced with iron balconies and clouded with creeping vines, red with the crimson and gold of a late Indian summer. The garden in front was gorgeous with choice dahlias and other autumn flowers that had not yet felt the frost, and on the basin of a small marble fountain in the centre stood several large aquatic lilies, from which the falling water-drops rained with a constant and sleepy sound.

Julia did not see all this at once, for the glance that she cast around was too wild and startled. She clasped the basket of flowers closer to her side, and stood motionless. Some potent spell seemed upon her.

"Can't you speak, child? Are those flowers for sale?"

Julia remained gazing in the man's face; her eyes, once fixed on those features, seemed immoveable. He stood directly before her, holding the iron gate which led to the cottage open with his hand.

"No—no—if you please, sir, they are ordered. A lady wants them."

"Then they are not paid for—only ordered. Come in here. There is a lady close by who may fancy some of those orange blossoms."

"No, no, sir—the other lady might be angry!"

"Nonsense! I want the flowers—not enough to be missed, though—just a handful of the white ones. Here is a piece of gold worth half your load. Let me have what I ask, and I dare say your customer will give just as much for the rest."

"I can't, sir—indeed I can't," said Julia, drawing a corner of her little plaid shawl over the basket; "but if you are not in a hurry—if the lady can wait an hour—I will leave these and get some more from the greenhouse."

The man did not answer, but, placing his hand on her shoulder, pushed the frightened child through the open gate.

"Let your customer wait—during the next hour you must stay here. It is not so much the flowers that I want as yourself!"

"Myself!" repeated poor Julia, with quivering lips.

"Go in—go in—I want nothing that should frighten you. Stay—just now I remember that face. Do you know I am an old customer?"

"I remember," answered Julia, and tears of affright rushed into her eyes.

"Then you recognise me again?—it was but a moment—how can you remember so long and so well?"

"By my feelings, sir. I wanted to cry then—I can't help crying now!"

"This is strange! Young ladies are not apt to be so much shocked when I speak to them. No matter. I want both your flowers and your services just now: oblige me, and I will pay you well for the kindness."

Julia had no choice, for as he spoke the gentleman closed the gate, and completely obstructed her way out.

"Pass on—pass on!" he said, with an imperative wave of the hand.

Julia obeyed, walking with nervous quickness as he drew close to her. The gentleman rang, a faint noise came from within, and the door was opened by a quiet old lady in mourning.

"Then you have come; you persist!" she said, addressing the gentleman!

"Step this way a moment," he answered in a subdued voice, opening the parlor door; "but first send this little girl up to Florence; if you still refuse, she must answer for a witness. Besides, she has flowers in her basket, and my sweet bride would think a wedding ominous without them!"

"Ominous indeed!" said the lady, pointing with her finger that Julia should ascend the stairs. "William, I will not allow this to go on; to witness the sin would be to share it."

"Mother," answered Leicester, gently taking the lady's hand, while he led her to the parlor, "tell me your objections, and I will answer them with all respect. Why is my marriage with Florence Craft opposed?"

"You have no right to marry—you are not free—cannot be so while Ada lives."

"But Ada is dead! Mother, say now if I am not free to choose a wife?"

"Dead! Ada Wilcox dead! Oh William, if this be true!"

"If! It is true. See, here are letters bearing proof that even you must acknowledge."

He held out some letters bearing an European post-mark. The old lady took them, put on her glasses, and suspiciously scrutinized every line.

"Are you convinced, mother, or must I go over sea, and tear the dead from her grave before your scruples yield?"

The old lady lifted her face; a tear stole from beneath her glasses.

"Go on," she said, in a deep solemn voice—"go on, add victim to victim, legally or illegally, it scarce matters—that which you touch dies. But remember—remember, William, every new sin presses its iron mark hard on your mother's heart, the weight will crush her at length."

"Why is maternal love so strong in your bosom that Scripture is revised in my behalf? Must my iniquities roll back on past generations?" said the son, with a faint sneer.

"No, it is because my own sin originates yours. Your father was a bad man, William Leicester, profligate, treacherous, fascinating as you are. I married him ; wo, wo upon the arrogant pride ; I married him, and said, in wicked self-confidence—'My love shall be his redemption.' My son—my son, you cannot understand me ; you cannot think how terrible iniquity is when it folds you in its bosom. There is no poison like the love of a profligate ; the fang of an adder is not more potent. It spreads through the whole being ; it lives in the moral life of our children. I said 'My love is all powerful, it shall reform this man whom I love so madly.' I made the effort ; I planted my soul beneath the Upas tree, and expected not only to escape but conquer the poison. Look at me, William ; can you ever remember me other than I am, still, cold, hopeless? Yet I only lived with your father three years. Before that I was bright and joyous beyond your belief.

"He died as he had lived. Did the curse of my arrogance end there ? No, it found new life in his son—his son and mine. In you, William—in you my punishment embodied itself. Still I hoped and strove against the evil entailed upon you. Heaven bear me witness, I struggled unceasingly ; but as you approached maturity, with all the beauty and talent of your father, the moral poison revealed itself also.

"Then the love that I felt for you changed to fear, and as one who has turned a serpent loose among the beautiful things of earth, I said, 'Let my life be given to protect society from the evil spirit which my presumption has forced upon it.' It was an atonement acceptable of God. How many deserted victims my roof has sheltered you know—how many I have saved from the misery of your influence it is needless to say. This one, so gentle, so rich in affection, I hoped to win from her enthralment, or, failing that, resign her to the arms of death, more merciful, more gentle than yours. I have pleaded with her, warned her, but she answers as I answered when those who loved me said of your father, 'It is a sin to marry him!' Must she suffer as I have suffered ? Oh! William, my son, turn aside this once from your prey. She is helpless—save her young heart from the stain that has fallen upon mine!"

"Nay, gentle mother, this is scarcely a compliment—you forget that I wish to marry the young lady."

How cold, how insulting were the tones of his voice—how relentless was the spirit that gleamed in his eyes! The unhappy mother stood before him, her pale hands clasped and uplifted, and words of thrilling eloquence hushed upon her lips, that no syllable of his answer might be lost. It came, that dry, insolent rejoinder; her hands fell; her figure shrunk earthward.

"I have done!" broke from her lips, and she walked slowly from the room.

"Madam, shall we expect you at the ceremony?" said Leicester, following her to the door.

She turned upon the stairs, and gave him a look so sad, so earnest, that even his cold heart beat slower.

"It is not important!" he muttered, turning back; "we can do without her. This little girl and the servant must answer, though I did hope to trust no one"

CHAPTER XVI.

THE BRIDAL WREATH.

The wreath of white jasmines is torn from her brow,
The bride is alone, and, oh, desolate now.

Julia Warren mounted the stairs in wild haste, as the caged bird springs from perch to perch when terrified by strange faces. Then she paused in her fright, doubtful where to turn or what room to enter. As she stood thus irresolute, a door was softly pushed open, and a fair young face looked out. The eyes were bent downward; the cheek and temples shaded with masses of loose ringlets, that admitted snowy glimpses of a graceful neck and shoulders, uncovered save by these bright tresses and a muslin dressing-down, half falling off, and huddled to the bosom with a fair little hand.

Imperceptibly the door swung more and more open, till Julia caught the outline of a figure, slender, flexible, and so fragile in its beauty, that to her excited imagination it seemed almost ethereal. Like a spirit that listens for some kindred sympathy, the young creature bent in the half-open door. The faint murmur of voices from below rose and fell upon her ear. No words could be distinguished; nothing but the low, deep tones of a voice, familiar and dear as the pulsations of her own heart, blended with the strangely passionate accents of another. The gentle listener could hardly convince herself that some strange woman had not entered the house, so thrilling and full of pathos was that voice, usually so calm and frigid.

Julia stood motionless, holding her breath. She saw nothing but the outline of a slender person, the shadowy gleam of features through masses of wavy hair, but it seemed as if she had met that graceful vision before—it might be in a dream—it might be—stay, the young girl lifted her head, and swept back the ringlets with her hand. A pair of dark, liquid eyes fell upon the flower girl, and she knew the glance. The eyes were larger, brighter, more densely circled with shadows than they had been, but the tender expression, the soft loveliness, nothing could change that.

The hand dropped from among the ringlets it held, away from that pale cheek, and a glow, as of freshly-gathered roses, broke through them as Florence drew her form gently up, and stood with her eyes fixed upon the intruder.

Julia came forward, changing color with every step.

"A gentleman—the lady, I mean—I—I was sent up here. If they want the flowers for you, I would not mind, though the other lady has spoken for them!"

Florence cast her eyes on the basket of flowers; a bright

mile kindled over her face, and drawing the girl into the :hamber, she took the heavy basket in her arms, and, overpowered by its weight, sunk softly down to the carpet, resting it in her lap. Thus, with the blossoms half buried in the white waves of her dressing-gown, she literally buried her face in them, while her very heart seemed to drink in the perfume that exhaled again in broken and exquisite sighs.

"And he sent them?—how good, how thoughtful! Oh! I ım too—too happy!"

She gathered up a double handful of the blossoms, and rained them back into the basket. Their perfume floated around her; some of the buds fell in the folds of her snowy muslin, that drooped like waves of foam over her limbs. She was happy and beautiful as an angel gathering blossoms in some chosen nook of Paradise.

There was something contagious in all this—something that sent the dew to Julia's eyes, and a glow of love to her heart.

"I am glad—I am almost glad that he made me come in," she said, dropping on her knees, that she might gather up some buds that had fallen over the basket. "How I wish you could have them all! He offered a large gold piece, but you know I could not take it. If we—that is, if grandpa and grandma were rich, I never would take a cent for flowers; it seems as if God made them on purpose to give away."

"So they are not mine, after all?" said Florence, with a look and tone of disappointment.

"Yes—oh, yes, a few. That glass thing on the toilet, I will crowd it quite full, the prettiest too—just take out those you like best."

"Still he ordered them—he tried to purchase the whole, in that lies happiness enough." The sweet, joyous look stole back to her face again; that thought was more precious than all the fragrance and bloom she had coveted.

The door-bell rang. Florence heard persons coming from the parlor, she started up leaving the basket at her feet.

"Oh, I shall delay him—I shall be too late; will no one

come to help me?" she exclaimed. "I dare not ask her, but you, surely you could stay for half an hour?"

"I must stay if you wish it; he will not let me go; but indeed, indeed, I am in haste. It will be quite dark."

"I do not wish to keep you by force," said Florence, gently; "but you seem kind, and I have no one to help me dress. Besides, she, his mother, will not stay in the room, and the thought of being quite alone, with no bridesmaid—no woman even for a witness—it frightens me!"

"What—what is it that you wish of me?" questioned Julia while a sudden and strange thrill ran through her frame.

"I wish you to stay a little while to help to put on my dress, and then go down with me. You look very young, but no one else will come near me, and it seems unnatural to be married without a single female standing by."

Florence grew pale as she spoke; there was indeed something lonely and desolate in her position, which all at once came over her with overwhelming force. Julia, too, from surprise or some deeper feeling, seemed struck with a sudden chill; her lips were slightly parted, the color fled from her cheek.

"Married! married!" she repeated, in a voice that fell upon the heart of Florence like an omen.

"To-night, in an hour, I shall be his wife!" How pale the poor bride was as these words fell from her lips! How coldly lay the heart in her bosom! She bent her head as if waiting for the guardian angel who should have kept better watch over a being so full of trust and gentleness.

"His wife! *his!*" said Julia, recoiling a step, "oh! how can you—how can you!"

A crimson flush shot over that pale forehead, and Florence drew up her form to its full height.

"Will you help me—will you stay?"

"I dare not say no!" answered the child; "I would not, if I dare."

Again the door-bell rang. "Hush!" said Florence, breathlessly; "it is the clergyman; that is a strange voice, and he—

Leicester—admits him. How happy I thought to be at this hour ; but I am chilly, chilly as death ; oh, help me, child !"

She had been making an effort to arrange her hair, but her hands trembled, and at length fell helplessly down. She really seemed shivering with cold.

"Sit down, sit down in this easy-chair, and let *me* try," said Julia, shaking off the chill that had settled on her spirits, and wheeling a large chair, draped with white dimity, toward the toilet. Lights were burning in tall candlesticks on each side of a swing mirror, whose frame of filagreed and frosted silver gleamed ghastly and cold on the pale face of the bride.

"How white I am ; will nothing give me a color ?" cried the young creature, starting up from the chair. "Warmth—that is what I want ! My dress—let us put on that first ; then I can muffle myself in something while you curl my hair."

She took up a robe of costly Brussels lace. "Isn't it beautiful ?" she said, with a smile, shaking out the soft folds. "He sent it." She then threw off her dressing-gown, and arrayed herself in the bridal robe ; the exertion seemed to animate her ; a bright bloom rose to her cheek, and her motions became nervous with excitement.

"Some orange blossoms to loop up the skirt in front," she said, after Julia had fastened the dress ; "here, just here !" and she gathered up some folds of the soft lace in her hand, watching the child as she fell upon one knee to perform the task. Florence was trembling from head to foot with the wild, eager excitement that had succeeded the chill of which she had complained, and could do nothing for herself. When the buds were all in place, she sunk into the easy-chair, huddling her snowy arms and bosom in a rose-colored opera cloak ; for, though her cheeks were burning, cold shivers now and then seemed to ripple through her veins. The soft trimming of swan's down, which she pressed to her bosom with both hands, seemed devoid of all warmth one moment, and the next she flung it aside glowing with over-heat. There was something more than agitation in all this, but it gave unearthly splendor to her beauty.

"Now—now," said Julia, laying the last ringlet softly down upon the neck of the bride; "look at yourself, sweet lady, see how beautiful you are."

Florence stood up, and smiled as she saw herself in the mirror; an angel from heaven could not have looked more delicately radiant. Masses of raven curls fell upon the snowy neck and the bridal dress. Circling her head, and bending with a soft curve to the forehead, was a light wreath of starry jessamine flowers, woven with the deep, feathery green of some delicate spray, that Julia selected from her basket because it was so tremulous and fairy-like. All at once the smile fled from the lips of Florence Craft; a look of mournful affright came to her eyes, and she raised both hands to tear away the wreath.

"Did you know it? Was this done on purpose?" she said, turning upon the child.

"What—what have I done?"

"This wreath—these jessamines—you have woven them with cypress leaves." Florence sunk into the chair shuddering; she had no strength to unweave the ominous wreath from her head.

"I—I did not know it," said the child greatly distressed; "they were beautiful—I only thought of that. Shall I take them off, and put roses in the place?"

"Yes! yes—roses, roses—these make me feel like death!"

That instant there was a gentle knock at the chamber door; Julia opened it, and there stood Mr. Leicester. The child drew back: he saw Florence standing before the toilet.

"Florence, love, we are waiting!"

He advanced into the chamber and drew her arm through his. She looked back into the mirror, and shuddered till the cypress leaves trembled visibly in her curls.

"My beautiful—my wife!" whispered Leicester, pressing her hand to his lips.

What woman could withstand that voice—those words? The color came rushing to her cheek again, the light to her eyes; she trembled, but not with the ominous fear that possessed her a moment before. Those words—sweeter than hope—shed warmth, and light, and joy where terror had been.

"Follow us!" said Leicester addressing the child.

Julia moved forward: a thought seemed to strike the bridegroom; he paused—

"You can write—at least well enough to sign your name?" he said.

"Yes, I can write," she answered, timidly.

"Very well—come!"

The parlor was brilliantly illuminated, every shutter was closed, and over the long window, hitherto shaded only with lace, fell curtains of amber damask, making the seclusion more perfect.

A clergyman was in the room, and Leicester had brought his servant as a witness. This man stood near the window, leaning heavily against the wall, his features immovable, his eyes bent upon the door. Julia started as she saw him, for she remembered the time they had met before upon the wharf, on that most eventful day of her life. His glance fell on her as she came timidly in behind the bridegroom and the bride; there was a slight change in his countenance, then a gleam of recognition, which made the child feel less completely among strangers.

It was a brief ceremony; the clergyman's voice was monotonous; the silence chilling. Julia wept; to her it seemed like a funeral.

The certificate was made out. Jacob signed his name, but so bunglingly that no one could have told what it was. Mr. Leicester did not make the effort. Julia took the pen, her little hand trembled violently, but the name was written quite well enough for a girl of her years.

"Now, sir—now, please, may I go?" she said, addressing Leicester.

"Yes, yes—here is the piece of gold. I trust your employer will find no fault—but first tell me where you live?"

Julia told him where to find her humble abode, and hurried

from the room. Her basket of flowers had been left in the chamber above; she ran up to get it, eager to be gone. In her haste she opened the nearest door; it was a bed-room, dimly lighted, and by a low couch knelt the old lady she had seen in the hall. Her hands were clasped, her white face uplifted; there was anguish in her look, but that tearless anguish that can only be felt after the passions are quenched. Julia drew softly back. She found her basket in the next room, and came forth again, bearing it on her arm. She heard Leicester's voice while passing through the hall, and hurried out, dreading that he might attempt to detain her.

Scarcely had the child passed out when Leicester came forth, leading Florence by the hand. He spoke a few words to her in a low voice: "Try and reconcile her, Florence. She never loved me, I know that, but who could resist you? To-morrow, if she proves stubborn, I will take you hence, or, at the worst, in a few days we will be ready for our voyage to Europe."

Florence listened with downcast eyes. "My father, my kind old father! he will not be angry; he must have known how it would end when he gave me to your charge. Still it may offend him to hear that I am married, when he thinks me at school."

"He will not be angry, love," said Leicester, and he thought of the letter announcing old Mr. Craft's death. "But the good lady up stairs; you must win her into a better mood before we meet again; till then, sweet wife, adieu!"

He kissed her hand two or three times—cast a hurried glance up stairs, as if afraid of being seen, and then pressed her, for one instant, to his bosom.

"Sweet wife!" the name rang through and through her young heart like a chime of music. She held her breath, and listened to his footsteps as he left the house, then stole softly up the stairs.

The clergyman went out while Julia was up stairs in search of her flowers. Jacob Strong left the parlor at the same time, but instead of returning, he let the clergyman out, and, moving back into the darkened extremity of the hall, stood there, concealed and motionless. He witnessed the interview between Leicester and Florence, and, so still was everything around, heard a little of the conversation.

Before Florence was half way up the stairs he came out of the darkness and spoke to her.

"Only a little while, dear lady, pray come back; I will not keep you long."

Florence, thinking that Leicester had left some message with his servant, descended the stairs and entered the parlor. Jacob followed her and closed the door; a few minutes elapsed—possibly ten, and there came from the closed room a wild, passionate cry of anguish. The door was flung open—the bride staggered forth, and supported herself against the frame-work.

"Mother! mother! oh, madam!" Her voice broke, and ended in gasping sobs.

A door overhead opened, and the old lady whom Julia had seen upon her knees came gliding like a black shadow down the stairs.

"I thought that he had gone," she said, and her usually calm accent was a little hurried. "Would he kill you under my roof? William Leicester!"

"He is not here—he is gone," sobbed Florence, but that man——" She pointed with her finger toward Jacob Strong, who stood a little within the door. He came forward, revealing a face from which all the stolid indifference was swept away. It was not only troubled, but wet with tears.

"It is cruel—I have been awfully cruel," he said, addressing the old lady—"but she must be told. I could not put it off. She thought herself his wife."

"I am his wife!—I am his wife!—*his wife*, do you hear?" almost shrieked the wretched girl. "He called me so himself. *You* saw us married, and yet dare to slander him!"

"Lady, she is not his wife!" said Jacob, sinking his voice, but speaking earnestly, as if the task he had undertaken were very painful. "He is married already!"

"He told me—and gave me letters from abroad to prove

that Ada, his wife, was dead." The old lady spoke in her usual calm way, but her face was paler than it had been, and her eyes were full of mournful commiseration as she bent them upon the wretched bride.

"Then he *was* married—he has been married before!" murmured Florence, and her poor, pale hands, fell helplessly down. The old lady drew close to her, as if to offer some comfort, but she had so long held all affectionate impulses in abeyance, that even this action was constrained and chilling, though her heart yearned toward the poor girl.

"Madam, did you believe him when he said his wife was no more?" questioned Jacob Strong.

The old lady shook her head, and a mournful smile stole across her thin lips; pain is fearfully impressive when wrung from the heart in a smile like that. Florence shuddered.

"And you—you also, his mother!" burst from her quivering lips.

"God forgive me! I am," answered the old lady.

"Then," said Jacob Strong, turning his face resolutely from the poor, young creature, whose heart his words were crushing: "Then, madam, you have seen his wife—you would know her again?"

"Yes, I should know her."

"This night, this very night, you shall see her then. Come with me; this poor young lady will not believe what I have said. Come and be a witness that Mrs. Ada Leicester is alive—alive with his knowledge. Two hours from this you shall see them together—Leicester and his wife, the mother of his child. Will you come? there seems no other way by which this poor girl can be saved."

"I—I will go! let me witness this meeting," cried Florence, suddenly arousing herself, and standing upright. "I will not take his word nor yours; you slander him, you slander him! If he has a wife, let me look upon her with my own eyes."

The old lady and Jacob looked at each other. Florence

stood before them, her soft eyes flashing, her cheeks fired with the blood grief had driven from her heart.

"You dare not—I know it, you dare not!"

Still her auditors looked at each other in painful doubt.

"I knew that it was false!" cried Florence, with a laugh of wild exultation. "You hesitate, this proves it. To-morrow, madam, I will leave this roof—I will go to my husband. The very presence of those who slander him is hateful to me. To-night; yes, this instant, I will go."

"Let her be convinced," said the old lady.

The strong nerves of Jacob gave way. He looked at that young face, so beautiful in its wild anguish, and shrunk from the consequences of the conviction that awaited her.

"It would be her death," he said. "I cannot do it!"

"Better death than that which might follow this unbelief."

The old lady placed her hand upon Jacob's arm, and drew him aside. They conversed together in low voices, and Florence regarded them with her large, wild eyes, as a wounded gazelle might gaze upon its pursuers.

"Come!" said Leicester's mother, attempting to lay her hand upon the shrinking arm of the bride; "it needs some preparation, but you shall go. God help us both, this is a fearful task!"

Florence was strong with excitement. She turned, and almost ran up the stairs. Jacob went out, and during the next two hours, save a slight sound in the upper rooms, from time to time, the cottage seemed abandoned.

At length a carriage stopped at the gate. Jacob entered, and seating himself in the parlor, waited. They came down at last, but so changed, that no human penetration could have detected their identity. The old lady was still in black, but so completely enveloped in a veil of glossy silk, that nothing but her eyes could be seen. A diamond crescent upon the forehead, a few silver stars scattered among the sombre folds that flowed over her person, gave sufficient character to a dress that was only chosen as a disguise.

Florence was in a similar dress, save that everything about her was snowy white. A veil of flowing silk had been cast over her bridal array, glossy and wave-like, but thick enough to conceal her features. Gleams of violet and rosy tulle floated over this, like the first tints of sunrise and the morning star, sparkling with diamonds, gathered up the veil on her left temple, leaving it to flow, like the billows of a cloud, over her form, and downward till it swept her feet. Without a word the three went forth and entered the carriage.

CHAPTER XVII.

AN HOUR BEFORE THE BALL.

The child stands, meekly, by her mother.
  Look, woman, in those earnest eyes!
Say, canst thou understand, or smother
  The deep maternal mysteries

That rise and swell within thy breast;
  That throb athwart thy aching brain,
Till, with deep tenderness oppressed,
  Hope, thought, and feeling turn to pain?

We take the reader once more to the residence of Ada Leicester—not as formerly, when the tempest raged around its walls, and darkness slept in its sumptuous rooms—when the wail of tortured hearts and sobs of anguish alone broke the gloomy stillness—not as then do we revisit this stately mansion. Now it is lighted up like a fairy palace; through the richly stained sashes, from the gables, and the ivy-clad tower, clouds of tinted light kindle the bland autumnal atmosphere to a soft golden haze. The tall old trees that surround the mansion seem bending beneath a fruitage of stars, so thickly are they beset with lamps that light up the depths of their ripe foliage. So broad is the illumination, so rich the tinted rays, you might see to gather fall flowers from the ground, even to their shaded extremity. White dahlias are amber-hued in that mellow light; wax balls hang like drops of gold in the thickets; the ivy leaves about the narrow windows of the tower seem dripping with starlight; and a woodbine that has crept up one of the young maples, a little way off, glows out along the golden foliage so vividly, that the branches seem absolutely on fire.

Julia Warren approached this mansion with wonder. It seemed like something she had read of in a fairy tale—the lamps gleaming among the trees and in the thickets; the foliage so strangely luminous; the crisp grass tinged with a brownish and golden green; all these things were like enchantment to the child whose life had been spent in a comfortless basement. She looked around in delighted bewilderment; the very basket upon her arm seemed filled with strange blossoms as she entered the lofty vestibule, and changed the richly hued atmosphere, without for the flood of pure gas-light that filled the dwelling.

"Oh! here she is at last—why, child, what has kept you?"

A pretty young woman, in a jaunty cap and pink ribbons, made this exclamation, while Julia stood looking about for some one to address. Her manner, her quick but graceful movements, had an imposing effect upon the child.

"Are you the lady?" she said.

"No—no!" answered the girl, with a pretty laugh, for the compliment pleased her. "Come up stairs—quick, quick—my lady has been *so* impatient."

They went up a flight of steps, the waiting-maid exchanging words with a footman who passed them, Julia treading lightly under her load of flowers. Her little feet sunk into the carpet at every step; once only in her life had she felt the same elastic swell follow her tread. Yet nothing could be more unlike than the dark mansion that rose upon her memory, and the vision-like beauty of everything upon which her eyes rested. The floors seemed literally trodden down with flowers. Rich draperies of silk met her eye wherever she turned. A door swung open to the touch of the waiting-maid. Julia remembered the room which they entered—the couch of carved ivory and azure damask—the lace curtains that hung against the windows like floating frost-work, and the rich blue waves that fell over them. Clearer than all she recognised the marble Flora placed near the couch, bending from its pedestal, with pure and classic grace, and gazing so intently on the white lilies in its hand,as if it doubted that the flowers were indeed but a beautiful mockery of nature.

Julia drew a quick breath as she recognised all these objects, but the waiting maid gave her but little time even for surprise. She crossed the room and opened a door on the opposite side. They entered a dressing-room, leading evidently to a sumptuous bed-chamber, for through the open door Julia could see glimpses of rose-colored damask sweeping from the windows, and a snow white bed, over which masses of embroidered lace fell in transparent waves to the floor. The dressing-room corresponded with the chamber, but Julia saw nothing of its splendor. Her eyes were turned upon a toilet richly draped with lace, and littered with jewels ; a standing-glass set in frosted silver, was lighted on each side by a small alabaster lamp, which hung against the exquisite chasing like two great pearls, each with perfumed flame breaking up from its heart.

It was not the sight of this superb toilet, though a fortune had been flung carelessly upon it, that made the child's heart beat so tumultuously, but the lady who stood before it. Her back was toward the door, but Julia *felt* who she was, though the beautiful features were only reflected upon her from the mirror.

The lady turned. Her eyes were bent upon the diamond bracelet she was attempting to clasp on her arm. Oh ! how different was that face from the tear-stained features Julia had seen that dark night. How radiant, how more than beautiful she was now ! Every movement replete with grace ; every look brilliant with flashes of exultant loveliness !

How great was the contrast between that superb creature,

in her robe of rich amber satin, heightened by the floating lustre of soft Brussels lace, which fell around her like a web of woven moonlight, and the humble child who stood there so motionless, with the flower-basket at her feet. The pink hood, faded with much washing, shaded her eyes; her hands were folded beneath the little plaid shawl that half concealed her cheap calico dress. Notwithstanding this contrast between the proud and mature beauty of the woman and the meek loveliness of the child, there was an air, a look—something indeed indescribable in one, which reminded you of the other. Ada turned suddenly, and moved a step toward the child; a thousand rainbow gleams flashed from the folds of her lace overdress as she moved; a massive wreath of gems lighted up the golden depths of her tresses, but its brilliancy was not more beautiful than the smile with which she recognized the little girl.

"And so you have found me again," she said, untying the pink hood, and smoothing the bright hair thus exposed with her two palms, much to the surprise of the waiting-maid. "Look, Rosanna, is she not lovely, with her meek eyes and that smile?"

The waiting-maid turned her eyes from the lady to the child.

"Beautiful! why, madam the smile is your own."

"Rosanna!" cried the lady, "this is flattery; never again speak of my resemblance to any one, especially to a child of that age. It offends, it pains me!"

"I did not think to offend, madam; the little girl is so pretty—how could I?"

Ada did not heed her; she was gazing earnestly on the little girl. The smile had left her face, and this made a corresponding change in the sensitive child. She felt as if some offence had been given, else why should the lady look into her eyes with such earnest sadness?

"What is your name?"

The question was given in a low and hesitating voice.

"Julia—Julia Warren."

That is enough. Rosanna, never speak in this way again!"

"Never, if madam desires it. But the flowers: see what quantities the little thing has brought. No wonder she was late—such a load."

"True, we were waiting for the flowers; here, fill my bouquet holder—the choicest, remember—and let every blossom be fragrant."

Rosanna took a bouquet-holder, whose delicate network of gold seemed too fragile for all the jewels with which it was enriched, and kneeling upon the floor, began to arrange a cluster of flowers. Her active fingers had just wound the last crimson and white roses together, when a footman knocked at the door. She started up, and went to see what was wanted.

"Madam, the company are arriving; two carriages have set down their loads already."

Ada had been too long in society for this announcement to confuse or hurry her, had no other cause of excitement arisen; as it was, the superb repose, usual to her manner, was disturbed.

"Who are they? have you seen them before?" she asked.

"Yes, madam, often."

"No stranger—no gentleman who never came before—you are certain?"

"None, madam."

There was something more in this than the usual anxiety of a hostess to receive her guests.

"I am insane to loiter here," she murmured, drawing on her gloves; "he might come and I not there; for the universe I would not miss his first look. The bouquet, Rosanna, and handkerchief—where is my handkerchief?"

"Is this it, ma'am?" said Julia, raising a soft mass of gossamer cambric and costly lace from the carpet, where it had fallen.

This drew Ada's notice once more to the child.

"Oh! I had forgotten," she said, going back to the toilet and taking up a purse that lay among the jewel cases; "I have not time to count it ; take the money, but some day you must bring back the purse—remember."

She took her bouquet hastily from the waiting-maid, and went out, leaving the purse in Julia's hand. After crossing the boudoir, she turned back.

"Remember, the flowers are for these rooms," she said, addressing the maid, and waving her hand, with a motion that indicated the bed-chamber and boudoir. "Let me find them everywhere."

With this command, she disappeared, leaving the doors open behind her.

Julia drew a deep breath, as the wave of her garments was lost in descending the stairs ; turning sorrowfully away, her eyes fell upon the purse; several gold pieces gleamed through the crimson net work.

"What shall I do—these cannot be all mine? the flowers did not cost half so much."

"No matter," was the cheerful reply; "she gave it to you. It is her way; keep it."

The child still hesitated.

"If you think it is not all right, say so when you bring back the purse," said the maid, good naturedly. "Who knows but it may prove a fairy gift? I'm sure her presents often do."

Julia was not quite convinced, even by this kind prophecy. Still, she had no choice but obedience, and so, bidding pretty Rosanna a gentle good night, she stole through the boudoir and away through the front entrance, for she knew of no other; and folding her shawl closer, as she encountered crowds of brilliantly dressed people she passed through the vestibule.

CHAPTER XVIII.

THE FORGED CHECK.

Secure in undiscovered crime
 The callous soul grows bold at length.
Stern justice sometimes bides her time,
 But strikes at last with double strength.

LEICESTER went to the Astor House after his marriage, for though he had accepted an invitation to Mrs. Gordon's fancy ball, which was turning the fashionable world half crazy, matters more important demanded his attention. Premeditating a crime which might bring its penalty directly upon his own person, he had made arrangements to evade all possible chance of this result, by embarking at once for Europe with his falsely married bride. In order to prepare funds for this purpose, the project for which Robert Otis had been so long in training, had been that day put in action. The old copy-book, with its mass of evidence, was, as he supposed, safe in Robert's apartment. The check, forged with marvellous accuracy, which we have seen placed in his letter case, passed that morning into the hands of his premeditated victim, and at night the youth was to meet him with the money. Thus everything seemed secure. True, his own hands had signed the check, but Robert had presented it at the bank, *he* would draw the money. When the fraud became known, *his* premises would be searched, and there was the old copy-book bearing proofs of such practice in penmanship as would condemn any one. Over and over again might the very signature of that forged check be found in the pages of this book, on scraps of loose paper, and even on other checks bearing the same imprint, and on the same paper. With proof so strong against the youth, how was suspicion to reach Leicester? Would the simple word of an accused lad be taken? And what other evidence existed? None--none. It was a fiendishly woven plot, and at every point seemed faultless. Still

Leicester was ill at ease. The consciousness that the act of this day had placed him within possible reach of the law, was unpleasant to a man in whom prudence almost took the place of conscience. The hour had arrived, but Robert was not at Leicester's chamber when he returned. This made the evil-doer anxious and restless. He walked the room, he leaned from the window and looked out upon the crowd below. He drank off glass after glass of wine, and for once suffered all the fierce tortures of dread and suspense which he had so ruthlessly inflicted on others.

At this time Robert Otis was in the building, waiting for Jacob Strong. That strange personage came at last, but more agitated than Robert had ever seen him. Well he might be; an hour before he had left Leicester's wretched bride but half conscious of her misery, and making heart-rending struggles to disbelieve the wrong that had been practised upon her. In an hour more he was to conduct her where she would learn all the sorrow of her destiny. Jacob had a feeling heart, and these thoughts gave him more pain than any one would have deemed possible.

"Here is the money; go down at once and give it to him; I heard his step in the chamber," he said, addressing Robert. "The count is correct, I drew it myself from the bank this morning."

"Tell me, is this money yours?" questioned the youth. "I would do nothing in the dark."

"You are right, boy; no, the money is not mine, I am not worth half the sum. I have no time for a long story, but there is one—a lady, rich beyond anything you ever dreamed of—who takes a deep interest in this bad man."

"What, Florence—Miss Craft?" exclaimed Robert.

"No, an older and still more noble victim. I had but to tell her the money would be used for him, and, behold, ten thousand dollars—the sum he thought enough to pay for your eternal ruin. My poor nephew!"

"Nephew, did you say, nephew, Jacob?"

"Yes, call me Jacob—Jacob Strong—Uncle Jacob—call me anything you like, for I have loved you, I have tried you—kiss me! kiss me! I haven't had you in my arms since you were a baby—and I want something to warm my heart. I never thought it could ache as it has to-night."

"Uncle Jacob—my mother's only brother—I do not understand it, but to know this is enough!"

The youth flung himself upon Jacob's bosom, and for a moment was almost crushed in those huge arms.

"Now that has done me lots of good!" exclaimed the uncle, brushing a tear from his eyes with the cuff of his coat, a school-boy habit that came back with the first powerful home feeling. "Now go down and feed the serpent with this money. You won't be afraid to mind me now."

"No, if you were to order me to jump out of the window I would do it."

"You might, you might, for I would be at the bottom to catch you in my arms! Here is the money, I will be in the drawing-room as a witness: it won't be the first time, I can tell you."

Leicester started and turned pale, even to his lips, as Robert entered his chamber, for a sort of nervous dread possessed him; and in order to escape from this, his anxiety to obtain means of leaving the country became intense. He looked keenly at Robert, but waited for him to speak. The youth was also pale, but resolute and self-possessed.

"The bank was closed before I got there," he said, in a quiet, business tone, placing a small leathern box on the table, and unlocking it, "but I found a person who was willing to negotiate the check. He will not want the money at once, and so it saves him the trouble of making a deposit."

Leicester could with difficulty suppress the exclamation of relief that sprang to his lips, as Robert opened the box, revealing it half full of gold; but remembering that any exhibition of pleasure would be out of place, he observed, with apparent composure—

"You have counted it, I suppose? Were you obliged to exchange bills with any of the brokers, as I directed, to get the gold?"

"No, it was paid as you see it," answered the youth, moving toward the door; for his heart so rose against the man, that he could not force himself to endure the scene a moment longer than was necessary.

"Stay, take the box with you," said Leicester, pouring the gold into a drawer of his desk; "I will not rob you of that."

Robert understood the whole; a faint smile curved his lip, and taking the box, he went out.

"No evidence—nothing but pure gold," muttered Leicester, exultingly, as he closed the drawer. "It is well for you, my young friend, that the holder of that precious document does not wish to present his check at once. Liberty is sweet to the young, and this secures a few more days of its enjoyment for you—and for me! Ah, there everything happens most fortunately. Why, a good steamer will put us half over the Atlantic before this little mistake is suspected."

Leicester was a changed man after this; his spirits rose with unnatural exhilaration.

"Now for this grand ball," he said aloud, surveying his fine person in the glass. "Surely a man's wedding garments ought to be fancy dress enough. Another pair of gloves, though. This comes of temptation. I must finger the gold, forsooth."

The ruthless man smiled, and muttered these broken fragments of thought, as he took off the scarcely soiled gloves, and replaced them with a pair still more spotlessly white. He was a long time fitting them on his hand. He fastidiously re-arranged other portions of his dress. All sense of the great fraud, that ought to have borne his soul to the earth, had left him when the gold appeared. You could see, by his broken words, how completely lighter fancies had replaced the black deed.

"This Mrs. Gordon—I wonder if she really is the creature they represent her to be. If it were not for this voyage to

Europe, now, one might—no, no, there is no chance now; but I'll have a sight at her." Thus muttering and smiling, Leicester left the hotel.

The evening was very beautiful, and Leicester always loved to enter a fashionable drawing-room after the guests had assembled. He reflected that a quiet walk would bring him to Mrs. Gordon's mansion about the time he thought most desirable, and sauntered on, resolved, at any rate, not to reach his destination too early. But sometimes he fell into thought, and then his pace became unconsciously hurried. He reached the upper part of the city earlier than he had intended, and had taken out his watch before a lighted window, to convince himself of the time, when a timid voice addressed him—

"Sir, will you please tell me the name of this street?"

He turned, and saw the little girl whom he had forced to become a witness to his marriage. She shrunk back, terrified, on recognizing him.

"I did not know—I did not mean it," she faltered out.

"What, have you lost your way?" said Leicester, in a voice that made her shiver, though it was low and sweet enough.

"Yes, sir, but I can find it!"

"Where do you live?—oh, I remember. Well, as I have time enough, what if I walk a little out of my way, and see that nothing harms you?"

"No, no—the trouble!"

"Never mind the trouble. You shall show me where you live, pretty one; then I shall be certain where to find you again."

Still Julia hesitated.

"Besides," said Leicester, taking out his purse, "you forget, I have not paid for robbing your basket of all those pretty flowers."

"No!" answered the child, now quite resolutely. "I am paid. The poor young lady is welcome to them."

Leicester laughed. "The poor young lady!—my own pretty bride! Well, I like that."

Julia walked on. She hoped that he would forget his object, or only intended to frighten her. But he kept by her side, and was really amused by the terror inflicted on the child. He had half an hour's time on his hand—how could he kill it more pleasantly? Besides, he really was anxious to know with certainty where the young creature lived. She was one of his witnesses. She had, in a degree, become connected with his fate. Above all, she was terrified to death, and like Nero, Leicester would have amused himself with torturing flies, if no larger or fiercer animal presented itself. His evil longing to give pain was insatiable as the Roman tyrant's, and more cruel; for while Nero contented himself with physical agony, Leicester appeased his craving spirit with nothing but keen mental feeling. The Roman emperor would sometimes content himself with a fiddle; but the music that Leicester loved best was the wail of sensitive heart-strings.

"I live here," said Julia, stopping short, before a low, old house, in a close side street, breathless with the efforts she had made to escape her tormentor. "Do not go any farther, Grandpa never likes to see strangers."

"Go on—go on," answered Leicester, in a tone that was jeeringly good-natured; "grandpa will be delighted."

Julia ran desperately down the area steps. She longed to close the basement door after her and hold it against the intruder, but as this idea flashed across her mind, Leicester stood by her side in the dark hall. She ran forward and opened the door of that poor basement room which was her home. Still he kept by her side. The basement was full of that dusky gloom which a handful of embers had power to shed through the darkness; for the old people, whose outlines were faintly seen upon the hearth, were still too poor for a prodigal waste of light when no work was to be done by it.

"Is it you, darling, and so out of breath?" said the voice of an old man, who rose and began to grope with his hand upon the mantel-piece. "What kept you so long? poor grandma has been in a terrible way about it." While he spoke, the grating of a match that would not readily ignite, was heard against the chimney piece.

"The gentleman, grandpa—here is a gentleman. He would come!" cried the child, artlessly.

This seemed to startle the old man. The match would not kindle; he stooped down and touched it to a live ember; as he rose again the pale blue flames fell upon the face of his wife, and rose to his own features. The illumination was but for a moment—then the wick began to fuse slowly into flame, but it was nearly half a minute before the miserable candle gave out its full complement of light. The old man turned toward the open door, shading the candle with his hand.

"Where, child? I see no gentleman."

Julia looked around. A moment before, Leicester had stood at her side. "He is gone—he is gone," she exclaimed, springing forward. "Oh, grandpa—oh, grandpa, how he did frighten me; it was the man I saw on the wharf, that day!"

CHAPTER XIX.

NIGHT AND MORNING.

We think to conquer circumstance, and sometimes win
A hold upon events that seemeth power.
But nothing stable waiteth upon sin;
God holds the cords of life, and in an hour
The strongest fabric built by human mind
Falls with a crash, and leaves a wreck behind.

Splendid beyond anything hitherto known in American life, was the ball, of which our readers have obtained but partial glimpses. At least a dozen rooms, some of them palatial in dimensions, others bijoux of elegance, were thrown open to the brilliant throng that had begun to assemble when the flower-girl left the mansion The conservatory was filled with blossoming plants, and lighted entirely by lamps, placed in alabaster vases, or swinging-like moons, from the waves of crystal that formed the roof. Masses of South American plants sheeted the sides with blossoms. Passion flowers crept up the crystal roof, and drooped their starry blossoms among the lamps. Trees, rich with the light feathery foliage peculiar to the tropics, bent over and sheltered the blossoming plants. An aquatic lily floated in the marble basin of a tiny fountain, spreading its broad green leaves on the water, and sheltering a host of arrowy, little gold-fish, that flashed in and out from their shadows. The air was redolent with heliotrope, daphnes, and cape-jessamines. Soft mosses crept around the marble basin, and dropped downward to the tesselated floor. It was like entering fairy land, as you came into this star-lit wilderness of flowers, from a noble picture-gallery, which divided it from the reception room. It was one of Dunlap's master-pieces. No artist ever arranged a more noble picture—no peri ever found a lovelier paradise. The silken curtains that divided the picture-gallery from the reception rooms were drawn back; thus a vista was formed down which the eye wandered till the perspective lost itself in the star-lighted masses of foliage; and on entering the first drawing-room, which was flooded with gas-light, a scene was presented that no European palace could rival, save in extent. Each of the tall, stained windows, had a corresponding recess, filled with mirrors that multiplied and reflected back every beautiful object within its range. Fresco paintings gleamed from the ceilings, but so delicately managed and enwrought in the light golden scrolls, that all over-gorgeousness was avoided. Each room possessed distinct colors, and had its own style of ornament; but natural contrasts were so strictly maintained, and harmonies so managed, that the rooms, when all thrown open, presented one brilliant whole, that might have been studied like the work of a great artist, and always found to present new beauties.

The rooms filled rapidly. The fancy dresses gave new éclat to the rooms. No royal court day ever presented a scene of greater magnificence. The flash of jewels—the wave of feathers—the glitter of brocades, had something regal in it, quite at variance with the simple republican habits with which our young country began its career among the nations of the earth. But in all this dazzling throng, our story deals more particularly with the four persons toward whom destiny was making rapid strides through all this glitter and gaiety.

William Leicester entered among the latest guests. The evening had been so full of events, that even his iron nerves were shaken, and he entered the mansion with pale cheeks and glittering eyes, as if conscious that he was rushing forward to his fate.

What was it that prompted the tantalizing wish to follow that young girl home, till she led him into the presence of that old couple, cowering over the fire in that dark basement? What evil spirit was crowding events so closely around him? He began to feel a sort of self-distrust; something like superstition crept over him, and he panted to place the Atlantic between himself and all these haunting perplexities.

A few distinguished persons had been allowed to attend the ball in citizens' dress, and among these, was Leicester, who appeared in the elegant but unostentatious suit worn at his wedding ceremony.

"Why, Leicester, you are pale! Has anything happened; or is it only the effect of that white vest?" said a young Turk, who stood near the entrance, removing his admiring eyes from the point of his own embroidered slipper, to regard his friend.

"Pale! No, I am only tired, making preparations for Europe, you know."

"A great bore, isn't it?" answered the young man, adjusting his cashmere scarf. "Isn't Mrs. Gordon beautiful to-night; the handsomest woman in the room, not to speak of uncounted pyramids! She'd be a catch—even for you, Leicester."

"She must have demolished some of her pyramids, before this paradise was created, I fancy," answered Leicester, looking down the vista of open rooms, now crowded with life and beauty.

"Yes, three at least," replied the juvenile Turk, planting one foot forward on the carpet, that he might admire the flow of his ample trousers; "one hundred and fifty thousand never paid for a place like this."

"So you, young gentleman, set fifty thousand down as a pyramid. Now, what if a lady chances to have only the half of that sum; how do you estimate her?"

"Twenty-five thousand!" repeated the exquisite; "a woman with no more than that isn't worth estimating; at any rate, till after a fellow gets to be an old fogy of two or three and twenty."

A quiet, mocking smile curved Leicester's lip. Though rather sensitive regarding his own age, he was really amused by this specimen of Young America.

"So, this widow, with so many pyramids—you think she would be a match worth looking after. What if I make the effort?"

"If you were twenty or twenty-five years younger, it might do."

Leicester laughed outright.

"Well, as I am too old for a rival, perhaps you will show me where the lady is; I have never seen her yet."

"What—never seen Mrs. Gordon, the beautiful Mrs. Gordon! I thought you old chaps were keener on the scent. I know half a hundred young gentlemen dead in for it."

"Then there is certainly no chance for me."

"I should rather think not," replied the youth, smiling complacently at his own reflection in an opposite mirror; "especially without costume. A dress like this, now, is a sort of thing that takes with women."

Leicester was getting weary of the youth.

"Well," he said, "if you will not aid me, I must find the lady myself."

"Oh, wait till the crowd leaves us an opening. There, the

music strikes up—they are off for the waltz; now you have a good view; isn't she superb?"

For one moment a cloud came over Leicester's eyes. He swept his gloved hand over them, and now he saw clearly.

"Which—which is Mrs. Gordon?" he said in a sharp voice, that almost startled the young exquisite out of his oriental propriety

"Why, how dull you are—as if there ever existed another woman on earth to be mistaken for her."

"Is that the woman?" questioned Leicester, almost extending his arm toward a lady dressed as Ceres, who stood near the door of an adjoining room.

"Of course it is. Come, let me present you, while there is a chance, though how the deuce you got here without a previous introduction, I cannot tell. Come, she is looking this way."

"Not yet," answered Leicester, drawing aside, where he was less liable to observation.

"Why, how strangely you look all at once. Caught with the first glance, ha?" persisted his tormentor

Leicester attempted to smile, but his lips refused to move. He would have spoken, but for once speech left him.

"Come, come, I am engaged for the next polka."

"Excuse me," answered Leicester, drawing his proud figure to its full height; "I was only jesting; Mrs. Gordon and I are old acquaintances."

"Then I will go find my partner," cried the Turk, half terrified by the flash of those fierce eyes.

"Do," said Leicester, leaning upon the slab of a music table that stood near.

And now, with a fiend at his heart and fire in his eye, William Leicester stood regarding his wife.

Ada had given this ball for a purpose. It was here, surrounded by all the pomp and state secured by position and immense wealth, that she intended once more to meet her husband. What hidden motive lay in the depths of her mind, I do not know. Perhaps—for love like hers will descend to strange humiliations—she expected to win back a gleam of his old tenderness, by the magnificence which she knew he loved so well. Perhaps she really intended to startle him by her queenly presence, load him with scornful reproaches, and so separate forever. This, probably, was the reason she gave to her own heart; but I still think a dream of reconciliation slept at the bottom of it all.

At another time Ada would have been dressed with less magnificence under her own roof: for her taste was perfect, and the elegant simplicity of her style was at all times remarkable. But now she had an object to accomplish—a proud soul to humble to the dust; and she loaded herself with pomp, as a warrior encases himself in armor just before a battle.

The character of Ceres, in which she appeared, was peculiarly adapted to the perfection of her beauty and the natural grace of her person. In order to increase the magnificence of this costume, she had ordered all her jewels to be reset at Ball & Black's, in wreaths, bouquets, and clusters, adapted to the character; and as Leicester gazed upon her from the distance, his eyes were absolutely dazzled with flashes of rainbow light that followed every movement of her person.

Her over-skirt of fine Brussels point was gathered up in soft clouds from the amber satin dress, by clusters of fruit, grass, and leaves, all of precious stones. Cherries, the size of life, cut from glowing carbuncles; grapes in amethyst clusters, or amber hued, from the Oriental topaz; stems of ruby currants; crab-apples, cut from the red coral of Naples; with wheat ears, barbed with gold, and set thick with diamond grain; all mingled with leaves and bending grass, lighted with emeralds, were grouped among the gossamer lace, whence the light came darting forth with a thousand sunset glories.

Her fair, round arms were exposed almost to the shoulder, where a quantity of soft lace, that fell like a mist across her bosom, was gathered up with clusters of fruit-like jewels. Her hair, arranged after the fashion of a Greek statue, flowed back from the head in waves and ringlets, and was crowned by a garland of jewels that shot rays of tinted light through all her golden tresses. The choicest jewels she possessed had been reserved for this garland, wreathed in both fruit and flowers. Here diamond fuschias, veined with rubies, and forget me-nots of torquoise, each with a yellow pearl at the heart, were grouped with diamond wheat ears and stems of currants, some heavy with ruby fruit, others beset with yellow diamonds. The grape leaves that fell around her temples were green with emeralds, and a single cluster of cherries, formed from carbuncles, that seemed to have a drop of wine floating at the heart, drooped over her white forehead. Great diamond drops were scattered like dew over these dazzling clusters, and fell away down the ringlets of her hair.

Ada stood beneath the blaze of a chandelier, that poured its light over the singular wreath, and struck the jewels of her girdle, till they sent it back in broken flashes. Waves of lace were gathered beneath this girdle, as we find the drapery around those antique statues of Ceres, still existing in fragments at Athens.

Leicester stood motionless, gazing upon his wife. Every gem about her person seemed to fix its value upon his mind. This surprise had overpowered him for a moment, but no event had the power to disturb him, even for the brief time he had been regarding her.

His resolution was taken. Self-possessed, and, but for a wild brilliancy of the eyes and a slight paleness about the mouth, tranquil as if they had parted but yesterday, he moved down the room.

The crowd was drawn off toward the dancing saloon, and at that moment the reception room, in which Ada stood, was somewhat relieved of the glittering crowd that had pressed around her but a moment before.

Still several persons were grouped near her, glad to seize upon every disengaged moment of the hostess; for never in her brightest mood had she been half so brilliant as now. Her lips grew red with the flashes of wit that passed through them. Her eyes flashed with animation, and a warm scarlet flush lay upon her cheek, burning there like flame, but growing more and more brilliant as the evening wore on. Sometimes she would pause in the midst of a sentence, and look searchingly in the crowd. Then a frown would contract her forehead, as if the jewelled garland were beset with hidden thorns that pierced her temples; but when reminded of this her smile grew brilliant again, and some flash of wit displaced the impression her countenance had made the moment before.

She had just made some laughing reply to a gentleman who stood near her, and turning away, cast another of those anxious looks over the room. She gave a faint start; her eye flashed, and drawing her form up to its full height, she stood with curved lips and burning cheeks, ready to receive her husband. He came down the room, slowly moving forward with his usual noiseless grace. He paused now and then as the crowd pressed on him, and it was a full minute after she first saw him, before he approached her near enough to speak.

"My dear lady, I shall never forgive myself for coming so late," he said, reaching forth his hand. "Why did not your invitations say at once that we were invited to paradise?"

For one moment Ada turned pale and lost her self-possession. The audacious coolness of the man astonished her. She had expected to take him by surprise, and promised herself the enjoyment of his confusion; but before his speech was finished the blood rushed to her cheek, her lips grew red again, and her eyes seemed showering fire into his. He had taken her hand, while speaking, and pressed it gently, but with a meaning that aroused all the pride of her nature.

Did he hope to practice his old arts upon her? Was she a school girl to be won back by a pressure of the hand and frothy compliments to her dwelling? The crafty man had mistaken her for once. She withdrew her hand with a laugh.

"So you were ignorant that the goddess of plenty reigned here."

There was meaning in the light words, and for an instant Leicester's audacious eyes fell beneath the glance of hers; but he recovered himself with a breath.

"The character is badly chosen. I could have selected better."

"What, pray—what would you have selected?" she asked, with breathless haste.

He stooped forward, and with a smile upon his lips, as if he had been uttering a compliment, whispered "A Niobe."

The tone in which this was uttered, more than the words, stung her.

She drew back with a suddenness that scattered the light like sunbeams from her jewelled garland.

"Everything that Niobe loved turned to stone. In that we are alike," she said, in a suppressed voice that trembled with feeling.

He bent his head and was about to answer in the same undertone, but she drew back with a low defiant laugh.

"No—no. It is a sad character, and I have long since done with tears," she answered, turning to a gay group that had gathered around her, "What say you, gentlemen, our friend here prefers a mournful character; do I look like a woman who ever weeps?"

"Not unless the angels weep," answered one of the group.

"Angels do weep when they leave the homes assigned to them," whispered Leicester, again bending towards her, "and it is fitting that they should."

She did not recoil that time. His words rather stung her into strength, and strange to say, Leicester seemed less hateful to her while uttering these covert reproaches, than his first adroit compliment had rendered him. A retort was on her lip, but that instant a group came in from the dancing saloon, laughing and full of excitement.

"Oh, Mrs. Gordon, such a droll character!" cried a flower girl, pressing her way to the hostess; "a postman with bundles of letters, real letters; you never saw anything like it. I'm sure Mr. Willis and some other poets here, that I could point out, have had a hand in getting up this mail, for some of the letters are full of delightful poetry. Only look here, isn't this sweet?"

The girl held up an open paper, in which half a dozen lines of poetry were visible.

"Read it aloud—read it aloud," cried several voices at once. "No one has secrets here!"

"Oh, I wouldn't for anything," answered the young lady, tossing the flowers about in her basket, with a simper; "Mrs. Gordon won't insist, I am sure.

Ada saw what was expected of her, and held the letter aloof, when the young lady made feints at snatching it away.

"But what if Mrs. Gordon does insist?" she said. "The postman has no business to bring letters here that are not for the public amusement."

"Well, now, isn't it too bad," cried the flower girl, striving to conceal her satisfaction with a pout. "I am sure it's not my fault."

"Read, read," cried voices from the crowd.

"No," said Ada, weary with the scene, and mischievously inclined to punish the girl for her affectation; "all amusement must be voluntary here."

The young lady took her note with a pout that was genuine, this time, and hid it in her basket.

During this brief scene, Leicester had glided from the room unobserved, and two strange characters took his place. This would hardly have been remarked in so large an assembly, but the costumes in which these persons appeared, were so arranged that they amounted to a disguise. One was robed as Night, the other as Morning; but the cloud-like drapery that fell around them, was of glossy, Florence silk, which allowed them to see what was passing, while their own features were entirely concealed. Neither of them spoke, and their presence cast a restraint upon the crowd close around the hostess. They seemed conscious of this, and gradually drew back, stationing themselves at last close by a pillar, that separated two rooms directly behind Ada and the group that surrounded her.

Leicester had only been to the gentleman's dressing-room, which was at that hour quite empty. He seemed hurried and somewhat agitated on entering. Going up to a light he took a letter-case from his bosom, and hastily shuffling over some papers it contained, selected one from the parcel. He opened this hurriedly, glanced at the first lines, and then looked around the room, as if in search of something.

Evidently the letters and poems from which the mock postman was supplied, had been arranged there, for a writing table stood in one corner littered with pens, fancy note-paper and envelopes.

"How fortunate," broke from Leicester, as he saw these accommodations; and he began to search among the envelopes for one of the size he wanted. Having accomplished this, he placed the paper taken from his letter-case open upon the table; and the light of a wax taper, that stood ready for use, revealed a tress of hair that lay curled within it.

Leicester pushed the curl aside with his finger, while he directed the envelope, refering to the paper every other letter, as if to compare his work with the writing it contained.

When this was accomplished and his hand removed, the light fell upon his own name written in a feminine running hand. He smiled as if satisfied with the address, replaced the lock of hair in the paper, and folded both in the envelope, which he carefully sealed. He left the room with a crafty smile on his lip, and beckoned to an attendant.

"Take this and give it to the postman you will find somewhere in the second drawing-room. Tell him Mrs. Gordon wishes him to deliver it when she is present; you understand."

"Oh, yes," said the French servant, charmed with a mission so congenial to his taste, "I've had a good many to carry down before to-night."

"Do this quietly—you understand—and here is something for the postage"

"Monsieur is magnificent," said the man, taking the piece of gold with a profound bow. "He shall see how invisible I shall become."

Leicester stole back to the reception rooms again, and glided into the group that still surrounded the hostess, unobserved as he thought; but those who watched Ada closely, would have seen the apathy, that had crept over her during his absence, suddenly flung off, while her manner and look became wildly brilliant once more. At this moment Night and Morning drew closer to the pillar, and sheltered themselves behind it.

"Here he comes—here comes the postman," cried half a dozen young ladies at once; "who will get a letter now? Mrs. Gordon, of course!"

One of the first lawyers of the State entered the room, acting the postman with great diligence and exactitude. He carried a bundle of letters on his arm, and held some loose in his hands. There was a great commotion among the young ladies when he presented himself, a flirting of fans and waving of curls that might have tempted any man from his course. He turned neither to the right nor left, but marching directly up to Leicester, presented a letter with "Two cents, sir, if you please."

Leicester as gravely took the letter, drew a five-cent piece from his pocket, and placed it in the outstretched hand of the postman, with, "The change, if you please."

A burst of laughter followed this scene; but the postman, no way disconcerted, placed the five-cent piece between his teeth, while he searched his pocket for the change. Drawing forth three cents, he counted them into Leicester's palm, and strode on again, as if every mail in the United States depended on his diligence. Leicester stood a moment with the letter in his hand, smiling and seemingly a little embarrassed about opening it!

Ada glanced sharply from the letter to his face. Even then she was struck with a jealous pang that made her recoil with self-contempt.

"No ! no—that will never do," called out voices all around, as Leicester seemed about to place the note in his pocket—"All letters are public property here—break the seal—break the seal !"

With a derisive smile on his lip, as if coerced into doing a silly thing, he broke the seal and unfolded the missive. A tress of golden hair dropped to his feet, which he snatched up hurriedly, and grasped in his hand. A burst of gay laughter followed the act.

"Read—read—it is poetry—we can see that—give us the poetry !" broke merrily around him.

"Spare me," said Leicester, apparently annoyed ; "but if the fair lady chooses to enlighten you, she has my consent."

Ada reached forth her hand for the paper. A strange sensation crept over her, with the first sight of it in the mock postman's hand, and it was with an effort that she conquered this feeling sufficiently to open the paper, with her usual careless ease.

She glanced at the first line. Her lips moved as if she were trying to speak ; but they uttered no sound, and by slow degrees the red died out from them.

Leicester watched her closely with his half averted eyes, and those around him looked on in gay expectation ; for no one else observed the change in her countenance. To the crowd, she seemed only gathering up the spirit of the lines, before she commenced reading them aloud. The paper contained a wild, impulsive appeal to him, after the first jealous outbreak that had disturbed their married life. As usual, when a warm heart has either done or suffered wrong, it matters little which, she had been the first to make concessions, and lavish in self-blame, poured forth her passionate regret, as if all the fault had been hers. In her first jealous indignation, she had demanded a tress of hair, for which he had importuned her one night at the old homestead.

He rendered it coldly back without a word. Wild with affright, lest this was the seal of eternal separation, she had sent back the tress of hair now grasped in Leicester's hand, with the lines which, with the plotting genius of a fiend, he had placed in her hand.

Poor Ada, she was unconscious of the crowd. The days of her youth came back—the old homestead—the pangs and joys of her first married life. While she seemed to read, a life-time of memories swept through her brain, which ached with the sudden rush of thought.

Leicester stood regarding her with apparent unconcern; but it was as the spider watches the fly in his net.

"She cannot read it aloud—I thought so," he said inly, "let her struggle—while her lips pale in that fashion she is mine; I knew it would smite her to the heart. Let the fools clamor, she is struck dumb with old memories."

Unconsciously a cold smile of triumph crept over his lips, as these thoughts gained strength from Ada's continued silence With her eyes on the paper, she still seemed to read.

At length her guests became politely impatient.

"We are all attention," cried a voice.

She did not hear it; but others set in with laughing clamor; and at length she looked up, as if wondering what all the noise was about. Her eyes fell upon Leicester. She saw the smile of which he was probably unconscious, and the present flashed back to her brain.

"He hopes to crush me with these memories," she thought with lightning intuition.

The life came back to her eyes, the strength to her limbs, and without hesitation or pause, her voice broke forth. As she went on, the fire of a wounded nature flashed over her face. Her voice swelled out rich and passionately. Her woman's heart seemed beating in every word.

TAKE back the tress! the broken chain,
  Its fragile folds have linked around us,
May never re-unite again!
  And every gentle tie that bound us,

The madness of a single hour—
  The madness of a word—has parted,
Leaving the marble in thy power:
  And me, ah more than broken hearted.

Take back the tress! I cannot bear
  To hold the link my hand has scattered;
It mocks me, in my dark despair,
  With scenes and hopes forever shatter'd;
It haunts me with a thousand things—
  A thousand words, half felt, half spoken—
When thy proud soul with eagle wings
  Stoop'd to the heart now almost broken.

It haunts me with the deep, low tones,
  That stir'd my soul to more than gladness
When we seemed in the world, alone,
  And joy grew deep almost to sadness.
Is there no charm to win thee back,
  To wake the love thy pride is crushing?
Has mem'ry left no golden track—
  No music which thy heart is hushing?

Is there within this little tress
  No thought but that which wakes thy scorning?
Oh say, was there no happiness
  Within thy breast that summer morning,
When from my brow the curl was shred
  With hand that shook in joy, and terror;
And love, half hush'd in trembling dread,
  Shrunk back, as if to feel were error?

My soul is filled with deep regret,
  That I who loved thee so, could doubt thee!
Sweep back thy pride, forgive, forget!
  Life is so desolate without thee.
I will not keep this tress of hair:
  As ravens from their gloomy wings
Cast shadows, it but leaves despair
  Upon the weary heart it wrings.

Where hope, and life, and faith are given,
  I send it back, perchance too late;
Go cast it to the winds of heaven,
  If it but rouse more bitter hate.

I will not rend a single thread
  That binds my willing soul to thine:
Take then the task; if love has fled,
  Despoil love's desolated shrine.

Her voice ceased to vibrate over the throng full half a minute, before the listeners breathed freely. The mesmeric influence of her hidden grief spread from heart to heart, till in its earnestness, the crowd forgot to applaud. Thus it happened that for some moments after she had done, there was silence all around her. The paper began to tremble in her hand—she tossed it carelessly toward Leicester.

"The lady is too much in earnest—she quite takes away my breath," she said, with an air of gay mockery; "a grand passion like that must be very fatiguing."

A flash rose to Leicester's brow. He took the paper, and refolding the curl of hair in it, placed both in his bosom. His manner was grave—almost humble. She had baffled him for once. But the game was not played out yet.

The crowd that observed nothing but the surface of this scene, was still somewhat subdued by it; but the ringing notes of a waltz that swept in from the dancing saloon, set the gay current in motion again.

"Who was it that engaged me for this waltz?" cried the hostess, glancing around the throng of distinguished men that surrounded her

Half a dozen voices gaily answered the challenge; but still, with a purpose at heart, she selected the most distinguished of the group, and was followed to the dancing saloon.

Leicester remained behind. Even his strong nerves were ready to break down under the excitement crowded upon him that evening. Never had he been placed in a position of such difficulty. With two important crimes, perpetrated almost the same hour, urging immediate flight to Europe, he found himself constrained to remain and secure the still richer prize, the discovery of that evening seemed to place within his grasp. He leaned against the pillar near which Ada had been stationed to receive her guests, and made a prompt review of his position.

"I must go," he thought, locking his teeth hard, as the necessity was forced upon him; "they must have time to put the boy up in Sing-Sing. The girl, too—fool that I was—she is the most troublesome part of the business. I will get her over sea, at once—the witnesses are nothing—she can't live over a few months—if she does——"

A fiendish expression crept over his face, and after a moment, he muttered, so audibly, that the two shrouded females close by the pillar heard him; "But women's hearts never do break; if they did, Wilcox's daughter would have been in her grave long ago."

A faint sob close by him, drove these evil thoughts inward again. There was a slight rustling near the pillar, and raising his eyes, he saw the two characters, Night and Morning, gliding away toward the dancers. He did not give the circumstance a second thought; but moved down the rooms toward the conservatory, where he could plot and think alone.

"Yes, I *must* go off and find a safe place for Florence. Thanks to my icy-hearted mother, who never had a visitor, there is no chance for gossip. Robert will be snugly-housed when I come back, and my man shall go with me."

But a new obstacle arose in his mind—the flower-girl, his other witness. The old people, whose faces he had so dimly seen—what if Ada should learn all from them? The thought was formidable; but at last he thrust it aside, as undeserving of anxiety.

"They will not meet; she has been years searching for them, and in vain; besides, I shall be back in a month or two. If that girl is obstinate and won't die, let her stay behind—that will settle it probably—the hectic is on her cheek now. But I must see this proud witch to-night. Poor Ada, how much trouble she takes to prove her love—I see it all; this grand display was for me—I was to be astonished, braved, taunted awhile, and after a tragic scene or two, my lady is meek as a lamb once more. The handsome wretch—she did outwit me with those lines; I thought they would have touched her to the heart. It was our first love quarrel. How the creature did go on then! Now I shall find her more difficult to bring under ; but the same heart is at the bottom. I didn't think she could have read those lines aloud—so dauntlessly too. Jove! I almost loved her as she did it. Fool that I was, to make this trip across the ocean necessary. But for that, I might take possession now. Ada Wilcox—my pretty rustic Ada, reigning here like a queen! Mrs. Gordon—Mrs. Gordon! Faith, it's a capital joke. She's managed it splendidly—out-generaled Mrs. Nash and Mrs. Sykes both. More than that, she has half out-generaled Leicester too."

CHAPTER XX.

THE LAST INTERVIEW.

Thy race is run—thy fate is sealed,
  Trust not the ties that bound thee;
A thousand snares, still unrevealed,
  Are woven close around thee.

Nor strength, nor craft availeth now;
  Thy stubborn will is riven;
The death drops hang upon thy brow,
  There's justice yet in Heaven.

It was over at last. The saloon, the banquet hall, the conservatory, sleeping in the moonlight shed from many a sculptured vase—all were deserted; wax candles flared and went out in their silver sockets; garlands grew dim and shadowy in the diminished light; half a dozen yawning footmen glided about extinguishing wax lights, and turning off gas, but they seemed ghost-like and dreary, wandering through the vast mansion.

But Ada Leicester felt no fatigue; she saw nothing of the gloom that was so rapidly spreading over the splendor of her mansion. Her boudoir was still lighted by those two pearl-like lamps. It was a dim, luxurious twilight, that seemed hazy with the perfume stealing up from a dozen snowy vases scattered through the dressing-room, the bed-chamber, and the boudoir. The doors connecting these apartments were ajar, but closed enough to conceal one room from the other.

Ada entered the boudoir. Her step was imperious; her cheek burning. Pride, anger and haughty scorn swelled in her bosom, as she seated herself to wait. One of those mysterious revulsions of feeling that are so frequent to a passionate and ill-disciplined nature, had swept over her heart. For the first time in her life she felt disposed to sting the foot that had trampled so ruthlessly upon her. In that moment, all the strong love of a lifetime seemed kindling into a fiery hate.

It was one of those hours when we defy destiny—defy our own souls. A few hours earlier and she could not have met him thus with scorn on her brow, rebellion in her heart. A few hours after she might repent in tears, but now she waited his approach without a thrill of pleasure or of fear. The very memory of former tenderness filled her with self-contempt. The marble Flora stood over her—crimson roses and heliotrope had been mingled with the sculptured lilies in its hand. A few hours before she had stolen away from her guests, to place these blossoms among the marble counterfeits, for they breathed his favorite perfume; now, she sickened as the fragrance floated over her, and tearing them from the statue, tossed them amid a bed of coals still burning in the silver grate.

She did not go back to the couch, but remained upon the ermine rug, with one arm resting upon the jetty marble of the mantel-piece. No footstep could be heard in that sumptuously carpeted house, but the proud spirit within her seemed to know when he stole softly forth from the conservatory, and approached the room where she was waiting.

Leicester was self-possessed; he had a game to play, more

intricate, more difficult than his experience had yet coped with, but this only excited his intellect. With a heart of stone the nerves hold no sympathy, and are obedient to the will alone: what or who had ever resisted Leicester's will!

But she also was self-possessed, and this took him by surprise. He moved toward the grate and leaned his elbow on the mantel-piece, directly opposite her. She held a superb fan, half open, against her bosom: it was fringed deep with the gorgeous plumage of some tropical bird, but no tumult of the heart stirred a feather. She held it there, as she had often done that evening, when homage floated around her, gracefully and quietly waiting to be addressed. This mood was one he had not expected; it deranged all his premeditated plan of attack. Instead of reproaching him, with that passionate anger that pants for reconciliation, she was silent.

"Ada!" The name was uttered in a voice that no heart that had loved the speaker could entirely resist. A faint shiver and an irregular breath were perceptibly ruffling, as it were, the plumage of her fan, but the proud woman only bent her head.

"Was it delicate—was it honorable to deceive your husband thus?" he said, "to grant him one interview after so many years, and then conceal yourself from his search under this disguise? I have sought for you, Ada, Heaven only knows how anxiously."

She smiled a cold incredulous smile, for well she knew how he had searched for her.

"You do not believe me," said Leicester, attempting to take her hand; but she drew back, pressing the fan harder to her bosom, till the delicately wrought ivory broke. The demon of pride grew strong within her. For the first time in her life she felt a knowledge of power over the man who had been her fate.

"Was I to seek you that your foot might be planted on my heart once more? Was I to offer my bosom to the serpent fang again and again? Have you forgotten our interview in the chamber overhead?—that chamber where I had hoarded every thing connected with the only happy months you ever permitted me to know—so full of precious memories? I thought they would touch even your heart."

He attempted to speak, but she would not permit him. "I did not know you, notwithstanding past experience. Your heart has blacker shades than I imagined! Not up there—not among objects holy from association with my child, should I have taken you, but here! here! do not these things betoken great wealth?" A scornful smile curved her lips, and she glanced around the boudoir.

There was one word in this speech that Leicester seized upon. "*Your* child, Ada. Great Heaven! would you exclude me from all share even in the love of our child!"

Even this did not soften her, though she was fearfully moved at the mention of her lost infant. He saw this, and his manner instantly changed.

"Why should I plead with you—why waste words thus?" he said, casting aside all affectation of tenderness:—"you are my wife—lawfully married—the mother of my child. If you have property, by the laws of this land that property is mine! I plead no longer, madam! Being the master of this house, if it is yours, my province is to command. Tell me, then! this wealth—for which people give their idol, *Mrs. Gordon*, so much credit—this mansion; are they real?—are they yours?—and therefore mine?"

The scorn that broke over Ada's face was absolutely sub lime.

"Yes," she said, "this wealth is mine, yours, if the law makes it so; but listen—then say if you will use it!"

She bent forward; her lips and cheek were pale as death, but across the snow of her forehead a crimson flush came and went, like an arrow shooting back and again.

"You asked me that night in the room above, if I had lived in Europe as the governess of that man's daughter—the governess only. I answered yes; a governess only. It was false!

Every dollar of the millions I possess comes from this man; he bequeathed them on his death-bed, that I might not again become your slave!" The haughty air gave way as she uttered this confession; her limbs trembled so violently that she was obliged to lean on the mantel-piece to keep from sinking to the floor. Pride, that treacherous demon, left her then, helpless as a child.

"This," said Leicester, with a stern, clear enunciation, "this in no way interferes with my claim on the property. Were it double, that would be poor atonement for the outrage to my affections—the disgrace brought upon my name."

She did not speak, but listened in breathless silence, trying to comprehend the moral enormity before her, with a confused sense that even yet she had not fathomed the black depths of his heart.

Leicester had paused, thinking that she would answer; but as she remained silent he spoke again, still calmly, and with measured intonation.

"But that which you have confessed becomes important in another sense. If the law gives me your property, it also enables me to divest it of the only incumbrance that would be unpleasant. Your confession, madam, entitles me to a divorce."

"You would not—oh, Heavens, no!" gasped the wretched woman.

"Now you seem natural—now you are meek again," he said with a laugh that cut to the heart. "So, you thought to dazzle me with your wealth—wither me with haughty pride—fool! miserable fool!"

"Mercy, mercy! Will no one save me from this man?" shrieked the wretched woman, flinging her clasped hands wildly upward.

Leicester was about to speak again, something fearfully bitter—you could see it in the curve of his lip—but her cry had reached other ears, and while the taunt was yet unspoken, Jacob Strong entered the boudoir. Leicester gazed upon him in utter amazement, for he advanced directly toward Ada, and taking the clasped hands she held out in both his, led her to the couch, trembling, and so faint that she was incapable of uttering a word.

"What is this? how came you here, fellow?" said Leicester, the moment he could break from the astonishment occasioned by Jacob's presence.

"My mistress called for help, and I came," was the steady answer.

"Your mistress! where—who?"

"This lady—your *first* wife! the other——"

"Villain! who are you?"

Jacob looked into his master's eyes with a calm stare: "Look at me, Mr. Leicester! I have grown since you saw me at old Mr. Wilcox's! No doubt you have forgotton the awkward boy, who tended your horse, and pointed out the best trout streams for you? But I—I shall never forget! No angry looks—no frowns, sir! The rocks we climbed together would feel them more than I do."

"Go on—go on—I would learn more," said Leicester, paling fearfully about the mouth. "You have been a spy in my service!"

"Yes—a spy—a keeper of your most dangerous secrets! I read the letter from Georgia—I have that old copy-book, which was to have sent Robert Otis, my own nephew, to state prison. There is a check of ten thousand, which I can lay my hand on at any moment—you comprehend! I saw it written—I saw it pass from your hand to his. I was in the back room. Villain! I am your master."

The palor spread up from Leicester's mouth to his temples, leaving a dusky ring around his eyes. For the first time in his life, this man of evil and stern will was terrified. Yet wrath was stronger in his heart than fear, even then. His white lips curled in fierce disdain. He turned towards Ada, who lay with her face buried in the silken pillows, conscious of nothing but her own unutterable wretchedness. She did not feel the fiendish glance that he cast upon her; but Jacob saw it, and his grey eyes kindled, till they seemed black as midnight: "If you wish to see another, come in here—come, I say! Victims are plenty about you; come in."

Jacob looked terribly imposing in this burst of indignation. His awkward form dilated into rude grandeur—his wrath, ponderous and intense, rolled forth like some fathomless stream, whose very tranquillity is terrible. He flung his powerful arm around Leicester, and drew him forward as if he had been a child.

Through the dressing-room, still flooded with soft light and redolent of flowers, and into the bed-chamber beyond, Jacob strode, grasping his companion firmly with one arm. He paused close by the bed. With an upward motion of his arms, he flung aside the cloud of lace that fell over it, and pointed to a form that lay underneath, pillowed, as it were, upon a snow drift. "Look! here is another!" said Jacob, towering above the man who had been his master—for there was no stoop in his shoulders then—"look! it is your last victim—to all eternity, the last!"

Leicester did look, for his gaze was fascinated by the soft eyes lifted to his from the pillow; the sweet, sweet smile that played around that lovely mouth. It went to his soul—that impenetrable soul—that Ada's anguish had failed to reach.

"She heard it all. She saw everything that passed between you and your wife," said Jacob.

"What—and smiles upon me thus?" There was something of human feeling in his voice. He stooped down, and put back some raven tresses that fell over the eyes that were searching for his.

Then the smile broke into a laugh so wild with insane glee, that even Leicester shuddered and drew back. Florence started up in the bed. The lace of her wedding garments was crushed around her form—her arms were entangled in the rich white veil which still clung, torn and ragged, to the diamond star fastened over her temple. The cypress and jessamine wreath, half torn away, hung in fragments among her black tresses. She saw that Leicester avoided her, and tearing the veil fiercely, set both her arms free. She leaned half over the bed, holding them out, as a child aroused from sleep, pleads for its mother. Leicester drew near, for a fiend could not have resisted that look. She caught both his hands, drew herself up to his bosom, and then began to laugh again.

That moment a female, whose black garments contrasted gloomily with the drift-like whiteness of the couch, came from the shadowy part of the room, and taking Florence in her arms laid her gently back upon the pillows. She had seen that of which Leicester and Jacob were unconscious—Ada Leicester, standing in the gorgeous gloom of her dressing-chamber, and watching the scene.

"Mother, you here also!" exclaimed Leicester, and his voice had, for the instant, something of human anguish in it. His mother pointed toward the dressing-room, and only answered—

"Would you drive her mad also?"

"Would to Heaven it were possible," answered Leicester, with a cold sneer. He bowed low, and with a gesture full of sarcastic defiance moved toward the dressing-room. Jacob followed him.

"Stay," said Ada, standing before them—"what is this—who are the persons you have left in my chamber?"

"One of them," answered Leicester, with calm audacity, "one of them is of little consequence, though you may find in her, my dear madam, an old acquaintance. The other is a young lady, very beautiful, as you may see even from here—to whom I had the honor of being married last evening. How she became your guest I do not know, but treat her with all hospitality, I beseech you, if it were only for the love that I bear her—love that I never felt for mortal woman before."

"Go," said Ada, stung into some degree of strength by his insolence, "or, rather let me go, if you are indeed the master here."

She took a shawl which had been flung across a chair, and folded it around her.

"Take everything, but let me go in peace. Jacob, oh, my friend, *you* will not abandon me now?"

"No," answered Jacob, with a degree of respectful tenderness that gave to his rude features something more touching than beauty. "Take off your shawl, madam—he has lost all power to harm you—there is desperation in his insolence, nothing more. His own crimes have disabled him."

"How? how? Not that which he hinted—not marriage with another? Tell me, that it was only bravado. Rather, much rather, could I go forth penniless and bare-headed into the street."

She approached Leicester, holding out her hands. He saw all the unquenched love that shed anguish over that beautiful face, and took courage. In this weakness, lay some hope of safety.

"Ada let me see you alone," he said, with an abrupt change of voice and manner. She looked at Jacob irresolutely. He saw the danger at once, and taking her hand, led her with gentle force into the bed-chamber. "Look," he said, pointing to Florence, who lay upon the couch—"ask her, she will tell you what it means."

Ada advanced toward the old lady, who came to meet her as one who receives the mourners who gather to a funeral.

"It is Leicester's mother," broke from the pale lips of Leicester's wife.

"My poor daughter," said the old lady, wringing the trembling hand that Ada held out.

"Will you—can you, call me daughter? oh madam, how long it is since that sweet word has fallen on my ear." The pathos of her words—the humility of her manner—melted the old lady almost to tears. She opened her arms, and received the wretched woman to her bosom.

Jacob went out and found Leicester in the boudoir.

"Will she come? I am tired of waiting," he said, as Jacob closed and locked the door leading to the dressing-room.

"Expect nothing from her weakness—never hope to see her

again. It is with me—not a weak, loving, forgiving woman, you have to deal."

"With you—her father's clownish farmer-boy—my own servant."

"I have no words to throw away, and you will need them to defend yourself," answered Jacob, with firm self-possession. "You have committed, within the last twenty-four hours, two crimes against the law. You have married a woman, knowing your wife to be alive. I am the witness, I, her playmate when she was a little girl, her protector and faithful servant in the trouble and sin which you heaped upon her after she was a woman. I went with her to the hotel that night, I witnessed all—all—to the scene last evening. Let that pass, for it *should* pass, rather than have her history connected with yours before the world. But another crime. This forged check—this attempt to ruin as warm-hearted and honest a boy as ever lived. In this, her name cannot, from necessity, appear; for this you shall suffer to the extent of the law; for this, you shall live year after year in prison, not from revenge, mark, but that she, Ada Wilcox, may breathe in peace. Leave this house, sir, quietly, for I must not have a felon arrested beneath her roof. Go anywhere you like, for a few hours, not to the hotel, for Robert Otis is waiting in your chamber with an officer; not to ferry, or steamboat, in hopes of escaping; men are placed everywhere to stop you; but till noon you are safe from arrest.

"I will not leave this house without speaking with Ada," said Leicester, in a whisper so deep and fierce, that it came through his clenched teeth like the hiss of a wounded adder.

"Five minutes you have for deliberation; go forth quietly, and as a departing guest, or remain to be marshalled out by half a dozen men, whom the chief of police has sent to protect the grounds—you understand, to protect the grounds."

Leicester did not speak, but a sharp, fiendish gloom shot into his eyes, and he thrust one hand beneath his snowy vest, and drew it slowly out; then came the sharp click of a pocket pistol. Jacob watched the motion, and his heavy features stirred with a smile.

"You forget that I am your servant; that I laid out your wedding dress, and loaded the pistol; put it up, sir—as I told you before, when I play with rattlesnakes, I take a hard grip on the neck."

Leicester drew his hand up deliberately, and dashed the pistol in Jacob's face. The stout man recoiled a step, and blood flowed from his lips. It was fortunate for him that Leicester had found the revolver which he was in the habit of wearing too heavy for his wedding garments. As it was, he took out a silk handkerchief, and coolly wiped the blood from his mouth, casting now and then a look at the tiny clock upon the mantelpiece. The fiendish smile excited by the sight of his enemy's blood was just fading from Leicester's lip, when Jacob put the handkerchief back in his pocket.

"You will save a few hours of liberty by departing at once," he said. "To a man, who has nothing but prison walls before him, they should be worth something."

"Yes, much can be done in a few hours," muttered Leicester to himself, and gently settling his hat, he turned to go.

"Open the door," he said, turning coolly to Jacob; "your wages are paid up to this time, at any rate."

Jacob bowed gravely, and dropping into his awkward way, followed his master down stairs. He opened the principal door, and Leicester stepped into the street quietly, as if the respectful attendance had been real.

The morning had just dawned, cold, comfortless, and humid; a slippery moisture lay upon the pavements, dark shadows hung like drapery along the unequal streets; Leicester threaded them with slow and thoughtful step. For once, his great intellect, his plotting fiend, refused to work. What should he do? how act? His hotel, the very street which he threaded perhaps, beset with officers; his garments elegantly conspicuous; his arms useless, and in his pockets only a little silver and one piece of gold. Never was position more desperate.

Hour after hour wore on, and still he wandered through the streets. As daylight spread over the sky, kindling up the fog that still clung heavily around the city, Leicester saw two men walking near him. He quickened his pace, he loitered, turned again, down one street and up another; with their arms interlaced, their bodies sometimes enfolded in the fog, distinct or shadowy, those strange wanderers had a power to make Leicester's heart quail within him.

All at once he started, and stood up motionless in the street. That child—those two old people! He had recognized them at once the night before as Mr. Wilcox and his wife, poor, friendless; he had striven to cast them from his mind, to forget that they lived. The after events of that night had come upon him like a thunder-clap; in defending himself or attacking others, he had found little time to calculate on the discovery of his daughter and her old grand parents. Now, the thought came to his brain like lightning. He would secure the young girl—Ada's lost child. The secret of her existence was his; it should redeem him from the consequence of his great crime. The old people were poor—they would give up the child to a rich father, and ask no questions. With this last treasure in his power, Ada would not refuse to bribe it from him at any price. Her self-constituted guardian, too, that man of rude will, and indomitable strength, he who had sacrificed a lifetime to the mother of this child, who had tracked his own steps like a hound, could he, who had given up so much, refuse to surrender his vengeance, also? This humble girl, from whom Leicester had turned so contemptuously, how precious she became as these thoughts flashed through his brain.

Leicester proceeded with a rapid step to the neighborhood that he had visited the previous night. He descended to the area, glided through the dim hall, and entered the back basement just as old Mr. Warren, or Wilcox we must now call him, was sitting down to breakfast with his wife and grandchild. A look of poverty was about the room, warded off by care and cleanliness, but poverty still. Leicester had only time to remark this, when his presence was observed. Old Mr. Wilcox rose slowly from his chair, his thin face grew pale as he gazed upon the elegant person of his visitor, and the rich dress, so strongly at variance with the place. A vague terror seized him, for he did not at once recognize the features, changed by time, and more completely still, by a night of agonizing excitement. At length he recognized his son-in-law, and sinking to his chair, uttered a faint groan.

Julia started up, and flung her arms around the old man's neck. Leicester came quietly forward.

"Have you forgotten me, sir?" he said, laying one hand softly upon the table.

"No," gasped the old man, "no."

"And the little girl, she seems afraid of me, but when she knows—"

"Hush," said the old man, rising, with one arm around the child, "not another word till we are alone. Wife, Julia, leave the room."

The old woman hesitated. She, too, had recognized Leicester, and dreaded to leave him alone with her husband. Julia looked from one to the other, amazed and in trouble.

"As you wish. I have no time to spare. Send them away, and we can more readily settle my demands and your claims."

"Go!" replied the old man, laying his hand on Julia's head. That withered hand shook like a leaf.

Julia and her grandmother went out, but not beyond the hall. There they stood, distant as the space would permit, but still within hearing of the voices within. Now and then a word rose high, and old Mrs. Wilcox would draw Julia's head against her side, and press a hand upon her ear, as if she dreaded that even those indistinct murmurs should reach her.

While these poor creatures stood trembling in the hall, a strange, fierce scene was going on over that miserable breakfast-table. Leicester had been persevering and plausible at first; with promises of wealth, and protestations of kindness, he had endeavored to induce the poor old man to render up the child. When this failed, he became irritated, and, with fiercer passions, attempted to intimidate the feeble being whom he had already wronged almost beyond all hopes of human forgiveness. *The old man said little, for he was terrified, and weak as a* child ; but his refusal to yield up the little girl was decided. "If the law takes her away, I cannot help it," he said, "but nothing else ever shall." Tears rolled down the old man's face as he spoke, but his will had been expressed, and the man who came to despoil him saw that it was immovable.

Despairing at last, and fiercely desperate, Leicester rushed from the basement. Julia and her grandmother shrunk against the wall, for the palor of his face was frightful. He did not appear to see them, but went quickly through the outer door and up to the side-walk. Here stood the two men, arm-in-arm, ready to follow him. He turned back, and retraced his steps, with a dull, heavy footfall, utterly unlike the elasticity of his usual tread. Further and further back crowded the frightened females. The old man was so exhausted that he could not arise from the chair to which he had fallen. He looked up when Leicester entered the room, and said, beseechingly, "Oh, let me alone! See how miserable you have made us! Do let us alone!"

"Once more—once more I ask, will you give up the child?"

"No—no."

A knife lay upon the table, long and sharp, one that Mrs. Wilcox had been using in her household work. Leicester's eye had been fixed on the knife while he was speaking. His hand was outstretched toward it before the old man could find voice to answer. Simultaneous with the brief "no," the knife flashed upward, down again, and Leicester fell dead at the old man's feet. Mr. Wilcox dropped on his knees, seized the knife, and tore it from the wound. Over his withered hands, over the white vest, down to his feet, gushed the warm blood. It paralyzed the old man; he tried to cry aloud, but had no power. A frightful stillness reigned over him; then many persons came rushing into the room.

A light shone in that pretty cottage—a single light from the chamber where Julia had robed Florence Nelson in her bridal dress. A bed was there, shrouded in drapery, that hung motionless, like marble, and as coldly white; glossy linen swept over the bed, frozen, as it were, over the outline of a human form. Death—death—the very atmosphere was full of death. On one corner of the bed, crushing the cold linen, wrinkled with her weight, Florence Nelson had seated herself, and with her black ringlets falling over the dead, sung to him as no human being ever sung before. Sometimes she laughed—sometimes wept. Every variation of her madness was full of pathos, sweet with tenderness, save when there came from the opposite room a pallid and grief-stricken creature, with drooping hands, and eyes heavy with unshed tears.

If this unhappy woman attempted to approach the bed, or even enter the room, Florence would spring up with the fierce cry of a wounded eagle; the song rose to a wail, then, with her waxen hands, she would gather up the linen in waves, over the dead, and if Ada came nearer, shriek after shriek rose through the cottage. Thus poor Ada Leicester, driven from the death-couch of her husband, would creep back to where his mother knelt in her calm, still grief. There, with her stately head bowed down, her limbs prone upon the floor, she would murmur, "Oh, God help me! It is just—but help me, help me! Oh, my God!"

CHAPTER XXI.

THE CITY PRISON.

He was a man of simple heart,
Patient and meek, the Christian part
Came to his soul as came the air
That heaved his bosom; hope, despair,
Were chastened by a holy faith!—
Meek in his life he feared not death.

Perhaps in the whole world there is not a building where all the horror, the wild poetry of sin and grief is so forcibly written out in black shadows and hard stone, as in the city prison of New York. A stranger passing that massive pile would unconsciously feel saddened, though entirely ignorant of its painful uses, for the very atmosphere fills him with a vague sensation of alarm. The Egyptian architecture, so heavy and imposing; the thick walls which no sunshine can penetrate, and against which cries of anguish might, unheard, exhaust themselves forever, chill the very heart. The ponderous columns, lost in a perspective of black shadows in the front entrance—piles of granite sweeping toward Broadway, and interlocking with the black prison that rises up, like a solid wall, gloomy, windowless, and penetrated only with loop-holes, like a fort which has nothing but misery to protect—fills the imagination with gloom.

The moment you come in sight of the building, your breath draws heavily; the atmosphere seems humid with tears—oppressive with sighs—a storm of human suffering appears gathering around. The air seems eddying with curses which have exhausted their sound against those walls; you feel as if sin, shame, and grief were palpable spirits, walking behind and around you; and all this is the more terrible, because the waves of life gather close up to the building, swelling against its walls on every side.

The prison sits like a monster, crouching in the very heart of a great city; the veins and arteries of social evil weave and coil close around it, like serpents born in the same foul atmosphere with itself. Placed on foundations lower than the graded walks, nestled in a dried up swamp that has exchanged the miasma of decayed nature for the miasma of human guilt; the neighborhood close at hand sunk, like this building, deep in the grade of human existence; is there on earth another spot so eloquent of suffering, so populous with sin?

"The Tombs," this name was given to the prison years ago, when its foundations were first sunk in the swampy moisture of the soil. Then you could see the vast structure sinking, day by day, into its murky foundations, and enveloped in clouds of palpable miasma. There the poor wretches huddled within its walls, died like herds of poisoned cattle; pine coffins were constantly passing in and out of those ponderous doors. Pauper death-carts might be seen every day lumbering up Centre street, on their road to Potter's Field. The man, innocent or guilty, who entered those walls, breathed his death warrant as he passed in.

This only continued for a season; it was not long before the tramp of human feet, and the weight of that ponderous mass of stone crushed the poisonous moisture from the earth, but the name which death had left still remained—a name deeply and solemnly significant of the place to all who deem moral evil and moral death as mournful as the physical suffering which had baptized it.

The main building, which fronts on Centre street, opens to a dusky and pillared vestibule, that leads to various rooms, occupied by the courts and officials connected with the prison. At the right, as you enter, is the police court, a spacious apartment, with deep casements. A raised platform, railed in from the people, upon which the magistrates sit, contains a desk or two, and beyond are several smaller rooms, used for private examinations.

In one of these rooms, the smallest and most remote, sat a mournful group, early one morning, before the magistrates had taken their seats upon the bench. One was an old man, thin, haggard and care-worn, but with a placid and even exalted cast of countenance, such as a stricken man wears when he has learned "to suffer and be strong." He sat near a round table covered with worn baize, upon which one elbow rested rather heavily, for he had tasted little food for several days; and the languor of habitual privation, joined to strong nervous reaction, after a scene of horror, impressed his person even more than his face. That, as I have said, was pale and worn, but tranquil and composed to a degree that startled those who looked upon him, for the old man was waiting there to be examined on a charge of murder, and men shuddered to see the calmness upon his features. It seemed to them nothing but hardened indifference, the composure of guilt that had ceased to feel its own enormity.

Close by this man sat two females, an old woman and a girl, not weeping, they had no tears left, but they sat with heavy, mournful eyes gazing upon the floor. Marks of terrible suffering were visible in their faces, and in the dull, hopeless apathy of their motionless silence. Now and then a low sigh rose and died upon the pale lips of the girl, but it was faint as that which exhales from a flower which has been trodden to death, and the poor girl was only conscious that the pain at her heart was a little sharper that instant than it had been.

The woman, pale, still, and grief-stricken in every feature and limb, did not even sigh. It seemed as if the breath must have frozen upon her cold lips, she seemed so utterly chilled, body and soul.

An officer of the police stood just within the room, not one of those burly, white-coated characters we find always in English novels, but a tall, slender and gentlemanly person, who regarded the group it had been his duty to arrest with a grave and compassionate glance. True, he searched the old man's face as those who have studied the human lineaments strive to read the secrets of a soul in their expression—but there was nothing rude either in his look or manner.

After awhile the officer remembered that his prisoners had not tasted food since the day previous, and, with a pang of self-reproach, he addressed them.

"You are worn out for want of food—I should have remembered this!" he said, approaching the table; "I will order some coffee."

The old man raised his head, and turned his grateful eyes upon the officer.

"Yes," he said, with a gentle smile, "they are hungry; a little coffee will do them good."

The young female looked up and softly waved her head; but the other continued motionless, she had heard nothing.

The officer whispered to a person outside the door, and then began to pace up and down the room like a sentinel, but treading very lightly, as if subdued by the silent grief over which he kept guard.

Directly the coffee was brought in, with bread and fragments of cold meat.

"Come now," said the officer, cheerfully, "take something to give you strength. The examination may be a long one, and I have seen powerful men sink under a first examination—take something to keep you up, or you will get nervous, and admit more than a wise man should."

"Yes," said the old man, meekly, "you are right, they will want strength—so shall I." He took one of the tin-cups which had been brought half full of coffee, and reached it toward the woman.

"Wife!" he said, bending toward her.

The poor woman started, and looked at him through her wild, heavy eyes.

"What is it, Wilcox? What is it you want of me?"

"You observe she is almost beside herself," said the old man addressing the officer, and his face grew troubled—"what can I do?"

"Oh! these things are very common. She must be roused!" answered the man, kindly. "Speak to her again."

The old man stooped over his wife, and laid his hand gently upon hers. She did not move. He grasped her thin fingers, and tears stood in his eyes; still she did not move. He stood a moment gazing in her face, the tears running down his cheeks. He hesitated, looked at the officer half timidly, and bending down, kissed the old woman on the forehead.

That kiss broke up the ice in her heart. She stood up and began to weep.

"You spoke to me, Wilcox—what was it you wanted? I am better now—quite well. What is it you wanted me to do?"

"He only wishes you to eat and drink something," said the officer, deeply moved.

"Eat and drink—have we got anything to eat and drink? That is always his way when we are short, urging us, and hungry himself."

"But there is enough for all," said the old man. "See, I too will eat, and Julia!"

"Why, if there is enough we will all eat, why not," said the poor woman, with a dim smile.

She took the coffee, tasted it, and looked around the room with vague curiosity.

"What is all this?—where are we now, Wilcox?" she said, in a low, frightened voice.

The old man kept his eyes bent on hers, they were full of trouble, and this stimulated her to question him again.

"Where are we? I remember walking, wading, it seemed to me, neck deep through a crowd, trying to keep up with you. Some one said they were taking us to prison; that I had done nothing, and they would not keep me. That you and Julia would stay, but I must go into the street, because a wife could not bear witness against her husband, but a grandchild could. Have I been crazy, or walking in my sleep, Wilcox?"

"No, wife, you are worn out—frightened; drink some more of the coffee, by and bye all will be clear to you."

The old woman obeyed him, and drank eagerly from the cup in her hand. Then she looked on her husband, on Julia, and the officer, as if striving to make out why they were all together in that strange place. All at once she set down the cup and drew a heavy breath.

"I remember," she said, mournfully—"I remember now that dead man, with his open eyes and white clenched teeth ; I know who he was—I knew it at first."

The officer drew a step nearer and listened, the spirit of his vocation was strong within him. There might be important evidence in her words, and for a moment the humane man was lost in the acute officer. The prisoner remarked this movement, and looked on the man with an expression of mild rebuke.

"Would you take advantage of her unsettled state, or of the words it might wring from me?" he said.

"No," answered the officer, stepping back, abashed. "No, I would not do anything of the kind, at least deliberately."

But this remonstrance had aroused distrust in the old woman, she drew close to her husband, and whispered to him—

"I cannot quite make it out, Wilcox. The people—the crowd said over and over again that they were taking us to prison. This is no prison! carpets on the floor, chairs, window blinds, all so pretty and snug, with us eating and drinking together. This is no prison, Wilcox, we have not had so nice a home these ten years."

"This is only a room in the prison, not the one they will give me by and bye!" answered the old man with a faint smile, "that will be smaller yet."

"You say *me!*" said the wife, holding tight to the hand that clasped hers. "Why do you not say that the room—let it be what it will—is large enough for us both, husband? I say you did not mean that it will not hold your wife too."

The old man turned away from those earnest eyes; he could not bear the look of mingled terror and entreaty that filled them.

"Remember, Wilcox, we have not spent one night apart in thirty years!"

"I know it," answered the old man with quivering lips.

"And now will you let me stay with you?"

"Ask him," said the old man, turning his face away, "ask him!"

She let go her hold of the prisoner's hand with great reluctance, and went up to the officer.

"You heard what he said, you must know what I want. We have lived together a great many years, more than your whole life. We have had trouble—great trouble, but always together. Tell me—can we stay together yet?"

"I do not know," said the man, deeply moved. "Your husband is charged with a crime that requires strict prison rules."

"I know, he is charged with murder! but you see how innocent he is," answered the wife, and all the holy faith, the pure, beautiful love born in her youth and strengthened in her age, kindled over those wrinkled features—"you see how innocent he is!"

The man checked a slight wave of the head, for he would not appear to doubt that old man's innocence, strong as the evidence was against him.

"You will not send me away!" said the old woman, still regarding him with great anxiety.

"I have no power—it is not for me to decide—such things have been done. In minor offences, I have known wives to remain in prison, but never in capital cases that I remember."

"But some one has the power. It is only for a little while—it cannot be for more than a week or two that they will keep him, you know."

"It may be—from my heart I hope so—but I can answer for nothing, I have no power."

"Who has the power?—what can we do?"

It was the young girl who spoke now. The entreaties of her grandmother—the tremulous voice of her grandsire, at length aroused her feelings from the icy stillness that had crept over them. The mist cleared away from her eyes, and though heavy with sleeplessness and grief, they began to kindle with aroused animation.

"No one at present, my poor girl—nothing can be done till after the examination."

Julia had drawn close to her grandmother, and grasped a fold of her faded dress with one hand. The officer could not turn his eyes from her face, so sad, so mournfully beautiful. He was about to utter some vague words of comfort, but while they were on his lips a door from the police-court opened, and a man looked through, saying in a careless, off-hand manner, "bring the old man in."

The court-room was crowded with witnesses ready to be examined, lawyers, eager for employment, and others actuated by curiosity alone, all crowded and jostled together outside the bar. As the prisoner entered, the throng grew denser, pouring in through the open door, and spreading out into the vestibule to the granite pillars, all pressing forward with strained eyes to obtain a view of one feeble old man.

They made a line for him to pass, crushing against each other with their heads thrown back, and staring in the old man's face as if he had been some wild animal, till his thin hand clutched the bar. There he stood as meek as a child, with all those bright, staring eyes bent upon him. A faint crimson flush broke through the wrinkles on his forehead; and his hand stirred upon the railing with a slight shiver, otherwise his gentle composure was unbroken.

The crowd closed up as he passed, but the two females clinging together, breathless and wild with fear, least they should be separated from him, pressed close upon his steps, forcing their way impetuously one moment, and looking helplessly around the next. Still resolutely following the prisoner, they won some little space at each step, not once losing sight of his grey head as it moved through the sea of faces, all turned, as they thought, menacingly upon him. At length they stood close behind the old man, and, unseen by the crowd, clung to his garments with their hands.

The judge bent forward in his leathern easy-chair, and looked in the prisoner's face, not harshly, not even with sternness.

12*

Had a lighter offence been charged upon the old man, his face might have borne either of these expressions, but the very magnitude of the charge under investigation gave dignity to the judge, and true dignity is always gentle.

He stooped forward, therefore, not smiling, but kindly in look and voice, informed the prisoner of his right, and cautioned him not to criminate himself ignorantly in any answer he might make to interrogations of the court.

The old man raised his eyes, thanked the judge in a low voice, and waited.

"Your name?"

"I am known in the city as Benjamin Warren, but it is not my real name."

"What is the real name then?"

"I would rather not answer."

The old man spoke mildly, but with great firmness. The judge bent his head. A dozen pens could be heard at the reporters' desk taking down the answer. A hush was on the crowd; every man leaned forward, breathless and listening. Those even in the vestibule kept still while the old man's reply ran among them in whispers.

"Did you know the man who was found dead in your house on the nineteenth of this month?"

"Yes, I knew the man well!"

"Where and when had you met before!"

"I do not wish to answer!"

"Did you see him on the evening of the eighteenth?"

"No!"

"Did evil feeling exist between you?"

The old man turned a shade paler, and his hand shook upon the railing; he hesitated as if at a loss for words which might convey an exact answer.

"I cannot say what his feelings were—but of my own I can speak, having asked this same question of my soul many times. William Leicester had wronged me and mine—but I forgave the wrong; I had no evil feeling against him."

"Were there not high words and angry defiance between you that morning?"

"He was angry—I was not; agitated, alarmed, I was—but not angry."

"Were you alone with him?"

"Yes!"

"How long?"

"Maybe ten minutes!"

"Once more," said the judge; "once more let me remind you that in another court these answers may be used to your prejudice. Now take time, you have no counsel, so take time for reflection before you reply. What business had Leicester with you?—what was the subject of conversation between you?"

The old man bent his forehead to the railing, and thus stood motionless without answering. His own honest sense told him that every question that he refused to answer gave rise to doubt, and kindled some new prejudice against him. His obvious course was silence, or a frank statement of the truth. He raised his head, and addressed the judge gently as he might have consulted with a friend.

"If I have a right to refuse answers to a part of what you ask me, may I not, by the same right, remain silent?"

"There is no law which forces you to answer where a reply will prejudice your cause."

"Will anything I can say help my cause?"

"No!"

"Then I will be silent. But I never lifted my hand against that man—never, so help me God!"

The judge felt this to be a wise conclusion, and a faint gleam of satisfaction came to his lips. The meek dignity of that old man, the beautiful pale face now and then peering out from behind his poverty-stricken garments—the feeble old woman crowding close to his side, all had aroused his sympathy. It was impossible to look on that group and believe any one of those feeble creatures guilty of the blood that had reddened their poverty-stricken hearth, and yet the evidence had been fearfully strong before the coroner's inquest.

Some commotion arose in the crowd after this. Men began to whisper opinions to each other—now and then a rude joke or laugh rose from the vestibule. People began to circulate in and out at the various doors, and during all this several witnesses were examined. These persons had seen a gentleman, well, nay, elegantly dressed, enter the miserable basement occupied by the prisoner and his family, very early on the morning of the nineteenth. One, a person who lived in the front basement, testified to high words, and a sound as if some one had stamped several times on the floor. Then he heard quick footsteps along the entry; saw the stranger an instant in the front area, and then heard him go back again. This excited considerable curiosity in the witness, who opened the door of his own room and looked out. He caught a glimpse of the stranger going, quickly, through the next door, and saw two females.

The old woman and girl now standing behind the prisoner were crouching in the back end of the entry, apparently much frightened, for both were pale; and the old woman wrung her hands while the girl wept bitterly. A little after, perhaps two minutes, this man heard a sound from the next room, as if of some heavy body falling; this was followed by a *hush* that made him shiver from head to foot. He went out and saw the two females clinging together, and creeping pale and terror-stricken up to the door, which the old woman tried to open, but could not, her hands shook so violently.

The witness himself turned the latch and looked in, leaning over the females, who, uttering a low cry, stood motionless, blocking up the entrance. He saw the stranger lying upon the floor, stretched back in the agony of a fierce death pang; his teeth were clenched; his eyes wide open; the chin protruded upward; and both hands were groping and clutching at the bare boards.

While the witness looked on, the limbs, half gathered up and strained against the floor, gave way, and settled down like ridges of withered grass. The room was badly lighted, but it seemed to the witness that there was some faint motion, after this a shudder, or it might be a fold of the dead man's clothes settling around him, but except this all signs of life went out from the body.

Then the witness had time to see the other objects in the room. The first thing that his eyes fell upon was the face of old Mr. Warren, the palest, the most deathly face he ever saw on a living man; he was stooping over the corpse, grasping what seemed a handful of snow, stained through and through with blood which he pressed down upon the dead man's side.

The witness grew wild with the terror of this scene. He pushed the two females forward and went in. The prisoner looked up, still pressing his hand upon the dead man; his lips moved, and he tried to speak, but could not. On stooping down, the witness saw that the stained mass clenched in the old man's fingers was one side of a white silk vest, clutched up with masses of fine linen, which the dead man had worn. He also saw a knife lying on the floor wet to the haft. After a minute or so, the prisoner spoke, apparently feeling the body grow stiff under his hand; he turned his head with a piteous look, and whispered—

"What can we do?"

The witness stated that his answer was "Nothing—the man is dead!"

Then the old man got up, and went to a bed huddled on the floor in one corner of the room, where his wife and grand-daughter had dropped, when the witness pushed them with unconscious violence from the threshold. He said something in a low voice to the woman, and she answered—

"Oh, Wilcox, tell me that you did not do it!"

The prisoner looked at her—at first he seemed amazed as if some horrid thought had just struck him, then he looked grieved, wounded to the heart. The expression that came upon his face was enough to make one cry, but his voice, when he spoke, was even worse than the look; it seemed choked up with tears, that he could not shed.

"My wife!" he said nothing more, but that was enough to make the old woman cover her face with both hands and sob like a child. Julia, his grandchild, who had been sitting white and still as death till then, lifted her eyes to the old man's face, and you could see them deepen with sorrowful astonishment, as if she too had been suddenly wounded. The look of horror died on her features, leaving them full of tenderness. She arose with the look of an angel, and clasping her hands over the old man's arm, as he stood gazing mournfully upon his wife, pressed her head against his side.

"Grandfather, she did not think it. It was the terror that spoke, not her, not my grandmother!"

The old man would have laid his hand upon her head, but it was crimson and wet. He saw this, and dropped it again.

The dim light, the pale faces, the man stark and dead upon the floor, made the scene too painful even for a strong man. The witness went out and aroused the neighborhood. He did not go back; more courageous men would have shrunk from the scene as he did.

I have given this man's evidence, not in his own words. He was a German, and spoke rude English; but the scene he described was only the more graphic for that. It impressed the judges and the crowd; it gratified that intense love of the horrible that is becoming a passion in the masses, and yet softened it with touches of rude pathos, that also gratified the populace. Here and there you saw a wet eye in the crowd. Men who were strangers to each other, exchanged whispered wishes that the prisoner might be found innocent. The old woman and her grand-daughter became objects of unceasing curiosity. Men pressed forward to get a sight at them. The reporters paused to study their features, and to take an inventory of their poverty-stricken garments.

Other witnesses were called, all testifying to like facts, that served to fasten the appearances of guilt more closely upon that fallen old man. When all had been examined but the grand-daughter, the excitement became intense; the crowd pressed closer to th bar; those in the vestibule rushed in, filling every corner of the room.

The poor girl moved when her name was pronounced, and with difficulty mounted the step which lifted her white face to a level with the judge. The little hands grasped the railing till every drop of blood was driven from the strained fingers; but for this she must have fallen to the earth, for there was no strength in her limbs, no strength at her heart, save that which one fixed solemn thought gave. There was something deeper than the pallor of fear in those beautiful features—something more sublime than sorrow in the clear violet eyes which she lifted to the magistrate. He saw her lips move, and bent forward to catch the sound of words that she seemed to be uttering,—

"I cannot answer any questions; don't ask me, sir, please don't!"

He caught these words. He saw the look of meek courage that spoke even more forcibly than the tremulous lips. No one saw the look, or heard the voice, but himself, not even the prisoner; for age had somewhat dulled his ear. The face, the look, the gentle bearing of this poor girl, filled the judge with compassion. It is a horrible thing for any law to force evidence from one loving heart that may cast another into the grave. The magistrate had never felt the cruelty so much before. The questions that he should have propounded sunk back upon his heart. It seemed like torturing a lamb with all the flock looking on.

Still, the magistrates of our courts learn hard lessons even of juvenile depravity; not to be suspicious would, in them, be a living miracle. This girl might be prompted by advice, and thus artfully acting as the tool of some lawyer. You would not look in her eyes and believe it, but soft eyes sometimes brood over falsehood that would make you tremble. No one is better aware of this than the acute magistrate; still there is something in pure simplicity that convinces the heart long before the judgment has power to act.

"Who told you not to answer my questions?" he said, in a low voice.

"No one!"

"Then why refuse?"

"Because my grandfather never killed the man, but what I should say, might make it seem as if he did."

"But do you know that is contempt of court—a punishable offence."

"I did not know it!"

"That I have power to make you answer?"

A faint beautiful smile flitted across her face. You might fancy a youthful martyr smiling thus when threatened with death by fire. It disturbed in no degree the humility of her demeanor, but that one gleam of the strength within her satisfied the magistrate.

Not even the reporters had been able to catch a word of the conversation. His dignity was in no way committed. He resolved to waive the cruel power, which would have wrung accusation from that helpless creature unnecessarily; for the evidence that had gone before was quite sufficient to justify a commitment.

"We shall not require the evidence of this young girl," he said, addressing a fellow-magistrate, who had been writing quietly during the proceedings.

"No," answered the magistrate, without checking his pen or raising his head, "what is the use? The story of that German was enough. I should have committed him after that. The poor girl is frightened to death. Let her go!"

"But in the other court, there she will be wanted!"

"True, she must be kept safe. Anybody forthcoming with the bonds?"

"I fear not. It seems hard to keep the poor thing in prison!"

"Like caging a blackbird!" answered the man, racing over the paper with his gold-mounted pen. "Hard, but necessary; bad laws must be kept the same as good ones, my dear fellow! Disgrace to civilization, and all that, but the majesty of the law must be maintained, even though it does shut up nice little girls with the offscourings of the earth."

"It goes against my heart ?" answered the sitting magistrate with a sigh. "It seems like casting newly fallen snow before a herd of wild animals. I never hated to sign my name so much!"

"Must be done though. You have stretched a point to save her. Just now, the reporters were eyeing you. Another step of leniency, and down comes the press!"

"I shall act rightly according to my own judgment, notwithstanding the press."

"A beautiful sentiment, only don't let those chaps hear it. Would not appreciate the thing at all!"

The sitting magistrate spoke the truth. Never in his life had he signed papers of commitment so reluctantly; but they were made out at length, and handed to the officer. The old man was conducted from the bar one way, and a strange officer took Julia by the hand, forcing her through the crowd in another direction. At first she supposed that they were going with her grandfather. When they were separated in the crowd, she began to struggle; a faint wail broke from her lips, and the officer was compelled to cast his arm around her waist, thus half carrying her through the crowd.

The woman had followed her husband and grandchild mechanically, but when they were separated, the cry that broke from Julia's lips made her turn and rush back; the crowd closed in around her; she cast one wild look after the prisoner, another toward the spot whence the wail came. They both were lost through a door in the dark vistas of the prison. She saw an arm flung wildly up as if beckoning her, and rushed forward. blindly struggling against the crowd. In the press of people, she was hurried forth into the vestibule, and there leaning, in dreary helplessness, against one of the massy stone pillars, she stood looking vaguely around for her husband and child. It was a heart-rending sight, but every day those ponderous walls witness scenes equally mournful.

CHAPTER XXII

THE IMPRISONED WITNESS.

When souls come freshly from their God,
They breathe the very air of Heaven!
To children on this earthly sod,
Angelic trusts are sometimes given.

And like bright spirits wandering through
The haunted depths of tears and sin,
Their gentle words drop down like dew,
Where wisdom fails, they charm and win.

It is strange—nay, it is horrible—that so much of barbarism still lingers in the laws and customs of a free land. Without crime or offence of any kind, a person may be taken, here in the city of New York, and confined for months among the most hideous malefactors; his self-respect broken down; his associations brutalized; and all, that the law may be fulfilled. What must that law be which requires oppression, that it may render justice?

In New York, the poor witness—a man who has the misfortune to know anything of a crime before the courts, is himself exactly in the place of a criminal. Like the malefactor, he must give bonds for his prompt appearance on the day of trial, or lacking the influence to obtain these, must himself share the prison of the very felon his evidence will condemn. Strangers thus—sea-faring men, and persons destitute of friends—are often imprisoned for months among the very dregs of humanity; innocent, and yet suffering the severest penalties of guilt.

This injustice, so glaring that a savage would blush to acknowledge it, exists almost unnoticed in a city overrun with benevolent societies, crowded with churches, and inundated with sympathies for the wronged of every nation or city on earth. If ostentatious charity would, for a time, give way to simple justice, New York like all the American cities we know of, would obtain for itself more respect abroad and more real prosperity at home.

It was under this law that Julia Warren, a young creature,

just bursting into the first bloom of girlhood, pure, sensitive, and guileless as humanity can be, was dragged like a thief into the city prison. She had known the deepest degradation of poverty, and that is always so closely crowded against crime in cities, that it seems almost impossible to keep the dew upon an innocent nature. But Julia had been guarded in her poverty by principle so firm, by love so holy, that neither the close neighborhood of sin nor the gripe of absolute want had power to stain the sweet bloom of a nature that seemed to fling off evil impressions as the swan casts off waterdrops from its snowy bosom, though its whole form is bathed in them.

This young creature, in all her gentle innocence, without crime, without even the suspicion of a fault, was now the inmate of a prison, the associate of felons, hand-in-hand with guilt of a kind and degree that had never entered even her imagination.

At first, when the officer separated the poor girl from her grandparents, she struggled wildly, shrieked for help, and at last fell to imploring the man, with eyes so wild and eloquence so startling, that he paused in one of the dark corridors leading from the court, and strove to soothe her, supposing that she was terrified by the gloom of the place.

"No, no!" she answered. "It is not that. I did not see that it was dark. I did not look at anything. My grandfather—poor grandma! Let me go with them. I'm not afraid. I don't care for being in prison, only let me stay where they are!"

"Your grandmother is not here!"

"Not here—not here!" answered the poor creature, wildly and aghast. "Then what has become of her? Let me go—let me go, I say. She will die!"

Julia unlocked the hands that she had clasped, flung back the hair from her face, and fled down the corridor so swiftly, that the keeper, taken by surprise, was left far behind. An officer, coming in from the court, seized her by the arm as she was passing him.

"Not so fast, canary bird; not quite so fast. It takes swifter wings than yours to get out of this cage."

Julia looked at the man, breathless with affright.

"What do you hold me for? Why can't I go?" she gasped forth.

"Because you are a prisoner, little one!"

"But I have done nothing!"

"Nobody ever does anything that comes here," said this man, with a contemptuous smile. "Never were so many innocent people crowded together."

As he spoke, the man tightened his hold on her arm, and moved forward, forcing her along with him.

The poor creature winced under the pain of his grasp.

"You hurt my arm," she said, in a low voice.

"Do I?" replied the man, affected by the despondency of her tone. "I did not mean to do that; but it would be difficult to touch a little, delicate thing like you without leaving a mark. Come, don't cry. I did not hurt you on purpose."

"I know it. It is not that," answered the girl, lifting her eyes, from which the big tears were dropping like rain.

"Well, well, go quietly to the women's department. They will not keep you long, unless you have been stealing, or something of that sort."

"Stealing!" faltered the girl, "stealing!" The color flashed into her pale, wet cheeks; a faint, scornful smile quivered over her lips.

The officer from whom she had fled now came up. "Come," he said, with a shade of impatience, "I cannot be kept waiting in this way."

"I am ready!" answered the poor girl, in a voice of utter despondency, while her head dropped upon her bosom. "If I am a prisoner, take me away. But what—what have I done?"

"Never mind; settle that with the court. I am in a hurry, so come along!"

Julia neither expostulated nor attempted to resist.

She gave her hand to the officer, who led her quickly forward. They threaded the dim, vault-like passage, and paused before a grated door, through which the trembling girl could see dark, squalid figures moving about in the dusky twilight that filled the prison. Two or three faces, haggard and fiend like, were pressed up against the bars. One was that of a negro woman, scarred with many a street brawl, whose inflamed eyes glared wickedly upon the innocent creature whom the laws had sent to be her companion.

"Get back—back with you!" commanded the officer, dashing his keys against the grating. "Your hideous faces frighten the poor thing!"

The faces flitted away, grinning defiance, and sending back a burst of hoarse laughter that made Julia shiver from head to foot. She drew close to the man, clinging to his garments, while he turned the heavy lock and thrust the door half open. The dim vista of a hall, with cells yawning on one side, and filled with gloomy light, through which wild, impish figures wandered restlessly to and fro, or sat motionless against the walls, met Julia's gaze. She shrank back, clinging desperately to her conductor—

"Oh, mercy, mercy! Not here—not here!" she cried, pallid and shivering.

The man raised her firmly in his arms, and passing through the door, set her down. She heard the clank of keys; the shooting of a heavy bolt. She saw the shadow of this, her last friend, fall across the grating; and then, in dreary desolation, she sat down upon a wooden bench, and leaning her cold cheek against the wall, closed her eyes. The tears pressed through those long, dark eyelashes, and rolled, one by one, in heavy drops, over her face. Her arms hung helplessly down; all the energies of her young life seemed utterly prostrated.

The hall was full of women of all ages, and bearing every stamp that vice or sorrow impresses on the countenance. Some, old and hardened in evil, stood aloof looking upon the heart-stricken girl with their stony, pitiless eyes; others, younger, more reckless and fierce in their sympathies, gathered around in a crowd, commenting upon her grief, some mockingly, others with a touch of feeling. Black and white, all huddled around the bench she occupied, pouring their hot breath out, till she sickened and grew faint, as if the boughs of a Upas tree were drooping over her.

"She's sick—she's fainting away!" cried one of the women "Bring some water!"

"No," cried another. "If we had a drop of brandy now But water, bah!"

"It's the horrors—see how she trembles," exclaimed a third, with a chuckle and a toss of the head.

"No such thing. She's too young—too handsome!"

"Oh, get away! Don't I know the symptoms?" interrupted the first speaker, with a coarse laugh. "Ain't I young—ain't I handsome? Who says no to that? And yet haven't you heard me yell—haven't you heard me rave with the horrors?"

"That was because the doctor prescribes brandy," interposed a sly-looking mulatto woman, folding her arms and turning her head saucily on one side. "When that medicine comes, you are still enough."

This retort was followed by a general laugh, in which the object joined, till the tears rolled down her cheeks.

In the midst of this coarse glee, Julia had fallen like a withered flower, upon the bench. That moment, the huge negress, who had so terrified the poor creature at the grating, plunged out from a cell in the upper end of the hall, and came toward the group with a tin cup full of water in her hand.

Had a fiend come forth on an errand of mercy, it would not have seemed more out of place than that hideous creature under the influence of a kind impulse. She came down the hall as rapidly as her naked feet, hampered by an old pair of slip-shod shoes, could move. The dress hung in rents and festoons of dirty and faded calico around her gaunt limbs, trailing the stone floor on one side, and lifted high above her clumsy ankles on the other.

The women scattered as she approached, giving her a full view of the fainting girl.

"So you've done it among you—smothered her. How dare you? Didn't you see that I took a fancy to her, before she came in? Let her alone. I want a pet, and she's mine."

"Yours!" Why, it was your face that frightened her to death. There hasn't been a bit of color in her lips since she saw you," answered the woman that had so eagerly recommended brandy, and who kept her place in spite of the formidable negress. "Here, give me the water, and get out of my sight."

The negress pushed this woman roughly aside, and kneeling down by the senseless girl, bathed her forehead with the water. Julia did not stir. Her face continued deathly white; a faint violet tinge lay upon her lips and around her eyes; her little hands fell down to the stone floor; her feet dropped heavily from the bench. This position, more than the still face even, was fearfully like death.

"Call a keeper," cried half a dozen voices, "she is scared to death!"

"The doctor!" urged as many more voices. "It will take a doctor to bring her out of that fit!"

"We won't have a doctor," exclaimed the old negress, stoutly. "He'd call it tremens, and give her brandy or laudanum. I tell you, she isn't one of that sort! Don't believe a drop of the ardent ever touched her lips!"

Again a coarse laugh broke up from among the prisoners.

The negress dashed a handful of water across the poor face over which that laughter floated like the orgies of fiends around a death couch. She rose to one knee, and turned her fierce eyes upon the scoffers.

I have never stained a page in my life with profane language, even when describing a profane person; never have placed the name of God irreverently into the lips of an ideal character. Sooner would I feel an oath burning upon my own soul, than register one where it might familiarize itself to a thousand souls, surprised into its use by their confidence in the author. Even here, where profanity is the common language of the place, I will risk a feebler description in my own language, rather than for one instant break through the rule of a life. Yet amid language and scenes which I could not force this pen to write, and creatures, most of them, brutalized by vice to a degree that I shrink from describing, this young guileless creature was plunged by the laws of an enlightened people. When she opened her eyes, that scarred, black face, less repulsive from a touch of kindly feeling, but hideous still, was the first object that greeted them.

The woman, as I have said, had risen to one knee. The holy name of God trembled on her coarse lips, prefacing a torrent of abusive expostulation that broke from them in the rudest and most repulsive language.

"You needn't laugh, don't I know better—fifty times better than any of you? Haven't I been here—this is the fifteenth time? Don't I go to my country-seat on Blackwell's Island every summer of my life? How many times have you been there, the best of you, I should like to ask? Twice, three times. Bah! what should you know of life? Stand out of the way. She's beginning to sob. You shan't stifle her again, I promise you It was the water did it. Which of you could be got out of a fit with water—tell me that? Here, just come one of you and feel her breath, while the tears are in it—sweet as a rose, moist as dew. I tell you, she never tasted anything stronger than bread and milk in her life!"

The woman clenched this truth with an imprecation on herself which made the young girl start up and look wildly around, as if she believed herself encompassed by a band of demons.

"What is the matter? Are you afraid?" said the white prisoner, that had formerly spoken, bending over her.

"Get out of the way," said the negress, with another oath. "It's my pet, I tell you."

The terrible creature, whose very kindness was brutal, reached forth her arm and attempted to draw Julia to her side, but the poor girl recoiled, shuddering from the touch, and fell upon her knees, covering her ears with both hands.

"Are you afraid of *me*? Is that it?" shouted the negress, almost touching the strained fingers with her mouth.

"Yes, yes!" broke from her tremulous lips, and Julia kept her eyes upon the woman in a wild stare. "I am afraid."

"This is gratitude," said the woman, fiercely. "I brought her to, and she looks at me as if I was a mad dog."

Julia cowered under the fiery glance with which these words were accompanied. This only exasperated her hideous friend, and with an angry grip of the teeth, she seized one little hand, forcing it away from the ear, that was on the instant filled with a fresh torrent of curses.

"Oh, don't! Pray, pray. It is dreadful to swear so!"

"Swear! Why, I didn't swear—not a word of it. Have been talking milk and water all the time just for your sake. Leave it all to these ladies, if I haven't!" said the woman, evidently impressed with the truth of her assertion, and appealing, with an air of simple confidence, to her fellow-prisoners; for profanity had become with her a fixed habit, and she was really unconscious of it.

A laugh of derision answered this singular appeal, and a dozen voices gave mocking assurance that there had been a mistake about the matter, saying,

"Oh, no! old Mag never swore in her life."

Tortured by the wild tumult, and driven to the very confines of insanity, Julia could scarcely forbear screaming for help. She started up, avoiding the negress with a desperate spring sidewise, and staggered toward the grated door. It seemed to her impossible to draw a deep breath, in the midst of those wretched beings!

"Mamma, mamma!" said a soft, sweet voice, from one of the cells, and as Julia turned her face, she saw through the narrow iron door-way the head of a child, bending eagerly forward and radiant with joyous surprise.

Julia paused, held forth both her trembling hands, and entered the cell, smiling through her tears as if an angel had called.

The child arose from the floor, for it had been upon its hands and knees, and putting back its golden hair, that broke into waves and curls in spite of neglect, with two soiled and dimpled hands, it gazed upon the intruder in speechless disappointment. Julia saw this, and her heart sank again.

"It was not me you wanted," she said, laying her hand tremblingly on the child's shoulder. "You are sorry that I came?"

"Yes," answered the child, and his soft, brown eyes filled with tears. "I thought it was mamma. It was dark, and I could not see, but it seemed as if you were mamma."

Julia stooped down and kissed the child. In that dim light, it was difficult to say which of those beautiful faces seemed the most angelic.

"But I love you. I am glad to see you," she said, in a voice that made the little boy smile through his tears. He fixed his eyes upon her in a long, earnest gaze, and then nestling close to her side, murmured, "And I love you!"

There was a narrow bed in the cell, and Julia sat down upon it, lifting the child to her knee. In return, she felt a little arm steal around her neck and a warm cheek laid against her own. The innocent nature of the child blended with that of the maiden, as blossoms in a strange atmosphere may be supposed to lean toward each other.

"Do they shut up children in this wicked place? How came you here, darling?"

"I don't know!" answered the child, shaking its beautiful head.

"But did you come alone?"

"Oh, no! *She* came with me."

"Who—your mamma?" questioned Julia, so deeply interested in the child, that for the moment, her own grief was forgotten.

"No, not her. They call her my mamma, but she isn't. Come here, softly, and I will let you see."

He drew Julia to the entrance, and pointed with his finger toward a female, who sat cowering by a stove a little distance up the passage. There was something so picturesque in the bold, Roman outlines of this woman's face, that it riveted Julia's attention. The large head was covered with masses of dull, black hair, gathered up in a loose coil behind, and falling down the cheeks in dishevelled waves. The nose, rising in a haughty and not ungraceful curve ; the massive forehead and heavy chin, with a large mouth coral red and full of sensual expression, gave to that head, bending downward with its side-face toward the light, the interest and effect of some old picture, which, without real beauty, haunts the memory like an unforgotten sin.

This woman had evidently received some injury on the forehead, for a scarlet silk handkerchief was knotted across it, the ends mingling behind with the neglected braids of her hair, which, but for it, must have fallen in coils over her neck and shoulders.

Her dress, of blue barége, had once been elegant, if not rich ; but in that place, faded and soiled, with the flounces half torn away, and the rents gathered rudely up with pins that she had found upon the stone-floor of her prison, it had a look of peculiar desolation. Every fold bespoke that flash poverty which profligacy makes hideous.

A book with yellow covers, soiled and torn, lay open upon this woman's lap ; and with her large, full arms loosely folded on her bosom, she bent over it with a look of gloating interest, that betrayed all the intensity of her evil nature. You could see her black eyes kindle beneath their inky lashes, as she impatiently dashed over a leaf, or was molested in any way by the noise around.

You could not look upon this woman for an instant without feeling the influence which a strong character, even in repose, fixes upon the mind. Powerful intellect and strong passions—the one utterly untrained, the other curbless and fierce—broke through every curve of her sensual person, and every line of her face.

As Julia stood in the cell-door, with one arm around the child, this woman chanced to look up, and caught those beautiful eyes fixed so steadily upon her. She returned the glance with a hard, impudent stare, which filled the young creature with alarm, while it served to fascinate her gaze.

The woman seemed enraged that her glance had not made the stranger cower at once. Crushing her book in one hand, she arose and came forward, sweeping her way through the prisoners with that sort of undulating swagger into which vice changes what was originally grace. She came up to Julia with an oath upon her lips, demanding why she had been staring at her so?

Julia did not answer, but shrunk close to the child, who cringed against her, evidently terrified by the menacing attitude and fierce looks that his temerity had provoked.

"Come here, you little wretch," exclaimed the termagant, securing him by the arm, and jerking him fiercely through the cell-door. "How dare you speak to anybody here without leave? Come along, or I'll break every bone in your body."

With a swing of the arm, that sent the child whirling forward in fierce leaps, she landed him at her old seat, and sitting down, crowded the beautiful creature between her and the hot stove, setting one foot, bursting through a white slipper of torn and dirty satin, heavily in his lap to hold him quiet, while she went on with her French novel.

The poor little fellow bent his head, dropped his pretty hands on the floor, each side of him, and sat motionless and meek, like some heavenly cherub crushed beneath the foot of a demon. Once he struggled a little, and made an effort to creep back, for the heat pouring from the huge mass of iron which stood close before him, had become insupportable.

The woman, without lifting her eyes from the book, put her hand down upon his shoulder with a fierce imprecation, and ordered him to be quiet. The poor infant dared not move again, though his face, his neck, and his little arms became scarlet with the heat, and perspiration stood upon his forehead like rain, saturating his golden hair, and even his garments He lifted his soft eyes, full of terror and of entreaty, to the hard face above him, but it was gloating over one of those foul passages with which Eugene Sue has cursed the world, and the innocent creature shrank from the expression as he had cowered from the heat. Tears now crowded into his eyes, and he turned them, with a look of helpless misery, upon the young girl who stood regarding him, with looks of unutterable pity.

Julia Warren could not withstand this look. She was no longer timid; the prison was forgotten now; her very soul went forth in compassion for the one being more helpless than herself, whom she might have the power to protect. She went softly up to the woman, and touched her upon the arm. Compassion gave the young creature that exquisite tact which makes generous impulses so beautiful.

"Please, madam, let the child stay with me a little longer; I will keep him very quiet while you read!"

The meek demeanor, the soft, sweet tone in which this was uttered, fell upon the sense like a handful of freshly gathered violets. The woman had loved pure things once, and this voice started her heart as if a gush of perfumed air had swept through it She looked up suddenly, and fixing her large, bold eyes upon the girl, seemed wondering alike at her loveliness and courage in thus addressing her.

Julia endured the gaze with gentle forbearance, but she could not keep her eyes from wandering toward the child, who, seizing her dress with one hand, was shrouding his face in the folds.

"How came you here?" demanded the woman, rudely.

"I don't know," was the meek answer.

"Don't know, bah! What have you done?"

'Nothing!"

Nothing!" repeated the woman, with a sickening sneer; "so you're not a chicken after all; know the ropes, ha! nothing! I never give that answer—despise it—always have the courage to own what I have the courage to act; it's original; I like it.

Take my advice, girl, own the truth and shame the—the old gentleman. He's an excellent friend of mine, no doubt, but I love to put the old fellow out of countenance with the truth now and then. The rest of them never do it ; not one of them ever committed a crime in their lives—unfortunate, nothing more."

"Will you let me take up the child?" said Julia, with a pleading smile; "see, the heat is killing him!"

The woman glanced sharply at the little creature, half moved her foot, and then pressed it down again, and drew back a little, dragging the child with her; but she resisted the effort which Julia made to release him.

"Not now, the child's mine; I'll make him as wicked as I like myself, but he shan't run wild among the prisoners!"

"Are you really his mother?" said Julia.

"Yes, I am really his mother!" was the mocking reply; "what have you against it?"

"Nothing, nothing—only I should think you would be afraid to have him here!"

"And your mother—she isn't afraid to have you here, I suppose."

"I have no mother!" said Julia, in a tone of sadness, that made itself felt even upon the bad nature of her listener.

"No mother, well don't mourn for that," said the woman, with a touch of passionate feeling. "Thank God for it, if you believe in a God; she won't follow you here with her white, miserable face; she won't starve to keep you from sin—or die—die by inches, I tell you, because all is of no use. You won't see her crowded into a pine coffin, and tumbled into Potter's Field, and feel—feel in the very core of your heart that you have sent her there. Thank God—thank God, I say, miserable girl, that you have no mother!"

The woman had risen as she spoke, her imposing features, her whole form quivering with passion. Tears crowded into her lurid eyes, giving them fire, depth, and expression. She ceased speaking, fell upon the seat again, and, covering her face with the soiled novel, sobbed aloud.

The child, released from the bondage of her foot, stood up, trembling beneath the storm of her words; but when she fell down and began to weep, his lips grew tremulous, his little chest began to heave, and climbing up the stool upon which his mother crouched, he leaned over and kissed her temple.

This angel kiss fell upon her forehead like a drop of dew; she dashed the novel from her face, and flung her arm over the child.

"Look!" she cried, with a fierce sob, turning her dusky and tear-stained face upon the young girl. "He has got a mother; look on her, and then dare to mourn because you have none!"

"But I have a grandfather and grandmother that love me as if I were their own child," said Julia, deeply moved by the fierce anguish thus revealed to her.

"And where are they?"

"My grandfather is here."

"Here! How came it about? What is he charged with?"

Julia's lips grew pale at the word "murder!" Even the woman seemed appalled by the mention of a crime so much more serious than she had expected.

"But you—they do not charge you with murder?" she questioned, in a subdued voice.

"No!" said Julia, innocently. "They charge me with being a witness!"

Once more a torrent of fiery imprecations burst from the lips of that miserable woman—imprecations against a law hideous almost as her own sins. Julia recoiled, aghast, beneath this profane violence. The child dropped down from the stool, and crept to her side, weeping. The woman saw this, and checked herself.

"Then you have really done nothing?"

Julia shook her head and smiled sadly.

"A beautiful country—beautiful laws, that send an innocent child to take lessons in life here, and from women like us. Oh, my dear, it's a great pity you haven't been in the Penitentiary half a dozen times; lots of benevolent people would be ready to reform you at any expense then."

Julia smiled dimly. She did not quite understand what the woman was saying.

"It makes my heart burn to see you here," continued the woman, vehemently; "it's a sin—a wicked shame; but I'll take care of you. There's some good left in me yet. Just get acquainted with that little wretch, and no one else; stay in your cell; the keeper won't let them crowd in upon you. The matron will be here by-and-bye. She'll be a mother to you; she's a Christian—a thorough, cheerful, hard-working Christian. I believe in these things, though I would not own it to every one. Kind, because she can't help it without going against her own nature. I like that woman—there isn't a creature here wicked enough not to like her."

"When shall I see her?" questioned Julia, brightening beneath this first gleam of hope.

"To-morrow morning—perhaps before—I don't know exactly. She's in and out whenever there is good to be done. But come, go into my cell—they haven't given you one yet, I suppose—the whole gang of them are coming this way again."

Julia looked up and saw a crowd of women coming up from the grated door, where they had been drawn by some noise in the outer passage. Terrified by the dread of meeting that horrible old negress again, she grasped the little hand that still held to her garments, and absolutely fled after the woman, who entered the cell where she had first seen the child.

The prisoners were amused by her evident terror, and gathered around the entrance; but as Julia sat down upon the bed, pale and panting with affright, her self-constituted guardian started forward and dashed the iron door in their faces, with a clang that sounded from one hollow corridor to another, like the sudden clang of a bell.

"There," she said, with a smile that for a moment swept away the fierce expression from her face, "I'd like to see one of them bold enough to come within arm's length of that. My home's my castle, if it is in a prison. I've been here often enough to know my rights. If the laws won't keep you free from that gang, I will!"

It was wonderful the influence that gentle girl had won over the depraved being who protected her thus. After she entered the cell, no rude or profane word passed the woman's lips. She seemed to have shut out half that was wicked in her own nature when she dashed the iron door against her fellow-prisoners. Her large, black eyes brightened with a sort of rude pleasure as she saw her child creep into Julia's lap, and lay his head on her bosom.

"How naturally you take to one another," she said, letting down the black masses of her hair, and beginning to disentangle the braids with her fingers, as if the pure eyes of her guest had reproached their untidy state. "When I was a little girl, we had plenty of wild roses in a swamp near the house. It is strange, I have not thought of them in ten years; but when I saw you and the child sitting there together, it seemed as if I could reach out my hands and fill them."

Julia did not answer; her eyes were bent on the child, who had ceased to cry, and lay quietly in her arms—so quietly that she could detect a drowsy mist stealing over his eyes. The woman went on threading out her long hair in silence. After awhile Julia, who had been watching the soft, brown eyes of the child as the white lids dropped over them gradually like the closing petals of a flower, looked up with a smile, so pure, so bright, that the woman unconsciously smiled also.

"He is sound asleep," said the young girl, putting back the moist curls from his forehead. "See what a smile, I have been watching it deepen on his face since his eyes began to close."

The woman put back her hair with both hands, and turned her eyes with a sort of stern mournfulness upon the sleeping boy.

"He never goes to sleep on my bosom like that," she said, at last, with a bitter smile, and more bitter tone. "How could he? My heart beats sometimes loud enough to scare myself; I wonder if wild flowers really do blossom over Mount Etna?

If they do, why should not my own child rest over my own heart?"

"My grandfather has told me that flowers *do* grow around volcanoes," said Julia, with a soft smile, "but it is because the fire never reaches them; if scorched once they would perish!"

"And my heart scorches everything near it. Is that what you mean?" said the woman, with a degree of mildness that was peculiarly impressive in a voice usually so stern and loud.

"When you were angry to-day, he trembled; when you wept he kissed you," answered the gentle girl, looking mildly into the dark face of her companion, whose fierce nature yielded both respect and attention to the moral courage that spoke from those young lips.

"Well, what if I do frighten him? We love that best which we fear most. It is human nature; at any rate it was my nature, and should be my child's," said the woman, striving to cast off the influence of which she was becoming ashamed.

"And did you ever fear any one?"

"Did I ever *love* any one?" was the answer, given in a voice so deep, so earnest, that it seemed to ring up from the very bottom of a heart where it had been buried for years.

"I hope so, I trust so—do you not love your child?"

The woman dashed back the entire weight of her hair with an impetuous sweep of one hand; then, with the whole Roman contour of her face exposed, she turned a keen look upon the young face lifted so innocently to hers. Long and searching was that look. The shadows of terrible thoughts swept over that face. Some words, it might be of passion, it might be of prayer—for bitterness, grief and repentance, all were blended in that look—trembled unuttered on her lips. Then she suddenly flung up her arms and falling across the bed, cried out in bitter anguish—"Oh, my God!—my God! can I never again be like her?"

CHAPTER XXIII.

THE THREE OLD WOMEN.

Why have we three gathered here,
  With aching hearts and aching brain?
Death must fill another bier,
  Before we three shall meet again.

"How do you do, madam? Anything in my way? Capital beets these—the most delicious spinach. Celery, bright and crisp enough to suit an alderman—sold five bunches for the supper-room at the City Hall, not half an hour since. Everything on the stand fresh as spring water, sweet as a rose. Two bunches of the celery, yes ma'am: anything else? not a small measure of the potatoes? Luscious things, always come out of the saucepan bursting their jackets; only one measure? Very well—thank you! Cranberries, certainly!"

Thus extolling her merchandise, busy as a bee, and radiant with good humor, stood our old huckster woman, by her vegetable stand in Fulton Market, on the morning after Julia Warren was cast into prison. No customer left her stand without adding something to the weight of his or her market-basket. There was something so hearty and cheerful in her appearance, that people paused spite of themselves, to examine her nicely arranged merchandise; and though all the adjoining stalls were deserted, Mrs. Gray was sure to have her hands full every morning of the week.

On this particular day she had been busy as a mother bird, serving customers, making change, and arranging her stall, now and then pausing to bandy a good-humored jest with her neighbors, or toss a handful of vegetables into some beggar's basket. The words with which our chapter opens, were addressed to a quiet old lady in deep mourning, who carried a small willow basket on her arm, and appeared to be selecting a few dainty trifles from various stalls as she passed along.

"Cranberries! Oh, yes, the finest you have seen this year, plump as June cherries; see, madam, judge for yourself."

The good woman took up a quantity of the berries as she spoke, and began pouring them from one plump hand to the other, smiling blandly now at the fruit, now at her quiet customer.

"Yes, they are very fine," said the old lady; "do up a small measure neatly, they are for a sick person."

Mrs. Gray looked over her stand for some paper, but her supply was exhausted. Nothing presented itself but the Morning Express, with which she usually occupied any little time that might be hers, between the coming and departure of her customers. This morning she had been too busy even for a glance at its columns; but as her neighbor seemed to be out of wrapping paper also, she took up the journal, and was about to tear off the advertising half, when something in its columns arrested her eye. She held the paper up and read eagerly. The rich color faded from her cheeks, and you might have detected a faint motion disturbing the repose of her double chin, a sure sign of unusual agitation in her.

"You have forgotten the cranberries!" said the customer, at length, looking with some surprise at the paper, as it began to rustle violently in the huckster woman's hands.

Mrs. Gray did not seem to hear, but read on with increased agitation. At length she sat down heavily upon her stool, her hands that still grasped the paper, dropped into her lap, and she seemed completely bewildered.

"Are you ill?" inquired the old lady, moving softly around the stand. "Something in the paper must have distressed you."

"Yes," answered the huckster woman, taking up the journal, and pointing with her unsteady finger to the paragraph she had been reading, "I am heart sick; see, I know all these people; I loved some of them. It has taken away my breath. Do you believe that it is true?"

The lady reached forth her hand, and taking the paper, read the account of Leicester's murder and Mr. Warren's arrest, to the end. Mrs. Gray was looking anxiously in her face, and, though it was white and still as the coldest marble, it seemed to the good woman as if it contracted about the mouth, and a look of subdued pain deepened around the eyes.

"Do you believe it?" questioned Mrs. Gray, forgetting that the person she addressed was an entire stranger.

"Yes," answered the lady, speaking with apparent effort—"yes, he is dead!"

"What! murdered by that old man? I don't believe it It's against nature!"

"He died a violent death," answered the lady, shrinking as if with pain.

"Then he killed himself," answered Mrs. Gray, recovering something of her natural energy, "it was like him."

"Oh! God forbid!"

The lady uttered these words in a low, gasping tone, as if Mrs. Gray's speech had confirmed some unspoken dread in her own heart. The noble old huckster woman saw that she was giving pain, and did not press the subject.

"Then some other person must be guilty; it was not old Mr. Warren; I haven't seen much of him, true enough, but he's a good man, my life on it! He's sat at my table—a Thanksgiving dinner, ma'am! I remember the blessing he asked, so meek, so full of gratitude, with as fine a turkey as ever came from a barn-yard tempting him to be short, and he with hunger stamped deep into every line of his face. I haven't heard such a blessing since I was a girl. This man charged with murder! I wouldn't believe it though every minister in New York swore against him."

The old lady opened her lips to speak again, but Mrs. Gray suddenly laid a hand upon her arm.

"Hush! you see that old woman coming up the market, it is his wife!—Mr. Warren's wife!—see how broken-heartedly she looks about from stall to stall; maybe it is this one she wants. Yes! how her poor eyes brighten. A friend in need is a friend indeed; she knows where to look, you see."

By this time the forlorn old woman, who came wandering like a ghost up the market, caught a glimpse of the portly figure and radiant countenance, that always made the huckster woman an object of attention. Her pale face did indeed brighten up, and she forced her way through the people, putting them aside with her hands in reckless haste.

Mrs. Gray left her customer by the stall, and went down the market in benevolent haste, the snowy strings of her cap floating out, and the broad expanse of her apron rippling with the rapidity of her steps. She met Mrs. Warren with a kindly, but subdued greeting, and, without releasing the thin hand she had grasped, led the heart-stricken woman up to her stall.

"There, now, sit down upon my stool," she said, giving another gentle shake of the withered hand, before she relinquished it. "You are tired and out of breath; there, there, keep quiet; cry away, if you like, I'll stand before you!"

The good woman had seen tears gathering into the wild eyes of her visitor from the first—for if tears are locked in a grateful heart, kindness will bring them forth—and with that intuitive delicacy which made all her acts so genial, she left the poor creature to weep in peace, shielding her from notice by the breast-work of her own ample person.

"Oh, the cranberries! I have kept you waiting!" she said to the customer who stood motionless by the stall, apparently unconscious of all that was passing, but keenly interested, notwithstanding this seeming apathy.

The lady started at this address, and without answer watched Mrs. Gray as she twisted half of the torn newspaper over her hand, and afterward filled it with berries. She took the paper, mechanically laid down a piece of silver, and waited for the change. All this was done in a cold, strengthless way, like one who does every thing well from habit, and who omits no detail of a life that has lost all interest. She stood a moment after receiving the parcel, and then drawing close to Mrs. Gray, whispered—

"Ask her where she lives!"

Mrs. Gray looked around, and saw that the pale face was bowed still, and that tears were pouring down it like rain. She leaned forward and whispered—

"Do you live in the old place yet?"

"No," was the broken answer, "I could not stay there alone, if the rent were paid. As it is they would not let me, I suppose."

"Where is your home, then? Where is your family?" said the lady, in her gentle way.

"They are in prison; my home is the street!"

"But where do you sleep?"

"Nowhere, I have not wanted to sleep since they took *him!*" was the sad reply. "I walk up and down all night; it is a little chilly sometimes, but a great deal better than sitting alone to think."

"She will go home with me," said Mrs. Gray, addressing her customer, and drawing one hand across her eyes, for their soft brown was becoming misty. "Of course she will—I don't know you, ma'am, but somehow it seems as if you would like to help this poor, unfortunate woman. She needs friends, and has got one, at any rate, but the more the better!"

"If—if you could only persuade the judge to let me stay in prison with them," said Mrs. Warren, lifting her face to the lady with an air of pleading humility. "I don't want a better home than that."

"They! Was it not they you said?" questioned the huckster woman. "Who is in prison besides Mr. Warren? Not Julia —not my little flower-angel—you do not mean that?"

"They let all go in but me!" answered Mrs. Warren, with a look of pitiful desolation.

"I never said it before!" exclaimed Mrs. Gray, untying her apron, rolling it up and twisting the strings around it with a degree of energy quite disproportioned to this simple operation —"I never said it before, but I'm ashamed of my country—it's a disgrace to humanity. I only wish Jacob knew it, that's all!"

"Hush!" said the lady, with her cold, low voice. "There's one stronger than the laws who permits these things for his own wise purposes."

Mrs. Warren looked up. A wan smile quivered over her face. "That is so like him—he said these very words."

"He is right! you must not feel so hopeless, or be altogether miserable—have faith! have charity!" added the gentle speaker, turning from the mournful eyes of Mrs. Warren, and addressing the huckster woman. "You cannot know how many other persons are suffering from this very cause. Let us all be patient—let us all trust in God."

She glided away as she spoke, and was lost in the crowd, leaving behind the hushed passion of grief and a feeling of awe, for the calm dignity of her own sorrow subdued the resentment which Mrs. Gray had felt, like the rebuke of an angel.

"Did you know her?" she questioned, drawing a deep breath, as the black garments disappeared. "One would think she understood the whole case."

Mrs. Warren shook her head.

"I suppose she was right," continued the huckster woman—"I *know* she was right, but we can't always feel the pious faith she wants us to have; if we did there would be no sorrow. Who minds wading a river when certain just how deep the water is, and while banks covered with flowers lie in full sight on the other side? It is plunging into a dark stream, with clouds hiding the shore, and not a star asleep in the bottom, that tries the faith. But after all, she speaks like one who knows what such things mean. So be comforted my poor friend, the river is dark, the clouds are heavy, but somewhere we shall find a gleam of God's mercy folded up in the blackness. Isn't there a hymn—I think there is—that says, 'earth has no sorrow that heaven cannot cure?'"

"Oh! if they would let me stay with him!" answered the poor old woman, with her wan smile, "I could have faith then, that is heaven to me!"

"You shall see him—you shall stay with him from morning till night, if you would rather! I'll go into court myself. I'll haunt the alderman like an office-seeker, till some of them lets you in. I'll—yes, I'll go after Jacob, he can do anything; you never saw Jacob—my brother Jacob, he's a man to deal with these courts. Strong as a lion, honest as a house-dog; been half his life in foreign parts. Knows more in ten minutes than his sister does in a whole year; he'll set things to rights in no time. Your husband is innocent—innocent as I am—we must prove it, that's all!"

Mrs. Warren did not speak the thanks that beamed in every lineament of her face; but she took the hand which Mrs. Gray had laid upon hers, and pressing it softly between her thin palms, raised it to her lips.

"Poh—poh, they will see you! Cheer up now, and let us consider how to begin. If Jacob were only here now, or even my nephew, Robert Otis, he would be better than nobody!"

"Thank you, aunt Gray—thank you a thousand times for this estimate of modest merit," said a voice at her elbow, whose cheerfulness was certainly somewhat assumed.

Mrs. Gray turned with a degree of eagerness that threatened to destroy the equilibrium of her stately person.

"Robert—Robert Otis," she cried, addressing the noble-looking youth, who stood with his hand extended, ready for the warm greeting that was sure to be his. "I was just wishing for you—so was poor Mrs. Warren; you remember Mrs Warren's grand-daughter—she is in trouble—great trouble!"

"Yes, I know," said young Otis, remarking the painful expression that came and went on that withered face. "I have been to the prison!"

"Did you see him? Did they let you in?" exclaimed Mrs. Warren, beginning to tremble. "Oh! tell me how he was—did he miss me very much? Was he anxious about his poor wife?"

"I was too early—they did not let me in," replied the young man, bending a pair of fine eyes, full of noble compassion, on the old woman; "but I learned from one of the keepers that your husband was more composed than persons usually are the first night of confinement."

The old woman sunk back to her seat, with an air of meek disappointment.

"And Julia, my grandchild—did you inquire about her?"

Robert's countenance changed; there was something unsteady in his voice, as he replied; it seemed embarrassed with some tender recollection.

"I saw her!"

"You saw her! How did she look?—what did she say?"

"I got admission to speak with Mrs. Foster, the matron, a fine, pleasant woman, you will be glad to know; but it was early for visitors, and I only saw your grand-daughter through the grating."

"Was she ill?—was she crying?—did she look pale?"

"She looked pale, certainly, but calm and quiet as an angel in heaven."

"Oh! she is like an angel, that dear grand-daughter!"

"She was leading a little child by the hand, up and down the lower passage—a beautiful creature, who kept his quiet, soft eyes fixed on hers, as we sometimes see a house-dog gaze on its owner. I had but one glimpse, and came away."

"Then she did not seem unhappy?" questioned the old woman.

"I could not say that. Her eyes were heavy, as if she had cried a good deal in the night, but she was calm when I saw her."

"Would they let me look at her as you did, if I promised not to speak a word?"

"There is no reason why you should not speak with her, and your husband too. If the keepers refuse, I will obtain an order from the sheriff."

"Do you think so, really? Can I see them to-day?"

"Be at rest; you will see them within a few hours, no doubt," replied the young man. "But your grand-daughter, at least, will, I trust, be at liberty. It was on this subject that I came to see you, aunt."

"And right glad I am you did come, nephew," replied the huckster woman. "I wanted to help the poor things somehow, but didn't know what on earth to begin with. I know just about as much of the law as a spring gosling, and no more. It costs heaps of money, that every one can tell you; but how it is to be spent, and what for, is the question I want answered."

"Well, aunt, the first step, I fancy, is to get the poor woman's grandchild out of that horrid place. I can tell you it made my blood run cold to see her among those women!"

"Yes—yes. But how is it to be done?"

"You must go up to court and give bonds for her appearance; that is, you agree to give five hundred dollars to the treasury, if this young girl fails to appear when her grandfather is put on trial. If she appears, you are free from all obligation. If she fails, the money must be paid."

"Fails! I thought better of you, nephew. How can you mention the word? Haven't I trusted her with fruit? Didn't I go security for half the flowers in Dunlap's green-house at one time within this very month? Robert, Robert, the world is spoiling you. How could you speak as if that girl—I love her as if she were my own niece, Robert—how could you speak as if she could fail, and her poor grandmother sitting by?"

Was it this energetic rebuke that brought the blood so richly into the young man's cheek, or was it the little word "niece" that fell so affectionately from the old huckster woman's lips? It could not be the former, for a bright smile kindled up the flush, and that, a rebuke, however kindly intended, was not likely to excite.

"You cannot feel more confidence in her than I do, dear Aunt Gray," he said; "but I thought it right to place the responsibility clearly before you!"

"That was right—that was like a man of business. Never mind what I said, nephew," cried the great hearted woman, shaking the youth's hand till the motion flushed his face once more. "Aunt Gray always was an old fool, seeing faults where they never existed, and making herself ridiculous every way, but never mind her—she'll give bonds for the poor child, of course; but then the old gentleman, how much will the law ask for him?"

"I'm afraid it will be out of your power to free him, aunt."

"What, they ask too much, ha? You think Aunt Gray must not run the risk; but she will, though. I tell you that old man is honest, honest as steel. They might trust him with the prison doors open; he will do what is right without fear or favor. I'll give bonds for him up to the last shilling of my savings, if the court asks it. He's innocent as a creeping babe, and I, for one, will let the world, yes, the whole world, know that this is my opinion."

"You will not hear me, out. Aunt Gray, I did not advise you against giving bonds, far from it; but Mr. Warren is charged with a crime for which no bonds can be received."

"I did not know that," answered Mrs. Gray, sinking her voice, "still something can be done; see how earnestly she is looking at us! My heart aches for her, Robert."

"Heaven knows I pity her," said the young man, "for I tell you fairly, aunt, the evidence against her husband is terribly strong."

"But you, Robert—you cannot think him guilty?"

"No, aunt, I solemnly believe Mr. Leicester killed himself But what is my belief without evidence?"

"Then you solemnly believe him innocent?"

"As I believe myself innocent, good aunt."

"I won't ask you to kiss me, Robert, because we are in the open market, and people might laugh—but shake hands again Next to faith in God, I love to see trust in human nature—faith in God's creatures—it's a beautiful thing! The good naturally have confidence in the good. That old man is a Christian, treat him reverently in his prison, nephew, as you would have bowed before one of the apostles; his blessing would do you good, though it came from the gallows."

"I believe all this, aunt; something of mystery there is about the man, but it would be impossible to think him guilty of murder! Still there must have been some connection between him and Mr. Leicester yet unexplained."

"I know nothing of this—nothing but what the papers tell me; but one thing is certain, Robert, no one ever had anything to do with Mr. Leicester without suffering for it. He was kind to you once, but somehow it seemed to wear out your young life. The flesh wasted from your limbs; the red went out from your cheeks. It made me heart-sick to see the boy I loved to pet like a child, shooting up into a thoughtful man so unnaturally. I remember once, when Leicester boarded at our house, Robert, there was a cabbage-rose growing in one corner of the garden. I haven't much time for flowers, but still I could always find a minute every morning before coming to market for those rose-buds when the blossom season came. That summer the bush was heavy with leaves, still there was but a single bud, a noble one, though, plump as a strawberry, and with as deep a red breaking through the green leaves. I loved to watch the bud swell day by day. Every morning I went out while the dew was heavy upon it, and saw the leaves part softly, as if they were afraid of the sunshine.

"One morning, just as this bud was opening itself to the heart, I found Mr. Leicester bending over the bush, tearing open the poor rose with his fingers. His hands were bathed in the sweet breath that came pouring out all at once upon the air. The soft leaves curled round his fingers, trying to hide, it seemed to me, the havoc his hands had made. It was hard to condemn a man for tearing open a half-blown rose, nephew, but somehow this thing left a prejudice in my heart against Mr. Leicester. The flower did not live till another morning. I told him of this, and he laughed.

"'Well, what then? I had all the fragrance at a breath,' he said. 'Never let your roses distil their essence to the sun, drop by drop, Mrs. Gray, when you can tear open the hearts and drink their sweet lives in a moment.'

"I remember his answer, word for word, for it came fresh to my mind many times, when I saw you, my dear boy, pining away as it were, under his kindness. It seemed to me as if he were softly parting the leaves of your young heart, and draining its life away !"

"And you really thought my fate like that of your rose dear aunt ?"

The youth uttered these words with a pale cheek and downcast eyes. The good woman's words had impressed him strangely.

"It kept me awake many a long night, Robert."

"But you did not think that Uncle Jacob was at hand ? Had he been in your garden, Leicester would not have found an opportunity to kill your pet rose—he might have breathed upon it, nothing more."

The huckster woman looked earnestly into that noble young face ; and Robert met her glance with a frank, but somewhat regretful smile.

"And Jacob, my brother, stood between you and this bad man," she said at length, with a degree of emotion that made the folds of her double chin quiver.

"He made me wiser and better—he was my salvation, Aunt Gray."

"God bless my brother—God bless Jacob Strong !" cried the huckster woman, softly clasping her hands, while her eyes were flooded with tears—grateful tears, that hung upon them like dew in the husks of a ripe hazelnut.

"Amen !" said the young man, in a low voice.

"Now, aunt, let us go to this poor woman—observe how earnestly she is watching us."

The aunt and nephew had stepped aside as their conversation became personal ; and old Mrs. Warren had been eagerly regarding them all the time. They were the only friends she had on earth. To her broken spirit, they seemed to hold the power of life and death over the beings she loved so devotedly. Robert had promised that she should see her husband and her grandchild; the heart-stricken woman asked for nothing more. She never, for an instant, questioned his power, but sat with her eyes turned reverently upon his fine person and noble features, as if he had been an angel empowered to unlock the gates of heaven for her.

Robert and his aunt approached her as their conference ended, and the young man took out his watch.

"Is it time? Would they let me in now?" questioned the poor woman, half rising as she saw the movement.

"Are you strong enough?" he answered, observing that she trembled.

"Oh, yes! I am strong—very strong. Let us go!"

With her thin, eager hands, she folded the shawl over her bosom and stood up, strong in her womanly affections, in her Christian humility, but oh, how weak every way else!

Mrs. Gray folded herself in an ample blanket shawl, and tying on her bonnet, led the way out of the market, forgetting for the first time in her life, that her stall was unattended.

CHAPTER XXIV.

THE FIRST NIGHT IN PRISON.

With the gloom of a prison, above and around,
He lay down at night, like a child to its sleep;—
His soul was at rest and his faith was profound,
His anchor was strong and God's mercy is deep!

If there is any portion of the city prison more cheerful than another, it is the double line of cells looking upon Elm street. Plenty of pure light pours in through the glazed roof, filling the space open from pavement to ceiling, with a pleasant atmosphere. The walls that form this spacious parade-ground are pierced with cells up to the very skylights. Each tier of cells is marked by a narrow iron gallery; and each gallery is bridged with that opposite, by a narrow causeway, upon which a keeper usually sits smoking his cigar, and idly reading some city journal.

In the day time the prisoners, who inhabit these various cells, take exercise and air upon the galleries. Even those committed for the highest crimes often enjoy this privilege, for the ponderous strength of the walls, and the vigilance of the authorities, render a degree of freedom safe here, which could not be dreamed of in less secure buildings.

I do not know that there is any rule requiring that persons charged with capital crime should be confined in the upper cells, but usually they are found somewhere in the third gallery, enjoying some degree of liberty till after sentence; but closed between that time and death, as it were, in a living tomb. Thick walls encompass them on every side. Doors of ponderous iron bolted to the stone, shut them in from the galleries. A slit in the walls, five or six feet deep, lets in all the breath and light of heaven which the wretched man must enjoy till he is violently plunged into a closer cell, whence breath and light are for ever excluded. A narrow bed, and perhaps a small, rude table, are all the furniture that can be crowded in with the prisoner. But books are seldom if ever denied him; and occasionally these little cells take a domestic air that renders them less prison-like, and less gloomy as the tastes and habits of the inmates develope themselves.

Old Mr. Warren was placed in one of these cells the day of his examination. He followed the officers along those dizzy galleries, submitting to the curious gaze of his fellow-prisoners with unshrinking humility, that won upon the kind feelings of his keepers. He entered the cell, looked calmly around, and then with a grateful and patient smile, thanked the officer for giving him a place so much better than he had expected.

The officer was touched by the grateful and meek air with

which he spoke these simple thanks, and replied kindly, "that he was willing to render any comfort consistent with the prison rules." After this he looked around to see that everything was in order, and went out, closing the heavy door with a kind regard to the noise, shooting the bolt as softly as so much iron could be moved.

And now the old man was alone, utterly alone, locked and bolted deep into that solitude which must be worse than death to the guilty soul. At first his brain was dizzy; the tragic events that cast him into prison had transpired too rapidly for realization. They rose and eddied through his mind like the phantasmagoria of a dream. He could not think—he could not even pray,

He sat down on the hard pallet, and bowing his forehead to his hands, made an effort to realize his exact situation. His eyes were bent on the floor. Once or twice his lips moved with a faint tremor, for in all the confusion of his ideas he could recollect one thing vividly enough. His wife and grandchild—the two beings for whom he had toiled and suffered, were torn from his side. His poor old wife—her cry, as she strove to follow him, still rang in his ear. She had not even the comforts of a prison.

He looked around the cell—it was clean and dry—the walls snowy with whitewash—the stone flags swept scrupulously. In everything but size it was more comfortable than the basement from which the officers had taken them. True, it was but a hole dug into the ponderous walls of a prison, but if she had been there the poor old man would have been content—nay, grateful, for as yet he had found no strength to realize the terrible danger that hung over him.

Thus, hour after hour went by, and he sat motionless, pondering over all the incidents of his examination like one in a dream. None of them seemed real—but the voice of his wife—the wild, white face of his grandchild as she was borne away through the crowd—these things were palpable enough. He tried to conjecture where his wife would go; what place of refuge she would find; not to their old home, the floor was still red with blood. She was a timid woman, dependent as a child. Without his calm strength to sustain her, what could she do? Perish in the street, perhaps; lie down, softly, upon some door-stone, and grieve herself to death.

There is nothing on earth more touchingly holy than the tenderness which an old man feels for his old wife. The most ardent love of youth is feeble compared to the solemn devotion into which time purifies passion. The mere habit of domestic intercourse is much, independent of those deeper and more subtle feelings which give us our first glimpses of Paradise through the joys of home affection. It was not the prison—it was not the charge of murder that held that old man spell-bound and motionless so long. His desolation was of the heart; his spirit fled out from those huge walls, and followed the lone woman who had been thrust rudely from his side, for the first time in more than thirty years.

It was not with this keen anguish that he thought of Julia, for in her character there was freshness, energy, something of moral strength beyond her years. She might suffer terribly, but something convinced the grandfather that the sublime purity of her nature would protect itself. She was not a feeble, broken-spirited woman like his wife. Yet his heart yearned as he thought of this young creature so pure, so beautiful, so full of sensitive sympathies, among the inmates of that gloomy dwelling.

It was of these two beings the old man pondered, not of himself. After awhile, this keen anxiety goaded him into motion. He stood up and began to pace back and forth in his cell. A narrow strip of the floor lay between his bed and the wall, and along this a little footpath had been worn in the stone by former prisoners.

Who had thus worn the prints of his solitary misery into the hard granite? What foot had trodden there the last sad step of destiny! This question drew the old man's attention for a moment from those he had lost. He became curious to know something of his predecessor—what was his crime? How did he look? Had he a wife and child to mourn? Did he leave the cell for liberty, other confinement, or death?

The word death brought a sense of his own condition for the first time before him. He became thoroughly conscious that a terrible charge had been made against him, and that appearances must sustain that charge. From that instant he stood still, with his eyes bent upon the floor, pondering the subject clearly in his mind. At length a faint smile parted his lips, and he began to pace the narrow cell again, but more calmly than before.

I will tell you why that old man smiled there, alone, in his prison cell, because it will convince you that nothing but guilt can make one utterly wretched. He had thought over the whole matter—the charge of murder—the impossibility of disproving a single point of the evidence. Nothing could be more apparent than the danger in which he stood—nothing more certain than the penalty that would follow conviction. But it was this very truth that sent the smile to those aged lips. What was death to him but the threshold of heaven? Death, he had never prayed for it, for his Christianity was too holy and humble for selfish importunity, even though the thing asked for was death. He was not one to cast himself at the footstool of the Almighty, and point out to His all-seeing wisdom the mercies that would please him best. No—no, the religion of that noble old man—for true religion is always noble—was of that humble, trusting nature that says, "Nevertheless, not my will, but thine, be done." He was only thinking when he smiled so gently, how much greater sorrow he had encountered than death could bring.

This gave him comfort when he thought of his wife also. She would go with him, he was certain of that as he could be of anything in the future. He remembered, with pleasure, that old people, long married, and very much attached, were almost certain to die within a few weeks or months of each other. How many instances of this came within his own memory. It was a comforting theme, and he dwelt upon it with solemn satisfaction.

The keeper, when he came to bring the old man's dinner, gazed upon his benign and tranquil features with astonishment. Never in his life had he seen a prisoner so calm on the first day of confinement. It was impossible for philosophy or hardihood to assume an expression so gentle, and full of dignity.

"Tell me," said the old man, as the keeper lingered near the door, "tell me who occupied this cell last? It is a strange thing, but with so much to distract my thoughts, a curiosity haunts me to know something of the man whose bed I have taken."

The officer hesitated. It was an ominous question, and he shrunk from a subject well calculated to depress a prisoner.

"I have made out a portion of the history," said the prisoner; "enough to know that he was a sea-faring man, and had talent."

"And how did you find this out?" inquired the officer.

"There, upon the wall, is a rough picture, but one can read a great deal in it!"

The old man pointed to the wall, where a few unequal lines, drawn with a pencil, gave a rude idea of waves in motion. In their midst was a ship, with her masts broken, plunging downward, with her bows already engulfed in the water.

"Poor fellow! I thought it had been whitewashed over," said the officer. "He did that the very week before—before his execution."

"Then he was executed?"

"Yes; nothing could have saved him."

"Was he guilty, then?"

"It was as clear a case of piracy as I ever saw tried; the man confessed his guilt."

"Guilty! Death must be terrible in that case—very terrible!" said the old man, with a mournful shake of the head.

"He was a reckless fellow, full of wild glee to the last, but a coward, I do believe. I found his pillow wet almost every morning. The last month he kept a calendar of the days over his bed there, pencilled on the wall. The first thing every morning he would strike out a day with his finger; but if any one seemed to pity him, he frequently broke into a volley of curses, or jeered at sympathy that he did not want."

"Have you ever seen an innocent man executed?" said the prisoner, greatly disturbed by this account; "that is, a man who met death calmly, neither as a stoic, a bravo, or a coward?"

"I have no doubt innocent men have been executed again and again, all over the world; but I have never seen one die, knowing him to be such."

The officer went out after this, leaving the old man alone once more. His face was sad now, and he watched the closing door wistfully.

"Why should I seek other examples?" he said, at length. "Was not *he* executed innocently? Is it not enough to know how my Lord and Saviour died?"

It was a singular thing, but, from the first, old Mr. Wilcox never seemed to entertain a hope of escaping from the prison by any means but a violent death. It was to this that all his Christian energies were bent from the earliest hour of confine ment.

The night came on, but its approach was perceptible only by the shadows that crept across the loop-hole which served as a window. In the darkness that soon filled the cell the old man lay down in his clothes and tried to sleep. Now it was that his soul yearned toward the poor old wife who had been so long sheltered in his bosom; the fair grand-daughter too—it seemed as if his heart would break as their condition rose before him in all its fearful desolation.

Deep in the night he fell asleep, and then his brain was haunted with dreams, bright, heavenly dreams, such as irradiate the face of an infant when the mother believes it whispering with angels. But this sweet sleep was of brief duration. He awoke in the darkness, and, unconscious where he was, reached out his arm. It struck the cold, hard wall, and the vibration went through his heart like a knife. She was not by his side.

Where, where was his poor wife? He asked this question aloud; his sobs filled the cell; the miserable pillow under his head soaked up the tears as they rained down his face. A dread of death could not have wrung drops from those aching eyes; but tears of affection reveal the strength of a good man. There are times when the proudest being on earth might be ashamed not to weep.

He did not close his eyes again that night, but wept himself calm with broken prayers. Low, humble entreaties for strength, for patience and for charity, rose from his hard bed. Slowly the cell filled with light, and then he saw, for the first time, a book lying on a small shelf, fastened beneath the window. He arose, eagerly, and took it down. A glow spread over his face. It was one of those cheap Bibles, which the Tract Society scatters through our prisons. As he opened the humble book, a sunbeam shot through the loop-hole, and broke in a shower of light over the page. Was it chance that sent the golden sunbeam? Was it chance that opened the book to one of the most hopeful and comforting passages of Scripture?

He took an old pair of steel spectacles from his pocket, and sat down to read. Hours wore away, still he bent over those holy pages as if they had never met his eyes before. And so it really seemed, for we must suffer before all the strength and beauty of the book of books can penetrate the heart. A noise at the door made him look up. His breath came fast. It required something heavier than that iron door, to lock out the sympathies of two hearts that had grown old in affection. His hands began to tremble; he took off the spectacles, and hastily put them between the pages of his Bible. It was of no use trying to read then.

The bolt was shot, the door swung open with a clang, and there stood a group of persons ready to enter.

"Husband! oh, husband!" cried old Mrs. Wilcox, reaching both hands through the door as she stooped to come in.

The prisoner took her hands in his, and kissed them as he had done years ago, when those poor withered fingers were rosy with youth. The door closed softly then, for old Mrs. Gray was not one to force herself upon an interview so mournful and so sacred.

CHAPTER XXV.

LITTLE GEORGIE.

As ivy clingeth round a ruin,
  Still green within the darkest cleft,
The human soul in its undoing
  Has still some lingering virtue left.

Julia slept little during the night. The state of nervous terror in which she had been thrown, the shrinking dread which made her quail and tremble at the approach of her fellow prisoners—even the rude kindness of the strange being who took a sort of tiger-like interest in her—frightened sleep from her eyes.

A cell had been arranged for her, and the woman, who still shielded her from the other prisoners, much as a wild beast might protect her young, consented that the infant boy should be her companion through the night. This was a great comfort to the poor girl. To her belief there was protection in the sleeping innocence of the child, who lay with his delicately veined temples pressing that coarse prison pillow, softly as if it had been fragrant with rose-leaves.

Julia could not sleep, but it was pleasant in her sad wakefulness to feel the sweet breath of this child floating over her face, and his soft arms clinging to her neck. To her poetic imagination it seemed as if a cherub from heaven had been left to cheer her in the darkness. Sometimes she would start and listen, or cringe breathlessly down to her pretty companion, for strange, fierce voices occasionally broke from some of the cells on either side—smothered sounds as of spirits chained in torment—wailing and wild shouts of laughter; for with some of those wretched inmates, memory grew sharp in the midnight of a prison, and others dreamed as they had lived—shouting fiercely in the sleep which was not rest, but the dregs of lingering inebriation.

Of the mind and heart of this young girl, we have said but little. The few simple acts of her life have been allowed to speak for her extreme youth; the utter isolation of her life, even more than her youth, would, in ordinary characters, have kept her still ignorant and uninformed. But Julia was not an ordinary character; there was depth, earnestness, and that extreme simplicity in her nature which goes to make up the beauty and strength of womanhood. Suffering had made her precocious, nothing more—it sent thought hand in hand with feeling. It threw her forward in life some three or four years. Gratitude, so early and so deeply enkindled in her young heart, foreshadowed the intensity of affection, nay, of passion, when it should once be aroused.

In this country, the most abject poverty need not preclude the craving mind from its natural aliment, books. Julia had read more and thought more than half the girls of her age in the very highest walks of life. Her first love of poetry was drawn from the most beautiful of all sources, the Bible. Her grandfather was a good reader, and possessed no small degree of natural eloquence. Gushes of poetry, of solemn, sweet feeling were constantly breaking through the prayers which she had listened to every night and morning of her life; the very sublimity of his faith, the simple trust which never forsook him in the goodness of his Creator—the cheerful humility of his entire character, all this had aroused sympathetic emotions in his grandchild's heart. It is the good alone who thoroughly feel how keen and sweet intellectual joys may become. When we water the blossoms of a strong mind with dew from the fountains of a good heart, the whole being is harmonious, and the rarest joys of existence are secured.

But though the Bible contains the safest and most beautiful

groundwork of all literature, history, biography, ethics, poetry, and even that pure fiction, which shadows forth truth in the parables, the mind that has first tasted thought there, will crave other sources of knowledge. A few old volumes, so shabby that the pawnbrokers refused loans upon them, and the second-hand book-stalls rejected them at any price, still remained in her basement home. These she had read with the keen relish of a mind hungry for knowledge. Then old Mrs. Gray had a few books at her farm-house. She had never read them herself, good soul, and whenever the beauties of "Paradise Lost," were mentioned, had only a vague professional idea that our first parents had been driven forth from a remarkably fine vegetable and fruit garden just before the harvest season. Still she had great respect for the man who could mourn so great a loss in verse, and delighted in lending the volumes to her young friend whenever she had time to read.

From these resources and the patient teachings of her grandfather, Julia had managed to obtain the most desirable of all educations. She had learned to think clearly and to feel rightly; but she felt keenly also, and a vivid imagination kindling up these acute feelings at midnight in the depth of a prison, made every nerve quiver with dread that was more than superstitious. One picture haunted her very sleep. It was her grandfather's white and agonized face stooping over that dead man. Never had the beautiful, stern face of the stranger beamed upon her so vividly before. She saw every lineament enameled on the midnight blackness.

She longed to arouse the child and ask it if the face were really visible, but was afraid to speak or move. The very sound of his soft breath as the boy slept terrified her. But while this wild dread was strongest upon her, the child awoke and began to feel over her face with his little hands. Softly, and with the touch of falling rose-leaves, his fingers wandered over her eyes, her forehead, and her mouth. They were like sunbeams playing upon ice, those warm, rosy fingers. The young girl ceased to feel frightened or alone. She began to weep. She pressed his hands to her lips, and drew the child close to her bosom, whispering softly to him, and pressing her lips to his eyes now and then, to be sure they were open. But all her gente wiles were insufficient to keep the little fellow awake; he began to breathe more and more deeply, and, overcome by the soft mesmerism of his breath, she fell asleep also.

It would have been a lovely sight had any one looked upon those two calm, beautiful faces pillowed together upon that prison bed. Smiles dimpled round the rosy lips, upon which the breath floated like mist over a cluster of ripe cherries. The bright ringlets of the child fell over the tresses that shadowed the fair temple close to his, lighting them up as with threads, and gleams of gold. It was a picture of innocent sleep those green walls had perhaps never sheltered before since their foundation. It was natural that Julia should smile in her sleep, and that a glow like the first beams of morning when they penetrate a rose, should light up her face. She was dreaming, and slumber cast a fairy brightness over thoughts that had perhaps vaguely haunted her before that night. Memories mingled with the vision and the scenes which wove themselves in her slumbering thought had been realities—the first joyous realities of her young life. She was at an old farm-house, half hid in the foliage of two noble maples, all golden and crimson with a touch of frost. Her grandparents stood upon the door-stone with old Mrs. Gray, talking together, and smiling upon her as she sat down beneath the maples, and began to arrange a lapful of flowers that somehow had filled her apron, as bright things will fall upon us in our sleep. These blossoms breathed a perfume more delicate than anything she had ever seen or imagined, and, though coarse garden flowers, their breath was intoxicating.

Dreams are independent of detail, and the sleeper only knew that a young man whose face was familiar, and yet strange, stood by her side, and smiled gently upon her as she bent over her treasure. Was her slumbering imagination more vivid than the reality had been, or had her nerves ever answered human look with the delicious thrill that pervaded them in this dream?

Was it the shadow of a memory haunting her sleep? Oh, yes, she had dreamed before—dreamed when those soft eyes had nothing but their curling lashes to veil them, and when the thoughts that were now floating through her vision left a glow upon that young cheek. It was true the angel of love haunted Julia in her prison.

The real and the imaginary still blended itself in her vision but indistinctly, and with that vague cloudiness that makes one sigh when the dream becomes a memory. An harassing sense that her grandfather was in trouble seemed to blend with the misty breath of the flowers. She still sat beneath the tree, and saw an old man in the distance, struggling with a throng of people, half engulphed in a storm-cloud that rolled up from the horizon. She could not move, for the blossoms in her lap seemed turning to lead, which she had no power to fling off. She struggled, and cried out wildly, "Robert—Robert Otis!"

The blossoms breathed in her lap again; flashes of silver broke up the distant cloud, and stars seemed dropping, one by one, from its writhing folds. Robert Otis was now in the distance, now at her side; she could not turn her eyes without encountering the deep smiling fervor of his glance. His name trembled and died on her lips in broken whispers, then all faded away. Balmy quiet settled on the spirit of the young girl, and she slept softly as the flowers slumber when their cups are overflowing with dew.

From this sweet rest she was aroused by a sharp clang of iron, and the tread of feet in the passage. The door of her own cell was flung open, and a tin cup full of coffee, with coarse, wholesome bread, was set inside for her breakfast. The dream still left its balm upon her heart, which all that prison noise had not power to frighten away. She smoothed her own hair, arranged her dress, and then arousing the child from its sleep with kisses, bathed and dressed him also. He was sitting upon her lap, his fresh rosy face lifted to hers, while she smoothed his tresses, and twisted them in ringlets around her fingers, when his mother entered the cell. She scarcely glanced at the child, but sat down, and supporting her forehead with one hand, remained in sombre stillness gazing on the floor. There was nothing reckless or coarse in her manner. Her heavy forehead was clouded, but with gloom that partook more of melancholy than of anger.

She spoke at length, but without changing her position or lifting her eyes from the floor.

"Will you tell me the name?—will you tell me who the man was they charge your grandfather with murdering? Was it—was it——" The low husky tones died in her throat; she made another effort, and added, almost in a whisper, "was it William Leicester?"

The question arrested Julia in her graceful task; her hands dropped as if smitten down from those golden tresses, and she answered in a faint voice, "that it was the name."

"Then he is dead; are you sure—quite sure?"

"They all said so; the doctor, all that saw him!"

"You did not see him then?"

"Yes—yes!" answered the young girl, closing her eyes with a pang. "I saw him—I saw him!"

"Why did your grandfather kill him? Had Leicester done him any wrong?"

"I do not know what wrong he had ever done," answered Julia; "but I am certain if he had injured him ever so much, grandpa would not have harmed a hair of his head."

"Who did kill him then?" said the woman sharply.

"I think," said Julia, in a low, firm voice—"I think that he killed himself!"

"No. It could not be that!" muttered the woman, gloomily. "No doubt the old man did what others had better cause for doing; tell me how it happened!"

Julia saw that the woman was growing pale around the lips as she spoke; her hand also looked blue and cold as it shaded her face.

"Don't be afraid of me. Go on, I could not harm a mouse this morning," she said, observing that Julia hesitated, and sat gazing earnestly upon her. "I have been in prison here two weeks, and never heard of his death till now!"

"Did you know Mr. Leicester?" questioned Julia.

"Yes, I knew him!"

There was something in the tone of her voice that surprised Julia; more of bitterness than grief, and yet something of both.

"Will you tell me what I asked you?" said the woman, with a touch of her usual impetuosity.

"Yes," answered Julia. "It distresses me to talk of it; but if you are really anxious to hear, I will!"

She went on with painful hesitation, and told the woman all those details that are so well known to the reader. The woman listened attentively, sometimes holding her breath with intense interest; again breathing quick and sharp, as if some strong feeling were curbed into silence with difficulty. When Julia ceased speaking, she folded both hands over her face, and lowering it down to her knees, rocked to and fro without sob or tear; but the very stillness was eloquent.

She got up after a little and went out. Half an hour after, Julia took the child to his mother's cell. The strange woman was lying with her face to the wall, motionless as the granite upon which her large eyes were fixed. She did not turn as they approached, but waved her hand impatiently that they should leave the cell.

Holding the child by his hand, Julia lingered in the passage. After a few careless, and in some cases, rude manifestations of interest, the prisoners left her unmolested, to seek what consolation might be found in observation and exercise.

Thus the day crept on. The confusion which her youth and terror created the day before, had settled down in that sullen apathy which is the most depressing feature of prison life. The women moved about with a dull, heavy tread; some sat motionless against the wall, gazing into the air, to all appearance void of sensation, almost of life; some slept away the weary time but depression lay heavily upon them all.

Julia lingered near the grating, for the gleams of sunshine that shot into the broad hall beyond, whenever the outer door was opened to allow access and egress to the officers, had something cheerful in it that filled her with hope. The child, too, felt this pleasant influence, and his prattle, now and then broken with a soft laugh, was music to the poor girl.

"Come, love—come, let us go away. People are at the door !" she cried all at once, striving to lead the child away.

"No—no. It is brighter here, I will stay," answered the little fellow, leaping roguishly on one side. "It's only the matron; don't you hear her keys jingle ? She will take me up into her pretty room, and you as well. Just wait till I ask her."

The door opened and a black-eyed little woman, full of animation and cheerful energy, stepped into the passage. She paused, for Julia stood in her way, making gentle efforts to free her dress from the grasp which the little boy had fixed upon it. The beauty of the young girl, her shrinking manner, and the crimson that came and went on her sweet face, all interested the matron at once. She smiled a motherly, cheering smile, and said at once—

"Ah, you have found one another out. George is a safe little playmate—ain't you, darling ? Come, now, tell me what her name is, that's a man."

"She hasn't told me yet," lisped the child, freeing Julia from his grasp, and nestling himself against the matron.

"My name is Julia—Julia Warren, ma'am," said the young prisoner, blushing to hear the sound of her name in that place.

"I thought so; I was sure of it from the first; there, there, don't be frightened, and don't cry. Come up to my room —come, George! Tell your young friend that somebody is waiting for her up there—some one that she will be very glad to meet."

"Tell me—oh! tell me who!" cried the poor girl, breathlessly.

"Your grandmother, so she calls herself—and——"

Julia waited for no more, but darted forward.

"There—there. You will never get on alone!" cried the matron, laughing, while she turned a heavy key bright with constant use in its lock, and opened the grated door. "Come, now, I and Georgie will lead the way."

Julia stood in the outer passage while the heavy door was secured again, her cheeks all in a glow of joy, her limbs trembling with impatience. Little George, too, seemed to partake of her eagerness; he ran up and down in the bright atmosphere like a bird revelling in the first gleams of morning. He seized the matron by her dress as she locked the door, and shaking his soft curls gleefully, attempted to draw her away. His sympathy was so graceful and cheering that it made both Julia and the matron smile, and though they mounted the stairs rapidly, he ran up and down a dozen steps while they ascended half the number.

Neither Julia nor her grandmother spoke when they met, but there was joy upon their faces, and the most touching affection in the eyes that constantly turned upon each other.

"And now," said old Mrs. Gray, coming forward with her usual bland kindness, "as neither of you seem to have much to say just now, what if Robert and I come in for a little notice?"

Julia looked up as the kind voice reached her, and there, half hidden by the portly figure of his aunt, she saw Robert Otis looking upon her with the very expression that had haunted her dream that night, in the prison. Their eyes met, the white lids fell over hers as if weighed down by the lashes, through which the lustrous eyes, kindling beneath, gleamed like diamond flashes. She forgot Mrs. Gray, everything but the glory of her dream, the power of those eloquent eyes.

"And so you will not speak to me—you will not look at me!" said the huckster woman, a little surprised by this reception, but speaking with great cordiality, for she was not one of those very troublesome persons who fancy affronts in everything.

"Not speak to you!" cried the young girl, starting from her pleasant reverie to the scarcely less pleasant reality. "Oh! Mrs. Gray, you knew better!"

"Of course I did," cried the good woman, with a laugh that made her neckerchief tremble, and she shook the little hand that Julia gave with grateful warmth, over and over again. "Come, now, get your bonnet and things."

Julia looked at the matron.

"But I am a prisoner!"

"Nothing of the sort. I've bought you out; given bonds, or something. Robert can tell you all about it; but the long and short is, you're free as a blackbird. Can go home with me—grandma too, I'm old—I'm getting lonesome—want her to keep house when I'm in market, and you to take care of her."

"But grandfather—where is he? Oh! where is he?"

Mrs. Gray's countenance fell, and she seemed ready to burst into tears.

"Don't ask me; Robert must tell you about that. I did my best; offered to mortgage the whole farm to those crusty old judges, but it was of no use."

"We couldn't leave him here alone!" said Julia, with one of her faint, beautiful smiles.

Robert Otis came forward now.

"It would be useless for either of you to remain here on his account, even if the laws would permit it. You will be allowed to see him quite as frequently if you live with my aunt, and with freedom you may find means of aiding him."

Julia raised her eyes to his face; her glance, instead of embarrassing, seemed to animate the young man.

"It admits of no choice," he added, with a smile. "Your grandfather himself desires that you should accept my aunt's offer, and she—bless her—it would break her heart to be refused."

"Grandfather desires it—Mr. Otis desires it. Shall we not go, grandma?"

"Certainly, child; he wishes it, that is enough; but I shall see him every day, you remember, ma'am. Every day when you come over, I come also. It was a promise!"

"Do exactly as you please—that's my idea of helping

folks," answered Mrs. Gray, to whom the latter part of this address had been made. "The kindness that forces people to be happy, according to a rule laid down by the self-conceit of a person who happens to have the means you want, is the worst kind of slavery, because it is a slavery for which you are expected to be very grateful. I have heard brother Jacob say this a hundred times, and so have you, Robert."

"Uncle Jacob never said anything that was not wise and generous in his life!" answered the young man, with kindling eyes.

"If ever an angel lived on earth, he is one!" rejoined Mrs. Gray, looking around upon her audience, as if to impress them fully with this estimate of her brother's character.

A sparkling smile broke over Robert's face.

"Well, aunt, I hope you never fancied the angels dressing exactly after Uncle Jacob's fashion!" he said, casting a look full of comic meaning on the old lady.

"Oh, Robert, you are always laughing at me!" replied the good-humored lady, turning from the young man to her other auditors. "It was always so; the most mischievous little rogue you ever saw. I thought he had grown out of it for a while, but nature is nature the world through."

Robert blushed. His aunt's encomiums did not quite please him, for the character of a mischievous boy was not that which he was desirous of maintaining just then. In the dark eyes turned so earnestly upon his face, he read a depth and earnestness of feeling that made his attempt at cheerfulness seem almost sacrilegious. Julia saw this, and smiled softly. She had not intended to rebuke him by the seriousness of her face, and her look expressed this more eloquently than words could have done.

When the heart is sorrowful, there are times when cheerfulness in those around us has a healthful influence. The joyous laugh, the pleasant word may fall harshly upon a riven heart at first, but imperceptibly they become familiar again, and at length sweep aside the gloom with which the mourner loves to envelope himself. Give the soul plenty of sunshine, and it grows vigorous to withstand the storm. When grief is pampered and cultivated as a duty, it often degenerates into intense selfishness Sorrow has its vanity as well as joy.

CHAPTER XXVI.

MRS. GRAY AND THE PRISON WOMAN.

Come with thy warm and genial heart—
Bring sunshine to the prison cell;
True goodness, without book or chart,
Sees the right path, and treads it well.

It was decided that Julia and her grandmother should accompany Mrs. Gray at once to her old homestead on Long Island. They were about to leave the room, when Julia remembered, with a pang, that she must surrender the little boy to his mother again. Her cheek blanched at the thought. The child had kept by her side since she first entered the room, and now grasped a fold of her dress in his hand almost fiercely. His cheeks were flushed, and his dimpled chin was beginning to quiver, as if he were ready to burst into tears at some wrong premeditated against him.

Tears swelled into Julia's eyes as she bent them upon the child.

"What shall I do? He seems to know that we are about to leave him," she murmured.

"Come with me, I will take you to mamma," said the matron, laying her hand on his head. "There, Georgie, be a little gentleman, dear!"

The tears that had been swelling in the little fellow's bosom broke forth now. He began to sob violently, and shaking off the matron's hand, clung to his new friend.

"Take me up, take me up—I will go too," he sobbed, lifting his little hands and his tearful face to the young girl.

Julia took him in her arms, and putting the curls back from his forehead, pressed a kiss upon it.

"What can I do?" she said, turning her eyes unconsciously upon Robert Otis.

Robert smiled and shook his head; but old Mrs. Gray, whose heart was forever creaming over with the milk of human kindness, came forward at once.

"What can you do? Why, take him along; the homestead is large enough for us all. It will seem like old times to have a little shaver like that running around, now that Robert is away."

"But he has a mother in the prison," said the matron—"a strange, fierce woman, who, somehow or other, has persuaded the authorities to leave him with her for the few days she will be here."

"His mother a prisoner, poor thing. Let me go to her, I dare say she will be glad enough to get a nice home for the boy," answered the good woman, hopefully.

"I'm afraid not," was the matron's reply; "she seems to have a sort of fierce love for the child, and is very jealous that he may become attached to some one beside herself. It was from this feeling she forced him from the poor woman who took him to nurse when only a few weeks old. He was very fond of her, and always fancies that any new face must be hers I wonder she submits to his fancy for this young girl!"

"But it's wrong, it's abominable to keep the little fellow here. I'll tell her so, I'll expostulate," persisted Mrs. Gray; "just let me talk with this woman—just let me into her cell, madam."

The matron shook her head, and gave the bright key in her hand a little, quiet twirl, which said plainly as words, that it was of no use; but she led the way down stairs, and conducted Mrs. Gray to the prisoner's cell.

The woman was still lying with her forehead against the wall, quite motionless, but she turned her face as the matron spoke, and Mrs. Gray saw that it was drenched with tears.

The huckster woman sat down upon the bed, and took one

of the prisoner's hands in hers. It was a large, but beautifully formed hand, full of natural vigor, but now it lay nerveless and inert in that kind clasp, and, for a moment, Mrs. Gray smoothed down the languid fingers with her own plump palm.

The woman, at first, shrunk from this mute kindness, and, half rising, fixed her great black eyes upon her visitor in sudden and almost fierce astonishment, but she shrunk back from the rosy kindness of that face with a deep breath, and lay motionless again.

Mrs. Gray spoke then in her own frank, cheerful way, and asked permission to take the little boy home with her. She described her comfortable old house, the garden, the poultry, the birds that built their nests in the twin maples, the quantity of winter apples laid up in the cellar. All the elements of happiness to a bright and healthy child she thus lay temptingly before the mother. Again the woman started up.

"Are you a moral reformer?" she said, with a sharp sneer.

"No!" answered Mrs. Gray, with a puzzled look. "At any rate not as I know of, but in these times you have so many new fangled names for simple things, that I may be one without having the least idea of it!"

"A philanthrophist then—are you that?"

"Haven't the least notion what the thing is," cried Mrs. Gray, with perfect simplicity.

"Are you one of those women who hang around prisons to pick up other people's children, while their own are running wild at home—who give a garret-bed and second-hand crusts to these poor creatures, and then scream out through society and newspaper reports for the world to come and see what angels you are? Who pick up a poor wretch from the cells here, and impose her off upon some kind fool from the country, whom she robs, of course; and before she has been tried three weeks, blaze out her reformation to the whole world, forgetting to tell the robbery when it comes?

"Do you want my boy for a pattern? Do you intend to have it shouted in some paper or anniversary report, how great a thing your society has done in snatching this poor little imp from his mother's bosom as a brand from the burning fire? In short, do you want to hold him up as a lure for the innocent country people who pour money into your laps, honestly believing that it all goes for the cause, and never once asking how yourselves are supported all the while? Are you one of these, I say?"

"Goodness gracious knows I ain't anything of the kind," answered Mrs. Gray. "Never set up for an angel in my life, never expect to on this side of the grave."

"Then you are not a lady president?"

"In our free and glorious country," answered Mrs. Gray, now more at home, for she had listened to a good many Fourth of July orations in her time; "in this country it's against the law for old women to be Presidents. At any rate, I never heard of one in a cap and white apron!"

A gleam of rich humor shot over the prisoner's face.

"Then you are not a member of any society?" she said, won into more kindly temper by the frank cordiality of her visitor.

Mrs. Gray's face became very serious, and her brown eyes shone with gentle lustre.

"It's my privilege to be a humble member of the Baptist church; but unless you have a conscience against immersion, I don't know as that ought to stand in the poor boy's way, especially as he may have been baptized already."

"Then you are not a charitable woman by profession? You are willing to take my boy for his own good? What will you do with him if I say yes?"

"Why, pretty much as I did with nephew Robert; let him run in the garden, hunt eggs, drive the geese home when he knows the way himself; and do all sorts of chores that will keep him out of mischief, and in health; as he grows old enough I will send him to school, and teach him the Lord's prayer myself. In short, I shall do pretty much like other people; scold him when he is bad, kiss him when he is good; in the end make him just such a handsome, honest, noble chap as my Robert is

—that nephew of mine. Everybody admits that he is the salt of the earth, and I brought him up myself, every inch of him !"

"And among the rest you will teach him to forget and despise his mother," said the woman, bending her wet eyes upon Mrs. Gray, with a look of passionate scrutiny.

"I never wilfully went against the Bible in my life. When the child learns to read, he will find it written there, 'Honor thy father and thy mother, that thy days may be long in the land which the Lord thy God giveth thee.'"

"Can I see him when I please ?"

"Certainly—why not ?"

"But I am a prisoner ; I have been here more than once."

"You are his mother," was the soft answer.

"You will be ashamed to have me coming to your house."

"Why so ? I have been a quiet neighbor—an upright woman, so far as my light went, all my life. Why should I fear to have any one come to my own house ?"

"But he will be ashamed of me ! With a comfortable home, with friends, schooling—my own child, will learn to scorn and hate his mother !"

"No," anwered Mrs. Gray, and her fine old face glowed with the pious prophecy—"no, because his mother will herself be a good woman, by-and-bye, *it is sure.* You are not dead at the root yet ; want care, pruning, sunshine ; will live to be a useful member of society before long—I have faith to believe it. God help you—God bless you. Now speak out at once, can I take the little fellow ?"

"Yes," answered the woman, casting herself across the bed, and pressing both hands hard against her eyes—"yes, take him —take him !"

And so Mrs. Gray returned to her old homestead with three new inmates that night. It was a bleak, sharp day, and the maple leaves were whirling in showers about the old house as they drove up. A crisp frost had swept every flower from the beds, and all the soft tints of green from the door-yard and garden. Still there was nothing gloomy in the scene ; the sitting-room windows were glowing with petted chrysanthemums, golden, snow-tinted and rosy, all bathed and nodding in a flood of light that poured up from the bright hickory-wood fire.

Robert had ridden on before the rest, bearing household directions from Mrs. Gray to the Irish servant girl. A nice supper stood ready upon the table, and a copper tea-kettle was before the fire, pouring out a thin cloud of steam from its spout, and starting off now and then in a quick, cheerful bubble, as if quite impatient to be called into active service. The fine bird's-eye diaper that flowed from the table—the little old-fashioned china cups, and the tall, plated candlesticks, from which the light fell in long, rich gleams, composed one of the most cheering pictures in the world.

Then dear old Mrs. Gray was so happy herself, so full of quiet, soothing kindness; the very tones of her voice were hopeful. When she laughed, all the rest were sure to smile, very faintly it is true; but still these smiles were little gleams won from the most agonizing grief. Altogether it was one of those evenings when we say to one another, "well, I cannot realize all this sorrow when the soul becomes dreamy, and softly casts aside the shafts of pain that goad it so fiercely at other times."

Little George fell asleep after tea, and Julia sat upon the crimson moreen couch under the windows, pillowing his head on her lap. The chrysanthemums rose in a flowery screen behind her, their soft shadows pencilling themselves on her cheek, and lying in the deeper blackness of her hair. Robert Otis spoke but little that night, and his dear, simple old aunt felt quite satisfied that the gaze which he turned so steadily toward the windows was dwelling in admiration on her flowers.

Be this as it may, his glance brought roses to that pale cheek, and kindled up the soft eyes that lay like violets shrouded beneath their thick lashes, with a brilliancy that had never burned there before. Julia's heart was far too sorrowful for *thoughts* of love, but there was something thrilling in her bosom deeper than grief, and more exquisite than any joy she had yet known.

But Robert Otis was more self-possessed. His thoughts took a more tangible form, and though he could not account to himself for the feeling of vague regret that mingled with his admiration, as he gazed upon the young girl, it was strong enough to fill his heart with sadness. Mrs. Gray noticed the gloom upon his brow as she sat in her arm-chair, basking in the glow of that noble wood fire. A dish of the finest crimson apples had just been placed on the little round stand before her, and she began testing their mellowness with her fingers, as a hint for her nephew to circulate them among her guests. Robert saw nothing of this, for he was pondering over the miserable position of that young girl, in his mind, and had no idea that his abstraction was noticed.

"Come—come," said Mrs. Gray, "you have been moping there long enough, nephew, forgetting manners and everything else. Here are the apples waiting, and no one to hand them round, for when I once get settled in this easy-chair"—here the good woman gave a smiling survey of her ample person, which certainly overflowed the chair at every point, leaving all but a ridge of the back and the curving arms quite invisible—"it isn't a very easy thing to get up again. Now bustle about, and while we old women rest ourselves, you and Julia, there, can try your luck with the apple-seeds.

"I remember the first time I ever surmised that Mr. Gray had taken a notion to me, was once when we were at an apple-cutting together down in Maine. Somehow Mr. Gray got into my neighborhood when we ranged round the great basket of apples. I felt my cheeks burn the minute he drew his seat so close to mine, and took out his jack-knife to begin work. He pared and I quartered. I never looked up but once—then his cheek was redder than mine, and he held the jack-knife terribly unsteady. By-and-bye he got a noble, great apple, yellow as gold, and smooth as a baby's cheek. I was looking at his hands sidewise from under my lashes, and saw that he was paring it carefully, as if every round of the skin was a strip of gold. At last he cut it off at the seed end, and the soft rings fell down over his wrist as I took the apple from his fingers.

"'Now,' says he, in a whisper, bending his head a little, and raising the apple-peel carefully with his right hand, 'I'm just as sure this will be the first letter of a name that I love, as I am that we are alive.' He began softly whirling the apple-peel round his head; the company was all busy with one another, and I was the only one who saw the yellow links quivering around his head, once, twice, three times. Then he held it still a moment, and sat looking right into my eyes. I held my breath, and so did he.

"'Now,' says he, and his breath came out with a quiver, 'what if it should be your name?'

"I did not answer, and we both looked back at the same time. Sure enough it was a letter S. No pen ever made one more beautifully. 'Just as I expected,' says he, and his eyes grew bright as diamonds—'just as I expected.' That was all he said."

"And what answer did you make, aunt?" asked Robert Otis, who had been listening with a flushed face. "What did you say?"

"I didn't speak a word, but quartered on just as fast as I could. As for Mr. Gray, he kept paring, and paring, like all possessed. I thought he would never stop paring, or speak a word more. By-and-bye he stuck the point of his knife into an apple, and unwinding the skin from around it, he handed it over to me. It was a red skin, I remember, and cut as smooth as a ribbon.

"'I shouldn't a bit wonder if that dropped into a letter G,' says Mr. Gray. 'Supposing you try it.'

"Well, I took the red apple-skin, and whirled it three times round my head, and down it went on to the floor, curled up into the nicest capital G that you ever sat eyes on.

"Mr. Gray, he looked at the letter, and then sort of sidewise into my face. 'S. G.,' says he, taking up the apple-skin, and eating it, as if it had been the first mouthful of a Thanksgiving dinner. 'How would you like to see them two letters on a new set of silver teaspoons?'

"I re'lly believe you could have lit a candle at my face, it burned so; but I couldn't speak more than if I'd been born tongue-tied."

"But did you never answer about the spoons?" asked Julia.

"Well, yes, I believe I did, the next Sunday night," said the old lady, demurely, smoothing her apron.

What was there in Mrs. Gray's simple narrative that should have brought confusion and warm blushes into those two young faces? Why, after one hastily withdrawn glance, did neither Robert Otis nor Julia Warren look at each other again that night?

CHAPTER XXVII.

STRUGGLES AND REVELS.

Wine, wine for the heart, in its struggle of pride,
And music to drown all this with'ring pain!
The arrow, the arrow is deep in her side!
Bring music and wine with their madness again.

THE passions take their distinctive expression from the nature in which they find birth. The grief that rends one heart like an earthquake, sinks with dead, silent weight into another, uttering no sound, giving no outward sign, and yet is powerful, perhaps, as that which exhausts itself in tumult. Some flee from grief, half defying, half evading it, pausing, breathless, in the race, now and then, to find the arrow still buried in the side, rankling deeper and deeper with each fierce effort to cast it out.

Thus it was with the woman to whom our story tends—Ada, the insulted and suffering widow of Leicester. There had been mutual wrong between the two; both had sinned greatly; both had tasted deep of the usual consequences of sin. During his life her love for him had been the one wild passion of existence; now that he was dead, her grief partook of the same stormy nature. It was wild, fierce, brilliant; it thirsted for change; it was bitter with regrets that stung her into the very madness of sorrow.

As an unbroken horse plunges beneath the rider's heel, the object of grief like this seeks for amelioration in excitement. It is a sorrow that thirsts for action; that arouses some kindred passion, and feeds itself with that.

Ada Leicester was not known to be connected, even remotely, with the man for whose murder old Mr. Warren was now awaiting his trial. She was a leader in the fashionable world; her very anguish must be concealed; her groans must be uttered in private; her tears quenched firmly till they turned to fire in her heart. All her life that man had been a pain and a torment to her. The last breath she had seen him draw was a taunt, his last look an insult; and yet these very memories embittered her grief. He had turned the silver thread of her life into iron, but it broke with his existence, leaving her appalled and objectless. She never had, never could love another; and what is a woman on earth without love as a memory, a passion, or a hope?

Her grief became a wild passion. She strove to assuage it in reckless gaiety, and plunged into all the excitements of artificial life with a fervor that made every hour of her existence a tumult. The opera season was at its full height. Society had once more concentrated itself in New York, and still Ada was the brightest of its stars. Morning dances by gas-light took place in some few houses where novelty was an object. Not long after Leicester's death her noble mansion was closed for a morning revel; every pointed window was sealed with shutters and muffled with the richest draperies. Light in every form of beauty—the pure gas-flame—the soft glow of wax-candles—the moonlight gleam of alabaster lamps flooded the sumptuous rooms, excluding every ray of the one glorious lamp which God has kindled in the sky. Dancers flitted to and fro in those lofty rooms; garlands of choice green-house flowers scattered fragrance from the walls, and veiled many a classic statue with their impalpable mist.

Never in her whole life had Ada appeared more wildly brilliant. Reckless, sparkling, scattering smiles and wit wherever she passed; now whirling through the waltz; now exchanging bright repartees with her guests amid the pauses of the music; fluttering from group to group like a bird of Paradise, dashing perfume from its native flower thickets, she flitted from room to room; now sitting alone in a dark corner of the conservatory, her hands falling languidly down, her face bowed upon her bosom, the fire quenched in her eyes, she felt the very life ebbing, as it were, from her parted and pale lips.

Thus with the strongest contrasts, fierce alike in her gaiety and her grief, she spent that miserable morning. The transition from one state to another would have been startling to a close observer, but the changes in her mood were like lightning; the pale cheek became instantly so red; the dull eye so bright, that her guests saw nothing but the most fascinating coquetry in all this, and each new shade or gleam that crossed her beautiful face brought down fresh showers of adulation upon her. The usual quiet elegance of her manner was for the time forgotten.

More than once her wild, clear laugh rang from one room to another, chiming in or rising above the music, and this only charmed her guests the more. It was a new feature in their idol. It was not for her wealth or her beauty alone that Ada Leicester became an object of worship that day. Like a wounded bird that makes the leaves tremble all around with its anguish, she startled society into more intense admiration by the splendor of her agony.

At mid-day her guests began to depart, pouring forth from those sumptuous rooms into the noontide glare, when delicate dresses, flushed cheeks and languid eyes were exposed in all the disarray which is sometimes picturesque when enveloped in night shadows, but becomes meretricious in the broad sunshine.

A few of her most distinguished guests remained to dinner that day, for Ada dreaded to be alone, and so kept up the excitement that was burning her life out. If her spirits flagged, if the smile fled from her lips even for an instant, those lips were bathed with the rich wines that sparkled on her board, kindling them into smiles and bloom again. The resources of her intellect seemed inexhaustible; the flashes of her delicate wit grew keener and brighter as the hours wore on.

Her table was surrounded by men and women who flash like meteors now and then through the fashionable circles of New York, intellectual aristocrats that enliven the insipid monotony of those changing circles, as stars give fire and beauty to the blue of a summer sky. But keen-sighted as these people were, they failed to read the heart that was delighting them with its agony. All but one, and he was not seated at the table, he spoke no word, and won no attention from that haughty circle, save by the subdued and even solemn awkwardness of look and manner, which was too remarkable for entire oblivion.

Behind Ada's seat there stood a tall man, with huge, ungainly limbs, and a stoop in the shoulders. He was evidently a servant, but wore no livery like the others; and those who gave a thought to the subject saw that he waited only upon his mistress, and that once or twice he stooped down and whispered a word in her ear, which she received with a quick and imperious motion of the head, which was either rejection or reproof of something he had urged.

Nothing could be more touching than the sadness of this man's face as the spirits of his mistress rose with the contest of intellect that was going on around her. He saw the bitter source from which all this brightness flowed, and every smile upon those red lips deepened the gloom so visible in his face.

"Now," said Ada, rising from the table, and leading the way to her boudoir, for it had been an impromptu dinner, and the drawing-room was yet in confusion after the dance; "now let us refresh ourselves with music. An hour's separation, a fresh toilet, and we will all meet at the opera—then to-morrow—what shall we do to-morrow?"

She entered the boudoir while speaking, and as if smitten by some keen memory, lifted one hand to her forehead, reflecting languidly, "To-morrow—yes, what shall we do to-morrow?"

"You are pale; what is the matter?" inquired one of the lady guests, in that hurried tone of sympathy which is usually superficial as sweet. "We have oppressed you with all this gaiety!"

"Not in the least—nothing of the kind!" exclaimed the hostess, with a clear laugh. "It was the perfume from those vases. It put me in mind—it made me faint!"

She rang the bell while speaking, and the servant, who stood all dinner-time behind her chair, entered.

"Take these flowers away, Jacob," she said, pointing to the vases, "there is heliotrope among them, and you know the scent of heliotrope affects me—kills me. Never allow flowers to be put in these rooms again. Not a leaf, not a bud—do you understand?"

"Yes, madam," answered the servant, with calm humility, "I understand! It was not I that placed them there now!"

Ada seated herself on the couch, resting her forehead upon one hand, as if the faintness still continued. Her lips and all around her mouth grew pallid. Though the flowers were gone, their effect still seemed to oppress her more and more. At length she started up with a hysterical laugh and went into the bed-chamber. When she came forth her cheeks were damask again, and her lips red as coral; but a dusky circle under the eyes, and a faint, spasmodic twitching about the mouth, revealed how artificial the bloom was. From that moment all her gaiety returned, and in her graceful glee her guests forgot the agitation that had for a moment surprised them.

Later in the evening, Ada drove to the Opera House, where she again met the gay friends who had thronged her dwelling at mid-day. Still did she surpass them all in the superb but hasty toilet which she had assumed, after the morning revel. Many an eye was turned admiringly upon her sofa that night, little dreaming that the opera-cloak of rose-colored cashmere, with its blossom-tinted lining and border of snowy swan's-down, covered a bosom throbbing with suppressed anguish. Little could that admiring crowd deem that the brilliants interlinked with burning opal stones that glowed with ever-restless light upon her arms, her bosom, and down the corsage of her brocade dress, were to the wretched woman as so many pebbles that the rudest foot might tread upon. Her cheeks were in a glow; her eyes sparkled, and the graceful unrest which left her no two minutes in the same position, seemed but a pretty feminine wile to exhibit the splendor of her dress. How could the crowd suppose that the heart over which those jewels burned, was aching with a burden of crushed tears.

She sat amid the brilliant throng, unmindful of its admiration. The music rushed to her ear in sweet gushes of passion. But she sat smilingly there, unconscious of its power or its pathos. It sighed through the building soft and low as the spring air in a bed of violets; but even then it failed to awake her attention. Unconsciously the notes stole over her heart, and feeling a rush of emotions sweeping over her, she started up, waved an adieu to her friends, and left the Opera House. Half a dozen of the most distinguished gentlemen of her party sprang up to lead her out. She took the nearest arm and left the house, simply uttering a hurried good-night as she stepped into the carriage. There was no eye to look upon her then. Those who had followed her with admiring glances as she left the opera, little thought how keen was her agony as she rolled homeward in that sumptuous carriage, her cheek pressed hard against the velvet lining; her fingers interlocked and wringing each other in the wild anguish to which she abandoned herself

CHAPTER XXVIII.

ADA LEICESTER AND JACOB STRONG

We drove him to that fearful gulf,
In the sharp pangs of his despair,
As angry hunters chase a wolf
From open field and hidden lair.

The servant who sat waiting in the vestibule was startled by the hard, tearless misery of Ada's face, as she entered her own dwelling that night. He looked at her earnestly, and seemed about to speak, but she swept by him with averted eyes and ascended the stairs.

It was the same man who had stood beside her chair at dinner that day. The look of anxiety was on his features yet, and he pressed his lips hard together as she passed him, evidently curbing some sharp sensation that the haughty bearing of his mistress aroused. He stood looking after her as she glided with a swift, noiseless tread over the richly carpeted stairs, her pale hand now and then gleaming out in startling relief from the ebony balustrade, and her stony face mocking the artificial scarlet of her mouth. She turned at the upper landing, and he saw her glide away in the soft twilight overhead. He stood a moment with his eyes riveted on the spot where she had disappeared, then he followed up the stairs with a step as firm and rapid as hers had been. Even his heavy foot left no sound on the mass of woven flowers that covered the steps, and the shadow cast by his ungainly figure moved no more silently than himself.

He opened several doors, but they closed after him without noise, and Ada was unconscious of his presence for several moments after he stood within her boudoir. A fire burned in the silver grate, casting a sunset glow over the room, but leaving many of its objects in shadow; for save a moonlight gleam that came from a lamp in the dressing-room, no other light was near.

Ada had flung her mantle on the couch, and with her arms folded on the black marble of the mantel-piece, bent her forehead upon them, and stood thus statue-like gazing into the fire. A clear amethystine flame quivered over the coal, striking the opals and brilliants that ornamented her dress, till they burned like coals of living fire upon the snow of her arms and bosom. Thus with the same prismatic light spreading from the jewels to her rigid face, she seemed more like a fallen angel mourning over her ruin than a living woman.

At length the servant made a slight noise. Ada lifted up her head, and a frown darkened her face.

"I did not ring—I do not require anything of you to-night," she said.

"I know it. I know well enough that you require nothing of me—that my very devotion is hateful to you. Why is it? I came up here, to-night, on purpose to ask the question—why is it?" answered the man, with a grave dignity, which was very remote from the manner which a servant, however favored, is expected to maintain toward his mistress. "What have I done to deserve this treatment?"

Ada looked at him earnestly for a moment, and then her lip curled with a bitter smile.

"What have you done, Jacob Strong! Can you ask that question of William Leicester's wife, so soon after your own act has made her a widow?"

"But how?—how did I make you a widow?" said he, turning pale with suppressed feeling.

"How?" cried Ada, almost with a shriek, for the passion of her nature had been gathering force all day, and now it burst forth with a degree of violence that shook her whole frame. "Who sat like a great, hideous spider in his web, watching him as he wove and entangled the meshes of crime around him? Who stung my pride, spurred on all that was unforgiving and haughty in my nature, till I too—unnatural wretch—who had wronged and sinned against him—turned in my unholy pride, and drove him into deeper evil? It was you, Jacob Strong, who did this. It was you who urged him into the fearful strait, that admitted of no escape but death. The guilt of this self-murder rests with you, and with me. My heart is black with his blood; my brain reels when the thought presses on it. I hate you—and oh! a thousand times more do I hate myself—the pitiful tool of my own menial!"

"Your menial, Ada Wilcox—have I ever been that?"

"No," was the passionate answer, "I have been *your* menial, your dupe. You have made me his murderer. I loved him, oh! Father of mercies, how I loved him!"

The wretched woman wrung her hands, and waved them up and down in the firelight so rapidly, that the restless brilliants upon them seemed shooting out sparks of lightning.

"I thought he would come back. He was cruel—he was insolent—but what was that? We might have known his haughty spirit would never bend. If he had died any other death—oh! anything, anything but this rankling knowledge, that I, his wife, drove him to self-murder!"

Jacob Strong left his position at the door, and coming close up to his mistress, took both her hands in his. He could not endure her reproaches. Her words stung his honest heart to the core.

"Sit down," he said, with gentle firmness—"sit down, Ada Wilcox, and listen to me. There is yet something that I have to say. If it will remove any of the bitterness that you harbor against me, if it can reconcile you to yourself, I can tell you that there is great doubt if your—if Mr. Leicester did commit suicide. Thinking it might grieve you more deeply, I kept the papers away that said anything of the matter; but even now a man lies in prison charged with his murder!"

"Charged with his murder!" repeated Ada, starting. "How?—when? She—his mother—said it was self-destruction!"

"She believes it, perhaps believes it yet, but others think

differently. He was found dead in a miserable basement, alone with the old man they have imprisoned. Why he went there no one can guess; but it is known that he was in that basement the night before, but a little earlier than the time when he appeared at your ball. If he had any portion of the money obtained from us about him, that may have tempted the old man, who is miserably poor."

Jacob was going on, but his mistress, who had listened with breathless attention, interrupted him.

"Do you believe this? Do you believe that he was murdered?"

"Very strong proofs exist against the old man," replied Jacob—"the public think him guilty."

Ada drew a deep breath.

"You have taken a terrible load from my heart," she said, pressing one hand to her bosom, and sinking down upon the couch with a low, hysterical laugh. "He is dead, but there is a chance that I did not kill him. I begin to loathe myself less."

"And me!—*me* you will never cease to hate?"

"You have been a good friend to me, Jacob Strong, better than I deserved," answered Ada, reaching forth her hand, which the servant wrung rather than pressed.

"And this last act," he said, "when I tried to free you from the grasp of a vile man, was the most kind, the most friendly thing I ever did!"

Ada started up and drew her hand from his grasp.

"Hush, not a word more," she said, "if we are to be anything to each other hereafter. He was my husband—he is dead!"

She sunk back to the cushions of her couch a moment after, and veiling her eyes with one hand, fell into thought. Jacob stood humbly before her; for though they spoke and acted as friends, nay, almost as brother and sister, he never lost the respectful demeanor befitting his position in Ada's household.

She sat up, at length, with a calmer and more resolute expression of countenance.

"Now tell me all that relates to his death," she said. "Who is charged with it? What is the evidence?"

Jacob related all that he knew regarding the arrest of old Mr. Warren. In his own heart he did not believe the poor man guilty, but he abstained from expressing this, for it was an intuition rather than a belief, and Jacob could not but see that his own exculpation in the eyes of the fair creature to whom he spoke, would depend upon her belief in another's guilt. Jacob had no courage to express more than known facts as they appeared in the case. The vague impressions that haunted him were, in truth, too indefinite for words.

Ada listened with profound attention. She had not been so still or so firm before, since her husband's death. It required time for feelings strong as hers to turn into a new channel, and the passage from self-hatred to revenge was still as it was terrible.

She remained silent for some minutes after Jacob had told her all, and when she did speak, the whole character of her face was changed.

"If this man is guilty, Leicester's death lies not here!" she said, pressing one hand hard upon her heart, as she walked slowly up and down the boudoir. "When he is arraigned for trial, I am acquitted or convicted. You also, Jacob Strong; for if this old man is not Leicester's murderer, you and I drove him to suicide."

Jacob did not reply. In his soul he believed every step that he had taken against William Leicester to be right, and he felt guiltless of his death, no matter in what form it came; but he knew that argument would never remove the belief that had fixed like a monomania upon that unhappy woman, and wisely, therefore, he attempted none.

"I have told you all," he said, moving toward the door. "In any case my conscience is at rest!"

She did not appear to heed his words, but asked abruptly,

"Are the laws of America strict and searching? Do murderers ever escape here?"

"Sometimes they do, no doubt," answered Jacob, with a grim smile, "but then probably quite as many innocent men are hung, so that the balance is kept about equal."

"And how do the guilty escape?"

"Oh, by any of the thousand ways that a smart lawyer can invent. With money enough it is easy to evade the law, or tire it out with exceptions and appeals."

"Then money can do this?"

"What is there that money *cannot* do?"

A wan smile flitted over Ada's face.

"Oh! who should know its power better than myself?" she said. Then she resumed. "But this man, this grey-headed murderer—has he this power?—can he control money enough to screen the blood he has shed?"

"He is miserably poor!"

"Then the trial will be an unprejudiced one. If proven guilty he must atone for the guilt. If acquitted fairly, openly, without the aid of money or influence, then are we guilty, Jacob Strong, guilty as those who hurl a man to the brink of a precipice, which he is sure to plunge down."

"No man who simply pursues his duty should reproach himself for the crime of another," was the grave reply.

"But have *I* done my duty? Can I be guiltless of my husband's desperate act?"

Jacob was silent.

"You cannot answer me, my friend," said Ada mournfully.

"Yes! I can. William Leicester's death, if he in fact fell by his own hand, was the natural end of a vicious life."

Ada waved her hand sharply, thus forbidding him to proceed with the subject, and entering her dressing-room, closed the door.

Jacob stood for a time gazing vacantly at the door through which she had disappeared, then heaving a deep sigh, the strange being left the boudoir, but a vague feeling of self-reproach at his heart, rendered him more than usually sad all the next day. True, he had changed the current of Ada's grief, had lifted a burden of self-reproach from her heart; but had he not filled it with other and not less bitter passions?

CHAPTER XXIX.

ADA'S SOLITARY BREAKFAST.

My tortured soul is sick, and every nerve
Answers its promptings with an aching strain,
Yet from my task I may not pause or swerve—
Rest is a curse, and every thought a pain.

For the first time since her husband's death, Ada slept soundly, till deep in the morning. But her slumber was haunted by dreams that sent shadows painful and death-like over her beautiful face. More than once her maid stole from the dressing-room into the rosy twilight of the bed-chamber, and stooped anxiously over her mistress as she slept, for the faint moans that broke from her lips, pallid even in that rich light, and parted with a sort of painful smile—startled the servant as she prepared her mistress's toilet.

It was almost mid-day when this unearthly slumber passed off, but the brightest sun could only fill those richly draped chambers with a twilight atmosphere, that allowed the sleeper to glide dreamily from her couch to the pursuits of life. When the mechanics throughout the city were at their noonday meal, Ada crept into her dressing-room, pale and languid as if she had just risen from a sick-bed. Upon a little ebony table near the fire, a breakfast service of frosted silver, and the most delicate Sèvres china stood ready. Ada sunk into the great easy-chair, which stood near it, cushioned with blossom-colored damask, which gleamed through an over drapery of heavy point lace. The maid came in with chocolate, snowy little rolls, just from the hands of her French cook, and two crystal dishes, the one stained through with the ruby tint of some rich foreign jelly, the other amber-hued with the golden honeycomb that lay within it. Delicate butter, moulded like a handful of strawberries, lay in a crystal grape-leaf in one corner of the salver, and a soft steam floated from the small chocolate urn, veiling the whole with a gossamer cloud.

Altogether, that luxurious room, the repast so delicate, but evidently her ordinary breakfast ; the lady herself in all the beautiful disarray of a muslin wrapper, half hidden, half exposed by the loosely knotted silk cord that confined a dressing-gown, quilted and lined with soft white silk—all this composed a picture of the most sumptuous enjoyment. But look in that woman's face ! See the dark circles beneath those heavy violet eyes. Mark how languidly that mouth uncloses, when she turns to speak. See the nervous start which she makes when the crystal and silver jar against each other, as the maid places them upon the table. Is there not something in all this that would make the rudest mechanic pause, before he consented to exchange the comforts won by his honest toil, for the splendor that seemed so tempting at the first glance ?

Ada broke a roll in two, allowed one of the golden strawberries to melt away in its fragments, then laid it down untasted. Her heart was sick, her appetite gone, and after drinking one cup of the chocolate, she turned half loathing from that exquisite repast.

" Move the things away !" she said, to the waiting-woman.

" Will madam chose nothing else ?" said the servant, hesitating and looking back as she carried off the tray.

" Nothing," replied her mistress.

The tone was one that forbade further inquiry ; so the maid left the apartment ; and Ada was alone, restless, feverish, unhappy.

She rose, and walking to the window, looked out ; but a few minutes spent thus appeared to tire her; and throwing herself again into her chair, she took up a book and attempted to read. But she still found no occupation for her thoughts. At last she flung down the volume, and rising, paced the chamber.

The reflection grew and grew upon her, that if the old man should be convicted of the murder, she would be free from the guilt of Leicester's death. Her mind had been in a morbid condition ever since that event, or she would not now have thought this, nor have before regarded herself as criminal. That the old man should be proved guilty, became an insane wish on her part. She clutched at it with despairing hope. The more she thought of this means of escape from her remorse, the wilder became her desire to see the prisoner convicted. Soon the belief in his criminality became as fixed in her mind as the persuasion of her own existence.

A stern, passionate desire for revenge now took possession of her. The very idea that the accused might yet escape, through some technicality, drove her almost to madness; and as she conjured up this picture, her eyes flashed like those of an angry tigress, and the workings of her countenance betrayed the tumult of her soul.

At last, catching the reflection of her person in a mirror, she started at her wild appearance; a bitter smile passed over her face, and she said—

"Why do I seek this old man's blood? Am I crazed, or a woman no longer? But heaven knows," she added, clasping her forehead with her hands, "that I have endured enough to transform me out of humanity."

With a heavy movement she rang the bell, ordered her maid to dress her, and directed the carriage to be in waiting.

When Ada Leicester descended to her carriage, radiant in majestic beauty, the last thought that would have presented itself to a spectator must have been that this queenly woman was unhappy. But the color in her cheek; the blaze of her brilliant eyes; and the proud, almost disdainful step with which she crossed the sidewalk, were deceptive as the fever of disease. The excitement which so increased her lofty beauty, was purchased with inexpressible pangs, as the hues of the dying dolphin are procured by intolerable anguish.

The day was bright; the breeze was fresh; everything around was beautiful and exhilarating. But the pleasant face of nature failed to allay the fever of Ada Leicester's soul. One thought only possessed her; "What if the old man should be acquitted?" This idea grew upon her, and still grew. She tried to shake it off. She endeavored to become interested in the equipages driving past on the Bloomingdale road, and failing there, turned her heavy eyes on the green fields along the North River, or the sailing vessels ploughing up and down its water. But it was all in vain; Ada had no interest in anything so quiet as those scenes.

That dark thought clung to her. Now it rose into a terror, and a new idea crossed her mind. If the murderer should escape, and her husband be unavenged, would not her guilt be then almost as great as if she had driven Leicester to suicide?

Everything became a blank around her; she was only conscious of this one thought. She saw nothing, heard nothing; for her entire soul was absorbed in one morbid idea. It became a monomania. Finally she pulled the check string, and, in a sharp tone, directed the coachman to drive back to the city.

The man looked around, startled by her voice; he was alarmed at the aspect of her countenance, which was almost livid. She did not notice it, but closed the curtain, and threw herself back on the cushions.

This terror was visible in his look. As they entered the city, the coachman asked if he should drive home.

This roused her from her stupor. A distance of five miles had been traversed since she had last spoken, yet the interval appeared to her scarcely a minute. She looked out with surprise. Recognizing the place, she pulled the check-string. and directed the servant to drive to the office of an advocate, renowned, especially in criminal cases, for his acute cross-examinations, not less than for his eloquence.

The lawyer was at home when the carriage drew up at his

door. He knew Ada Leicester as a leading star in society, and was surprised to see her enter his office so abruptly. He rose, bowed profoundly, and handed her a chair.

His visitor hesitated a moment, and then said,

"There is a man now in prison, charged with the murder of one William Leicester—you know the case, perhaps—and I have called on you to make it impossible for the prisoner to escape unless he is really innocent." She uttered these last words slowly, with her eye fixed on the advocate as she spoke.

"There is such a thing, I believe, as the friends of a guilty man securing legal assistance when the commonwealth proves lax or indifferent."

"Oh! yes, madam," said the lawyer. "The thing is of common occurrence."

"Very well," said Ada, slowly, taking a note of large value from her *porte-monnaie*. "I wish you to see the district-attorney, and assist him in this trial."

"You would retain me—I understand your wish," said the lawyer, too polite to touch the note which she laid before him, yet unable to prevent a glance at its denomination; and bowing again profoundly, as his visitor rose to go, he continued, "the guilty man shall not escape, madam."

Ada Leicester drove home with a lighter heart, feeling as if a great duty had been discharged.

CHAPTER XXX.

THE PRISON WOMAN IN ADA'S DRESSING-ROOM.

Look not so haughtily, imperious dame;
Chance digs the gulf that lies between us two:
Mine is the open, yours the hidden shame;
The vulture soars with me, but skulks with you.

Ada Leicester had scarcely gained her apartment, when Jacob Strong entered it. He came in with a tread so heavy, that it made itself heard even through the turf-like swell of the carpet. She looked up at him wearily, yet with surprise. Jacob, so phlegmatic, so sturdy in all other cases, never was self-possessed with his mistress; one glance of those eyes, one wave of that hand was enough to confuse his brain, and make the strong heart flutter in his bosom like the wings of a wild bird.

"Madam," he stammered, shifting his huge feet unsteadily to and fro on the carpet, "there is a woman down stairs who wants to see you."

"I can see no one this morning; send her away!"

"I tried that, madam, but she answers that her business is important, and, in short, that she *will* see you."

Ada opened her eyes wide, and half turned in her chair. This insolent message aroused her somewhat.

"Indeed! What does she look like? Who can it be?"

"She is a very common-looking person, handsome enough, but unpleasant."

"You never saw her before, then?"

"No, never!"

"Let her come up; I cannot well give the next ten minutes to anything more miserable than myself," said Ada; "let her come up!"

Jacob left the room, and Ada, aroused to some little interest in the person who had so peremptorily demanded admission to her presence, threw off something of her languor as she saw the door swing open to admit her singular guest.

A woman entered, with a haughty, almost rude air. Her dress was clean, but of cheap material, and put on with an effort at tidiness, as if in correction of some long-acquired habits which she had found it difficult to fling off. A black hood, lined with faded crimson silk, was thrown back from her face, revealing large Roman features, fierce dark eyes, and a mouth that, in its heavy fullness, struck the beholder more unpleasantly even than the ferocious brightness of those large eyes.

The woman looked around her as she entered the dressing-room, and a faint sneer curled her lip, while she took in, with a contemptuous glance, all the elegant luxury of that little room. Ada had not for an instant dreamed of inviting a creature so unprepossessing to sit down in the room so exquisitely fitted up for her own enjoyment; but the woman waited for no indication of the kind. She cast one keen glance on the surprised and somewhat startled face turned upon her as she entered, another around the room, which contained only two chairs beside the one occupied by its mistress, and seizing one, a frail thing of carved ebony, cushioned with the most delicate embroidery on white moire, she took possession of it.

At another time Ada would have rung the bell and ordered the woman to be put from the room; but now there was a sort of fascination in this audacious coolness that aroused a reckless feeling in her own heart. She allowed the woman to seat herself, therefore, without a word; nay, a slight smile quivered about her lip as she heard the fragile ebony crack, as if about to give way beneath the heavy burden cast so roughly upon it.

The strange being sat in silence for some moments, examining Ada with a bold, searching glance, that, spite of herself, brought the blood to that haughty woman's cheek. After her fierce black eyes had roved up and down two or three times, from the pretty lace cap to the embroidered slipper, that began to beat with impatience against the cushion which it had before so languidly pressed, the woman at last condescended to speak.

"You are rich, madam; people say so, and all this looks like it. They say, too, that you are generous, good to the poor; that you give away money by handsful. I want a little of this money!"

Ada looked hard at the woman, who returned the glance almost fiercely

"You need not search my face so sharply," she said, "I don't want the money for myself. One gets along on a little in New York, and I can always have that little without begging of rich women. I would scrub anybody's kitchen floor from morning till night, rather than ask you or any other proud aristocrat for a red cent! It isn't for myself I've come, but for a fellow prisoner, or rather one that was a fellow-prisoner, for I'm out of the cage just now. It's for an old man I want the money, a good old man that the night-hawks have taken up for murder!"

Ada started, but the woman did not observe it, and went on with increasing warmth.

"The old fellow is a saint on earth—a holy saint, if such things ever are. I know what crime is. I can find guilt in a man's eye, let it be buried ever so deep; but this old man is not guilty; a summer morning is not more serene than his face! Men who murder from malice or accident do not sit so peacefully in their cells, with that sort of prayerful tenderness brooding over the countenance."

"Of whom are you speaking, woman? Who is this old man?" demanded Ada, sharply. "What is his innocence or his guilt to me?"

"What is his innocence or guilt to you? Are you a woman?—have you a heart and ask that question? As for me I *might* ask it—I who know what crime is, and who should feel most for the criminal! But you, pampered in wealth, beautiful, loving, worshipped—who never had even a temptation to sin—it is for you to feel for a man unjustly accused—the innocent for the innocent, the guilty for the guilty. Sympathy should run thus, if it does not!"

"This is an outrage—mockery!" said Ada starting from her chair. "Who sent you here, woman?—how dare you talk to me of these things?—I know nothing of the old man you are raving about; wish to know less. If you want money, say so, but do not talk of him, of crime, of—of murder!"

She sunk back to her chair again, pale and breathing heavily. Her strange visitor stood up, evidently surprised by a degree of agitation that seemed to her without adequate cause.

"So the rich can feel," she said; "but this is not compassion. My presence annoys you—the close mention of sin makes you shudder. You look, yes, you do look like that angel child when I first laid my hand upon her shoulder."

"What child?--of whom do you speak?" questioned Ada, faintly, for the woman was bending over her, and she was fasinated by the power of those wild eyes.

"It is the grandchild of that old man—the old murderer they call him—the old saint *I* call him; it is his grandchild that your look reminded me of a moment ago; it is gone, now, but I shall always like you the better for having seemed like her only for a minute!"

"Her name, what is her name?" cried Ada, impelled to the question by some intuitive impulse, that she neither comprehended nor cared to conceal. "What is the child's name, I say?"

"Julia Warren."

"A fair, gentle girl, with eyes that seems to crave affection, as violets open their leaves for the dew when they are thirsty; a frail, delicate little thing, toiling under a burden of flowers! I have seen a young creature like this more than once. She haunts me—her name itself haunts me—and why, why!—she is nothing to me—I am nothing to her?"

Ada spoke in low tones, communing with herself; and the woman looked on, wondering at the words as they dropped so unconsciously from those beautiful lips.

"It is the same girl, I am sure of it," said the woman, at last. "She had no flowers when I saw her tottering with her poor wet eyes into the prison; but her face might have been bathed in their perfume, it was so full of sweetness. It was so—so holy I was near saying, but the word is a strange one for me. Well, madam, this young girl has been in prison with me, and the like of me!"

"She must come out—she shall not remain there an hour!" said Ada, searching eagerly among the folds of her dress for a purse, which was not to be found. "It is not here, I will ring for Jacob; you want money to get this young girl out of prison; that is kind, very kind; you shall have it. Oh, heavens! the thought suffocates me—that angel child—that beautiful flower spirit in prison! Woman, why did you not come to me before?"

"I was in prison myself—the officers don't let us out so easily. We are not exactly expected to make calls; besides, how should I know anything about you, except as one of those proud women who gather up their silken garments when we come near, as if it were contagion to breathe the same atmosphere with us."

"But how is it that you have come to me at last?"

"She told me about you!"

"*She* sent you to me then?" questioned Ada, with sparkling eyes; "bless her, she sent you!"

"No, she told me about you. I came of my own accord."

Ada's countenance fell; she was silent for a moment, subdued by a strange feeling of disappointment.

"But she is in that horrid place; no matter how you came; not another hour must she stay in prison, if money or influence can release her."

"But she is not in prison now!" said the woman.

"Not in prison!—how is this. What can you desire of me if she is not in prison?"

"But her grandfather—the good old man, he is in prison, helpless as a babe—innocent as a babe. It is the old man who is in prison."

"Why am I tormented with this old man? Do not mention him to me again—his crime is fearful; *I* am not the one to save him, the murderer of—of——"

"He is the young girl's grandfather!"

Ada had started from her chair, and was pacing rapidly up and down the room, her arms folded tightly under the loose sleeves of her dressing-gown, and the silken tassels swaying to and fro with the impetuosity of her movements. There seemed to be a venomous fascination in that old man's name that stung her whole being into action. She had not comprehended before that it was connected with that of the flower-girl; but the words "he is the young girl's grandfather," arrested her like the shaft from a bow. Her lips grew white, she stood motionless gazing almost fiercely upon the woman who had uttered these words.

"That girl the grandchild of Leicester's murderer!" she exclaimed. "Why the very flowers I tread ón turn to serpents beneath my feet!"

"The old man did not kill this Leicester," answered the woman, and her rude face grew white also; "or if he did, it was but as the instrument of God's vengeance on a monster—a hideous, vile monster, who crawled over everything good in his way, crushing it as he went. If he *had* killed him—if I believed it, no Catholic saint was ever idolized as I would worship that old man!"

"Woman, what had Leicester done to you that you should thus revile him in his grave?"

A cloud of inexplicable passion swept over the woman's face. She drew close to Ada, and as she answered, her breath, feverish with the dregs of intoxication, and laden with words that stung like reptiles, sickened the wretched woman to the heart's core. She had no strength to check the fierce torrent that rushed over her; but folded her white arms closer and closer over her heart, as if to shield it somewhat from the storm of bitter eloquence her question had provoked.

"What has Leicester done to me?" said the woman. "Look, look at me, I am his work from head to foot, body and soul, all of his fashioning!"

"How? Did *you* love him also?"

A glow of fierce disgust broke over the woman's features, gleaming in her eye and curling her lip.

"Love him, I never sunk so low as that; he scarcely disturbed the froth upon my heart, the wine below was not for him. Had I loved him, he might have been content with my ruin only; as it was, madam, it is a short story, very short, you shall have it—but I'll have drink after."

"Compose yourself—do not be so violent," said Ada, shrinking from the storm she had raised, with that sensitiveness which makes the wounded bird shield its bosom from a threatened arrow, "I do not wish to give you pain!"

"Pain!" exclaimed the woman, with a wild sneer, "I am

beyond that. No one need know pain while the drug stores are open! You ask what Leicester has ever done to me You knew him, perhaps—no matter, you are not the first woman whose face has lost its color at the sound of his name ; but he will do no more mischief, the blood is wrung from his heart now."

Ada sunk back in her chair, holding up both hands with the palms outward, as if warding off a blow. But the woman had become fierce in her passion, and would not be checked.

"You ask if I loved him, I, who worshipped my own husband, my noble, beautiful, young husband, with a worship strong as death, holy as religion. Leicester, this fiend, who is now doing a fiend's penance in torment—this demon was my husband's friend, he was my friend too, for I loved everything that brightened the eye, or brought smiles to the lip of my husband—a husband whom I worshipped as a devotee lavishes homage on a saint—loved as a woman loves when her whole life is centered in one object. I was never good like him—but I loved him—I loved him ! You look at me in astonishment —you cannot understand the love that turns to such fierce madness when it is but a past thing—that drugs itself with opium, drowns itself in brandy !"

Ada answered with a faint sob, and her eyes grew wild as the great black orbs flashing upon her. The woman saw this, and took compassion on what she believed to be purely terror at her own violence. She made a strong effort and spoke more calmly, but still with a suppressed, husky voice that was like the hush of a storm.

"We were poor, madam. I kept a little school ; my husband was a clerk, at very low pay, with very hard labor. It was a toilsome life, but oh, how happy we were ! I don't know where James first saw Mr. Leicester, but they came home together one evening, and I remember we had a little supper, with wine, and some game that Leicester had ordered on the way. If you have never seen that man, nothing can convey to you the power, the fascination of his presence. Soft, persuasive, gentle as an angel in seeming ; deep, crafty, cruel as a fiend in reality—if you had a foible or a weakness, he was certain to detect it with a glance, and sure to use it, though it might be to your own destruction. I was young, vain, new to the world, and not altogether without beauty. I doubt if Leicester ever saw a woman without calculating her weaknesses, and playing upon them if it were only for mere amusement, or in the wanton test of his own diabolical powers.

"I was strong, for heart and soul I loved my husband; he saw this and it provoked his pride; else in my humility I might have escaped his pursuit; but I was vain, capricious, passionate. A little time he obtained some influence over me, for his subtle flattery, his artful play upon every bad feeling of my nature had its effect. But the woman who loves one man with her whole strength, has a firm anchorage. My vanity was gratified by this man's homage, nothing more—still he attained all that he worked for, a firmer influence over my husbard. Had I been his enemy he could not have wormed himself around that simple, honest nature. I helped him, I was a dupe, a tool, used for the ruin of my own husband. It is this thought that brandy is not strong enough to drown, or morphine to kill!

"He was our benefactor—you understand—without himself directly appearing in the business, except to us upon whom his agency was impressed; a place, with much higher salary, was procured for my husband. We were very grateful, and looked upon Leicester as a guardian angel. Very well—a few months went on, still binding us closer to the man who had benefited us so much. One day he stood by my husband's desk. It was a rich firm that he served, and James had charge of the funds. It was just before the hour of deposit; ten thousand dollars lay beneath the bank-book. Leicester seemed in haste; he had need of a large sum of money that day, which he could easily replace in the morning, five thousand; something had gone wrong in his financial matters, and he proposed that James should lend that sum from the amount before him.

"My husband hesitated, and at length refused. Leicester

did not urge it, but went away apparently grieved. By that time it was too late for the bank, and James brought the money home, thinking to deposit it early the next day. Leicester came in while we were at dinner, he looked sad and greatly distressed. I insisted upon knowing the cause, and at last he told me of his embarrassment, dwelling with gentle reproach on the refusal of my husband to aid him.

"I was never a woman of firm principle; the holiest feeling known to me was the love I bore my husband; all else was passion, impulse, generous or unjust as circumstances warranted. I did not understand the rectitude of my husband's conduct. To me it seemed ingratitude; my influence over him was fatal. When Leicester left the house, five thousand dollars—not ours nor his—went with him.

"The next day we did not see him. My poor husband grew nervous, but it was not till a week had passed that I could force myself to believe that the money would not be promptly repaid. Then James inquired for Leicester at his hotel. He had gone south.

"My husband had embezzled his employers' money. He was tried, found guilty, sentenced to the state prison for seven years. I—I had done it! When he went up to Sing Sing, linked wrist to wrist with a band of the lowest felons, I followed to the wharf, and my little boy, his child and mine, only a few weeks old, lay crying against my bosom. I watched the boat through the burning tears that seemed to scorch my eyes, and when it was lost, I turned away still as the grave, but the most desolate wretch that ever trod the earth. Seven years, it was an eternity to me! I had no moral strength—I was mad. But his child was there, and I struggled for that!"

The woman paused. Her voice, full of rude strength before, grew soft with mournful desolation.

"I went often to see him; I struggled for a pardon, it was his first offence, but he must stay a year or two in prison; there was no hope before then—I have told you how innocent he really was. But a sense of shame, the hard fare, the toil—he drooped under these things! Every visit I found him thinner; his smile more sad; his brow more pallid. One day I went to see him with the child, and they told me to go home, for my husband was dead.

"I went home quietly as a lamb that has been numbed by the frost. That night I drank laudanum, intending to be nearer my husband before morning, but there was not enough. It threw me into a sleep, profound as death, except that I could not find him in it. The potion did not kill, but it taught me where to seek for relief, how to chain sleep. It was my slave then, we have changed places since."

Ada sat cowering in her chair, while the woman went on with her narrative. It seemed as if she herself were the person who had inflicted the great wrong to which she had listened; as if the fierce anger, the just reproaches of that woman were levelled at her own conscience.

"What atonement can be made? What can be done for you?" she faltered, weaving her pale fingers together, and lifting her eyes beseechingly to the woman's face, which was bent down and haggard with exhausted anguish.

"What atonement can be made?" cried the woman, throwing back her head till the crimson hood fell half away from her dark tresses. "He is making atonement now—now—ha! ha!"

The laugh which followed this speech made Ada cower as if a mortal hand had fallen upon her heart. She looked piteously at the woman, and after a faint struggle to speak, fell back in her chair quite insensible.

This utter prostration—this deathly helplessness, touched the still living heart of the woman. She could not understand why her terrible story had taken such effect upon a person, lifted as it seemed so far above all sympathy for one of her wretched cast; but she was a woman, had suffered and could still feel for the sufferings of others. A gush of gentle compassion broke up through the blackness and rubbish which had almost choked up the pure waters of her heart, humanising her countenance, and awaking her womanhood once more.

She stole into the bed-chamber, and taking a crystal flask full of water from a marble slab, dashed a portion of its contents over the pale face still lying so deathly white against the damask cushions.

This, however, had no effect. She now took the cold hands in hers, chafing them tenderly, removed the dainty cap and scattered water-drops over the pale lips and forehead. With a degree of tact that no one would have expected from her, she refrained from calling the household, and continued her own efforts till life came slowly back to the bosom that a moment before seemed as marble.

Ada opened her eyes heavily, and closed them again with a shudder, when she saw the woman bending over her.

"Go!" she said, still pressing her long eyelashes together; "leave word where you live, and I will send you money."

"For the old man?"

"No; for yourself, not for *his* murderer?"

"I did not ask money for myself," answered the woman, sullenly. "If you give it, I shall pay the lawyers to save him!"

"Then go, I have nothing for you or him—go," answered Ada, faintly, but in a voice that admitted no dispute; and, rising from her chair, she went into the bed-room and closed the door.

The woman looked after her with some anger and more astonishment; then drawing down her hood she tied it deliberately, and strode into the boudoir, down the stairs, and so out of the house, without deigning to notice the servants, who took no pains to conceal their astonishment, that a creature of her appearance should be admitted to the presence of their mistress.

CHAPTER XXXI.

THE TOMBS LAWYER.

As reptiles haunt a prison wall,
And search its broken cliffs for food;
Some human beings cringe and crawl
For daily bread where sorrows brood.

Mrs. Gray found more difficulty in performing her benevolent intentions with regard to the Warrens, than she had ever before encountered. Ignorant as a child of all legal proceedings, she found no aid either in the old prisoner, his wife, or his grandchild, who were more uninformed and far less hopeful than herself. Her brother Jacob, on whom she had depended for aid and counsel, much to her surprise, not only refused to take any responsibility in her kind efforts, but looked coldly upon the whole affair.

It was not in Jacob Strong's nature to shrink from a kind action; for his rude exterior covered a heart true and warm as ever beat. But the part he had already taken in those events that led to William Leicester's death; the almost insane fear that haunted his mistress, lest the murderer should escape punishment; the taunts that had wrung his strong heart to the core, but which she had so ruthlessly heaped upon him—all these things conspired in rendering him more than indifferent to the fate of a man whom he had never seen, and whom he wished to find guilty. He received his good sister's entreaties for counsel, therefore, with reproof, and a stern admonition not to meddle with affairs beyond her knowledge.

Thus thrown upon her own resources, the good woman, by no means daunted, resolved to conduct the affair after her own fashion. Robert, it is true, had volunteered to aid her, and had already applied to an eminent lawyer to conduct old Mr. Warren's defence; but the retainer demanded, and the large sum of money expected, when laid before the good huckster woman, quite horrified her. The amount seemed enormous to one who had gathered up a fortune in pennies and shillings. She had heard of the extortions of legal gentlemen, of their rapacity and heartlessness, and resolved to convince them that one woman, at least, had her wisdom teeth in excellent condition.

So Mrs. Gray quietly refused all aid from Robert, and went into the legal market as she would have boarded a North River craft laden with poultry and vegetables. Many a grave lawyer did she astonish by her shrewd efforts to strike a bargain for the amount of eloquence necessary to save her old friend. Again and again did her double chin quiver with indignation at the hard-heartedness and rapacity of the profession.

Thus time wore on; the day of trial approached, and, with all her good intentions, Mrs. Gray had only done a great deal of talking, which by no means promised to regenerate the legal profession, and the prisoner was still without better counsel than herself.

One day the good huckster woman was passing down the steps of the City Prison—for she invariably accompanied Mrs Warren to her husband's cell every morning, though it interfered greatly with her harvest hour in the market—she was slowly descending the prison steps, as I have said, when a man whom she had passed, leaning heavily against one of the pillars in the vestibule, followed and addressed her.

On hearing her name pronounced, Mrs. Gray turned and encountered a man, perhaps thirty-five or forty years of age, with handsome but unhealthy features, and eyes black and keen, that seemed capable of reading your soul at a glance, but too weary with study or dissipation for the effort.

"I beg your pardon," said the stranger, lifting his hat with a degree of graceful deference that quite charmed the old lady. "I believe you are Mrs. Gray, the benevolent friend of that poor man lodged up yonder on a charge of murder. My young man informed me that a lady—it must have been you, none other could have so beautifully answered the description—had called at my office in search of counsel. I regretted so much not being in. This is a peculiar case, madam, one that enlists all the sympathies. You look surprised. I know that feeling is not usual in our profession, but there are hearts, madam—hearts so tender originally, that they resist the hard grindstone of the law. It is this that has kept me poor, when my brother lawyers are all growing rich around me."

"Sir," answered Mrs. Gray—her face all in a glow of delight—reaching forth her plump hand, with which she shook that of her new acquaintance, which certainly trembled in her grasp, but from other causes than the sympathy for which she gave him credit, "Sir, I am happy to see you—very happy to find one lawyer that has a heart. I don't remember calling at your office without finding you in, though I certainly have found a good many other lawyers out."

Here the blessed old lady gave a mellow chuckle over what she considered a marvellous play upon words, which was echoed by the lawyer, who held one hand to his side, as if absolutely compelled thus to restrain the mirth excited by her facetiousness.

"And now, my dear lady, let us to business. The most exquisite wit, you know must give place to the calls of humanity. My young man informed me of your noble intentions with regard to this unhappy prisoner. That out of your wealth so honorably won, you were determined to wrest justice from the law. I am here with my legal armor on, ready to aid in the good cause. If I were rich now—if I had not exhausted my life in attempting to aid humanity, nothing would give me so much pleasure as to go hand-in-hand with you to his rescue, without money and without price; as it is, my dear madam—as it is, 'the laborer is worthy of his hire.'"

This quotation quite won the already vacillating heart of poor Mrs. Gray. She shook the lawyer's thin hand again, with increased cordiality, and answered—

"True enough—true enough, my dear sir. I declare it is refreshing to hear Bible words in the mouth of a lawyer. It's what I didn't expect."

"Ah, madam," cried the lawyer, drawing a white handkerchief from a side pocket, and returning it as if he had determined to suppress his emotions at any cost—"ah, madam, do not apply a general rule too closely. Our profession is bad enough, I do not defend it. What man with a conscience void of offence, could make the attempt? But there exist exceptions—honorable exceptions. Permit me to hope that your clear mind can distinguish between the sharper and the man who sacrifices the world's goods for conscience's sake. Believe me, dear lady, there are such things as honest lawyers, as pious men in the profession."

"Well, I must say the idea never struck me before," answered Mrs. Gray, with honest simplicity.

"Permit me to hope, that from this hour you will no longer doubt it," answered the lawyer, gently passing one hand over the place which anatomists allot to the human heart. "And now, madam, suppose we walk to my office and settle the preliminaries of our engagement. A cool head and warm heart, that is what you want; fortunately such things may be found. Pray allow me to help you; the steps are a little damp, accidents frequently happen up this avenue; my office is close at hand; many a poor unfortunate has learned to bless the way there—take my arm!"

Mrs. Gray hesitated; a blush swept over her comely cheek at the thought of walking arm-in-arm with so perfect a gentleman, and that in the open streets of New York. It was a thing she had not dreamed of since the death of poor Mr. Gray. But there was a leaven of feminine vanity still left in the good woman's nature. The shrewd swindler, who stood there so gracefully presenting his arm, had not altogether miscalculated the effect of his flattery, and he clenched it adroitly, with this act of personal attention.

Mrs. Gray hesitated, blushed, drew on her glove a little tighter, and then placed her substantial arm through the comparatively fragile limb of the lawyer, softly, as if she quite appreciated the danger of bearing him down with her weight.

Thus the blessed old woman was borne along, sweeping half the pavement with her massive person, and crowding the poor lawyer unconsciously out to the curb-stone every other minute.

He, exemplary man, bore it all with gentle complacency, cautioned her against every little impediment that came in her way, and consoled himself for the somewhat remarkable figure he made in the eyes of the police-officers that haunt that neighborhood, by a significant twirl of his disengaged hand in the direction of his own face, and a quick drooping of the left eyelid, by which they all understood that the Tombs lawyer had brought down his game handsomely that morning.

Mrs. Gray was certainly somewhat disappointed in the style of the lawyer's office into which she was ushered with so much ceremony. A rusty old leathern chair; a table with the green baize half worn off, with a bundle or two of dusty papers upon it; a standish full of dry ink, and a steel pen rusted down to the nib, all veiled thickly with dust, did not entirely meet her ideas of the prosperous business she had anticipated. The lawyer saw this, and hastened to sweep away all unfavorable impressions from her mind.

"This is my work-shop, you see, madam, the tread-mill in which I grind out my humble bread and my blessed charities—no foppery, no carpets, nothing but the barest necessaries of the profession. I leave easy-chairs, &c., for those who have the conscience to wring them from needy clients. You comprehend, dear lady. Oh! it is pleasant to feel that now and then in this cold world, a good life meets with appreciation. John, bring me another chair?"

"My young man," whom the lawyer had mentioned so ostentatiously, came forward in the shape of a lank Irish lad, taller than his master by three inches, which might be accurately measured by the space visible between the knee of his nether garments and the top of his gaiter boots. The closet door, from which he issued, revealed a lurking encampment of dusty bottles, a broken washstand, and two enormous demijohns, the wickerwork suspiciously moist, and with a stopper of blue glass chained to the neck.

The lawyer made a quiet motion with his hand, which sent the Irish boy in haste to close the door. Then taking the unstable chair which the lad had disinterred from the closet, he sat down cautiously, as a cat steals to the lap of her mistress, whose temper is somewhat doubtful, and glided into the business on hand. The Irish boy stood meekly by, profiting by the scene with a knowing look, which deepened into a grin of delight as he saw Mrs. Gray draw forth her pocket-book, and place bank-notes of considerable amount into the lawyer's hand. When the good woman had thus deposited half the sum which the lawyer assured her would save old Mr. Warren's life, she arose with a sigh of profound satisfaction, shook out her voluminous skirts, and left the office, fully satisfied with the whole transaction.

The lawyer and "his man" followed her to the door. When she disappeared down the street, the lawyer turned briskly, and in the joy of his heart seized the Irish boy by the collar that had lately graced his own neck, and gave him a vigorous shake.

"What are you grinning at, you dog? How dare you laugh at my clients? There now, get along; take that and fill both the demijohns; buy a clean pack of cards, and a new supply of everything. Do you hear?"

The Irish boy shook himself back into his coat, and seizing the money, plunged into the street, resolved not to return a shilling of change without first securing the month's wages, for which his master was, as usual, in arrears.

The lawyer threw himself into the leathern chair which Mrs. Gray had just left, stretched forth his limbs, half closed his eyes, and rubbing his palms softly together, sat thus full ten minutes caressing himself, and chuckling over the morning's business

CHAPTER XXXII.

THE LAWYER'S VISIT TO HIS CLIENT.

I am his wife; full forty years
This head was pillowed on his breast;
I shared his joy, I shared his tears,
And in deep sorrow loved him best.

Yes, tempter, I am still his wife!
I hold the glory of his name!
To purchase liberty or life
I would not dim its light with shame!

If those who think that happiness exists only in those external circumstances that surround a man, could have seen old Mr. Warren in his prison, they would have been astonished at the placidity of his countenance, at the calm and holy atmosphere that had made his cell emphatically a home. His wife and grandchild haunted it with their love, and it seemed to him—so the old man said—that God had never been quite so near to him as since he entered these gloomy walls. He might die; the laws might sacrifice him, innocent as he was; but should this happen, he only knew that God permitted it for some wise purpose, which might never be explained till the sacrifice was made.

True, life was sweet to the old man; for in his poverty and his trouble two souls had clung to him with a degree of love that would have made existence precious to any one. All that earth knows of heaven, strong, pure affection had always followed him. It is only when the soul looks back upon a waste of buried affection, a maze of broken ties, that it thirsts to die. Resignation is known to every good Christian, but the wild desire which makes men plunge madly toward eternity, comes of exhausted affections and an insane use of life. Good and wise men are seldom eager for death. They wait for it with still, solemn faith in God, whose most august messenger it is.

There was nothing of bravado in the old man's heart; he

made no theatrical exhibition of the solemn faith that was in him; but when visitors passed the open door of his cell—for, being upon the third corridor, there was little chance of escape—and saw him sitting there with that meek old woman at his feet, and an open Bible on his lap, a huge, worn book that had been his father's, they paused involuntarily, with that intuitive homage which goodness always wins, even from prejudice.

A few comforts had been added to his prison furniture; for Mrs. Gray was always bringing some cherished thing from her household stores. A breadth of carpet lay before the bed; a swing shelf hung against the wall, upon which two cups and saucers of Mrs. Gray's most antique and precious china, stood in rich relief; while a pot of roses struggled into bloom beneath the light which came through the narrow loop-hole cut through the deep outer wall.

Altogether that prison-cell had a home-like and pleasant look. The old man believed that it might prove the gate to death, but he was not one to turn gloomily from the humble flowers with which God scattered his way to the grave. He lifted his eyes gratefully to every sunbeam that came through the wall; and when darkness surrounded him, and that blessed old woman was forced to leave him alone, he would sit down upon his bed, and murmur to himself, "Oh! it is well God can hear in the dark!"

Thus as I have said, the time of trial drew near. The prisoner was prepared and tranquil. The wife and grandchild were convinced of his innocence, and full of gentle faith that the laws could never put a guiltless man to death. Thus they partook somewhat of his own heavenly composure. Mrs. Gray was always ready to cheer them with her genial hopefulness; and Robert Otis was prompt at all times with such aid as his youth, his strength, and his fine, generous nature enabled him to give.

One morning, just after Mrs. Gray had left the cell—for she made a point of accompanying the timid old woman to the prison of her husband—Mr. Warren was disturbed by a visitor that he had never seen before. It was a quiet demure sort of personage, clothed in black, and with an air half-clerical, half-dissipated, that mingled rather incongruously upon his person. He sat down by the prisoner, as a hired nurse might cajole a child into taking medicine, and after uttering a soft good morning, with his palm laid gently on the withered hand of the old man, he took a survey of the cell.

Mrs. Warren stood in one corner, filling the old china cup from which her husband had just taken his breakfast, with water; two or three flowers, gathered from the plants in Mrs Gray's parlor windows, lay on the little table, whose gentle bloom this water was to keep fresh. To another man it might have been pleasant to observe with what care this old woman arranged the tints, and turned the cup that its brightest side might come opposite her husband.

But the lawyer only saw that she was a woman, and reflected that the sex might always be found useful if properly managed. Instead of being struck by the womanly sweetness of her character, and the affection so beautifully proved by her occupation, he began instantly to calculate upon the uses of which she might be capable.

"Rather snug box this that they have got you in, my good friend," said the lawyer, turning his eyes with a sidelong glance on the old man's face, and keeping them fixed more steadily than was usual with him, for it was seldom a face like this met his scrutiny within the walls of a prison. "Trust that we shall get you out soon. Couldn't be in better hands, that fine old friend of yours, a woman in a thousand, isn't she?—confides you to my legal keeping entirely!"

"Did Mrs. Gray send you? Are you the gentleman she spoke to about my case?" inquired the old man, turning his calm eyes upon the lawyer, while Mrs. Warren suspended her occupation and crept to the other side of her husband. "She wished me to talk with you. I am glad you have come!"

"Well, my dear old friend, permit me to call you so—for if the lawyer who saves the man from the gallows isn't his friend,

I should like to know who is. When shall we have a little quiet chat together?"

"Now, there will be no better time!"

"But this lady; in such cases one must have perfect confidence. Would she have the goodness just to step out while we talk a little?"

"She is my wife. I have nothing to say which she does not know!" answered the old man, turning an affectionate look upon the grateful eyes lifted to his face.

"Your wife, ha!" cried the lawyer, rubbing his palms softly together, as was his habit when a gleam of villainy more exquisite than usual dawned upon him. "Perhaps not, we shall see! may want her for a witness! but we can tell better when the case is laid out. Now go on; remember that your lawyer is your physician; must have all the symptoms of a case, all its parts, all its capabilities. Now just consider me as your conscience; not exactly that, because one sometimes cheats conscience, you know—after all there is nothing better—think that I am your lawyer—that I have your life in my hands—that I must know the truth in order to save it—cheat conscience, if you like, but never cheat the lawyer who tries your case, or the doctor who feels your pulse."

"I have nothing to conceal. I am ready to tell you all," answered the old man.

The calmness with which this was said took the lawyer somewhat aback. He had expected that more of his cajoling eloquence would be necessary, before his client would be won to speak frankly. His astonishment was greatly increased, therefore, when the old man in his grave and truthful way related everything connected with the death of William Leicester exactly as it had happened. Nothing could be more discouraging than this narrative, as it presented itself to the lawyer. Had the man been absolutely guilty, his counsel would have found far less difficulty in arranging some grounds of defence. Without some opening for legal chicanery the lawyer felt himself lost. Unprincipled as he was, there still existed in his mind some little feeling of interest in any case he undertook, independent of the money to be received. He loved the excitement, the trickery, the manœuvering of a desperate defence. He had a sort of fellow feeling for the clever criminal that sharpened his talent, and sent him into court with the spirit of an old gambler.

But a case like this was something new. He did not for a moment doubt the old man's story; there was truth breathing in every word, and written in every line of that honest countenance. Indeed it was this very conviction that dampened the lawyer's ardor in the case. It seemed completely removed from his line of position. He had so long solemnly declared his belief in the innocence of men whom he knew to be steeped in guilt, that he felt how impossible it was for him to utter the truth before a jury with any kind of gravity. His only resource was to make this plain, solemn case as much like a falsehood as possible.

"And so you were entirely alone in the room?"

"Entirely."

The lawyer shook his head.

"You have no witnesses of his coming in, or of the conversation, except this old lady and your grandchild?"

"None!"

"Your neighbors, how were you situated there? No kind fellow in the next casement who heard a noise, and peeped through the key-hole, ha?"

The old man looked up gravely, but made no answer.

"I tell you," said the lawyer sharply, for he was nettled by the old man's look, "yours is a desperate case!"

"I believe it is," was the gentle reply.

"A desperate case, to be cured only with desperate measures. Some person must be found who saw this man strike the blow himself."

"But who did see it, save God and myself?"

"Your wife there, she must have seen it. The door was not quite closed; she was curious—women always are; she looked through, saw the man seize the knife; you tried to arrest his hand; he was a strong man; you old and feeble. You saw all this, madam!"

The old woman was stooping forward, her thin fingers had locked themselves together while the lawyer was speaking, and her eyes were fixed on him, dilating like those of a bird when the serpent begins its charm. At first she waved her head very faintly, thus denying that she had witnessed what he described; then she began to stoop forward, assenting, as it were, to the force and energy of his words, almost believing that she had actually looked through the door and saw all that the lawyer asserted.

"No, she did not see all this," answered the prisoner, quietly; "and if she had, how would it be of use?"

"You did see it, madam!" persisted the lawyer, without removing his eyes from the old woman's face, but fascinating her, as it were, with his gaze—"you did see it!"

"I don't know. I—I, perhaps—yes, I think."

"But you did see it; your husband's life depends on the fact. Refresh your memory; his life, remember—his life!"

"Yes—yes. I—I saw!"

It was not a deliberate falsehood; the weak mind was held and moulded by a strong will. For the moment that old woman absolutely believed that she had witnessed the scene, which had been so often impressed upon her fancy. The lawyer saw his power, and a faint smile stole over his lip, half undoing the work his craft had accomplished. The old woman began to shrink slowly back; she met the calm, sorrowful gaze of her husband, and her eyes fell under the reproach it conveyed.

The lawyer saw all this, and without giving her time to retract, went on.

"By remembering this you have saved his life—saved him from the gallows—his name from dishonor—his body from being mangled at the medical college."

The old woman wove her wrinkled fingers together; the ker chief on her bosom quivered with the struggle of her breath.

"I saw it—I saw it all!" she cried, lifting up her clasped hands and dropping them heavily on her lap. "God forgive me, I saw it all!"

"Wife!" said the old man, in a voice so solemn that it made even the lawyer shrink. "Wife!"

She did not answer; her head dropped upon her bosom; those old hands unlocked and fell apart in her lap, but she muttered still, "God forgive me, I saw it all!"

It *was* a falsehood now, and as she uttered it the poor creature shrunk guiltily from her husband's side, and attempted to steal out of the cell.

"One moment," said the lawyer, beginning to kindle up in his unholy work. "Another thing is to be settled, and then you have the proud honor, the glorious reflection that it is to you this good, this innocent man owes his life. How long have you been married?"

The old woman looked at a gold ring on her finger, worn almost to a thread, and answered—

"It is near on forty years."

"Where?"

The old woman looked at her husband, but his eyes were bent sorrowfully downward, giving her neither encouragement or reproach, so she answered with some hesitation—

"We were married Down East, in Maine, !"

"So much the better. Is the marriage registered anywhere?"

"I don't know!"

"The witnesses, where are they?"

"All dead!"

The lawyer rubbed his hands with still greater energy.

"Very good, very good indeed; nothing could be better! Just tell me, could you prove the thing yourselves?"

"Prove what?" said Mrs. Warren, half in terror, while the prisoner remained motionless, paralyzed, as it seemed, by the weakness of his wife.

"Prove?—why, that you were ever married. The truth is, madam, you could not have been married to the prisoner—never where the thing is impossible. It spoils you for a witness—do you understand?"

"No," said the old woman—"no, how should I? What does it mean?"

"Mean?—you are not his wife!"

"Not his wife—not his wife! Why, didn't I tell you we had lived together above forty years?"

"Certainly; no objection to that, a beautiful reproof to the slander that there is no constancy in woman. Still you are not his wife—remember that!"

"But I *am* his wife. Look up, husband, and tell him if I am not your own lawfully married wife."

"Madam," said the lawyer, in a voice that he intended should reach her heart. "In order to save this man's life you must learn to forget as well as to remember. You saw Leicester kill himself, that is settled. I shall place you on the stand to prove the fact—a fact which saves your husband from the gallows. His *wife* would not be permitted to give this evidence; the laws forbid it—therefore you are not his wife. They cannot prove that you are; probably you could not easily prove it yourself. I assert, and will maintain it, no marriage ever existed between you and the prisoner."

"But we have lived together forty years; more than forty years!" cried the old woman, and a blush crept slowly over her wrinkled features till it was lost in the soft grey of her hair. "What am I then?"

"What matters a name at your time of life. Besides, the moment he is clear you may prove your marriage before all the courts in America for aught I care; they can't put him on trial a second time."

"And you wish me to deny that we are married—to say that I am not his wife."

The old woman, so weak, so frail, grew absolutely stern as she spoke; the blush fled from her face, leaving it almost sublime. The lawyer even, felt the moral force of that look, and said, half in apology—

"It is the only way to save his life!"

"Then let him die; I could bear it better than to say he is not my husband—I not his wife." She sunk to the floor as she spoke, and bowing her forehead to the old man's knee, sobbed out, "Oh, husband—husband, say that I am right now—did you hear—did you hear?"

The old man sat upright. A holy glow came over his face, and his lips parted with a smile that was heavenly in its sweetness. He raised the feeble woman from his feet, and putting the grey hair gently back from her forehead, kissed it with tender reverence. Then, holding her head to his bosom, he turned to the lawyer. "You may be satisfied, she does not think her husband's poor life worth that price," he said. "Now leave us together."

The lawyer went out rebuked and crest-fallen, muttering to himself as he passed from one flight of steps to another, "Well, let the stubborn old fellow hang, it will do him good; the prettiest case I ever laid out spoiled for an old woman's fancy. It was badly managed, I should have taken her alone! I verily believe the old wretch is innocent, but they will hang him high as Haman, if the woman persists."

CHAPTER XXXIII.

THE TRIAL FOR MURDER.

It is a wrong and monstrous thing,
That from young hearts where love is deep,
Justice herself the words should sing
That sends a kindred soul to sleep.

THE day of trial came at last. Such cases are frequent in New York, and, unless there is something in the position or history of the criminal to excite public attention, they pass off almost unnoticed. Still there is not a single case that does not sweep with it the very heart-strings of some person or family, linked either to the prisoner or his victim ; there is not one that does not wring tears from some eyes and groans from some innocent bosom. We read a brief record of these things; we learn that a murderer has been tried, convicted, sentenced ; we shudder and turn away without being half conscious that the history thus briefly recorded embraces persons innocent as ourselves, who must endure more than the tortures of death for the sin that one man is doomed to expiate.

Old Mrs. Warren and her grand-daughter stood at the prison doors early that morning. It was before the hour when visitors could be admitted, but they wandered up and down in sight of the entrance with that feverish unrest to which keen anxiety subjects one. All was busy life about the neighborhood. It was nothing to the multitude that passed up and down the steps, that a fellow being was that morning to be placed on trial for his life. A few remembered it, but with the exception of old Mrs. Gray and her nephew, it passed heavily upon the heart of no living being save those two helpless females.

How strange all this seemed to them! With every thought and feeling occupied, they looked upon the indifferent throng with a pang; the smiling faces, the bustle, the cheerfulness, all seemed mocking the heaviness of their own hearts.

The hour came at last, and they entered the prison. Old Mr. Warren received them affectionately as usual; he exhibited no anxiety, and seemed even more cheerful than he had been for some days. The Bible lay open upon the bed, and there was an indentation near the pillow, as if his arms had rested heavily there while reading upon his knees.

He spent more than an hour conversing gently with his wife and grand-daughter, striving to give them consolation rather than hope; for, from the first, he had believed and expressed a belief that the trial would go against him. With no faith in his counsel, and no evidence to sustain his innocence, how could he doubt it? Perhaps this very conviction created that holy composure, which seemed so remarkable in a man just to be placed on a trial of life and death.

When the officers came to conduct him to the City Hall, he followed them calmly, solemnly, as a good man might have gone up to a place of worship. It was a bright, frosty morning, and he had been some weeks in prison. Still his heart must have been wonderfully at ease when the clear air, and the busy life around could thus kindle up his eye and irradiate his face. A crowd gathered around the prison to see the old murderer come forth, but the people were disappointed. Instead of a fierce, haggard being, wild with the terrors of his situation, ready to dart away through any opening like a wild animal from its keepers, they saw only a meek old man, neatly clad, and walking quietly between the officers with neither the bravado or the abject humility of guilt. The fresh air did him good; you could see that in his face, and so grateful was he for this little blessing, that he almost forgot the gaze and wonder of the crowd.

"This is very beautiful," he observed to one of the officers, and the man stared to see how simple and unaffected was this expression of enjoyment. "Had I never been in prison, how could I have relished a morning like this?"

"You expect to be acquitted?" answered the man, unable to account for this strange composure in any other way.

"No," replied the old man, a little sadly—"no, I think they will find me guilty—I am almost sure they will!"

"You take it calmly, upon my honor—very calmly!" exclaimed the man. "Have you made up your mind, then, to plead guilty at once?"

"No, that would be false—they must do it—I will not help them. All in my power I must do to prevent the crime they will commit in condemning me. Not to do that would be suicide!"

There was something in this reply that struck the officer more than a thousand protestations could have done. Indeed the entire bearing of his charge surprised him not a little. Seldom had he conducted a man to trial that walked with so firm a step, or spoke so calmly.

"Have you no dread of the sentence—no fear of dying, that you speak so quietly?"

The old man turned his head and looked back. Two females were following him a little way off. They had gone across the street to avoid the crowd of men and boys that hung like a pack of hounds about the prisoner, but were gazing after him with anxious faces, that touched even the officer with pity, as his glance fell upon them. The old man saw where his eyes rested, and answered very mournfully—

"Yes, I have a dread of the sentence. It will reach *them!* Besides, it is a solemn thing to die—a very solemn thing to know that at a certain hour you will stand face to face with God!"

"Still, I dare say, you would meet death like a hero!"

"When death comes, I will try and meet it like a Christian," was the mild answer.

As the old man spoke, they were crossing Chambers street to a corner of the Park, but their progress was checked by a carriage, drawn by a pair of superb horses, and mounted by two footmen in livery, that dashed by, scattering the crowd in every direction.

Mrs. Warren and her grand-daughter were on the opposite side, and had just left Centre street to cross over. Julia uttered a faint scream, and attempted to draw her grandmother back, for the horses were dashing close upon them, and the old woman stood as if paralyzed in the middle of the street. She did not move; the horses plunged by, and the wheels made her garments flutter with the air they scattered in passing. The old woman uttered a cry as the carriage disappeared, and ran forward a step or two, as if impelled by some wild impulse to follow it; Julia darted forward and caught hold of her arm.

"Grandmother, grandmother, where are you going? What is the matter?"

"Did you see that?" said the old woman.

"What, grandmother?"

"That face—the lady in the carriage. Did you see it?"

"No, grandmother; I was looking at you. It seemed as if the horses would trample you down."

The old woman listened, evidently without comprehending. Her eyes were wild, and her manner energetic.

"Where is your grandfather?—I must tell him. It was *her* face!"

"Whose face, grandmother?"

"Whose! Why, did you not see?" The old woman seemed all at once to recollect herself. "But how should you know—you, my poor child, who never had a mother?"

"Oh! grandmother, has trouble driven you wild?" cried the poor girl, struck with new terror, for there was something almost insane in the woman's look.

"No, I am not wild; but it was her—see how I tremble. Could anything else make me tremble so?"

"I have been trembling all the morning," said Julia.

"True enough, but not deep in the heart—not—oh! where is your grandfather? They have taken him off while we are standing here. Come, child, come—how could we lose sight of him?"

They hurried into the Park, and across to the City Hall, which they reached in time to secure a single glance of the prisoner as he was conducted up the staircase, still followed by the rabble.

The court-room became crowded immediately after the prisoner was led in, and it was with considerable difficulty that an officer forced a passage for the unhappy pair to the seats reserved for witnesses. Mrs. Gray was already in court, a little more serious than usual, but still so confident of her protégé's innocence, and filled with such reverence for the infallibility of the law, that she had almost religious faith in his acquittal. She smiled cheeringly when Mrs. Warren and Julia came up, and her black silk gown rustled again as she moved her ponderous person that they might find room near her. Mrs. Warren was a good deal excited. She even made an effort to reach her husband, as they were conducting him through the court, but the crowd was too dense, and, spite of herself, she was borne forward to the witnesses' seats, without obtaining an opportunity to whisper a word of what was passing in her heart. The judges were upon the bench; the lawyers took their places, and all the preliminaries of an important trial commenced. The prisoner remained calm as he had been all the morning, but there was nothing stupid or indifferent in his manner. When informed of his right of challenge to the jury, he examined each man as he came up, with a searching glance, and two or three times gave a peremptory challenge. He listened with interest to the questions put by the court, and sunk back in his seat, breathing deeply, as if an important duty was over, when the jury was at length empannelled.

The district attorney opened his case with great ability. He was a keen, eloquent man, who pursued his course against any person unfortunate enough to be placed before him, with the relentless zeal of a bloodhound, yielding nothing to compassion, feeling no weakness, and forgiving none. His duty was to convict—his reputation might be lessened or enhanced by the decision of a jury—that thought was ever in his mind—he was struggling for position, for forensic fame. The jury before him was to add a leaf to his yet green laurels, or tear one away. What was a human life in the balance with this thought?

To have watched this man one might have supposed that the feeble old prisoner, who sat so meekly beneath the fiery flash of his eyes, and the keen scourge of his eloquence, had been his bitterest enemy. Even in opening the case, where little of eloquence is expected, he could not forbear many a sharp taunt and cruel invective against the old man, who met it all with a sort of rebuking calmness, that might have shamed the dastardly eloquence which was in no way necessary to justice.

You should have seen dear Mrs. Gray, as the lawyer went on. No winter apple ever glowed more ruddily than her cheek; no star ever flashed more brightly than her fine eyes. The folds of her silken dress rustled with the indignation that kept her in constant motion; and she would bend first to old Mrs. Warren, and then to Julia, whispering—

"Never mind, dears—never mind his impudence! Our lawyer will have a chance soon, then won't that fellow catch it! Don't mind what he says; it's his business; the State pays for it—more shame for the people. Our man will be on his feet soon. I ain't the State of New York, but then he's got a fee that ought to sharpen his tongue, and expects more when it's over. Only let him give that fellow his own again with interest—compound interest—and if I don't throw in an extra ten dollars, my name isn't Sarah Gray. Oh, if I could but give him a piece of my mind now! There, there, Mrs. Warren, don't look so white! it's only talk. They won't convict him—it's only talk!"

Mrs. Gray was drawn from this good-natured attempt to cheer her friends by the proceedings of the court, that each moment became more and more impressive.

The prosecution brought forth its witnesses, those who had appeared in the preliminary trial, with many others hunted out by the indefatigable attorney. Never was a chain of evidence more complete—never did guilt appear so hideous or more firmly established. Every witness, as he descended from the stand, seemed to have thrown a darker stain of guilt upon that old man. The sharp cross-examinations of the prisoner's counsel, only elucidated some new point against him. His acute wit and keen questioning brought nothing to light that did not operate against the cause—a better man might have been excused for abandoning his case in despair.

It seemed impossible that anything could overthrow all this weight of evidence; even the desperate plea of insanity would be of no avail. No one could look on the solemn, and yet serene face of that old man, without giving him credit for a steadiness of mind that no legal eloquence could distort.

Among the last witnesses brought up was Julia Warren. Her determination not to give evidence, which had just escaped legal censure on the examination, had been reasoned away by her grandfather who, believing, himself that the laws should be obeyed in all things, leaving the result with God, had succeeded in convincing the mind of this young girl that her duty was obedience. She arose, therefore, when summoned to the stand, turned her eyes upon her grandfather, as if to gather courage from his strength, and moved forward tremulously, it is true, but with more fortitude than might have been expected in a creature so young and so delicately sensitive.

With her usual good sense, Mrs. Gray had taken care that her protégé should be neatly dressed, but spite of the little cottage bonnet with its rose-colored lining, that face was colorless as a snow-drop.

A thrill of sympathy passed through the crowd, as this young girl stood up in the public gaze. She was known as the grandchild of the accused, and to possess knowledge that could but deepen the charges against him. This of itself was enough to enlist the generous impulses of a people, more keenly alive than any on earth, to the claims and dependencies of womanhood. But the shrinking modesty of her demeanor—the exquisite purity of her loveliness—her youth, the innate refinement that breathed about her like an atmosphere, all conspired to make her an object of generous pity. There was not a face present, even to the officers, that did not exhibit some sign of this feeling when the first view of her features was obtained. The face in which this tender compassion beamed most eloquently was that of the old prisoner. For the first time that day tears came into his eyes, but when her glance was turned upon him with a look that pleaded for strength and for pardon, eloquently as eyes ever pleaded to a human soul, the grandfather answered it with a smile that kindled up her pale face, as if an angel had passed by, which no one had the power to see, save her and the old man.

She touched her lips to the sacred volume, and turned with a look of angelic obedience toward the judges. When the prosecuting attorney commenced his examination, she answered his questions with a degree of modest dignity that checked any desire he might have felt to excite or annoy her with useless interrogations. Nothing could be more absorbing than the attention paid to every word that dropped from her lips. She spoke low, and faltered a little now and then ; but the tones of her voice were so sadly sweet, the tears seemed so close to her eyes without reaching them, that even the judges and the jury leaned forward to catch those tones, rather than break them by a request that she should speak louder.

CHAPTER XXXIV.

THE TWO WITNESSES.

Woman, thy haughty pride shall fall—
Thy very soul shall quake and quail.
Those words are weaving shroud and pall,
And truth itself may not avail.
To save the life thy sin has taken—
To save thy father's whitened head—
Thy soul to its proud depth is shaken—
Say, canst thou raise him from the dead

I WILL not give Julia's entire evidence as she uttered it in detail, because most of my readers know already the events which she had to relate ; I have attempted no melodramatic effect by an effort at mystery. The truth which that court could not know, is already made manifest to those who have followed my story up to this point. When questioned if she had known the deceased, Julia answered that she had seen him three times in her life. Once upon a wharf near the Battery, where she had wandered with flowers and fruit, which she wished to sell. He then purchased a few of her flowers, and presented them to a lady who had left a southern vessel with him but a few moments before. She described how he had driven away with the lady at his side, and said at that time she never expected to have seen him again

"But you did see him again," said the examining counsel. "Tell us where and how?"

"It was in October, the evening before he—before he died. I was going up town with some flowers, which a lady had ordered for a ball she gave that night. It was rather late when I started from Dunlap's, and I walked fast, fearing to lose my way after dark. This man saw me as I was passing a house with a flower-garden in front, and a pretty fountain throwing up water among the dahlias and chrysanthemums; I was out of breath, and walked a little slower just then, for the water-drops as they fell were like music, and everything around was so lovely that I could not find it in my heart to walk fast. I did not stop; but Mr. Leicester saw me and wanted me to sell my flowers. I told him no; but he *would* have them, and almost pushed me, basket and all, through the gate and into the house."

"Well, what passed in the house?"

"He took me up stairs into a chamber, and there I saw the same lady that was with him on the wharf, alone, and dressing herself in some beautiful clothes that lay about. She asked me to help her, and I did. She took some of my flowers for her hair and her dress. I was in a great hurry, and wished to go, but she begged me to stay a few minutes longer, and I could not refuse. After she was dressed, we went down stairs, and this lady was married to Mr. Leicester in a room below. The wedding seemed like a funeral; the lady cried all the time, and so did I.

"When it was all over they let me go, and I carried the rest of my flowers to the lady who had ordered them. It was getting late when I went back; I lost my way; a gentleman stood looking into a window at the corner of some street; I asked him to tell me the way home without looking in his face; he turned. It was Mr. Leicester; he *would* go home with me; I did not like it, and would rather have been lost in the streets all night; but all that I could say against it did no good. He followed me home, down the basement steps, and to the door of grandfather's room. There was no light in the room; and while grandpa was kindling a match, Mr. Leicester went away. I do not know how, but when the candle was lighted I looked round for him, and he was gone!"

"Did you tell your grandfather that he had followed you?"

"Yes, I always tell grandfather everything!"

"So you told him that this man had followed you home against your will?"

"Yes, I told him."

"Was he angry?"

"My grandfather never is angry!"

"But what did he say?"

"Nothing particular. He kept his arm around me a good while, I remember, as I was warming myself, and seemed to feel sorrowful about something. He asked several questions about the man, how he looked, and what he said."

"And was that all he said or did?"

"No. He prayed for me that night before we went to bed more earnestly than I had ever heard him before. I remember, he asked God to protect me from harm, and said that he was old, so old that he was of no use, and well stricken in years. It was not the first time I had heard him say this, but that night I remember well, for it made me cry!"

"When was the next time you saw Mr. Leicester?"

Julia grew pale as she replied to this question, and her voice became so faint that she could scarcely be heard.

"I saw him the next morning!"

"At what hour?"

"I do not know exactly; but we had just done breakfast when he came into the basement where we lived, and attempted to speak with my grandfather!"

"Did your grandfather know him? Did he call Mr. Leicester by name?"

"He did not call him by name; but I think they must have known each other!"

"Why do you think so?"

Because grandfather turned so pale and looked so dreadfully; I never saw him look so before."

"Well, what passed after he came in?"

"I don't know; he sent us both out of the room, grandma and me."

"Where did you go?"

"Into the entry; we had no other place!"

"Did you hear nothing after?"

"Yes, the sound of voices, but no words; then Mr. Leicester rushed through the door, and out to the area; we thought he was gone, but in a minute he came back and went into the basement again; we heard no words after that, but a heavy fall. We went in, Mr. Leicester lay on the floor; grandpa was close by; there was blood about: but I do not know anything else, my head grew dizzy; I remember clinging to grandmother that I might not fall."

"And this is all you know?"

"Yes, it is all!"

It is impossible to describe the effect this young girl's evidence produced upon the court. She did not weep or blush as most girls of her age might have done. The feelings that gave her voice those tones of thrilling sadness, the subdued pain so visible in her sweet countenance, were all too strong and deep for these more common manifestations. You saw that this young creature was performing a solemn duty, when she stood up there to testify against the being whom she loved better than anything on earth—that the single hour which she occupied on the stand would leave behind it such memories as weigh upon the heart forever.

Julia descended from the gaze of that crowd, older at heart by ten years than ordinary events would have left her. Great suffering brings painful precocity with it. It takes but a few moments to harden iron into steel; but the fire is hot, and the blows hard which accomplish the transformation.

The defence refused all cross-examination, and Julia was told that she might leave the stand. As the permission was given, she lifted her heavy eyes and turned them once more upon her grandfather. Oh, what a world of anguish lay in that look. The old man answered it with another smile. She saw it but dimly, for her eyes were filling with tears, but its sad sweetness made her faint. She tottered back to the seat by her grandmother, leaned her head against the wall, and without a sigh or a motion became as insensible as the wall itself.

It was strange, but the evidence of this young girl, strongly as it bore against the prisoner in fact, created a feeling in his favor with the jury, and disposed the crowd to more charitable thoughts of the old man who could make himself so beloved by a creature like that. As for Mrs. Gray, she absolutely sobbed till the chair shook under her, all the time that Julia was speaking. But the grandmother sat motionless, only turning her eyes slowly from her husband to the jury, and from them to the judges, striving, poor creature, to gather some ray of hope from their faces.

It was a strong proof of the influence which the truthfulness of this young creature had upon the court, that there was a good deal of legal informality permitted in the examination. She had been allowed to tell her story after her own gentle fashion, without undue interference from the lawyers ; and for a little time after she left the stand, there was profound silence in the crowd, as if no one could break, even by a whisper, the impressions which her evidence had left.

This silence was broken by the prisoner, who arose, all at once, and attempted to move toward his grand-daughter. While all others were absorbed, he had seen her head droop against the wall, the heavy lids settle like snow-flakes over her eyes, and the color quenched around her mouth. The sight was too much for him, and he started up, as I have described, but only to feel the officer's gripe upon his arm.

"See, see, you have killed her," said the old man, pointing with his finger to the insensible girl. "Let me go to her, I say—one minute—only a minute ! No one else can bring her to life !"

The officer attempted to resist the old man.

"Sit down—sit down," he said, "it disburbs the court. She shall have care, only be quiet."

The prisoner resisted this friendly violence, and struggled against the man with all his feeble strength.

"She is dead; I tell you it has killed her, poor thing! Poor darling, she is dead!" he repeated, and tears rolled heavily down his face. "Will no one see if she is quite, quite gone?"

As if in answer to this pathetic cry for aid, a young man forced his way up from a corner of the room, where he had stood all day regarding every stage of the trial with the keenest interest, and taking Julia in his arms, carried her to an open window.

"Give me water," he said to the officer; "there is some before the judge;" then turning toward Mrs. Gray, who, occupied by the prisoner, had been quite insensible to Julia's situation, he said, abruptly, "Have you no hartshorn?—nothing about you, aunt, that will be of use?"

"Dear me, yes," answered the good lady, producing a vial of camphor from the depths of her pocket, "I thought something of the kind might happen; here is the water too; there, her eyelids begin to move."

"She is better—she will soon be well," said Robert Otis, turning his face toward the prisoner, who stood up in the midst of the court, looking after his grandchild, with eyes that might have touched a heart of stone.

"Thank you, thank you!" said the old man; and without another word, he sat down, covered his face with both hands, and wept like a child.

After a little, Julia was led back to her seat, and Robert Otis withdrew into the crowd again. Another witness was examined and dismissed. Then there came a pause in the proceedings. The witnesses' stand was for a time unoccupied. The district attorney sat restlessly on his chair, casting anxious glances toward the door, as if waiting for some person important to his cause. The judge was just bending forward to desire the proceedings to go on, when a slight bustle near the door caused a movement through the whole crowd. Those persons near the entrance were pressed back against their neighbors by two officers in authority, who thus made a lane up to the witnesses' stand, through which a lady passed, with rapid footsteps, and evidently much excited by the position in which she found herself.

A whisper of surprise, not unmingled with admiration, ran through the crowd, as this lady took her place upon the stand. She hesitated an instant, then, with a graceful motion, swept the veil of heavy lace back upon her bonnet, and turned toward the judges. The face thus exposed had something far more striking in it than beauty. It was a haughty face, full of determination, and with a calmness upon the features that was too rigid not to have been forced. Notwithstanding this, you could see that the woman trembled in every limb, as she bared her features to the crowd.

It was not the bashful tremor which might have brought crimson to the brow of any female, while so many eyes were bent upon her, but a strong nervous excitement, which lifted her above all these considerations. The contrast of a black velvet dress flowing to her feet, and fitted high at the throat, might have added somewhat to the singular effect produced by a face at once so stern and so beautiful. Certain it is, that a thrill of that respect which strong feeling always carries with it, passed through the crowd; and though she was strikingly lovely, people forgot that, in sympathy for the emotions that she suppressed with such fortitude. The rapidity with which she had entered the court, and the position which she took on the stand, prevented a full view of her face to Mrs. Warren and Julia; but as she turned slowly toward them, in throwing back her veil, the effect upon these two persons was startling enough.

The old woman half rose from her chair, her lips moved, as if a smothered cry had died upon them, and she sat down again, grasping a fold of Mrs. Gray's gown in her hands. It was the face she had seen in the carriage that morning.

Julia also recognized the lady, with a start. It was the woman who had purchased flowers of her so often, who had been so invariably kind, and whose fate had been strongly blended with her own since the first day when she had purchased violets from her flower basket.

There was something startling to the young girl in this sudden apparition of a person who had been to her almost like fate itself. At that solemn moment she drew her breath heavily, and listened with painful attention for the first words that might fall upon the court. Mrs. Gray also was filled with astonishment, for she saw her own brother, Jacob Strong, enter the court, walking close behind the lady, until she mounted the stand, with the air and manner of an attendant. When the lady took her position, he drew back toward the door, and stood motionless, gazing anxiously upon her face, without turning his eyes aside even for an instant. It was in vain Mrs. Gray motioned with her hand that he should approach her; all his senses seemed swallowed up by keen interest in the lady. He had no existence for the time but in her.

Of all the persons in that court-room, there was not one who did not exhibit some unusual interest in the woman placed so unexpectedly upon the witnesses' stand, except the prisoner himself. He had been, during some moments, sitting with his forehead bent upon his clasped hands, lost in thought, or, it might be, in silent prayer to the God who had, as it seemed, almost abandoned him. He did not look up when the lady entered, and not till the examination had proceeded to some considerable length, was he aware of her presence.

It was worthy of remark, that the prosecuting attorney addressed this witness with a degree of respect which he had extended to no other person. His voice, hitherto so sharp and biting, took a subdued tone. His manner became deferential, and the opening questions, in which he was usually abrupt, almost to rudeness, were now rather insinuated than demanded.

He waived the usual preliminaries regarding tne age and name of the witness, and even apologized for the necessity which had compelled him to bring her oefore the court.

The lady listened to all this with a little impatience; she was evidently in no state of mind for commonplace gallantries, and seemed relieved when he commenced those direct questions which were to place her evidence before the court.

"Mrs. Gordon, that is your name, I believe !"

The lady bent her head.

"Did you know Mr. William Leicester when he was living ?"

A faint tremor passed over the lady's lips, but she answered clearly, though in a very subdued voice—

"Yes, I knew him !"

"He visited at your house sometimes ?"

"Yes !"

"When did you see him last ?"

"On the——" Her voice became almost inaudible as she uttered the date; but the lawyer had keen ears, and forbore to ask a repetition of the words, for her face changed suddenly, and it seemed with a violent effort that she was able to go on.

"At what hour did he leave your house ?"

"I do not know the exact hour !"

"Was it late ?"

"Yes, I gave a ball that night, and my guests generally remained late !"

"Did you observe anything peculiar in his manner that night ? Did he act like a man that was likely to commit suicide in the morning ?"

It was half a minute before the lady gave any reply to this question; then she spoke with an effort, as if some nervous affection were almost choking her.

"I cannot judge—I do not know. It is a strange question to ask me !"

"I regret its necessity !" said the attorney, with a deferential bend of the head; "our object is," he added, addressing the judge, "to show by this witness, how the deceased was occupied during the night before his murder. I believe it is the intention of the defence to claim that William Leicester killed himself; that it was a case of suicide instead of the foul murder we will prove it to have been. I wish to show by this lady that he was a guest in her mansion up to a late hour; that he joined in the festivities of a ball, and was among the most cheerful revellers present. I must repeat the question, madam—did you remark anything singular in his manner—anything to distinguish him from other guests?"

The lady parted her lips, struggled, and answered—

"No, I saw nothing!" She lifted her eyes after this, as if impelled by some magnetic power, and met those of the tall, gaunt man, who had followed her into court. His look of sorrowful reproach seemed to sting her, and she spoke again, louder and more resolutely. "There was nothing in the words or acts of William Leicester, that night, which warranted an idea of suicide—nothing!"

A faint sound, not quite a groan, but deeper than a sigh, broke from Jacob Strong; and he shrunk back into the crowd, with his head drooping like some animal stricken with an arrow, and anxious to hide the wound. That moment, as if actuated by one of those impulses that seem like the strides of fate toward an object, the district attorney said, as it seemed in the very wantonness of his professional privilege,

"Look at the prisoner, madam. Did you ever see him before?"

The lady turned partly round and looked toward the prisoner's seat. The old man had his head bowed, for the sight of his insensible grandchild had left him strengthless, and she could only distinguish the soft wave of grey hairs around his temples, and the stoop of a figure venerable from age.

"Stand up," commanded the judge, addressing the old man; "stand up that the witness may look upon your face!"

The old man arose and stood upright. His eyes were lifted

slowly, and met those of the woman, which were filled with cold abhorrence of the being she was forced to look upon. I cannot describe those two faces as their eyes were riveted upon each other; both were instantly pale as death. After a moment, in which something of doubt mingled with its corpse-like pallor, that of the woman took an expression of almost terrible affright. Her pale lips quivered; her eyes distended with wild brilliancy. She lifted one hand that shook like an aspen, and swept it across her eyes once, twice, as if to clear their vision. She did not attempt to speak; the sight of that old man chilled her through and through, body and soul. She seemed freezing into marble.

The change that came upon the prisoner was not less remarkable. At first there settled upon his face a look of the most painful astonishment. It deepened, changed, and as snow becomes luminous when the sunshine strikes it, the very pallor of his features brightened. Affection, tenderness, the most thrilling gratitude beamed through their whiteness, and while her gaze was fascinated by his, he stretched forth his arms. This scene was so strange, the agitation of these persons so unaccountable, that it held the whole court breathless. You might have heard an insect stir in any part of that vast room. It seemed with every breath as if some cry must burst from the old man—as if the lady would sink to the earth, dead, so terrible was her agitation. But the prisoner only stretched forth his arms, and it seemed as if this slight motion restored the lady to herself. Her face hardened; she turned away, withdrawing her gaze slowly, as if the effort cost her a mortal pang. Then she answered,

"No, I do not recognize him!"

Her lips were like marble, and her voice so husky that it made the hearers shrink, but every word was clearly enunciated.

The old man fell back to his seat; his arms dropped heavily down; he too seemed frozen into stone.

For a moment the witness stood mute and still; then she started all at once, turned and descended into the crowd.

Mrs. Warren, whom no one had observed during this scene, arose from her seat as the lady passed, and followed her. The crowd closed around them, but the old woman struggled through, and laid a trembling grasp upon the velvet dress that floated before her like the waves of a pall. The lady turned her white face sharply round, and it came close to that of the old woman. A convulsion stirred her features ; she lifted her arm as if to fling it around that frail form, then dashed it down, tearing her dress from that feeble grasp, and walked steadily out of the court.

CHAPTER XXXV.

THE VERDICT.

Tread lightly here—let outraged justice weep!

THERE had been a severe change in the weather since morning. The pure frosty air, that invigorated everything it touched, hardened toward night, into one of those cold storms—half snow, half ice—that chill you to the vitals. A coating of this sleety snow lay upon the Park, icing the trees with crystal, and bending every twig as with a fruitage of pearls. The stone pavement and the City Hall steps were carpeted an inch deep by the storm; and the hail crackled sharply under foot if any one attempted to pass over them. In short, it was one of those nights when everything living seeks shelter, and no human being is seen abroad, save those given up to wild desolation, either of body or mind.

Miserable and stormy as the night was, two persons had been wandering in it for hours, sometimes lost in the blackness of the storm, sometimes gliding by the lamps that seemed struggling to keep themselves alive—and again stealing up the curving staircase within the City Hall, ghost-like and shadowy, only to come forth in the tempest and wander as before.

In the darkness, it would have been difficult to judge of the sex or condition of those persons. Both were muffled in garments black as the clouds that hung over them. Both were tall, and, sometimes as they walked, the outlines of their persons blended together, till they seemed scarcely more than a mass of moving darkness. It was remarkable that, standing or walking, they never lost sight of a range of windows in one wing of the City Hall, where lights shone gloomily into the mist, not wandering about as the lamps of a happy household often do, but motionless, like watchfires, half smothered by the dense atmosphere.

Once more these two persons ascended the steps and entered the vestibule, from which the horse-shoe staircase diverges. A shower of sleet followed them, and the wind swept wailing over their heads as they went in. A lamp burned near the staircase, and for a moment, the faces of those two wanderers became visible. The one that struck you first, was that of a female. Tresses, that had of late been curled, hung in dripping masses down each side of her face, that was not only as white, but seemed cold also as marble. A pair of wild eyes, really blue, but blackened with the smothered fire that protracted suspense leaves behind it, gleamed out from the shadow of her bonnet, around which the folds of a heavy lace veil dripped in sodden masses to her shoulders. The velvet cloak which shrouded her was heavy with rain ; its lustre all gone, and its rich fringes, frozen together with sleet, rattled against the balustrades as she pressed them in passing. Her companion—but even as we attempt to describe him, the woman turns, with her hand upon the balustrade, and addresses him—thus giving his identity better than any description could convey.

"What was that, Jacob? A noise—the stirring of feet! Oh, my God—my God—they are coming in!"

She caught hold of Jacob's rough over-coat with one hand The gleam of her teeth, as they knocked together, made the strong man recoil. It gave an expression of fearful agony to her face. He listened.

"No, it is the wind breaking through the hall."

"How it sobs! How like a human voice it is! Do you hear it? Death!—death!—that is what it says!"

"You shudder—you are cold. How your teeth chatter!" said Jacob, folding the half-frozen cloak about her. "What can I do? If you would only go home, I will come the first minute after the verdict. Do—do go!"

"Hush! it is there again. Are the winds human, that they moan so?"

"It is a fierce storm, nothing more," said Jacob.

A woman came down the steps that moment. She had no cloak on, and a thin shawl hung in limp folds over her shoulders. An old hood lay back from her face, revealing features large and stern, but for the instant softened with sorrow. She came from the vestibule overhead. In that direction lay the court-room. Ada saw the woman, and holding out both her hands, shivering and purple with cold, walked slowly up to meet her. These two females had seen each other but once in the world. One was from a prison, the other from a palatial home; yet they stood face to face, on equal terms, now. I am wrong; the woman of the prison looked down with something of stern rebuke upon the lady. She said in her heart, "The blood of this old man be upon her head! Did she not deny me the gold that might have saved him?" But when she looked upon that face, her resentment gave way. She paused on the steps, instead of pushing roughly by, and said, in a tone that sounded peculiarly gentle from its contrast with her appearance and bearing—

"This is a bitter night, madam."

"Tell me—tell me," gasped Ada, seizing the woman's shawl, and raising her hand toward the court-room, "have they—have they—"

"Poor thing! so you repent at last," answered the woman, comprehending her gesture with that quick magnetism which is the lightning of some hearts. "No, they have not come in; but it is of no use waiting—the poor old man is as good as hung, depend on it."

Ada uttered a faint cry, very faint, but it seemed to her that it sounded through the whole building, ringing above the storm like a yell. She dropped the woman's shawl, and stood motionless, looking helplessly in her face.

"You had better take the lady home," said the woman, turning kindly to Jacob; "she is wet through—the ice rattles on her clothes; she will catch her death of cold. I would stay and help her, for she seems in trouble; but there is worse trouble coming for the poor creature overhead. I thought I had seen hard sights before; but this—there is no brandy strong enough to make me forget this!"

"There is no news—the jury are still out?" questioned Jacob. "Tell me!"

"No, no—I have nothing to say—the jury are out yet—the judge waiting—the old man—"

"Hush!" said Jacob, "she is listening."

"Stay—tell me all—the old man—tell me all!" cried Ada, hurrying down two or three steps after the woman.

"I cannot wait, lady; the jury may come in any moment. Those poor watchers will want a carriage. I must find one somewhere. Nobody thought of that but me. They might not feel the storm, for the verdict will numb them; but it is a piercing night."

"You have no cloak—scarcely more than summer clothes. I will go," said Jacob.

"I am used to battling with the weather," was the answer. "Thank you, though."

"Stay with her," answered Jacob, and he hurried down the steps.

"How the wind blows!—it is a terrible night," said the woman, drawing her scant shawl together, and sitting down by Ada, who had sunk upon the cold steps, as if all the strength had withered from her limbs the moment Jacob left her.

"You tremble—your teeth chatter—these poor hands are like ice; there, there, let me rub them between mine."

Ada submitted her shivering hands meekly as a child, and a drop, that was not rain, stole down her face.

"You told me once," she said, "that money would save him; will thousands—hundreds of thousands do it now?"

"It is too late," answered the woman, sadly.

The tempest rose just then, and, to Ada's almost frenzied mind, it seemed as if every swell of the wind answered back, "too late—too late!" She shuddered, and cowered down by the woman, as if a death sentence were ringing over her.

When Jacob returned, he found the two women sitting together, upon the steps. Ada rose to her feet, and, without speaking, began rapidly to mount them. Jacob followed.

"Where are you going! Not there, I hope—not there!"

"Yes, *there!*"

She rushed forward, her frozen garments crackling and shedding ice-drops as she moved. All the high-bred dignity of her mien was gone; all the richness of her toilet drenched away. The woman who followed her scarcely looked more poverty stricken—did not look so utterly desolate. She opened the court-room door, and crept in. All the audience was gone. Empty benches flung their long, gloomy shadows athwart the room. Dim lamps flared across the wall, leaving patches of blackness in the angles and around every object that could catch and break the weak gleams of light. The judge was upon his seat, pale and still as a statue of marble. Weary with excitement and the protracted trial, he sat there in the gloomy midnight, waiting for the death-word, face to face with that old man, whose life lay in the breath on his lip. Constantly his eyes turned upon the prisoner, and always they were met with a glance that penetrated his heart to the core. A light, overhead, fell upon the old man's temple, silvering the broad, high forehead, gleaming through the white locks and glancing downward, shedding faint rays upon his beard and bosom. I have seen a picture of Rembrandt's, so like my idea of the old man, that it has haunted me ever since. The calm, deep-set eyes, the holy strength slumbering within them—the expanse of forehead, the whole head, were so perfectly the embodiment of my thought, that it startled me. That which I saw in the picture, it was, which penetrated to the heart of the judge, as he gazed upon the living man.

A group of police-officers hung about the door; some asleep, with their caps down over their eyes, others yawning and stretched at full length upon the benches, making the scene more gloomy by the contrast of their indifference with the anguish that surrounded them.

Away, in the darkest corner, was another group of persons —three females and a man. No word, no whisper passed among them. It scarcely seemed as if they drew breath; but as you looked that way, the glitter of wild eyes struck you with a sort of terror; and if the least sound arose, the shadows around those women changed sharply, as if they felt something of the anguish which made their principals start. Ada Leicester crept noiselessly along the darkened wall, followed by the prison woman, and sat down a little way from the rest. No one seemed to regard her, and there she remained in the gloom, motionless as the figures upon which her dull eyes were now and then turned. Thus an hour went by; all within the court room was silent as death; without was the storm, wailing and sobbing around the windows, shaking them angrily, like evil spirits striving to break in, then rushing off with a hoarse disappointed howl. This terrible contrast—the stillness within—the wild tumult without—made even the officers cower closer together, and filled the other persons present with intense awe. It seemed as if heaven and earth had combined in hurling denunciations against that hapless old man. It was after midnight, and for an instant there was a hush in the storm—a hush in the vast building. Then came the sharp closing of a door, the tramp of heavy feet, and twelve figures glided, one after another, into the court-room. They ranged themselves in a dark line along the jury-box, and stood motionless, their cloaks huddled around them, like folds of a thunder-cloud, their faces white as marble.

The judge arose, leaning heavily with one hand upon the desk before him. His lips moved, but it was not till a second effort that they gave forth a sound ; but when it did come, his voice broke through the room like a trumpet.

" Prisoner, stand up and look upon the jury !"

The old man arose, and turning meekly around, lifted his eyes to the twelve jurors. * * *

" Guilty or not guilty ?"

" Guilty !"

The storm began to howl again, but all was still in the court-room.

CHAPTER XXXVI.

THE PARENTS, THE CHILD AND GRANDCHILD

Nor sin, nor shame, nor sense of wrong,
Can yet a mother's love control;
It waiteth, watcheth, hopeth long,
And grows immortal with the soul.

The next morning, a carriage, one of the few superb equipages that give an air of elegance to Broadway, equal to that of any public drive I have yet seen, stopped at the corner of Franklin street. The grey horses and deep green of the carriage were well known in that thoroughfare, and it had been too often seen before Stewart's, and Ball & Black's, for any one to remark the time during which it remained in that unusual place.

Had any one seen Ada Leicester as she descended from the carriage and walked hurriedly toward the City Prison, it might have been a matter of wonder, how a creature so elegant and so fastidious had forced herself to enter a neighborhood which few women visit, except from force or objects of philanthropy.

Jacob Strong walked by the side of his mistress. Few words passed between them, for both seemed painfully preoccupied. Jacob betrayed this state of mind by a more decided stoop of the shoulders, and by knocking his great feet against every loose brick in the sidewalk, as he stumbled along. The lady moved on as one walks in a dream, her eyes bent upon the pavement, her ungloved hand grasping the purple velvet of her cloak and holding it against her bosom. The people who passed her thought it a pretty piece of coquetry, by which she might reveal the jewels that flashed upon the snow of that beautiful hand. Alas, how little we can judge of one another! The delicate primrose gloves had dropped from her grasp unheeded, and lay trampled in the mud close by her own door. The maid had placed them in her palsied hand, as she had performed all other duties of the toilet that morning, but the wretched woman was quite unconscious of it all.

They entered the prison. A few words passed between Jacob and the warden in an outer office; then a door was flung open, and they entered an open court within the walls; stone buildings ranged all around, casting gaunt shadows athwart them. They crossed the court, passed through a low door, and entered the hall where male prisoners are kept. Ada was scarcely conscious that a score of eyes were bent on her from the galleries overhead, along which prisoners charged with lighter offences were allowed to range. At that moment a regiment of soldiers might have stood in her way, and she would have passed through their midst, unconscious of the obstruction. She mounted to the third gallery, following after Jacob, until he paused at one of the heavy iron doors which pierced the whole wall at equal distances from pavement to ceiling. An officer, who had preceded them, turned the key in the lock, and flung the door open, with a clang that made Ada start, as if some one had struck her.

"Shall I go in with you?" said Jacob.

She did not answer, save by a short breath, that seemed to tear her own bosom without yielding a sound, and entered the cell. Jacob leaned forward, and closing the door after her, began to walk up and down the gallery, but never passing more than six or eight paces from the cell.

Ada Leicester stood face to face with her father. He had been reading, and had laid the old Bible on the bed by his side as the noise of her approach disturbed him. His steel-mounted spectacles were still before his eyes, dimmed, it may be, by traces of tears, shed unconsciously, for he could not distinguish clearly through them, and with a motion so familiar that it made her tremble, he folded them up and placed them within the pages of the book.

She paused, motionless, after taking one step into the room, and but for the shiver of her silk dress, which the trembling of her limbs disturbed, as the leaves are shaken in autumn, she might have been a draped statue, her face and hands were so marble-like.

The old man looked at her, and she at him. He did not attempt to speak, and a single word died on her lip again and again, without giving forth a sound. At length that one word broke forth, and rushed like an arrow from her heart to his—

"Father!"

It was the first word that her infant lips had ever uttered. The old man was blinded by it. He saw nothing of the stately pale woman, the gleaming eyes, the rich drapery; but a little girl, some twelve months old, seemed to have crept to his knees. He saw the ringlet of soft golden hair, the large blue eyes, the little dimpled shoulder peeping out from its calico dress; he reached forth his hands to press them down upon these pretty shoulders, for the vision was palpable as life. They descended upon the bowed head of the woman, for she had fallen crouching to his feet. He drew those hands back with a moan. The innocent child had vanished; the prostrate woman was there.

"Father!"

He held his hands one instant, quivering like withered leaves, over her head, and then dropped them gently down upon her shoulders.

"My daughter!"

Then came a rush of tears, a wild clinging of arms, a shaking of silken garments, and deep sobs, that seemed like the parting of soul and body. Ada clung to her father. She laid her cold face upon his knees, and drew herself up to his bosom.

"Forgive me! forgive me!—oh, my father, forgive me!"

The old man lifted her gently in his arms, and seated her upon the bed. He took off her bonnet, and smoothed the rich hair it had concealed between his hands.

"And so you have come home again, my child!"

"Home!"

She looked around the cell, and then into the eyes of her father.

"I have given you this home—I, who have sought for you—prayed—prayed, father, not as you pray, but madly, wildly prayed for one look, one word—pardon, pardon! I have got it—I see it—you pardon me with your eyes, my father; but oh, how wretched I am—I, who gave you a home like this!"

"No, not you, but God!" answered the old man. "I knew from the first that our Father who is in heaven had not afflicted his servant for nothing. All will be well at last, Ada."

"But you will die! Even to-day will they sentence you!"

"I know it, and am ready; for now I begin to see how wisely God has willed that the last remnant of an old man's life shall be the restoration of his child."

"But you are innocent, and they will kill you!"

"They cannot kill more than this old body, my child. Even now it feels the breath of eternity. What though the withered leaf is shaken a moment earlier from its bough!"

Ada held her breath, and gazed upon her father, filled with strange awe. The quiet tone, the gentle resignation in his words, tranquillized her like music. She could not realize that he was to die. Her soul was flooded with love; her eyes answered back the holy affection that beamed in his. For that moment she was happy. Her childhood came softly back She forgot her own sin alike with her father's danger.

"Now," said the old man, "tell me all that I do not know. By what means has God sent you here?"

At these words Ada half arose; all the joy went out from her face; her eyes drooped; the lines about her mouth hardened again; she attempted to look up, failed, and with both hands shrouded her guilty features.

"How much do you know?" she inquired, in a hoarse voice.

"I know," said the old man, "that you left an unworthy husband and a happy child, to follow a stranger to a strange land."

"But you did not know," said Ada, still veiling her face, "you did not know how cruelly, how dreadfully I was treated; how I was left days and weeks together in hotels and boarding houses, without money, without friends, exposed to all sorts of temptation. You cannot know all the circumstances that combined to drive me mad. Still do not say I abandoned the child. Did I not send her to you? Did I not give her up when she was dear as the pulses of my own heart, rather than cast the stain of my example upon her? Oh, father, was this nothing?"

"We took the child, and strove to forget the mother," said the old man sadly.

"But could not—oh, you could not! This thought was the one anchor which kept me from utter shipwreck, you could not curse an only child—wicked, erring, cruel though she was!"

"No, we did not curse her—we had no power to forget."

"I came back—Jacob Strong will bear me witness—I lost no time in searching for you at the homestead. Strangers were there. Had we met then—had I found the old place as it was—you, my mother, my daughter there—how different all this might have been!"

"God disposes all things," muttered the prisoner. "We left our home when disgrace fell upon us We who had been sinfully proud of you, Ada, went forth burdened by your shame to hide ourselves among strangers; we could not look our old neighbors in the face, and so left them and gave up the name our child had disgraced."

"Father—father, spare me—I am wretched—I am punished—spare me, spare me!"

"Ada," said the old man solemnly, "do you heartily repent and forsake your sin?"

"I do repent—I have forsaken—he is dead for whom I left you; it was a solitary fault, bitterly, oh, bitterly atoned for."

The old man looked at her earnestly—at the glowing purple of her garments—at the delicate veil she had gathered up to her face with one hand. The other had fallen nervelessly down. The old man took it from her lap and gazed sadly on the jewels that sparkled on her fingers. She felt the touch, and the trembling hand became crimson in his clasp.

"And yet you wear these things!"

She shrunk away, and the glow of her shame spread and burned over every visible part of her person.

"Cast them from you, daughter—come to me in the pretty calico dress that became you so well—give up these wages of shame—become poor, honest and humble, as we are; then will your mother receive you; then your child may know that she has a mother living; then your old father can die in peace, knowing that his life has not been sacrificed in vain."

The old man looked wistfully at her, as he spoke. He saw the struggle in her face—the reluctance with which she understood him, and tightened his grasp on her hand.

"What—what would you have me do?" she said.

"Cast aside all that you possess, save that which comes of honest labor, and earn the forgiveness you ask."

"Father, I cannot do this; the wealth that I possess is vast; it was devised to me by will upon his death-bed; it was an atonement upon his part."

"The wages of sin are death."

"Death, father, death! Surely you are right. Leicester is

dead; they will murder you. Nothing but this money, this very wealth that I am ordered to cast aside, can save you."

"And that never shall save me!" answered the old man with grave dignity; "the price of my daughter's sin, let it be millions, shall never buy an hour of life for me, were it possible thus to bribe the law."

"Oh father, father, do not say this; it crushes my last hope."

"Daughter," and the old man stood up, while his face glowed as with the light of prophecy, "it is not this ill-gotten wealth that shall purchase my life; but it is the death I shall suffer, which will purchase the salvation of my child. The way of providence is made clear to me now; I see it plainly, as if written upon the wall that has seemed so blank to my eyes till now."

The hand fell from her face. She gazed upon him with awe, for the solemn faith that beamed in his eyes held her breathless. That moment the cell door was opened, and Mrs. Warren came in, followed by her grand-daughter. The old woman paused motionless upon the threshold, hesitating and pallid. Ada stood up trembling and afraid in the presence of her mother. A moment the two stood face to face, gazing at each other; then the old woman stretched forth her arms, and tears rolled down her cheeks. Ada would have thrown herself forward, but the old prisoner interposed.

"No, wife, not yet; the time is at hand when our child shall come back to your bosom, like the lamb that was lost; but God has a work to accomplish first; have patience and let her depart."

"Patience, patience! Oh, Wilcox, she is our child Ada, Ada!"

He was not strong enough to keep them apart. Their arms were interwoven; they clung together, filling the cell with soft murmurs and smothered sobs. Broken syllables of endearment —all the pathetic language with which heart speaks to heart in defiance of words, gave power to the scene. Remember, reader, it was a mother meeting her only child—her sinful, erring child—for the first time in years. They met in a prison, with death shadows all around. Was it wonderful that, forgiving, forgetting, they clung together? Or that the turnkey, as he looked in, felt the tears bathing his cheek?

It is a mercy that intense feeling has its limits, else a scene like this might have broken the two hearts that rushed together, as torrents meet in a storm. Their arms unlocked at length, and the two women only held by each other from weakness.

"And this is my child, my little Julia," said Ada, turning her eyes upon the young girl who stood by, troubled and amazed by all she saw.

She bent forward, and would have kissed the girl, but the old man interposed again solemnly, almost sternly.

"Not yet—the lip must be purified, the kiss made holy, which touches the forehead of this innocent one."

"I will go, father, I will go—this is bitter, but perhaps just. I will go while I have the strength."

Ada left the cell. We will not follow her to the scene of her solitary and splendid anguish. We will not remain in the prisoner's cell. The scene passing there was too holy and too pathetic for description; yet was there more happiness that day in the prison, than Ada Leicester found in her palace-home. Truly it is much better to suffer wrong, than to do wrong!

CHAPTER XXXVII.

THE DAWNING OF LIGHT.

As sunshine falls upon a flower
 That storms have beaten to the ground,
Her heart began to feel the power
 Of his deep love and faith profound.

The sentence was pronounced; the time of execution fixed. Each morning, as the prisoner awoke, he said to himself, another is gone ; so many, and so many days are left. I dare not say that this man did not occasionally shrink from the agony that awaited him ; or that the clouds of doubt did not grow black above his head, more than once ; but at all times his mien was tranquil, his words full of resignation. Some hope, some sublime faith, stronger than death, seemed to bear him up.

His daughter came to him more than once, and always left the cell with a changed manner and subdued aspect. While there was a hope of saving the prisoner, she had been excited and almost wild in her demeanor. She appealed to the governor in person. She lavished gold. On every hand the great power of her personal influence was all tested to the utmost, but in vain. There exist cases in which the fangs of the law fasten deep, and no human power can unloose them. In this instance, mercy veiled her face, and justice became cruelty.

At no time did the old man sanction or partake of his daughter's efforts. Shall I say, that he did not even desire them to succeed? One sublime idea had taken possession of his mind, and when he prayed, it was not that he might be saved from death, but that the pang which sent him into eternity might open the gates of paradise to his child.

I have said that the old man was feeble, and scenes through which no human being could pass with unshaken nerves, had gradually undermined the little strength that age and privation had spared. Those who saw him every day scarcely noticed this, the change was so gradual; but the sheriff, who came but once each week, remarked how frail he was becoming, and how difficult it was for him to support the irons with which they had manacled his limbs. More than once he said to himself, " It will scarcely be more than a shadow that they force me to strangle." Still, as his strength gave way, the holy faith within him beamed out stronger and brighter, as a flame becomes more brilliant from increased purity of the oil on which it feeds.

All hope was gone—and Ada saw her father every day, always alone, and her visits lasted for hours. At such times, Jacob Strong, who kept sentinel at the door, would pause and hold his breath, struck, as it were, by the sweet, solemn tones that came through the door. Sometimes you might have seen him brush one huge hand across his eyes; and then, bowing his head upon his bosom, pace slowly to and fro, with a mournful but not altogether dissatisfied look.

After these visits, Ada would come forth with a subdued and gentle air, which no person had ever witnessed in her before. The entire character of her beauty changed. Her features became thin; her person lost something of its roundness, but gained in that refined grace which is indescribable. Her eyes grew darker and softer from the shadows that deepened under them. Something of holy light there was too, that brooded sadly there in place of the brilliancy that had kindled them so often almost into wildness. If Ada had been beautiful when we first knew her, she was far lovelier now. The heart yearned toward her as it felt the glance of her eyes. The earthly was becoming purified from her being, and the resemblance between her and the old man seemed to have found a spiritual link. Truly the solemn faith within him was near its reward

CHAPTER XXXVIII.

GATHERING FOR THE EXECUTION.

He was a man of simple heart,
Patient and meek; the Christian part
Came to his soul as came the air
That heaved his bosom; hope, despair,
Were chastened by a holy faith!
Meek in his life he feared not death.

THE day of execution arrived, and every hearth-stone in the great metropolis was shadowed by a knowledge that at an hour to be fixed between sunrise and sunset, a human being was to be strangled to death—forced brutally into the presence of his Maker. Children whispered to one another in the grey dawn as they crept awe-stricken from their little couches. Mothers—those who had hearts—grew sad as they thought of the household ties which the law would that day tear asunder.

I do not say that this law of blood for blood, which some good men cling to so tenaciously, should be altogether abolished. Women who from the natural and just arrangement of social life, have no share in forming laws, can scarcely arrogate to themselves the right of advancing or of condemning those which owe their existence to the greatest masculine intellect; and we, who reason so much from the heart, can never be sure that the angel of mercy, whom we worship, may not sometimes crowd Justice from her seat. But there is no law that should permit a solemn act of justice to become a jubilee for the mob. Executions, if they must darken the history of a nation, should be still as the grave—solemn as the eternity to which they lead.

Two wardens had been placed over the prisoner that night, for the sheriff feared that the poor old man might attempt suicide. It was a useless precaution for one who was so close to death, and yet slept so calmly. There he lay in the deep slumber which is so sweet to old age. The men kept a light in the cell, and it streamed softly over those calm, pale features, revealing a faint smile upon the lips, and the impalpable shadows scattered over his forehead by the white hair that lay around his temples. Sometimes, as the men gazed upon this picture, and thought of the morrow, with all its death horrors, they turned from each other with a sort of terror, and sat with downcast eyes, gazing upon the floor, for it made them heart-sick —the contrast of that peaceful slumber and the brutal death-sleep into which they were guarding the old man.

At the most, it was but a brief gleam of life that the law claimed; and even that had grown faint within the last few days, so faint that it seemed doubtful if the officers of the law would not be compelled to lift its victim to the scaffold, when the hour of sacrifice came. The day dawned quietly, and shed a sort of still, holy light over the slumbering man. Then, for the first time, his keepers remarked how deathly pale was the serene countenance—how feeble was the breath that scarcely stirred the coarse linen on his bosom.

Everything was still. The cold dawn, the quiet city, and the prison lying heavy and grim in its bosom. All at once this stillness was broken by the fall of a hammer, distinct and sharp as the beat of a death-watch. It made the officers start and look at each other with meaning eyes; but the old man slept on, and the sound might have been the sigh of an angel, instead of the hideous death-signal that it was, for it only disturbed that tranquil slumber pleasantly, as it would seem. A faint smile dawned upon the face, and he folded his hands softly upon his bosom, with a deeper breath, as if some vision of ineffable happiness filled his thought.

It seemed a cruelty to disturb the last sleep he was ever to know on earth, and so the morning deepened, and the prison was filled with that sort of muffled tumult which bespeaks the opening day within those walls, before the old man awoke.

Other persons than the keepers were in the cell then. The wife, who was so soon to be a widow, and the grandchild, half orphaned at heart, were seated at the foot of the bed, watching him dimly through their tears. He held forth his hands on seeing them, and with the same smile that had haunted his slumber, asked after their welfare. You should have seen that aged couple, in their humble but sublime sorrow, that day, for it was a beautiful sight, and one which is not often witnessed within the walls of a felon's cell. There they sat, hand in hand, linked together by that beautiful love that outlives all things, comforting each other with gentle earnestness—he reading passages from the Bible to her now and then, and she more than once smiling hopefully through her tears, when he spoke of their great age, and of the little time that they could possibly be kept asunder. It did not seem as if they were talking of death, but of some important and not unpleasant journey, in which the wife would soon follow her husband to a new home.

The grandchild sat by in silent grief. It seemed a long time for her to wait, she was so young, so cruelly full of life. She could not, with her sensitive feelings and quick imagination, cast off the consciousness of all the horrors that would that day overwhelm her grandfather. Her eyes were heavy with weeping. At every sound a shiver of terrible apprehension ran through her frame, and she would grasp at the old man's hand, as if scared with dread that they might tear him away before the appointed time.

Then came another—and that prison cell was crowded full of grief. Ada Leicester, modestly clad, with all the jewels stripped from her hands, and her superb beauty veiled and toned down by suffering, such as wrings all bitterness from the heart, stood with her parents once more, a portion of the household her own errors had desolated. Then the old man arose in his bed, and his benign features lighted up with such joy as the angels know over a sinner that repenteth.

"My child," he said, opening his arms to receive her, "my child, who was lost and is found!" For a moment he held her to his bosom; then lifting his head, he reached forth one hand, and drew his grandchild forward.

"It is your mother, Julia, your own mother; she has been far away for many years; God has sent her back. Ada, kiss your daughter; Julia, my grandchild, love your mother, reverence her, for this day shall I be one of those that rejoice over her in heaven."

Ada turned to her daughter, and timidly held forth her arms. A thrill so exquisite that it swept all the tears from her heart, passed over the bereaved girl. She moved forward; she nestled close to the bosom of her mother; she murmured the name over and over again, "Mother—mother—mother!"

I have dwelt upon this scene, perhaps, tediously, and only, gentle reader, because my heart and nerves shrink from a description of that which was going on without the prison. It is so much better to describe that which is holy and strong in human nature, than to yield oneself up to scenes that shock and revolt every pure feeling, every gentle affection. But in portraying life as it is, an author cannot always choose the flower nooks, or keep back the clouds that darken human nature.

It was a winter's day, cold and drear, without being stormy. The sky was clouded a little, and of that pale, hard blue which is more desolate than absolute storm. The air seemed full of snow, but none fell; and the sunshine, when it did penetrate the atmosphere, streamed mournfully to the brown, frozen earth. Had you gone into the streets that day, something in the aspect of the populace would have told you that an event of no common interest was about to transpire. Men were grouped at the corners and around the doors. Business was in a degree suspended. But few females were abroad, and they walked hurriedly, as if necessity alone had called them from home.

The time of execution was fixed at five in the afternoon, an hour when the gay world usually throngs Broadway. But for once that noble promenade was deserted; and though the cross streets began to fill long before noon, it was not by the class who usually make the great thoroughfare so full of life.

It was a singular thing; but that day, a little after twelve, a star became visible, hanging, pale and dim, like a funereal lamp in the cold sky. At every corner you saw groups of men and boys gazing upward, with superstitious awe, as if there must be some connection between this star and the human soul about to be launched into eternity. It might have been only the grey light; but every one who went forth that morning must have noticed how pallid were the faces that met his view in the streets. It is difficult to excite the masses of a great city; but in this case there had been so much to interest the public, that for once the multitude seemed perfectly aroused. The age of the prisoner, the exceeding beauty and touching loveliness of his grandchild, the position and fashionable associations of William Leicester—all conspired to arouse public interest to a state of unusual excitement. Hours before the time of execution, the city prison was besieged by an eager mob. Mechanics left their work; women of the lower classes went forth, some with infants in their arms, some leading sons and daughters by the hand, all eager and full of open-mouthed curiosity to see a fellow-creature strangled to death in the face of high heaven.

It had been given forth that this execution would be private, in the court of the prison; that is, three or four hundred persons, favorites of the sheriff, or members of the press, might have the exquisite satisfaction of seeing how an old man could die, and these would duly report his struggles and his agonies, the next morning, through the daily press, that the crowd, heaving, swearing, and jostling together without the walls, might have their horrid curiosity satisfied.

All the cross streets around the prison filled rapidly up; and Centre street, down to Reade and above White, was crowded full of human beings. Then they began to swarm closer, filling the housetops and windows, choking up the door passages and alleys, till every standing-place within sight of the prison was crowded full of eager, brutal life. I am saying now what might be deemed a cruel perversion of probability in fiction, but which many of my readers well know to be a disgraceful truth. But in the windows, and on the roofs of almost every house that overlooked the prison, appeared that day women *not* of the lowest classes, who came there to witness a scene at which the very soul revolts—women whom, with all the proud love of country thrilling at the heart, an American blushes to call countrywomen. When the time drew near, this ocean of human life began to heave and swell tumultuously against the prison walls. Many climbed upwards, fierce for a sight of bloodshed, though at the peril of life and limb, creeping like animals along the massive stonework, or hoisted up on the shoulders of those below, till they hung on the gateway and walls, literally swarming there, like bees seeking for a hive.

As the hour drew near, the mob became more compact and more eager. Excitement grew ferocious; faces, before only curious, now gleamed upwards in groups and masses, haggard with impatient brutality. Ten minutes had gone by—ten minutes beyond the time, and the gallows still loomed up from the prison yard empty. Then the crowd began to murmur and bandy rude jests, like men who had paid for an exhibition, and feared to be baffled out of their amusement. Shouts went up; oaths ran from lip to lip; those upon the walls leaned over, with open mouths and gloating eyes, gazing down into the yard, then telegraphed their companions, or shouted their disappointment to the mob, while others crept up from the mass, crowding the possessors from their places, and occasionally casting one headlong downward.

All at once, when the whole mob was tumultuous with impatience, a cry of fire rung up from the prison walls. The crowd caught the sound, and echoed it fiercely, heaving to and fro, and trampling each other down, eager to see the flames burst forth. There was a wooden steeple or watch-tower, over the front building of the prison. Through the huge timbers of this structure the flames leaped upward, flinging long gleams of light over the upturned faces of the multitude, and adding another horrid feature to a scene already terrible. The alarm bells sounded; the crowd rushed to and fro, shouting, heaving up in waves, beating itself fiercely against the prison walls. Through the masses thundered three or four engines, and a stream of firemen swept through the tumult, pouring noise upon noise, with their trumpets and their voices.

The prison gates were flung open, and as the firemen entered, a portion of the crowd, now furious with excitement, forced through after them, with a sudden rush, filling the inner courts like a torrent let loose.

With nothing but bare timbers to feed upon—for the prison itself was fire-proof—the flames soon burned themselves out, after scattering brands and sparks among the throng, leaving a red glare and a cloud of smoke hovering luridly over the scene When the mob saw the fire dying away, its attention was once more turned upon the execution, and the clamor became deaf ening both within and without the prison walls. The hour of death had gone by. Were the people to be cheated and pu off with a burning watch-tower? Were mechanics, who had lost half a day's time, in order to see a man hanged, to be kept waiting, when their appetite was whetted for a sight of blood? They packed the prison courts more densely; they swarmed close up to the gallows, and pushed forward into the prison corridors, abusing the sheriff, and calling on him vociferously to come forth and explain the meaning of all this delay.

He did come forth, at last, looking white as death; but this was nothing. All were pale then, either from compassion or wrath. He came slowly forth from the prisoner's cell, and standing upon the third gallery, looked down upon the mob.

"Bring the old fellow out—let's see him—no put off with us!" Shouted a man near the staircase.

"I cannot bring him out, he is ——"

They drowned the sheriff's voice with clamor.

"Cheated the gallows—stabbed himself."

The sheriff again attempted to speak, but the tumult grew louder.

"Bring him out—dead or alive, bring him out!"

The officer waved his hand and pointed into the cell. Half a dozen men sprang up from the masses, and ran from one gallery to another, shouting to the crowd below.

"We'll see for ourselves—it's all sham—they mean to let him escape!"

Like a troop of wild animals they plunged forward, pushed themselves past the sheriff, and entered the cell. There they stood motionless, all their brutal ferocity struck dumb within them. They had their wish. The old man was before them; the last gleam of life in his eyes; the last breath freezing upon his lips. God had been very merciful, more merciful than the law.

CHAPTER XXXIX.

HEARTS AND CONSCIENCES AT REST.

The storms of life with her are passed,
Stern memory leaves her soul at rest;
She finds a tranquil home at last,
Content with blessing, to be blessed.

Mrs. Gordon never appeared again in the gay world. The reason was a mystery that no one could explain. The rich furniture, the statues and pictures that had made her home a palace, were quietly sold, and the rooms filled with everything essential to comfort, without the slightest approach to former profuse luxuriousness. Plain carriages and less spirited horses, took the place of her former superb equipage. The grounds still bloomed with flowers, the hot-houses teemed with fruit, but Ada seldom tasted the one or inhaled the other. She was far too busy and useful for the indulgence, even of her most harmless love of the beautiful. She had literally gone out by the wayside and hedges, forcing the poor to come in and partake of her hospitality. For months Jacob Strong might have been observed, side by side with his mistress, threading the alleys, searching in attic chambers, for objects of just charity. Old men and women, generally of the educated poor, who could not work, and were too proud for begging, soon became the inmates of those splendid saloons. Any day, when you passed that mansion, some old lady in her snow-white cap might be seen looking quietly from the casement, while others strolled in the gardens, or amused themselves in the marble vestibule. Occasionally Jacob Strong might be seen loitering about the door, but all the servants were changed. The very atmosphere of the place seemed that of another region. No French maids, no liveried footman, lent a foreign and meretricious air to the dwelling now. In the place of former splendor, gay tumult and heartless display, reigned a calm and pure tranquillity. Every face was serene; every being you met looked soberly content.

In truth, the little paradise—for still the beautiful reigned throughout that dwelling—did indeed at times seem haunted by an angel; for flitting about, now in the sunshine of the garden, now in the more bland sunshine of her mother's smile, Julia grew in beauty and in all those sweet qualities which are the essence of loveliness. If painful memories sometimes haunted the maiden—if a prison cell and an old man blessing her with his last breath—a tumult of people, and wild shouts that seemed terrible to her, even then, sometimes broke upon her in the still morning, or the more stilly night, it was but a passing cloud; and with tears in her eyes, she would thank God, that those who loved that good old man had been saved the crowning horror of his death.

And the old grandmother—it should have been no cause of grief when the meek woman went softly to sleep one night and awoke with her husband in heaven. It was the home she had pined for even when surrounded closest by her children's love. They laid her by his side in Greenwood, with many tears, for though certain that happiness awaits the departed, those who are left must mourn, or they cannot have loved.

Now we have one scene to describe, and our story is done. It was three years after the death of old Mr. Wilcox, and once more the home of Ada Leicester was lighted up for guests. The boudoir which we have so often mentioned was redolent with flowers, and the pure muslin curtains floated to and fro in the summer air that came balmily through the open windows. Beyond, was the bed-chamber. You could hear the rustle of light footsteps on the India matting, and see the gleam of snowy drapery, waving like a cloud in the distance. All was exquisitely chaste and full of simplicity. How unlike the gorgeous luxuriousness of those rooms, in other days!

The rooms filled, not with guests such as had made them brilliant once, but with persons who may interest the reader far more. The first person whom Jacob Strong ushered into the boudoir, was his own sister, Mrs. Gray. Never in her whole life had the good lady appeared so radiantly happy. Her gown of silver grey silk rustled cheerfully as she walked, white satin ribbons knotted the lace cap under her chin and floated in glistening streamers adown the white muslin kerchief folded over her bosom. A pair of gloves—man's size, but white as snow—were neatly buttoned about her plump wrists. This, with her beautiful grey hair, her cheeks softly red like a mellow winter apple, and the double chin that had taken a triple fold since we last saw her, would have warmed your heart had you been a guest at that house, as she was. Then there was a quiet little old lady in black, who glided in like a shadow, and was completely lost behind the rotundity of Mrs. Gray's person ; and another gentle creature clothed in black also, but of a beauty that made your heart ache, the sweet face was so touchingly sad, the countenance so waxen in its whiteness, and every movement was so painfully shy. It seemed as if the poor young creature might turn and flee, like a frightened doe, if an unfamiliar eye were turned upon her. Reader, these two persons are no strangers to you; they are the mother and the victim of William Leicester. Poor Florence, her mind was shaken yet, but not as it had been. She was gentle and mournfully sad, but not insane. Still it was a painful thing to see a creature so young, with that utter hopelessness of countenance. She sat down close to the little, aged woman, and looked up in her face, with meek, trusting eyes, holding shyly to a fold of her dress all the while. Not even the sunny smile of Mrs. Gray, could win a gleam of joy to those large eyes. Then there was a large woman with black eyes and an abundance of raven hair, that kept bustling in and out of the bed-chamber with a look of happy importance, that made her strong features quite handsome. You would hardly have recognized the prison woman, in that neatly clad rosy cheeked female, the expression and whole appearance was so changed. Home and care had done everything for her, and at this time she was housekeeper in the mansion. Had you asked her character of the old ladies who found an asylum there, the account would have astonished you. After all, where real strength of character exists, there is always hope of reformation. It is your weak sinner for whom one despairs the most. As this woman passed through the room, she always turned her eyes, beaming with fondness, on a little boy, half concealed by the flow of Mrs. Gray's gown. It was quite wonderful how much that gown could shelter ; and the mother spoke in that glance eloquently as ever love was uttered in words.

Then there was Jacob Strong himself, with a new coat in its first gloss, too short for his long arms, and cut after a fashion of his own, which made him look more round-shouldered and ungainly than ever. A buff vest, and gloves of a deeper yellow, gave an air of peculiar smartness to his costume, which bespoke some very important occasion ; for it was not often that Jacob gave way to weaknesses regarding his toilet ; and when he did, the effect was indisputably striking.

Besides the persons we have mentioned, were a score of nice aged women in snowy caps and chintz dresses, looking the very pictures of contented old age, who whispered cosily together, and watched a door that led to the stairs with the greatest interest, as if some very important person was expected to enter from that way.

Their impatience was gratified at last ; for a clergyman with flowing robes came sweeping through, escorted by Jacob Strong, who had been wandering about the dim vestibule during the last ten minutes. Directly after, the room opposite was flung open, and Robert Otis came forth, leading a fair young girl by the hand. There was something heavenly in the loveliness of that gentle bride, as the blush deepened and faded away beneath the gossamer sheen of her veil.

Jacob Strong rubbed his yellow gloves softly together, as he gazed upon her ; and the rustle of Mrs. Gray's dress was absolutely eloquent of all the restless pride she felt in seeing the two beings she most loved united for ever.

Of all the persons present, Ada Leicester alone was sad. She remembered her own marriage, and the shadow of many a painful thought swept across her face, as the solemn benediction was uttered over her child.

When the ceremony was complete Florence arose, and quietly placing a folded paper in the lap of the bride, stole away, as if terrified by the strange eyes that followed her movement. Julia took up the paper, half unfolded it, and then, with a blush and a smile, placed it in the hand of her young husband. With that paper Florence had conveyed two thirds of her fine property to the daughter of William Leicester—the man who had swept every blossom from the pathway of her own life.

THE END.

AN ORIGINAL AMERICAN ROMANCE.

Annie Grayson;

OR,

LIFE IN WASHINGTON.

BY MRS N. P. LASSELLE.

Complete in one vol. 12*mo.* 345 *pages, cloth,* 75 *cts., paper* 50 *cts.*

"The aim of the fair authoress seems to have been to impress upon the young mind the danger of giving the heart up to a love of pleasure and outward display. She seems to have been extremely happy in the attainment of her object, and has been successful in producing a very entertaining volume."—*New-Bedford Standard.*

"We should judge it to be not only a good representation of the prominent phases of society in Washington, but well calculated to convey to the young heart the danger of giving itself up to a love of pleasure and outward display."—*Springfield Republican.*

"It is designed to show off the peculiarities of fashionable society in that city, and at the same time to impress the value of a life of piety in contrast to a life of pleasure."—*New York Literary Gazette.*

"'Annie Grayson.'—Such is the modest title of a new and deeply interesting American novel, by Mrs. N. P. Lasselle—a novel founded upon real incidents, most of which transpired amid the circles of the fictitious society of Washington city. We have seldom read a work with a better relish—the characters being boldly and truthfully drawn—knowing as we do the extreme vulnerability of fashionable life at the capital."—*Boston Mail.*

BY THE AUTHOR OF "EVELINA."

Cecilia;

OR THE

MEMOIRS OF AN HEIRESS.

BY MISS BURNEY.

AUTHOR OF "CAMILLA," "DIARY AND LETTERS OF MAD. D'ARBLY," ETC.

One vol. 12*mo.*, 312 *pages. Cloth, gilt,* 75 *cts.; paper covers,* 50 *cts.*

"The publishers have done the reading public a service in resuscitating a work that could draw from that *ursa major*, Dr. Johnson, honeyed compliments, and unmeasured eulogium, and from the eloquent Burke his warmest commendations, and could even beguile Sheridan from the wine-cup, and Fox from the gaming-table; and obtain the unqualified approval of that fastidious and hypercritical cynic, Walpole. Such endorsements are sufficient to recommend 'Cecilia' to all who have not perused the work, while its intrinsic merits will confirm the verdict of the past age. For a more graphic and delightful picture of society, as it existed in the middle of the last century, does not exist."—*Home Journal.*

"'Cecilia' has a world-wide reputation, and on its first publication established beyond all controversy, the fame of its author. It was first published in 1782, and it is said that 'no romance of Sir Walter Scott, was more impatiently awaited, or more eagerly snatched from the counters of the booksellers. High as public expectation was, it was amply satisfied; and Cecilia was placed, by general acclamation among the classical novels of England;'—a place that it has held with honor until the present time." —*Northern Budget.*

"As a story for the 'home circle,' we know of no other more capable of enlisting the sympathies of both old and young, while in morals it is almost superfluous to say it is unimpeachable."—*Golden Rule.*

BUNCE & BROTHER, PUBLISHERS,
184 NASSAU STREET, NEW YORK.